"Rise, Sir ⋯⋯⋯⋯ leaving the sword on his left shoulder.

At that Sommers risked a glance at her expression, and saw a wry smile.

"Do you swear fealty to me, upon your honor as a knight?"

"Forever," he answered lightly.

"Then I require a service of you."

"You have only to ask," he said, relaxing slightly. He rose and took the saber from her.

"Kiss me." She was perfectly composed; he had stopped breathing. "I understand you are going to send me away, but I've never been kissed and before I leave I want you to kiss me."

"Ask me for something else." His voice was strained. "Please." He was looking at the floor and could feel himself trembling.

"I know you are married—" She swallowed. "I saw the pictures in your strongbox. But surely you could kiss me just once, even so."

He was on the point of denying he was married when he realized her misunderstanding was potentially his best safeguard.

"Very well," he said stiffly. He sat down on the stairwell next to her, trying to keep his legs from touching hers, and leaned over to kiss her on the forehead. Unfortunately, the result was not what he had envisioned. Before he could stop her, Elizabeth had twisted slightly, reached up, and pulled his head down. He found himself kissing not her forehead, but her lips. He gave a little sigh and surrendered.

BOOK YOUR PLACE ON OUR WEBSITE AND MAKE THE READING CONNECTION!

We've created a customized website just for our very special readers, where you can get the inside scoop on everything that's going on with Zebra, Pinnacle and Kensington books.

When you come online, you'll have the exciting opportunity to:

- View covers of upcoming books
- Read sample chapters
- Learn about our future publishing schedule (listed by publication month *and author*)
- Find out when your favorite authors will be visiting a city near you
- Search for and order backlist books from our online catalog
- Check out author bios and background information
- Send e-mail to your favorite authors
- Meet the Kensington staff online
- Join us in weekly chats with authors, readers and other guests
- Get writing guidelines
- AND MUCH MORE!

**Visit our website at
http://www.kensingtonbooks.com**

THE EXILES

Nita Abrams

ZEBRA BOOKS
KENSINGTON PUBLISHING CORP.

http://www.kensingtonbooks.com

ZEBRA BOOKS are published by

Kensington Publishing Corp.
850 Third Avenue
New York, NY 10022

All Kensington titles, imprints and distributed lines are available at special quantity discounts for bulk purchases for sales promotion, premiums, fund-raising, educational or institutional use.

Special book excerpts or customized printings can also be created to fit specific needs. For details, write or phone the office of the Kensington Special Sales Manager: Kensington Publishing Corp., 850 Third Avenue, New York, NY 10022. Attn. Special Sales Department. Phone: 1-800-221-2647.

Zebra and the Z logo Reg. U.S. Pat. & TM Off.

First Printing: June 2002
10 9 8 7 6 5 4 3 2 1

Printed in the United States of America

For MKM

Prologue

Lille, June 1813

Deputy-Commissioner Launay glanced once more at his visitor and coughed nervously. A month under arrest, even under fairly lenient conditions, had not improved Meillet's temper, which had never been amiable. The gray eyes were ice cold; the tall figure stood rigidly at attention, heels together on the Indian carpet. He had declined a chair.

"Monsieur Meillet," he faltered. "What more can I say? You have been grievously wronged, we are all agreed. The minister himself has sent a personal letter of apology. Everyone was duped. The resemblance was remarkable."

The blond head notched up an inch. "I was not duped," Meillet reminded the commissioner.

"Yes of course, of course, it is simply dreadful that this English masquerader, this spy, was able to impose on all of us, to assume the identity of Monsieur Arnaut, to order your arrest . . ."

Meillet slammed his fist down on the marquetry panel

of the desk between them with a sudden blaze of anger. The plump little commissioner jumped in his chair. *"Nom d'un nom!* My arrest is the least of it; the man was in charge of the entire northern sector for three months! Three months! My God! He has the names of fifty of our informants in England now, and has personally inspected every one of the coastal patrols! It is a disaster!''

"But no, my dear Meillet, hardly that; the situation can be retrieved. We have every confidence that under your supervision, the office at Lille can recover very quickly. The minister has confirmed your appointment in advance and has charged me to offer you any funds you need to expedite the reorganization of our surveillance operations in Lille. Or you may have more men, if you wish. We can transfer them from Calais and place them under your jurisdiction.''

"I will not be remaining in Lille. You must give the appointment to someone else.''

Launay was astounded. Meillet had been angling for the position of chief inspector of the Lille *Sûreté* for nearly a year. He had been livid with rage when Arnaut had been appointed over his head, and his suspicions of Arnaut, unfortunately, had been ascribed to professional jealousy and ignored until it was too late. "But— surely you are not resigning?''

"I have requested permission from the minister to trace the false Arnaut. He himself has not been seen, but a servant of his has been spotted near Vienna.''

"He will not grant you that permission,'' said the commissioner firmly. "You are needed here. To track this Englishman, this 'Rover,' as they so childishly name him, is an exercise in futility.''

The gray eyes bored into him. "The minister will follow your recommendation, will he not?''

Launay shifted uncomfortably in his chair. "At the

moment I could not recommend that he grant you leave for such a purpose, monsieur. It is only natural that you should wish to pursue this man who has wronged you, but personal vengeance must yield to the national interest."

Meillet put both hands on the desk and leaned over until his face was only inches from Launay's. "Supposing I were to tell you that the traitor Southey, the double-dealing courier who supplied Arnaut with his false reports from England, is not dead, as we initially thought, but alive, and also reported to be in Vienna? Supposing I were to tell you that Colonel White, Southey's former commanding officer, has recalled the courier Nathanson from Spain, and ordered him to Vienna as well? Would a visit to Vienna still be considered personal vengeance, or do you think there might be good reason to discover why all these spies are converging there?"

Launay was silent. Napoleon himself was ensconced in Dresden, not far from the Austrian capital, negotiating with the European powers. There could indeed be good reason to investigate the sudden British interest in the area.

"I was right before," added Meillet softly. "When I doubted Arnaut."

"Very well," conceded Launay reluctantly. "I will request a temporary stay of the appointment in Lille from the minister. Let me know within forty-eight hours how many men you will take with you, and the papers for your party will be ready by Friday."

A brief and wintry smile appeared, the first smile Launay had seen. "My thanks, commissioner. Tell His Excellency I will try not to tread on any toes in Vienna." He clicked his heels in the Prussian manner, bowed, and left.

How did he know, thought Launay uneasily, *that I was just about to warn him to be careful not to offend the Austrians?*

Perhaps the surveillance office at Lille would suffer from Meillet's absence, but personally, Launay was relieved to think he would not see the man for a while. Meillet frightened him.

One

Elizabeth DeQuincy looked at the boy and scowled. He scowled back. Not totally implausible, she thought, surveying the figure in front of her. Not bad at all, in fact. He appeared to be in his teens, slight, face and features somewhat thin but passable, reasonably tall for a boy who had not yet reached his full growth. He would probably not attract much notice; he looked like an ordinary boy. Only the eyes were distinctive: blue in the center, with an odd dark-gray rim.

As always, the eyes reminded her of Robin, and she bit her lip, but forced herself to continue her scrutiny. The breeches fit well, she noticed, pleased. The hair was too long, of course; she would need to cut it, but that would have to wait until just before she left. And then there were the boots. She had sent Anna, their young housemaid, to fetch them from the cobbler. If she was lucky, there would not be too many awkward questions. Hands on her hips, she studied the stockinged feet. The boy in the mirror did the same.

"You're a shabby fellow," she said with some humor to her image. The shirt was worn at the cuffs and elbows, and there was a stain on the breeches at the knee. When she had abstracted her uncle's things from the mending basket and altered them, she had known perfectly well that any garment which was new and clean was unlikely to be sitting neglected in her aunt's room. But she did not dare run the risk of stealing something finer, which might be missed. If her uncle knew to look for a boy instead of a young lady, it would be much easier for him to find her. "Never mind," she consoled the boy. "Shabby travelers attract less attention; it will be safer this way."

"Fräulein?" The maid's voice outside the closed door sounded alarmed. "Is someone here with you?"

Anna! She should not have been back for another hour! Elizabeth scrambled frantically for her dress and realized she could never get it on in time; not only that, but the shirt would show underneath her bodice. "I'm just talking to myself, Anna," she called out in German. "Everything is fine." In desperation, she seized her cloak, which was lying on the bed, and threw it around herself. Their young housemaid had an unfortunate habit of coming in without knocking.

Anna peered around the edge of the door and froze, her eyes wide. "Fräulein?" she said doubtfully. "Are you feeling ill?" It was a very warm day in late June; the cloak had not been a wise choice. Her wrap would have been better. She could have said she had put it on while mending her dress. Since she owned only the one black dress, it would make perfect sense. Now Anna would know something was wrong.

"Not at all," said Elizabeth, improvising recklessly. "I am—I am doing some sewing, and I thought I might need to raise the hem on my cloak. It is a bit too long, I believe." She looked at herself in the mirror, pretending to consider the fall of the hem at her ankles, and suddenly realized she was wearing her uncle's stockings. Perhaps Anna would not notice.

Anna did not notice the stockings, but only because

her attention was caught by something else. "Fräulein Elizabeth!" she cried in dismay. "What has happened to your cloak?"

Good Lord, what an idiot she was! She had forgotten that she had taken off the trim so it would look more like a boy's cloak. Loose threads from the ripped-out overstitching were sticking up all the way down the front opening of the cloak. "I did not like that color braid. I am going to buy some new trim, in silver," she announced. Anna was still staring at the ruined cloak. How to get rid of her? "Why are you back so soon?" she tried. "I thought you were going to the cobbler."

Anna stepped all the way into the room. She was only sixteen, and in this odd household, where she was now the only servant, she sometimes behaved more like a younger sister than a maid. "Look what I did!" she said, laughing and holding out a small purse, which Elizabeth mechanically accepted. A few small coins clinked disconsolately inside. "I took the wrong one! And I did not want to ask Herr Schuler for the boots without the rest of the money." She pouted for a moment, but her good humor returned as she looked over at the nightstand, where a much larger purse sat, heavy with coins, leaning against a candlestick.

Elizabeth sighed with exasperation. Now she would not have the boots until tomorrow. Only a scatterbrain like Anna could have set off to the cobblers with an empty money bag and not noticed—or, for that matter, barged in without knocking. But Anna had been a wonderful nurse while her aunt had been ill. It was not her fault she lacked training. Elizabeth had been too busy taking care of her aunt and running the household to worry about instructing Anna in proper etiquette.

Clearly, the Austrian girl thought the wasted errand a great joke. She was chattering away in German, describing the handsome young drayman who had given her a ride back to the Fleischmarkt after hearing her tale of woe. Inspiration came to Elizabeth. "Anna, do you think you could go back?" she asked, interrupting. "Could you find someone to give you a ride so you would reach the shop before it closed?"

"Yes, Fräulein, if you wish. But I could walk, also. Herr Schuler will open the shop for me. He is my mother's cousin. I have often told him about you and the Dear Lady, may she rest in peace, and he is the one who made your black slippers to go with your black dress."

'Dear Lady' was Anna's term for Elizabeth's late aunt. She *had* been a dear lady. Elizabeth had never regretted joining her as a companion and nurse after her father had died, in spite of her mistrust of her uncle and in spite of their unsettled life in an endless series of seedy rooms in various European capitals. But now, of course, things were different.

Elizabeth reached for the larger purse, and was about to pass it over to the maid, when she suddenly paused. If the cobbler was a relative and knew of their household, he would know already that there was something odd about this order. Why had Fräulein DeQuincy sent her maid with a sketch, rather than coming in herself to be measured?

What is more, Anna, who thought the English very odd, might not have been surprised that Elizabeth was requesting boots which looked like men's boots—but the cousin, who was more knowledgeable, would realize that even English ladies would never wear such footgear. If Anna returned after hours, calling attention to the urgency of the purchase, he might grow suspicious enough to mention something to Anna. Or, worse, to her uncle.

"Never mind," she said, attempting a casual tone. "It is late; there will be time to go tomorrow morning. Besides"—quickly seizing on a plausible errand— "you need to go get some coffee. We are nearly out." Anything to distract the inquisitive Anna! She nearly pushed the girl out into the anteroom before closing the door firmly. It was like an inferno inside the wool cloak; she tore it off and threw it on the bed with a sigh of relief. Then she turned back to the mirror. Before she took off the shirt and breeches, she should check the hems she had pinned up once more, to make sure the legs were even.

The door popped open, and Anna reappeared, carrying the coffee tin. "Fräulein, you forgot to give me the money for the . . ." Her voice died in her throat as she caught sight of Elizabeth. Anna was young, but she was not dull-witted. "You are running away," she whispered finally, looking horrified.

Slumping onto the bed in surrender, Elizabeth nodded wearily.

"Why?" The little maid's eyes narrowed. "Is it Herr Stourhead?" She pronounced the name stiffly; no 'Dear Gentleman' title for Elizabeth's uncle. Anna was terrified of the bad-tempered Englishman, with his bulging eyes and enormous gray mustaches.

Elizabeth nodded again.

"I will help you," the maid said fiercely. "You do not need to wear these dreadful clothes and pretend to be a boy. You can go to my grandmother's house; she will take care of you, I promise."

Elizabeth gave a shaky smile. "Thank you, Anna, but I must go home to England. And it is not easy for me to travel so far alone, as a young woman. Nor do I want my uncle to be able to trace me. He would find me at your grandmother's easily, and then he could make things very unpleasant for your family, even though I am of age now and he is no longer my guardian."

"He should hire a companion and a manservant for you and send you back to England, if you wish to go," Anna said angrily. "For how many years is it now that you have been nursing the Dear Lady and taking charge of the house? He owes you at least that."

"I asked him," replied Elizabeth bitterly. "He said no. He needs me here, he says. I am an ungrateful girl, who does not remember that he and my aunt took me in when I was penniless."

"It is not proper for you to be here, now that your aunt is gone to Heaven." Anna's chin jutted out stubbornly. "Your uncle is a widower, and you are a nice unmarried young lady. I am not old enough to be a chaperone for you."

"I told him that, too. He laughed." Elizabeth clasped her hands between her knees. It was rather an odd sensation to have no skirt fabric underneath them. She started to speak again, then stopped herself. Her discomfort in her uncle's presence was no business of Anna's, and her imagination had probably exaggerated his intentions.

"Gott im Himmel!" Anna, who had her own experiences fending off her employer to guide her, read Elizabeth's expression easily. She dropped the coffee tin onto the bed and sank down on her knees by Elizabeth, looking up at her in concern. "Frau Wedlein would come back, I think, if you asked her." Their former housekeeper and cook had been let go when doctors' bills began to strain her uncle's erratic income.

"I mentioned her, but he said no. And I cannot force him to give me enough money to travel home properly escorted, either. He can be very difficult, Anna." Their eyes met. Joseph Stourhead was a hectoring bully of a man who was, Elizabeth guessed, involved in some very questionable business transactions with some even more questionable associates. She did not think he had many scruples. "I do not like the idea of running away, but it is by far the easiest solution. My aunt gave me some jewelry; I can sell it to pay my fare and lodging."

"I will ask about coaches on my way back from the grocer," Anna promised. "The grooms at the livery stable will know something, I am sure." She patted Elizabeth's shoulder in a motherly fashion. "Don't worry, Fräulein. You make a fine boy; you have a nice, low voice and not much hips. And if you change your mind,

I will take you to my grandmother." She marched out the door with a decisive nod.

Anna's calm acceptance of the situation made Elizabeth feel very much better. The thought of traveling alone across a continent blockaded by Napoleon's troops was terrifying enough. Maintaining her disguise would make it all the more difficult. And yet what else was she to do? She had thought at first of taking refuge with some of her aunt's friends. But she had no idea whether the English ladies she had met earlier in the year were even still here. Once her aunt had become really ill, Elizabeth had seen no one except a few elderly harridans who had called to make sure her aunt was closer to death than they were.

Briefly, she had then considered trying to find work as a music teacher. She had rejected that idea almost at once. A female with only passable German trying to obtain a post teaching music in Vienna? And her uncle would be able to locate her easily if she stayed here. It was imperative that she find a way to get back to England.

Robin's friends would help her obtain a position with a good English family who could protect her from her uncle—although she suspected England itself was enough protection. Her uncle had not put one foot on English soil for as long as she had known him.

At last she had come, reluctantly, to the decision to run away. Such cowardice was bad enough for a sister of Robin DeQuincy, but to run away in disguise was surely worse. And Elizabeth, who had inherited rather strict notions of propriety from her aunt, felt this particular disguise was the most disgraceful part of the whole scheme. Still, Anna had not been very shocked. Elizabeth conveniently forgot that Anna's notions of decorum were her greatest failing as a maidservant.

Slowly, Elizabeth took off the breeches and shirt and resumed her dress. "A girl of little beauty and no fortune," her uncle had called her when he sneered at her request to be sent back to England.

The figure in the mirror now offered no contradiction to her uncle's harsh assessment of her prospects. A thin, flat-chested girl in a hideous black frock looked out at her, a girl with clumsily styled light brown hair and red-rimmed eyes. No, she had no illusions she would be able to find a husband when she returned to England. She would find another post as a companion, or as a governess. She was certainly plain enough.

It was very late. Even the tavern was closed, the noisy patrons all dispersed, the great iron lantern which hung at the entrance to the courtyard quenched. Below her window all lay in darkness.

Why was it, Elizabeth wondered irritably, that when boys ran away they simply climbed down a trellis, but when girls ran away it required hours of tedious preparation? She stabbed her thumb again with the back of the needle and hissed in pain. At some point she had lost her thimble, and now did not dare go into her aunt's room to look in her workbox. If her uncle was still awake, she wanted him to think she had gone to sleep and left the candle burning, as she often did, in spite of his grumbles about the cost of tapers.

Someday, she supposed, she would live in a house where she did not need to count every penny. It had not happened so far. The Chapman women did not marry very well. Her aunt had chosen Joseph Stourhead, and her mother had fallen in love with a handsome wastrel whose father had already disowned him. And then she had died, leaving her improvident husband with a schoolboy and a nine-year-old girl. Her father had promptly proved his own family had been right to cast him off by quarreling so bitterly with the Chapmans that they had washed their hands of Elizabeth and Robin.

Another stab of the needle, and Elizabeth sighed and wrenched her thoughts back to her seam. She had already hemmed the breeches and mended some stockings, which only needed a few darns to be wearable. Now she was working on the shirt. Ideally she should have two shirts, but she was not certain she could force herself to stay awake that long, and she was determined to leave tomorrow, as soon as she could pick up the boots. Delaying until Thursday would mean running the risk of her uncle discovering her plan.

She looked over at the small valise she had concealed behind the bed. It held very little. At the bottom were her valuables, including her aunt's jewelry. Then came her best summer traveling dress and slippers for when she arrived in England, undergarments, sewing supplies, and, on top, her mangled cloak. She must hope the weather would stay warm and dry, since she did not think it looked like a boy's garment even in its denuded state.

The minutes went by, and she stitched on, blinking with fatigue. A thunderous rumble startled her, and the needle slipped yet again as she jumped in surprise. It was her uncle, snoring.

Enough, then. She would go and get the thimble; her uncle would not hear her. She rose stiffly and tiptoed across the hall with the candle to the large front room which had been her aunt's. It was eerie in here, she thought, with the curtains open to the blackness outside and the light of her candle shining back at her from the windows. In haste, she went over to the walnut chest where her aunt kept her workbasket and looked through it quickly. No thimble. Then, as she turned in resignation to leave, the light of the candle swept across the lid of the pianoforte.

It was the one luxury in that nomadic household. Elizabeth and her aunt had both loved music, and her aunt had decided Elizabeth must have an instrument. Tears came to Elizabeth's eyes as she looked at the silent

bed where the sick woman had spent hours listening to
Elizabeth play. Her lovely, gentle aunt, who had insisted
that Elizabeth have dancing masters, had herself tutored
her niece in voice and drawing, and had invited catty
little aristocratic ladies to tea so Elizabeth could keep
up her French. Who had made a destitute girl of seventeen feel welcome and needed, rather than an awkward
encumbrance, who had rejoiced with her every time
one of her brother's rare letters had arrived from Portugal. Who had sat up with her for two nights when the
terrible news of his death had reached them in—where
were they then? Berlin? Zurich?

There was a stack of sheet music on top of the piano;
Elizabeth had spent most of her pin money at the print-
er's since they had arrived in Vienna. On impulse, she
swept up all but two or three pieces, decoys to fool her
uncle, and retreated back to her room. She packed
them carefully at the bottom of the valise with her other
treasures: the little bag of jewelry, her identification
papers, Robin's letters, the miniature showing him looking impossibly neat and handsome in his new uniform.
And the last letter, from three officers in his division,
softening the blow of the grim news they reported by
telling her Robin had spoken of her at the very end
and had taken their promise to serve her should she ever
need their assistance. She would go back to England and
claim that assistance now.

Suddenly she was very tired. She replaced the clothing
on top of the papers and added the second shirt. Surely
she could find time to alter it while she traveled. It
would be as much as she could manage to finish the
first one before she fell asleep right here in the chair
beside her bed.

Two

It was not as simple as she had thought it would be to sell her aunt's jewelry. She had gone first to the shop her aunt had patronized—not to buy, for her uncle was too stingy for that, but to have pieces repaired. This was down on the Kohlmarkt, a commodious and well-lit establishment with uniformed doormen and assistants who spoke French. Elizabeth the young lady had never drawn the notice of the doormen, but now they made it very clear that young men in wrinkled shirts, worn breeches, and no jacket who wished to sell ladies' jewels had best be prepared to speak with the police before proceeding further. One man had even asked to see her papers, and Elizabeth had realized in horror that her papers were in her own name. Not only that, but the name was prefixed by the inevitable *mademoiselle,* in large, clear letters.

Now she was striding along in her new boots down a less prosperous street, hoping jewelers in this quarter would not ask so many questions. Her valise was getting heavy, and she put it down for a moment to rest. At once a rather seedy-looking man shuffled over, his eyes on the valise. Elizabeth gasped and snatched it up, only to see as the man drew closer that his eyelids were crusted shut with scars, and he tapped his way with a cane. He was holding out his hand, chanting in a plaintive whine, "Alms, of your charity, kind sir, kind madam, alms."

Ashamed of her reaction, Elizabeth set down the bag again and fumbled with the purse tucked into her breeches. She had both the jewels and the money inside, and had to dig down for a coin, so she missed the gleam beneath the scabbed eyelids. Embarrassed by his effusive thanks, she hurried on, shifting her bag from hand to hand, and darted gratefully into a small shop a few doors along which proclaimed:

> JEWELRY. WATCHES. CLOCKS. FINE REPAIRS.
> CUSTOM ORDERS.
> PROPRIETOR M. SCHLEWIG.

"May I help you, young sir?" asked an elderly man as she came in.

"If you please," said Elizabeth in her best German, "I should like to sell some jewelry given me by my late aunt to obtain funds to travel."

The man scrutinized her sharply, noting both the ragged haircut and the fine leather of the boots, and switched to French. "You are Dutch? English?"

"English," said Elizabeth firmly.

Another long stare, and he gestured her to a small stool in front of a counter piled with tiny gears and watch springs. "Of course you will wish to go home now," he commented.

Elizabeth was puzzled.

"You have not heard the news? There was a great battle. Your countrymen have driven the French out of Spain. Napoleon is beside himself, they say."

A cry of delight broke from her, and she thought, *if only Robin could hear this!* Then she realized this news might well put a period to the armistice between the allies and France which had been negotiated earlier in the month. She must leave at once. "I had not heard, no," she said, flustered. "You are right, it is a matter of some urgency, even more so now."

"Let me see what you have," he said curtly. He took the pieces in silence and examined them under a small lamp. On the ruby brooch he used a loupe. Elizabeth had pushed the diamond earrings aside, and when he reached for them, she shook her head. "Not for sale?" he said, surprised. "They would bring more than the rest all together, you know."

Elizabeth tightened her lips. If she was forced to, she would sell them when she reached England. But she should have enough to make the journey without parting with her most treasured gift from her aunt. "I would like to save something of hers," she said to the jeweler, almost apologetically.

He looked at her oddly, then resumed his study of the four items she had given him. "Sixty florins for the lot," he said at last. It was less than the pieces were worth, Elizabeth knew, but far better than she had dared hope. Her purse was very heavy indeed as she left the shop and made her way down the street towards the Judenplatz. Her thoughts were busy. What was she to do about her papers? People traveled with false papers all the time; she herself had a second set of Swiss papers for travel through French-held territory. But her uncle had procured them, and she had no idea how to set about buying some—for she was sure they were for sale, if one knew where to look.

Suddenly she heard a shout, then felt a body slam into her from behind. She staggered and nearly fell, and clutched desperately at her valise. Had she been wiser in the ways of the street, it would not have been the bag she would have clutched. A tug at her waist, a quick glimpse of a blade, and her purse had been cut away from her belt. A young man was running down the street, the 'beggar' just ahead of him beckoning him on.

"Stop, thief!" screamed Elizabeth, forgetting that she was not in England. Then she ransacked her memory for the right words: "*Dieb! Halt!*" She was running after them, dragging her valise, but the new boots were slippery. Suddenly her left foot gave way and she fell hard onto the cobblestones. Something stabbed her in the stomach, and she thought the thief had left his dagger in her waistband. She was cut, she was robbed, she would never get back to England; she would bleed to death on the streets of Vienna. Overwhelmed, she groaned and doubled over, sobbing in pain and fright and misery.

"Sir, are you hurt?" asked an anxious voice in English. Then, as she looked up, surprised to hear that language spoken, the voice changed. "Why, it's a boy! What is this, then?" And a face was peering down at her with real concern. She realized first that the pain in her stomach was gone, and then that boys did not cry. Humiliated and bewildered, she struggled up to a sitting position and looked at her protector.

At first she thought him an older man, because there were streaks of gray in the brown hair. But then she looked more closely at his face. It was a youthful face, very tan, with hazel eyes and a fine, thin mouth. In spite of the tan, the face was a bit drawn. He must have been ill, thought Elizabeth. Perhaps that was why his hair had turned gray. Then she became conscious she was staring, and blushed.

The Englishman squatted down next to her. "They are long gone," he said. "I am sorry. I thought you were hurt, and chose to stay with you rather than pursue them. Did they take anything valuable?"

"Everything I own," said Elizabeth bleakly. "I had just sold my aunt's jewels to pay for my journey back to England." She bowed her head in despair. Now she would have to go back to her uncle. Wearily she got to her feet and started to pick up her bag.

"Are you certain you are not hurt?" said the young-old man. "May I assist you at all?"

Elizabeth looked down at her belt. There was a tiny spot of blood at the waist of her shirt, and something sticking out of the cloth—a piece of metal, or a pin? She reached down and pulled at it. Then she understood what it was, and impatiently she ripped a hole in the shirt to pull it out. It was one of the diamond earrings. It must have come out of the purse as it was cut off, she thought, and suddenly the whole situation struck her as terribly amusing. She started to laugh, but there was an odd edge to the laughter.

The stranger was smiling wryly. "You, my lad," he said, "need a beer. Allow me to aid a fellow countryman at least to that extent." And he picked up her valise and started off down the street.

Not at all an old man, she concluded, observing the easy, athletic stride and the slender build. Her bag seemed to weigh nothing as he swung it lightly up to his shoulder. Oddly, Elizabeth did not have any qualms about trusting him with it. She followed, limping along quite confidently.

He turned back suddenly. "You had best put that gewgaw in your pocket," he advised. "Especially if it is all that remains of your family fortune."

Elizabeth realized she was still holding the earring between her thumb and index finger. Hastily, she tucked it away.

He was still surveying her. "You are limping," he said accusingly.

"My foot," said Elizabeth. "I twisted it just now, running. Otherwise I think I could have caught them."

"While hauling along this lot?" queried her helper cheerfully. "Mighty heavy for such a small bag."

I should be carrying it, realized Elizabeth belatedly. *I am a young man, not a young lady. I should not let an older man carry my things.* She grabbed for the valise, but he swung it away.

"Not until we check your foot," he said, with an air of authority. And then, as though he could not help himself, "How old are you, if you do not mind my asking?"

"Seventeen," said Elizabeth, trying to look dignified. A derisive snort was the response.

"Turned sixteen," she tried in a small voice, thinking, *what would he say if I told him I was twenty-two?*

He still looked skeptical, but they walked on in silence until they reached a café. He seemed to be known here, for the waiter showed him to a table in the corner and stood politely waiting for orders. There was an awkward moment as Elizabeth waited for her chair to be pulled out. Then she quickly tumbled into it, recollecting her part.

"Two beers," said her host. "And a plate of sausages." He turned to Elizabeth. "Permit me to introduce myself. Michael Sommers, at your service."

"Edward," stammered Elizabeth, fishing quickly for a family name. A piece of music dangled in front of her memory. "Edward Purcell. And I am very grateful to you, sir, for your assistance."

Sommers waved his hand deprecatingly. "It is of no moment. Indeed, I hope I may assist you further. You were planning to travel back to England, you say? What now, with your money gone? Have you family here in Vienna? Or acquaintances?"

"No, not any longer. I was traveling with my aunt," said Elizabeth, making a sudden decision to conceal the existence of her uncle. "She died some weeks ago, and I was on the point of setting out for home when I was robbed, as you saw." She added ruefully, "I was a ripe pigeon for their plucking, I'm afraid. Tales of such tricks had reached me, but I was not on my guard, as I should have been."

The beer and sausages arrived, and Elizabeth suddenly was very hungry. She helped herself to a sausage and tentatively took a swig of the beer. It was horrid, and she had to school her face not to show her disgust. But after she had had more sausage, she was thirsty and took up the beer again. It tasted better now.

The waiter came and refilled her glass. Sommers was chatting lightly, remarks about Vienna, and about possible routes back to England, but he was watching her keenly. She took another pull at the beer. It was delicious. Another large draft. She gave Sommers a lopsided grin.

He grinned back, reached over, and pulled away the beer. "I thought so," he said dryly. He summoned the waiter with an imperative gesture. "The bill, please." Then he looked meaningfully at Elizabeth. "It is clear you have no acquaintance with Austrian beer, my boy."

A delightful dizziness was filling Elizabeth, running up her knees and through her chest into her head. What a kind man, this Sommers! It was too bad her purse had been stolen, but she would sell the diamond earring for fifty florins—no, eighty, at least. There was nothing to be concerned about. She could manage everything. Sommers had turned away momentarily to pay the waiter, and she snatched back her beer. How dare he treat her like a schoolgirl? She had had wine before, and even champagne once. She saw Sommers's brows snap together as he noticed what she was doing, and defiantly she put her head back and drained the entire glass.

"That's torn it," she heard Sommers say with a groan. She started to protest, to assert her adult dignity. Then there was a wave of not-so-delightful dizziness, and another wave of something even less delightful. Speaking was out of the question. It was a struggle even to stay upright. Her companion was looking at her with growing concern. She wanted to tell him she would be fine in a moment, but suddenly she knew it was not true. With a choking sound she bolted from the table,

staggered outside to the street, and was violently ill into
the gutter. She knelt there, shaking, as the staid Viennese passersby drew away with shocked murmurs.

"Congratulations," said a calm voice behind her.
Sommers was leaning against the wall of the café, regarding her with resigned amusement. "I did not think you
would make it all the way to the street." He had her
valise, she saw now. "Come along, Purcell. You had best
come home with me until your head shakes off your
first meeting with Viennese brewing. It's quite a bit
stronger than English ale. I should have known better."

"Frau Renner!" called Sommers as they came into a
small courtyard off the alley. "Frau Renner, I have a
guest! Could you make us some tea?"

Elizabeth's head had cleared a bit, although the walk
had not been very long. She looked around with interest.
The gate they had come through, from the alley, opened
onto a small stone pavement set between two walls of a
house. The upper floor of the house ran over the gate
and pavement, connecting the two walls. Behind this
was a dirt yard, roped off into several squares. On either
side of the pavement was a set of stone steps leading
up to two identical wooden doors, painted bright blue.
One of these opened now and a tiny old woman came
out, wiping her hands on her apron.

"Herr Sommers, you are back already?" she asked,
in an accent so thick Elizabeth could hardly follow her
German.

"Yes, I found a countryman who had been set upon
and robbed in the Kurrentgasse," he replied. "I brought
him home to see if we could help him."

Frau Renner gasped in sympathy, and Elizabeth felt
two bright blue eyes peering at her. Furtively, the old
woman took out a pair of spectacles, held them up to
her face, and then quickly replaced them in an apron
pocket.

"He is only a boy!" said Frau Renner indignantly. "What is this world coming to, then, when boys are attacked and robbed on the streets of the Emperor's city! You go on upstairs, *mein Herr,* and I will bring you up some tea and cakes." Elizabeth paled at the thought of food.

"No cakes," said Sommers quickly. "For the moment, at least." He winked at Elizabeth and went in the other door, which opened onto a set of stone stairs. Still carrying her bag, he ran up ahead of her lightly, and she followed more slowly. The door on the first landing stood open, and she could see a large, bare room with a mirror hung on the end wall—quite a big mirror, she thought. There was a glimpse of hooks, with strange sacks hanging from them. They were still climbing, and came out at the top of the staircase. Here there was no door. There was an outer room with a couch, a battered armchair, some old wooden chests, and a small table. Two doors were partly ajar in the far wall, leading to other rooms, she supposed. They were up under the roof; the windows were tiny and set high in the wall, and the ceiling had stains in it.

"It leaks," said Sommers, following her glance. "There is a small attic up there, with pigeons nesting in it, so do not be alarmed if you hear noises from overhead." He disappeared into one of the two inner rooms. "Go ahead and wash up, if you wish," he called. "The basin is in the other room."

Elizabeth looked down. Her hands were filthy, there was a bloodstain on her shirt, and her breeches were covered with dust. She moved hesitantly into the indicated room and stopped with a gasp. The basin was there, as promised, on a washstand. So were two pitchers of water, and some faded towels. But the rest of the room was full of swords. They hung from hooks, evidently organized by size, because the hooks nearest the door had small, thin swords, and the hooks back against the far wall held only one weapon apiece, huge, flat-bladed affairs which reminded her vaguely of knights in armor.

"Admiring my collection?" asked Sommers behind her. "Tools of my trade, Purcell. I am a fencing instructor, and quite fortunate to have been able to purchase this lot at a good price when I parted from my former master ten days ago."

So that is what the room downstairs is for, thought Elizabeth. *And the roped-off squares in the courtyard.*

She mumbled some reply, and poured water into the basin, scrubbing her face and hands vigorously. The shirt would have to wait; she was bitterly regretting now that she had not stayed up all night to finish the second one. She tucked it down into her breeches to conceal the stain, and brushed ineffectively at the dust on her legs. She finished up with an attempt to smooth down the cowlicks on her head.

"Who cut your hair?" asked Sommers, with raised eyebrows, as she reemerged.

She blushed. "I did. My aunt liked it long." She had cut it off this morning without a qualm and stuffed the gleaming hanks of brown and gold hair viciously under the mattress of her bed. Anna never turned the mattresses; they would lie there for eternity, probably.

"I can tell," he told her, leading the way to the tiny table. A pot of tea and two mugs sat there; Frau Renner must have come in while she was washing. There was a plate of cakes, which she looked at with loathing. Sommers hastily whisked them away. "Couldn't stop her," he apologized. "Frau Renner believes beverages without cakes are the work of the devil. Try some tea. Perhaps you'll feel more the thing once you do."

Elizabeth sipped her tea obediently. The cold water on her face had helped immensely. After a few minutes she got up, went over to the sideboard, and retrieved the cakes, silently offering one to Sommers before taking one herself and returning to the couch.

"Well, Master Purcell," mused Sommers after she

had eaten her cake. "What are we to do with you?" He was sprawled in the armchair, watching her as she tried unobtrusively to brush the crumbs off her lap.

"I am much obliged to you," responded Elizabeth, "and I must apologize for my behavior in the café. But I would not wish to inconvenience you any further." She glanced at the windows and saw that the light was slanting obliquely through the thick panes. It was getting late. "I should be on my way, in fact," she added politely. "I would like to sell the earring today to pay for my lodging tonight."

"You are a young fool," said Sommers, but without any malice in his tone. "How much do you think you will get for that earring?"

"Thirty—maybe forty florins," stammered Elizabeth.

"And that is all the money you have?"

"Yes. Well," Elizabeth corrected, "I put a few coins in my pocket after I sold the jewels so I would not have to open my purse every time I purchased something."

"You know that much, at least," he commented. "Do you think you could travel back to England on forty florins—if you could indeed realize that sum from the earring?"

She looked at him in dismay.

"It is possible," he said, answering his own question. "But you would have to stay in the kind of places your friend the cutpurse frequents, or travel all the way through without resting overnight anywhere. Even so, you might run out of funds before you arrived if the weather were bad or soldiers stopped the coaches. It would be very risky. I will wager, moreover, that you only have English papers. With the news of Wellington's victory today, it will be impossible to travel through French territory without a decent set of forged papers. And they do not come cheap."

"What am I to do, then?" asked Elizabeth, sinking back down onto the couch. She tightened her fists. She would *not* go back to her uncle, she vowed. She would

set out for England and get as far as she could. Perhaps
she could get a position somewhere closer to home and
earn the rest of her fare.

"Are you quite sure you have no family, no friends,
here?" said Sommers, looking at her intently.

"Quite sure," lied Elizabeth.

"Your aunt—she was unmarried? A widow?"

"Yes"—Elizabeth paused to make a choice. "A
widow," she decided.

"And your uncle? He is not going back to England?"

"No," said Elizabeth without thinking. "He has business here . . ." Her voice died in her throat. "Oh, you
are despicable!" she said, furious at Sommers and at
herself.

"Not as despicable as your uncle, I take it," he said
quietly. "Or you would not have run away from him.
Would it be so terrible to return to him?"

Elizabeth flinched at the thought, and Sommers's
face tightened. "Never mind," he said hastily. "I am
sure we can contrive something."

"Mr. Sommers," said Elizabeth, struggling to reassert
herself, "there is no reason for you to concern yourself
with my affairs. I am perfectly able to take care of myself,
in spite of my tender years." This last was said with some
sarcasm. To her astonishment, he looked ashamed.

"I beg your pardon," he said, embarrassed. "I did
not mean to insult you. My father—well, I myself was
thrown on my own resources quite young, and it was
not a pleasant experience. I am not offering you charity,
you understand." He paused, considering the well-
made boots, the cultured accent, and the courtesy,
weighing them against the shirt, the breeches, and the
haircut.

"You are a gentleman, I think?" he said after a
moment.

"I suppose so," said Elizabeth slowly.

"I will make you a proposal, then," he said. "If you
will give me your word that you have good and sufficient

reasons for refusing to return to your uncle, I will hire you on as my assistant for a month so that you can earn enough money to travel safely back to England. I would make you a loan, but after purchasing my stock of weapons so recently I have not the money on hand, and in any case it will take some time to procure your new papers.''

"Your assistant?'' Elizabeth was taken aback. "What would my duties be?''

Sommers misinterpreted her hesitation. "Nothing untoward, for a well-educated young man. Help me take equipment to those pupils who require me to teach them at their homes, instruct the youngest students in the basics, carry messages, clean and polish the swords. Frau Renner and her girl do all the housework and cooking, you would not have to do anything unseemly. You do speak French, do you not? Most of my pupils think it shameful to speak German except with their servants.''

"Yes, I speak French,'' said Elizabeth. "But I do not know how to fence.''

"Not at all?'' Sommers was incredulous. "Well, boxing, then. They are somewhat similar.''

She shook her head.

"You have never been taught boxing or fencing? Are you a scholar?'' asked Sommers, noting the slight build and the pale complexion.

"I am a useless fribble, Mr. Sommers,'' said Elizabeth wearily. "I speak a little German and Italian, good French, and play the piano. That is the sum of my accomplishments.'' She suppressed the urge to tell him she had been cooking for her uncle's household for the past two months. He already had Frau Renner, and any mention of cooking might give away her disguise immediately.

"Well, I could hire you to play piano whilst my noble pupils practice their feints,'' laughed Sommers. Then he sobered. "My offer still stands," he said seriously. "Have you at least been taught to dance?"

Elizabeth nodded.

"Then I can teach you enough to take the youngest pupils as soon as your foot is better."

He rose to his feet. "I will go ask Frau Renner to lend me a cot, and to set another place for supper."

Numb and exhausted, Elizabeth simply nodded. It occurred to her that she should tell him she could not accept his kind offer. She could go and stay in a hotel for tonight and consider what to do tomorrow. She could not possibly sleep in a loft with a fencing master; it was unthinkable. But he had vanished.

She pulled off her boots, curled up on the couch and went to sleep, and woke only once, when he hoisted her up and marched her to the cot. There was one bad moment when he tugged at her shirt, presumably intending to undress her, but when he felt her shrink away he dropped his hand, and merely covered her with what felt like one of the towels. Through half-closed eyes she saw the dim gleam of metal on the walls. The cot must be in the sword-room, then, not in the other room, where presumably her host slept. Reassured that she was at least not sharing a bedchamber with a fencing master, she fell back to sleep.

Three

In her dream, her uncle was chasing her, his fish-like eyes protruding even more with the effort of running. She could hear a series of thumps as his feet hit the floor—or was it a street? Or stairs? The thumps sounded like stairs. He was making an odd purring noise, and just as he came up with her, he picked up a lantern and shone it full in her face.

With a gasp, Elizabeth opened her eyes. There was a light shining in them, so she closed them again. The thumps were gone, but she still heard the purring.

Not purring, she remembered. Cooing. It was the pigeons. She was in the loft, the fencing-master's loft; it was all dreadfully improper, but it did not matter because she was never going to be able to get home to England in any case. Gloomily, she sat up, and the light vanished, but looking down at the cot, she saw a fiercely bright triangle where her head had been. Sunlight was coming in through the tiny windows near the ceiling and had angled off one of the swords straight onto the cot. Shocked, she realized it must be very late in the morning.

She scrambled up at once. The basin and pitchers were gone, but looking through the open door to the bare outer room she could see them sitting on one of the chests. She went out and washed her face and rinsed her teeth. Then she looked down at her stained and wrinkled clothing with a sigh. No decent hotel would give her a room at any price, she thought. Not looking like this. And yet she must leave and find some other place to stay.

A light step on the stairs, and Sommers appeared, panting slightly. His shirt was clinging to his spare frame, and a fine sheen of perspiration coated his face and neck. "Up at last, slugabed?" he inquired, grinning. "I've already had two sets of pupils here. A fine assistant you are."

"Mr. Sommers—" began Elizabeth.

He had disappeared momentarily into the other room. When he reemerged, he was carrying a larger towel and clean linens. "I'm going down to bathe," he announced. "In addition to her many other virtues, Frau Renner has the very latest in bathtubs. When the landlord bought her the new stove, they installed some kind of tank for the water. Would you like a bath?" he added, looking at her disordered clothing. "I thought I could lend you one of my shirts. I looked in your valise, and your clean one appears to have a hole in it." He tossed her a large white piece of cloth, and Elizabeth caught it.

"No," she managed, "I am fine for the moment. Thank you." She took a breath and started on her speech again. "Mr. Sommers—"

But he was off down the staircase before she could continue. She sat down on the couch in a daze, still clutching the shirt. Should she just leave? No, that would be dreadfully rude. She looked at the shirt. It was very clean, and neatly pressed. Everything in the place was clean, she realized, except her. Books neatly lined up, crockery set out just so on the table.

On impulse, she walked over to the other room and looked in the door. There was a small trundle, which had already been made up with mathematical precision, a tiny table with some papers on it—squared into symmetrical stacks—and another washstand with a smaller basin. The one which had been in her room must be for pupils, she realized.

She went back into the sword-room and closed the door. She desperately needed a clean shirt. Surely she could pay him for it? It was lucky he had not noticed the other shirt was far too big for her when he had looked in her valise.

Then a dreadful thought struck her: her papers were in the valise. Her papers with her real name. A sudden panic overtook her. At once it became supremely important that this Mr. Sommers should not know how she had deceived him. She opened the valise, relieved to see that the shirt, as she remembered, was on top, and that nothing else seemed to have been disturbed. Snatching out the bundle of letters and papers from the bottom, she pulled out both sets of documents, and refolded the letters.

How long would his bath take? She had no idea. In her experience, most of bath time was waiting for hot water to be carried in, and it seemed as though that was not the case here.

In a fever of haste, she made a decision she would later deeply regret. She snatched up the papers, sank them with both hands into the basin, still full of water, and tore the sodden sheets into tiny pieces. Then she scraped up the limp shreds, squeezed the water out of them until they made a sticky ball, and shoved it up the chimney as far as she could reach.

It seemed as though this decision calmed her and made other decisions easier. She went back into the little room, closed the door, and put on his shirt. It was only a little large—Sommers was of medium height, and fairly slender. Then she pulled out a clean pair of stockings and started to put them on, only to stop as there was a quick rap at the door and Sommers reappeared, smelling strongly of soap.

"Let's take a look at your foot," he said briskly, apparently not concerned that his shirt was still open and that he was not wearing stockings or shoes. Come to think of it, her own feet were bare, and her legs exposed to the knee. A ferocious blush rose up her neck and over her face.

But there was worse; he had her bare foot and was twisting it carefully, frowning down at the slight swelling. "It needs to be bound up," he said, and disappeared into his own room. A moment later he came back in with a strip of flannel and, unconscious of her embarrassment, wound it very firmly around her instep. "Try that," he commanded, sitting back on his heels. Warily, she took a step. The relief was enormous.

"You are a miracle worker, sir," she said warmly.

"Good," he replied. "We can have our first lesson after you have something to eat. If you can eat, after yesterday."

She lowered her head, embarrassed, but he laughed.

"I've no students this afternoon. Some immensely wealthy Spanish noblewoman has arrived in Vienna and is giving a fete to which nearly all my pupils are invited. Unaccountably, however, I have received no card of invitation, which leaves me free to start your training."

After I've had some food, thought Elizabeth. *I'll tell him then. It would be rude to leave right now, and I need to think of a way to offer him money for the shirt without offending him.*

A week later, Elizabeth would have stared blankly at anyone who addressed her as Miss DeQuincy. She was Purcell—or occasionally Ned, when Sommers slipped out of his normally respectful manner and treated her like the young pup he thought she was. And whoever she was, she ached everywhere. He had been shocked by the weakness of her arms, and had set her to practicing two-handed with the heaviest sabers until her shoulders trembled with fatigue. Lunging—which she did for what seemed like hours every day—had produced a continuous, aching band across the front of her thighs. For two days, in fact, she could barely go down the stairs, but Sommers had just laughed heartlessly at her dismay and told her it would wear off.

Already she was greeting pupils at the salle, taking their coats, and bringing down their weapons from the sword room. She also accompanied him to most of his classes in private homes, carrying the masks and foils and, for beginners, the burlap coats she had mistaken for sacks on her first sight of the fencing salon.

She herself had now had several lessons with these. The student put on the smock, which was of dark brown burlap, as did the instructor or sparring partner. Then both took up wooden rods and dipped them in a bucket of chalk. Hits were reckoned by counting chalk marks on the burlap. Elizabeth's single ambition now was to one day put at least a trace of chalk on Sommers. At the moment he did not even bother to put on the burlap when they practiced. Comparing herself to her teacher, she felt clumsy and inept. She could not recognize how much and how quickly she was learning—or how urgently she would soon need her new skills.

Her uncle's breeches had not survived two days of lunging. If she had bothered to consider why they were in the workbasket, she would have looked at them more closely. The back panel was worn so thin that light shone through it. Sommers had lent her a pair, which were far too long, for the rest of the day, and Frau Renner had quickly found her some secondhand ones of the proper size.

One day, five days after her arrival, she had looked over at one of the mirrors in the salle. There, facing her, was a barefoot, panting young man wearing Sommers's shirt and breeches handed down from Frau Renner's nephew. Not one item in the mirror was familiar. Even her face looked different—younger, less feminine. At that point, horrified, she had resolved yet again to leave, but Sommers was coming at her with the dreaded chalk-tipped staff, and she had forgotten all about it by the time their bout was finished.

"Today is the children's class," Sommers told her at breakfast a week after her first lesson. "They did not come last week because of the fete. I think you are ready to take them."

"Surely you are joking!" protested Elizabeth, horrified. "I cannot even demonstrate the first four positions properly yet."

"These are eight- and nine-year-olds," he advised. "They just began in May. If you can keep them from clouting each other, you will be doing more than I have succeeded in doing so far. For the most part, they are spoilt, undisciplined brats who have no business studying fencing. But such is the fashion for swordplay these days that their parents have eagerly descended on me. The wealthiest have private lessons at their homes, of course. Still, most of those pupils have remained with my old master." He scowled. "Sometimes I think the main reason he helped set me up in my own establishment was to be rid of the children's lessons."

"But are you certain I am able to take a class?" asked Elizabeth, her eyes round with anxiety. "Even beginners?"

"So certain that I have booked two advanced students at the same time," was the response. "And since the extra fees are the source of your wages, you should be eager to prove me right." He looked at her critically. "You know, there is one thing we need to attend to before the lesson." He looked at the clock on the mantel. "We have time, come along." He strode into his bedchamber, and Elizabeth followed reluctantly. "Sit there," he said, waving at the trundle bed.

Timidly, Elizabeth sat down.

He was fishing around in a trunk which he had opened, and emerged at last with a small pair of scissors. "Been meaning to do this since the first day," he commented. "Hold still."

He took a full twenty minutes at it, working very patiently, with a sheet spread out on the coverlet to catch the clippings. "Not bad," he said at last, well pleased. "I should have made someone a very fine valet, I believe." He handed Elizabeth a small glass and she looked, curious, then gasped in shock.

When she had cut her own hair, she had simply hacked it off at the neck, leaving the raw ends just below ear length. Now Sommers had trimmed the ragged edges and cut it short all over, and it was already curling gently around her brow. She looked so much like Robin that it hurt, and something of her thoughts must have shown on her face, because Sommers pulled the glass away and looked at her with concern.

"Is something wrong? Did I make it too short?"

Elizabeth shook her head; she did not trust her voice. Obeying an unaccountable impulse, she went into her room and pulled the oval case out of the valise, then handed it to Sommers, who had followed her. He looked at the portrait, and then at her. The likeness was unmistakable, especially the eyes. 'Chapman eyes,' her father had called them. He had lost—or more likely gambled away—the miniature of her mother, but had told both children often that their unusual eyes were his best reminder of his dead wife.

"It is not you, is it?" he said very slowly. "Too old. Your father? No, of course not, the subject has a short haircut like the one I gave you. And he is in one of the new uniforms. A brother?"

"My older brother," said Elizabeth, turning away so he could not see her face.

"He is dead?"

She nodded.

Sommers squeezed her shoulder.

"He—he was with Wellington in Portugal, and his unit was betrayed to the French by a Portuguese guide who was taking them through the hills." She felt Sommers stiffen abruptly and withdraw his hand.

"I am very sorry," he said quietly. Then he strode off to his own room, and made something of a fuss about gathering up the clippings to give Elizabeth time to recover.

In the end, Elizabeth did not have to give much of a lesson. Shortly after she began, with seven unruly boys, the advanced pupils arrived. While they warmed up and then sparred with each other, she was able, with some difficulty, to put her class through three or four basic exercises.

But in the middle of demonstrating different grips, she saw two of her students looking over at the other side of the yard. This would not have surprised her, except that they were two of the three who were holding actual swords, a privilege they had all demanded vociferously. It must be something compelling to draw their attention under those circumstances. And it was.

When she turned around herself, she saw that Sommers had a foil in each hand and had taken on both of his students simultaneously. She motioned to her class to put their weapons in the rest position and watched along with them. The speed and the complexity of the engagement, which would have been meaningless to her a week earlier, was now terrifying and beautiful. Her students were spellbound. Eventually, Sommers disengaged and withdrew. The class let out a collective breath; they had been standing motionless.

"Can you do that?" demanded one of the smaller students, a dark-haired boy with a rather haughty air.

"No," said Elizabeth with a small sigh. "I, however, did not begin my training early, as you are doing." She had no more trouble with them for the rest of the lesson, and they said their good-byes in a markedly more courteous manner than they had used when they first arrived.

Sommers came over to her as she was gathering up rods and sacking and said with something rather different from his usual detached manner, "Ned, that was more profitable than I had imagined. How were the brats?"

"Fine," answered Elizabeth. "They watched you for a quarter hour. So did I, for that matter. It was well worth watching."

"Apparently one of my pupils agrees with you," said Sommers with a faint smile. "That lesson was by way of being an audition. I have been engaged to teach the emperor's son."

"The crown prince?" Elizabeth frowned. She had seen him, from a distance, at several musical soirees. He was a year or so younger than she was, an odd-looking young man with a vacuous stare who was rumored to be feeble-minded.

"No, his younger brother, Francis Charles." He stooped down and helped her gather up equipment. "He is only ten or eleven. It is a great compliment to be asked to instruct him. We will be going over to the Reitschule next week."

"We?" gasped Elizabeth. So much for her hopes of remaining inconspicuous while she earned her coach fare! It was one thing to help carry equipment to the homes of bourgeois pupils; quite another to take the risk of venturing into the palace complex, which teemed with people at all hours—including people who had seen her with her aunt.

"Purcell, have you no sense yet of my consequence?" demanded Sommers. "Think you that anyone in that rabbit warren of an imperial palace will consider me fit to instruct a prince if I do not have an attendant to lend me dignity?"

Elizabeth was still trying to decide whether or not he was serious as he strode off towards the stairs with an armful of wooden rods. Perhaps that was what impelled her, when the two English gentlemen came hesitantly into the courtyard a few moments later inquiring for Sommers, to ask for a card and to inform them, doing her best imitation of a butler, that she would see if the master was receiving visitors.

When she handed Sommers the card, he looked at her suspiciously. "Have you turned footman, then?" he asked, glancing at the card. Then he froze. "Hell and the devil!" he muttered. "No help for it, it will be even worse as I deny myself to him. Play your part, Purcell; show him up."

"There are two gentlemen," said Elizabeth, worried. "Would you like them both to come up?"

"I suppose so," said Sommers, distracted. He vanished into his bedchamber. "Go down and fetch them," he called, "while I wash off some of this dust."

Elizabeth looked down at the card, which he had left on the table. It read, *Major Thomas Sommers Cox.* Puzzled, she ran down the stairs.

"Please come up," she said politely to the two visitors, looking at them more closely. One must be family— but which one? Neither looked much like her employer. The taller and younger of the two was a dark-haired officer in a uniform which looked vaguely familiar to her. But the insignia showed his rank as captain, not major. The other man, in quiet but well-made clothing of a distinctly British cut, was a round, pleasant-looking type with pale hair, pale eyes, pale eyebrows, and pale lips. He looked rather washed-out next to his companion.

"You go first, Cox," said the officer, a glint of mischief in his eye. "I'll warrant he is mighty anxious to see you."

"You've a cruel streak, by Jove," responded the other man, but he started up the stairs. Elizabeth could hear him chuckling to himself. He emerged into the Spartan sitting-room just behind her, where her employer was waiting, a slight frown between his brows. He showed no sign of recognizing the visitor. *Something is wrong,* thought Elizabeth.

"Mr. Sommers? Mr. Michael Sommers?" inquired the round man genially. "Allow me to introduce myself. I am Thomas Sommers Cox, your cousin. It happens that business calls me to Vienna, and I desired to make your acquaintance."

"I am very happy to meet you, sir," said Sommers, "but I must disclaim any ties of kinship. Mine is a rather small branch of the family; I do not believe I have any male cousins."

The second visitor had mounted the stairs very quietly and was leaning against the wall at the top of the staircase, watching Sommers narrowly. "Oh, come now," he interrupted. "You can do better than that, surely. Tell him your father poisoned himself after being disowned and you therefore have sworn an oath never to receive any of your relatives."

"Nathanson!" gasped Sommers. He looked from his alleged cousin to the newcomer and back again. Suspicion dawned on his face, and evolved into a relieved grin. "You unfeeling monster," he accused, "you sent him up alone deliberately to scare me witless. Confess it."

"Well," conceded Nathanson, "I did think it might prove amusing. Did I give you a bad moment or two?"

"Or two," replied Sommers ruefully. "Why have you returned? Is your friend here in truth a Sommers?" He was looking around, distracted. "Please come in and sit down. I'll send Purcell down for some refreshments."

He nodded at Elizabeth, who went off in haste in search of Frau Renner and the ubiquitous cakes. She tried to efface herself while they were there, which was not easy in such a small space, but they stayed for only three-quarters of an hour.

Elizabeth gave a sigh of relief when they left; she had

seen the one called Nathanson give her several hard
stares during the conversation. Then it was time to prepare for an afternoon lesson at a palace over by the
Freyung. By the time they had returned, she was
exhausted and had dismissed the incident from her
mind.

When Sommers informed her that he was meeting
his friends for dinner at their hotel, she gladly went
down to Frau Renner's kitchen for an early supper.
Now she could catch up on her rest, which seemed in
perpetually short supply these days. It was still daylight,
in fact, when she tumbled onto her cot, and only when
she was delightfully comfortable did she remember that
she needed to leave a lamp lit for Sommers. Yawning,
she got up, lit the lamp, and returned to the cot. In less
than a minute she was fast asleep.

She did not awaken when he returned, although perhaps at some level she was aware that he was moving
around in the sitting room. But the knock on the door
at the bottom of the stairs did rouse her. She sat up,
thinking perhaps it was morning and she should answer
it. It was still full dark, however, and she heard Sommers
running down the stairs. Then two sets of feet came
back up, and Sommers must have relit the lamp; she
saw a glow under her door.

"My apologies," said Nathanson's voice. "It took him
forever to decide to retire. The man drinks brandy as
though it were water."

"He'll do well here, then," commented Sommers.
"They admire men who can drink. Not as much as
the Prussians, do, of course. Would you like something
yourself? Or did you have enough trying to keep pace
with my 'cousin'?"

"Enough and more than enough," said Nathanson
wearily. She heard the horsehair in the couch crinkle
as someone seated himself.

You are eavesdropping, she accused herself. But what
could she do? She was wide awake, and the rooms were

so small that no matter how quietly they spoke, she would hear every word. Perhaps she should ostentatiously reveal that she was not asleep—come out of her room, or make a noise. But just then she heard her name.

"Where did you get that angel-faced boy? Purcell, you called him?"

"I adopted him, in a manner of speaking," answered Sommers curtly. "He was robbed of all his money on the point of setting out to return to England, and I hired him on as an assistant so he could earn enough to make the trip."

"He'll break some hearts in a few years," observed Nathanson.

Sommers laughed. "There speaks one who knows," he mocked. "How many beauties have you left languishing in Spain?"

It was true, thought Elizabeth, Nathanson was startlingly handsome.

Nathanson ignored that gibe. "Was it not a bit risky to 'adopt' someone? What if he discovers your wig, for example?"

Sommers sighed. "Pray do not remind me of it. I wear it all the time now. And it is deuced uncomfortable. But Frau Renner is so inquisitive, and fusses over me so constantly, I should have been doing so all along."

Now Elizabeth was listening intently. She felt a strange mixture of disgust and curiosity. Clearly her host was not what he seemed, and perhaps she was in danger, staying here with him. It was only prudent for her to find out more about him. And yet it seemed very disloyal, after all he had done for her.

"You will need to be on your guard even more. Meillet is loose, and White has let it be known that you are not dead."

There was a long pause. Then Sommers said, "Do you think Meillet is coming here?"

"I am nearly certain of it. He has sworn to find you

and my father, and rumor now places you both in this area."

"That is not good news," said Sommers heavily. "You found me easily, even though I had moved since you were here a month ago."

"I went to Signor Fratelli's *salle d'armes,* and he told me where to find you," said Nathanson scornfully. "Not that Meillet will have any difficulty tracing you once he gets word there is a left-handed English fencing master in town. But Fratelli told me something else, as well. A rather interesting story."

"What was that?" asked Sommers. Elizabeth heard him shifting in the armchair.

"He told me that after you had been working for him for several weeks, he suggested you should get a new jacket, since you were now going to the homes of some wealthy pupils. And when you delayed, he began to wonder, since he was—as he claims—paying you quite well."

"Go on," said Sommers savagely. "Did he think I was gambling?"

"I suppose something of the sort might have occurred to him. At any rate, he explained to me, very apologetically, that fencing masters must be careful of their reputation, because pupils associate fencing with the code of honor. And since he had hired you off the street, with no references, he grew worried. So he sent Teobaldo to follow you when you left the *salle.*"

"The devil he did!" said Sommers in furious tones.

"He had a perfect right to do so," said Nathanson sternly. "Shall I go on, or is your indignation blocking your ears?"

There was a grumble of assent.

"He told me that Teobaldo found you living in what was described to me as a garret. And since this is hardly the lap of luxury, I take it your previous lodgings— which you would not let me see—were rather grim."

"They were inexpensive," muttered Sommers.

"As was your food, I gather."

"What did Teobaldo do, watch me eat?" demanded Sommers, clearly angry again.

"No. It was a simple matter of arithmetic. He followed you to my uncle's bank and watched you give them a rather large sum of money to be forwarded to an office in London. And then he bribed the clerk to tell him how much you sent back, how often. I have already told my uncle to sack the clerk, by the way." There was a long silence. "It will not help your family in England if you starve to death, you know."

"I am perfectly well," growled Sommers. "And, as you see, in relatively respectable quarters now. Are you implying Fratelli set me up in my own *salle* because he was sorry for me?"

"He did not say so," was the reply. "How far will your pride take you? Will you storm over to the Degenstrasse and throw it back in his face?"

"No," said Sommers slowly. "He desperately needed an assistant when I arrived. He was so overbooked that he was losing pupils who were annoyed at being kept waiting. And we made an agreement when I moved over here: he would send me his left-handed students, or the very advanced ones, who wished to practice against a left-handed opponent, and I would take the children's class and then send them back to him when they were civilized. Thank God for Purcell. I was tearing hair out of my wig every time I had to teach those little rogues."

"Is the boy a decent fencer, then?"

Sommers gave a crack of laughter. "Would you believe it, Nathanson? He is clearly a gentleman's son, but has never been taught to box or fence! Nor instructed in any other sport, I'll wager; he is as weak as an invalid. But he moves well and never complains, although I see him shifting the sword bags from shoulder to shoulder when we go off to give lessons. In a week he has learned enough to take the children on. He's quite a good lad, I think."

At these words, Elizabeth felt a warm rush of happiness flooding through her. She would work twice as hard, she vowed. She would practice in front of the mirrors downstairs in her spare time. She would pay attention when he talked to her about the history of fencing after dinner. She would read some of his books. The rest of their conversation drifted over her unheeded as she fell back to sleep, savoring Sommers's offhand praise and wondering if he, too, thought she had an angel face.

Four

"Well, coz?" said Cox, with a challenging air. He and Nathanson had watched politely as Sommers and Elizabeth put away the equipment from the morning lessons and had trooped up the stairs with them and waited while they cleaned up. Now the two visitors sat on the sofa, waiting for Sommers to answer their query.

"Why on earth do the two of you want me to attend these ghastly parties?" demanded Sommers, exasperated. "I've plenty of contacts through my fencing lessons, and now I will be going to the palace once a week as well—to the Riding School, at least," he corrected.

"The whole point of asking your cousin to visit you in Vienna was so that he could sponsor you socially," said Nathanson impatiently. "Your good friend Colonel White was most anxious that you should make the acquaintance of important people in Vienna. It will not hurt you to sit through an hour of singing and drink a few glasses of wine." At the mention of White's name, Sommers stiffened and shot a quick glance at Elizabeth, but she had fastened on something else.

"Is there to be music at this event?" she said, before she could stop herself.

"Yes. Do you know of Johann Vogl?" asked Sommers. "He is to perform at the home of my would-be hostess this evening."

"You must go, then!" Elizabeth, her face glowing. "He has the most beautiful voice and is very witty and charming as well. I have only heard him once, and would give anything to have another chance."

"I would be a boor, then, to refuse, in your eyes?" he laughed, enjoying Elizabeth's enthusiasm. Then he eyed her thoughtfully and said slowly to Nathanson, "Do you suppose we could take Purcell?"

"Not in those clothes," was the frank response. "Unless we take him to help the coachman with the horses. But I suppose that with his looks he would have no trouble persuading a maidservant to station him someplace inconspicuous where he could at least hear the performance."

Sommers made a face. "My fault. I've been meaning to get him a jacket and another set of breeches. We've been so cursed busy. Since the palace engaged me to teach the young prince, every well-born twelve-year-old in Vienna seems to want private lessons. But I still think it rather questionable for the fencing master of the morning to appear as a gentleman in the evening, though he be escorted by twenty genteel cousins."

"For heaven's sake, man, even I have been invited," snapped Nathanson. "And there are many refugees of good breeding these days in Vienna who have turned their hand to teaching dancing, or French, or Italian. Think you that you will be the only one there who works for his bread? This Doña Maria has invited nearly the entire population of Vienna to some affair or another since she arrived."

"My pupils are talking of little else, it is true. Who is she? Do you know?"

Cox frowned. "I cannot remember her full name and

all her titles. It was not familiar to me, that I know, and I was in Spain for some months two years ago. Her family is not well-known or influential and, to be frank, I would wager that even the prospect of excellent entertainment might not lure so many to the house she has rented here did she not travel with a ravishing young lady as her companion.''

"Well, no wonder you want to go then, Nathanson," said Sommers with a mocking smile. "And here I thought Vienna would be a dull place for you."

The young officer flushed and his mouth tightened, but he said nothing more. It was left to Cox to make arrangements to call for them later that afternoon in a hired carriage. "Since," he informed them, "Nathanson is unwilling to borrow his uncle's."

"My aunt has put a horrid great crest on the panels," muttered Nathanson. "I refuse to set foot in the thing, and so would you had you once seen it in all its garish glory."

Perhaps, thought Elizabeth that evening, a garish carriage would have been just the thing. What must have been a rather dignified stone house a few miles southwest of Vienna had been transformed for the evening into a display of how dangerous it was to combine money and a habit of lavish entertaining with an utter disregard for good taste. The lanterns in the driveway had been painted with silver—very hastily, from the appearance of the posts—and hung with enormous baskets of yellow flowers. It was still light, of course; the days were long just now, but Elizabeth found a distinct trace of scent on the air and wondered if when they were lit they would be burning perfumed oil.

A large terrace at the top of the front steps was covered with a gilded cloth strewn with flower petals, and the great doors, wide open, had garlands of blossoms and foil hung over them. More glittering floor covers were visible in the front hall, as were liveried footmen with powdered wigs and coats stiff with silver braid. It was almost a relief to escape to the stableyard, where the horses were unharnessed, and to go into the kitchen with the coachman.

Inside there was complete confusion. Four cooks were screaming at assistants, servants who had arrived with other guests were darting around trying to grab something to eat or drink before they were pushed off into a side room, footmen and maids were dashing in and out with trays. Elizabeth wondered if there was any point in asking about some means to hear the music upstairs. It did not look as simple as Nathanson had made it seem back in the loft. She was certainly in the way here, she decided, and she began to edge her way toward the door leading to the side room.

Halfway there, she was seized from behind and spun around. An enormous woman dressed all in black demanded fiercely in very bad German, "Do you speak French?" When Elizabeth nodded, she broke into a huge smile. "Come here, then, child," she said in that language. "What a liar, that Hessel, to try to tell me those village boys could say anything beyond *bonsoir!* Would you mind very much working upstairs, instead of in the kitchen?" And then, as she and Elizabeth fought their way out of the kitchen into the lower hall, she took a better look at her. "*Madre de Dios!* You are not one of ours!"

"I would not mind helping," said Elizabeth quickly. "If it is not anything difficult. I would very much like to hear the singing."

"I will send you into the main salon, then," said the woman. "You are to bring chairs to the ladies, and send the waiters with trays to anyone who requests something to drink, and generally be available to carry messages down to the staff here below—if someone calls for their carriage or if Monsieur Vogl wishes anything special to eat or drink after he sings."

She was pulling a blue and silver jacket out of a cupboard as she spoke. Then she turned and looked at what Elizabeth was wearing. "Boots!" She raised her hands in horror. "Wait here." A few minutes later, she reappeared with white stockings, pumps, and a wig. The pumps were too big, but not unmanageably so, and Elizabeth was relieved to think that with the wig, no one who had seen her with her aunt could possibly recognize her.

As a footman escorted her up the stairs, she had a moment of panic. What was she doing here, acting as a page boy in the rented home of a mad Spanish aristocrat? How could she possibly deceive anyone? She had no notion of how a footman should behave, nor any idea of how to summon a waiter or send for a carriage. But as she was entering the crowded salon, she saw that people were drifting in, settling themselves for the concert, and she hurried over to arrange chairs.

After that, she was so busy she had no time to worry.

The hostess was receiving her guests in a small salon across the hall from the room where Vogl had just finished singing. Many guests were lingering in the larger room, chatting with each other or sampling drinks and tidbits from the gilded trays offered by hovering attendants. Cox, however, having been introduced to Doña Maria, was determined to perform the same service for Nathanson and his fictional cousin, and he hustled them away. There was a crowd around the chair where the lady was greeting visitors, so that at first Nathanson could not even see her. Then a gap opened up, and the two younger men stood in awed silence as they took in her appearance.

"Incredible!" said Nathanson at last, in a faint voice. "What has White embroiled us in, now, do you think?" They were moving forward, bowing, as Cox presented them with a trumpet-blast of Spanish syllables.

Nathanson was trying not to stare. The old woman who sat so imperiously in the chair had barely an inch of her own flesh showing. Her hair was clearly a wig, a very elaborate and ancient one, which she had powdered in a style thirty years gone by. There was even more powder on her face, which fairly cracked under the layers. A black gown beaded copiously with jet was of the same vintage as the wig, and opened out over enormous hoops. Silver lace gloves covered her ladyship's hands, but rings and bracelets were jammed on over the gloves. A matching silver shawl covered her neck and shoulders, although the evening was warm. An overpowering aroma of lily water radiated out from where she sat.

"Well, Monsieur," demanded the lady in a high, imperious voice. Her French was excellent, save for a trace of a lisp, common among gentry from northern Spain. "Are you thinking my gown a trifle outmoded? You are quite right, quite right!" She gave a cackle of laughter. "You would not wish to see me in damped muslin, I do assure you! These hoops and corsets are far better for me, though some of my contemporaries do all of us a disservice by attempting to wear the newer modes." And she glared across the room at a plump matron in a gauze robe, an unfortunate choice on that sultry evening. Nathanson heard a stifled sound from Sommers which sounded something like a fish swallowing. To his disgust, both his companions had managed to avoid the gorgon's notice by keeping their eyes modestly lowered, and now they were edging away. His attempt to follow them was forestalled when the beady eyes swung back and pinned him in place.

"Allow me to present my companion, Mademoiselle Mendez," said Doña Maria, gesturing airily to her left. "She, at least, can wear the latest designs *à merveille.*" Nathanson tore his eyes away from the caked masses of powder and turned towards a graceful young lady who had moved towards them, hearing her name. Then he looked again. His eyes widened momentarily. A girl with dark blond hair and green eyes in a classic oval face stood regarding him with friendly interest. Her own expression was calm as she allowed him to bow over her hand. Of course. She had presumably seen him as he approached Doña Maria and had not been caught by surprise, as he had. Long training asserted itself. He regained control over his features and murmured some polite phrases.

"Captain Nathanson and I are acquainted already, madame," he heard the girl say. The sheer effrontery amazed him. "We met in England last year." She turned to him with a dazzling smile. "It grows very warm, do you not think? Perhaps madame will excuse us for a few moments; we could walk in the garden."

Mechanically he offered his arm and moved out through the room, ignoring the protests of what seemed to be an enormous group of young men professing themselves mademoiselle's devoted cavaliers. An older woman in a plain black dress had detached herself from a position near the hostess and was following them out onto the back terrace. *A duenna,* Nathanson thought. That might make things a bit difficult. He forced himself to walk slowly down the terrace steps, assisting his companion ostentatiously.

Once they were out of sight of the house, the languid courtesy vanished. Gritting his teeth, he pulled her along at a virtual run along a small avenue of cherry trees, so that the duenna had to trot after them to stay in sight. In his wake, the paper lanterns strung between the saplings began to dance crazily as he brushed impatiently through them.

"Does she speak English?" he asked in a low voice, when they had gained a bit of distance.

"French, yes; English, no. Or only a few words."

"And is she discreet?"

She looked up at him archly. "Quite discreet. Unless you try to kiss me, of course."

"Kiss you!" he hissed in a fury, "Kiss you! Elena, you little baggage, you will be fortunate an I do not box your ears! What are you doing here? You are supposed to be on your way to Italy to marry Anthony!"

She settled herself demurely under one of the lanterns on a small bench and admired him as he glowered down at her.

"My, you are glorious when you are in a temper, Cousin James," she said sweetly. "I *am* on my way to Italy. I simply took a small detour. In a few weeks, Uncle Leon will escort me down to Milan, and Anthony and my aunt will come and meet me there."

He was not mollified. "A small detour? Four weeks of jaunting all over the continent? Flirting outrageously with every man Doña Maria entertains, I warrant? Does your mother know about this?"

Elena was enjoying herself. She opened her fan and then closed it, rapping it on the palm of her hand to emphasize her point as she spoke. "Firstly." Rap. "My mother has given her permission. Secondly." Rap. "Anthony himself was informed. Thirdly." Rap. "Your father knows and approves."

For the first time Nathanson betrayed surprise. "You have seen him, then? Where?"

"In—in Gibraltar, of course. You were there, too. In March."

Nathanson muttered under his breath and returned grimly to his original argument. "I'll go bail Anthony would not have agreed if he knew you as well as I do. There is enough uncomfortable talk to plague him, what with my sister breaking her engagement to him and marrying a Gentile. It is outrageous of you to carry on in this fashion under the circumstances."

"Is it my fault if your sister fell in love with one of your fellow couriers?" she retorted, stung. "Surely she is the one to reproach, not me."

"I am warning you, Elena," said Nathanson, with a stern look. "It is not only Anthony's interests which concern me. There is an epidemic of dueling in Vienna and Prague right now, and you are already the talk of the town. If one single hint of scandal attaches to you, or if your true identity is discovered, or if any of the young officers, even the French officers, are injured on your account, I will personally see to it that you are held accountable.''

Her eyes dropped. "Very well," she said in a low voice. "I will be sure to flirt with all of them, and be as silly as possible. But you have no idea how dreary it has been in Gibraltar this past year." Her tone grew wistful. "I only wanted to travel a bit and see something of society before Aunt Amelia makes me into a model daughter-in-law."

"Don't try to cozen me," growled her cousin. "Your life seemed none so dreary when I last saw you, dangling officers from every finger on your graceful little hand." Still, he thought, he could not blame her for chafing at the restrictions their odd social status imposed. "We should not stay away too long," he said abruptly. "That will create the very problem I wish to avoid." He offered his arm again, but she did not rise.

"You have not told me what you are doing here," she pointed out.

"No, I have not," he agreed.

She did get up then, and stamped her foot in irritation. "You have not changed one bit!" she flared. "You expect me to tell you everything I hear or see or do, and you never, ever confide in me! Do you think I am not to be trusted?"

"Officially, I am here to act as a liaison between English residents of Vienna and the British military advisors to the Allies. Does that satisfy you?"

"Not if you preface it with the word 'officially,' " said Elena darkly. "I heard you were almost captured by the French last month. You and your father seem to take a perverse delight in frightening the rest of the family half out of our wits with your capers."

"I do not appear to be in great danger here in Vienna." They had turned back towards the house. "I hear the armistice has been extended until the middle of August. Things are quite peaceful here at the moment."

As if to contradict him, from the other side of one of the trees came a small feminine shriek and the sound of tearing cloth. Elena and Nathanson looked at each other in astonishment and Nathanson said in a low voice: "I believe I must leave you for a moment. May I entrust you to your dragon woman?" He did not wait for an answer, but pushed his way through the saplings and shrubs to the other path.

Two figures, stiff with anger, faced each other on opposite sides of the gravel walk, neither aware, yet, of his presence. Closer to Nathanson was a young man of something less than middle height, rather broad in the shoulder and neck. Nathanson could not see his face in the dim light. He had a better view of the petite young woman who stood glaring at him, clutching her reticule in her hands. It was brocade, to match the trim on her dress, and it was badly torn; the contents were spilling out into her hands. That must have been the ripping sound, thought Nathanson. And yet the young man did not look like a thief. He was wearing an elegant jacket and his breeches fit like a glove.

The girl caught sight of him first out of the side of her eye, and gasped. Then her opponent turned, and Nathanson saw that his first impression was correct. This was no thief; arrogance was stamped on that face from birth, he thought. Perhaps his initial interpretation of the shriek and ripping noise was correct after all. The reticule might have been interposed by the girl as her escort reached for some other target. He felt a sudden desire to plant his fist in the sneering face, but he simply bowed slightly to the girl, ignoring her companion, and said pointedly, "May I be of some assistance, mademoiselle?"

"You see, Fritz?" she said to the young man furiously. "This is what comes of behaving so outrageously! What will people think of us?" She turned belatedly to Nathanson. "Pray excuse us, monsieur. My brother and I have had a—a disagreement, and when my reticule was torn accidentally, I am afraid I gave a small scream." Clear blue eyes, tears still hanging on the lashes, looked up at him.

This is the most beautiful creature I have ever seen in my life, he thought, noting the fact in what seemed at the time a rather disinterested fashion. Next to her, his cousin Elena was a clumsy giant. Her arms and wrists, her feet peeking out from under the brocaded gown, were indescribably tiny and graceful. He could probably span her waist with his two hands. Every feature of her face looked as though it had been carved out of ivory. Even her hair was extraordinarily fine, worked into tiny gold curls caught up at the nape of her neck in a brocaded ribbon which matched the gown and the reticule. He realized he must be gawking like a peasant, and he wrenched his gaze away and bowed to the brother without even seeing him.

"I beg your pardon, then, for intruding. Monsieur, mademoiselle, your servant."

"Ah, no, monsieur, surely your chivalry deserves some reward. When you came so gallantly to my aid you did not know it was merely a family quarrel."

"Mademoiselle," he replied, some of his address returning to him, "your thanks are ample recompense."

"It is madame," she informed him. "Fritz, pray introduce us." Having ascertained Nathanson's name, which provoked a raised eyebrow, the brother introduced himself as Graf Friedrich von Werzel and his sister as the Countess of Brieg.

"I felicitate Monsieur le Comte," said Nathanson.

"Her husband is no longer in any case to accept your congratulations," said the brother in acid tones. "Although I assure you that while he was still alive he was the recipient of many similar remarks, which my sister did nothing to discourage.''

The countess dimpled. "Now, Fritz," she scolded. "Do not embroil the poor captain in our quarrel. You will have him think either that I am a heartless flirt or that you are a most ungracious brother.''

Nathanson had already made his choice. The scowling Friedrich seemed to him a boorish lout. It was difficult to believe he was that incomparable creature's blood kin. Still, for her sake, he would be civil to the man. The little countess was looking up at him.

"Could I trouble you to escort me back to the house?" she said timidly. "I fear my brother is still feeling a bit warm, and will wish to remain outside where it is cooler." He bowed and offered his arm.

"Theresa!" hissed the brother. He strode across the path and took her other arm urgently, breaking into German. "Do you know who he is? I will not permit this!"

"Excuse us one moment, Captain," said the countess calmly, quelling her brother with a warning frown. They stepped a few paces away, and she looked back to make sure that Nathanson was out of hearing.

"Of course I know who he is," she retorted. "And surely you do not believe that tale that he is the liaison officer to the British military advisers. He is a spy, and it is my duty as a servant of the emperor to become acquainted with him."

"Your sense of duty is not by chance influenced by the combination of a handsome face and a social standing which makes marriage impossible? What of your duty to our family name? Have you thought of that?"

She stamped her foot. "Fritz, have done! You are becoming a dreadful bore! I begin to be grateful I no longer bear that name." She turned away, then swung back. "And by the way, he speaks fluent German. His family is originally Hessian." She drifted gracefully down to where Nathanson waited, his face impassive.

"I apologize for my brother, Captain Nathanson," she said. "Shall we walk on?"

Elizabeth was the undisputed center of attention on the ride home. It began with a remark she made to Sommers as the carriage got under way. "I had no idea," she confessed, "how much servants gossip. You would not believe what I was told by complete strangers! I will never be careless about what I say or do in front of servants again."

"What sorts of things?" demanded Cox. "Did you learn anything about our hostess, for example?"

"Let me see," said Elizabeth. "She is a widow, from a rather poor region of Spain. Evidently she had French troops billeted on her estates several years ago and they did extensive damage to her home and her orchards. For the last month or so she has been traveling all over Europe, first to Paris, then to Dresden, and now here, trying to obtain compensation from French officials. Napoleon refused to see her in Dresden, and she went round to all of his marshals who were posted nearby to ask them to intercede, but without success. She has visited some of them two or three times, and sits for hours in their offices demanding to see some soldier now under their command who was billeted on her land in Spain. Then she records their names and ranks in an enormous leather casebook and waves the book at all the French commanders.

"Now she has come on to Vienna in the hopes that the emperor might be able to help her, or so that she can appeal to the allies, since they presently hold Spain. She travels with four coaches, two ladies-in-waiting, two priests, and her own chef. Her Spanish servants give themselves dreadful airs and refuse to speak German. And her Austrian housekeeper thinks she is mad, and told me at the rate she is spending money here in Vienna no Spanish estate could possibly be worth the expense and trouble, even if she does eventually obtain some redress.''

There was a stunned and rather impressed silence. ''We have been wasting our time, gentlemen,'' said Nathanson at last, ''attending the ladies upstairs. We should have been downstairs washing dishes. Who else was dissected?'' he asked Elizabeth.

''Hmmmm,'' she said, remembering. ''The young lady, Doña Maria's companion—I cannot remember her name—is thought to be a bit wild, and she went off into the garden with some man tonight; there were a number of comments, especially since he is evidently not *comme il faut*.''

Sommers burst out laughing. ''There you are, Nathanson!''

''Oh, I beg your pardon!'' gasped Elizabeth. ''I did not know it was you, sir!''

''No matter,'' said Nathanson. ''They are quite right. She is a shocking flirt, and I am not at all good *ton*. Pray continue.''

''There was another lady—the Duchess of Sagan— evidently she is Metternich's mistress. And the duchess's sister is a spy for the emperor's secret police.'' This was old news to the three men, who wondered where Elizabeth had been for the last three months that it was fresh to her. ''The duchess was to attend tonight and then sent word she was ill, but the servants say Metternich must be coming back tonight from Prague, and that is why she would not come.''

''How astute they are in the kitchen,'' commented Cox. ''I believe Metternich is indeed due here for a meeting tomorrow morning between the emperor and representatives of Prussia, but I did not think it was widely known.''

''Did you hear anything of a Countess of Brieg?'' asked Nathanson suddenly.

''Is she very tiny and blond?'' asked Elizabeth, frowning.

"Yes."

"I saw her in the Grand Salon during the music. Her servants were complaining about her downstairs. Her family married her to a very wealthy man when she was quite young; he was some fifty years older than she. Since he died last year, she has returned to Vienna. Her housekeeper left her service because she disapproved of her immodest behavior. But she has recently been appointed a lady-in-waiting to the Princess Maria Louisa. Her servants think this is shocking and claim the scandals were only overlooked because their mistress, too, spies for the secret police. And," concluded Elizabeth with relish, "she has a dreadful temper and beats her maids with the hot curling irons."

Luckily, it was dark in the carriage, and no one could see Nathanson's face. "I would imagine even the maidservants of such a woman are jealous, and spread rumors about her," he said lightly.

As the carriage pulled up at the entrance to Frau Renner's, Nathanson put out a hand and detained Sommers momentarily. He waited until Elizabeth had gone in the door, and then said emphatically, "You should get rid of that boy,"

"Why?" said Sommers. "I made a bargain with him, and I intend to keep it."

"It is too dangerous for you to have him here. He already knows you are not really Cox's cousin, and we have been fairly indiscreet in front of him. I could lend him the money to travel home. He does not need to slave for you for another three weeks."

"He could not leave yet; he has no papers," said Sommers, who found himself in no hurry to lose Purcell's help and companionship.

Nathanson made an impatient gesture. "Papers can be bought, and for the right price, bought quickly."

"The boy has no money," retorted Sommers. "What

he does have is pride. I do not think he is a danger to your plans. As for me, I have no plans and nothing to lose. What is galling you, my friend, is that remark he made about the little countess. I saw you looking at her like a sheep after you came in from your jaunt to the garden."

"That is not what is galling me, as you so crudely put it," flashed Nathanson. "He reminds me of someone, and I cannot remember who it is. I do not think his name is Purcell, that is certain."

"I am quite sure it is not. He made it up on the spot when I introduced myself. I could see the wheels turning behind those strange eyes of his."

"Well, then?"

"What of it? He did not want me to force him to return to his uncle, who apparently had treated him brutally. Thus it was only prudent to give me a false name. That does not prove him untrustworthy."

"I don't like it," muttered Nathanson. "You could be liable for prosecution. He is a minor, and his uncle is presumably his guardian. What makes you think the uncle is such a villain?"

"He flinched when I mentioned him. And he will never so much as take off his shirt where anyone can see him."

Nathanson was silent. He had seen the scars on Sommers's back and legs. Some arguments were unanswerable.

Five

With some reluctance, Elizabeth climbed out of the tin bathtub and hastily began to dress. She was always worried someone would come into the little room behind the kitchen when she was bathing, but it seemed as though soaking in hot water was the only way to prevent the sore muscles in her arms and legs from locking permanently into an aching spasm.

Tonight, with Sommers off at a reception, had seemed an ideal time to do some sewing. There was her second shirt, and the two jackets and dress breeches she had hastily bought secondhand after Sommers threatened to take her to a tailor. Then, struggling into the more formal of the two jackets, she had ripped one of the improvised breast bands she used to conceal what little curvature she had.

Altogether, the alterations and mending had taken quite a while, but when she had finished it was barely dark. Sommers would be gone for hours yet, and Frau Renner retired early, hence the extra indulgence of a long bath. Her spare band, now reasonably clean, was slung over the edge of the tub; she would have to think of some inconspicuous place to hang it up to dry.

Even fresh from the warm water, her legs protested as she climbed the stairs slowly. She knew, though, that she was growing stronger by the day. Her lunges were deeper and surer, and her wrists no longer sagged when she held a saber. There was a spring in her step, and her hands sometimes seemed to move of their own accord as Sommers attacked. When she had observed the prince's first lesson earlier that day, she had been very pleased to find that she recognized nearly everything Sommers demonstrated.

Wrapped up in such self-satisfied reflections, she noticed only at the last minute that a lamp had been kindled in the loft. Hastily she pulled her towel over the damp breast band and peered around the corner at the top of the stairs. Could Sommers have returned so early? There was no sound or movement in the room, and at first she did not see him. He must have been back for some little while; a decanter of brandy was on the table, and a glass. His good jacket was hanging over the back of the chair, and he himself was slumped over his folded arms, his head down on the table.

Was he drunk? Ill? She moved closer, giving an involuntary cry of concern. Then she saw the tension in the shoulders and the white knuckles of the fist clenched under his bowed head. He started up when he heard her and twisted around in the chair.

His habitual expression of calm irony was gone; he looked haggard and his eyes were empty.

"What is wrong?" cried Elizabeth, horrified at the look on his face. "Have you had some news from home? What is it?"

He turned his head away and got up abruptly from the chair. Not drunk, then; he moved easily, and she noticed the decanter was still quite full. Still not facing her, he said in a carefully controlled voice, "I found that Viennese society did not agree with me, so I left early." Walking over to the crooked little bookshelf behind the armchair, he ostentatiously selected a book and sat down.

"I beg your pardon," said Elizabeth stiffly, feeling for some reason indignant and hurt. *What business is it of yours?* she told herself as she went into her room and hung up the breast band underneath the towel on the washstand. *You have only known him a few weeks, and you will be leaving shortly.* Her sewing things were still out on the cot; she knelt on the floor and began to pack them away.

"You mended your other shirt?" inquired Sommers, in a neutral tone. "And got a decent jacket, I see." He was standing in the doorway, his face expressionless. Then he made a sudden fierce gesture. "Did you ever find yourself in a room full of mirrors? Unable to hold a conversation, or take a glass of wine from a servant, or bow to an acquaintance without seeing hundreds of you on every wall doing the same thing? And did you ever look at those shimmering copies and think that every one of them might be the real you, and you the reflection, and wish with all your heart that it were so?"

Openmouthed, Elizabeth stared at him. The hazel eyes were glittering; he looked feverish. What on earth was he talking about? Perhaps her first conjecture was correct and he was ill. Certainly he had been working himself to the bone the last week. A pang of guilt assailed her—the extra work was probably so that he could pay her while still sending money home to England.

He sat down on her cot with a groan. "My apologies, Ned. I'm talking nonsense, am I not? I mislike this scheme of Nathanson's, that is all. I have no place in the world of receptions and dances and elegant badinage."

"You did once, though," said Elizabeth slowly, studying him. She was still kneeling by his feet.

"I did once," he agreed. "But now I am no one. I have nothing. No family, no identity, no country. A man who is so alone does best not to look at mirrored walls in crowded rooms.''

"Surely you exaggerate," protested Elizabeth. "Comrades cannot replace family, but they are not so easily discounted. Nathanson seems to value you."

"He and I worked together, that is all."

"What of your other friends?"

"I have no friends," he answered bitterly. "Only former friends, and very few of those."

"What am I, then?" she flared, outraged. "Your servant? Your debtor?"

The tightness left his face and he had the grace to look embarrassed. "I suppose I had thought of you as something like a young cousin."

Elizabeth thought for a moment. "It might well be so, in fact," she said without thinking. "The Sommerses and Coxes are related, and I am nearly certain the Coxes are cousins of—my mother." She had only just in time stopped herself from saying "the Chapmans".

Sommers looked at her, amused. "My dear young cousin," he drawled. "I regret to inform you that in view of the price on my head in France, I have taken the liberty of borrowing a sobriquet. Sommers is not my real name."

Elizabeth flushed. "I suppose I have known that since Cox and Nathanson visited last week," she admitted. "I had forgot for the moment." And then, in a burst of frankness prompted by the odd intimacy of their conversation, she confessed, "Purcell is not my name, either."

Sommers thought of retorting that a ten-year-old would have seen through that hesitant announcement in the café, but he said only, "Nathanson thinks your uncle could charge me with kidnapping if he finds you."

Elizabeth stared at him in alarm.

"Should I be worried about such a possibility? Is there anyone here in Vienna, or nearby, who has a legal right to take charge of you?"

"There is not; I swear it," said Elizabeth firmly. She

was silent for a minute, remembering her twenty-first birthday. Her uncle had been away, and her aunt had surprised her by presenting her with the diamond earrings, which she had deliberately not worn for many months so that Elizabeth would be willing to accept them.

"Friends, then, since we are agreed we are not cousins?" He held out his hand. Looking up, she saw a wistful smile on Sommers's face. An odd sensation manifested itself in the middle of her chest. Had she seen him smile like that before? Surely not, or she would have remembered it.

"Friends," said Elizabeth hastily, suddenly conscious that her eyes had been fixed on his face for what seemed like five minutes. She gripped his hand in her best imitation of a manly handclasp, only to see him wince.

"Take it easy, Purcell," he warned. "No need to prove your loyalty by crushing my bones, you know." The ironic mask was back. He rose and sauntered out into the main room. "By the way, this brandy is dreadful stuff," he called back to her. "Lucky thing, or I'd not give much for my chances against Nathanson in our bout tomorrow morning."

Sommers did not seem to be exerting himself much, thought Elizabeth, watching the two men flash their foils through the bands of early morning light in the *salle*. It was raining lightly, and they had elected to fence inside. On the other hand, Nathanson, who was clearly quite a competent swordsman, was not pushing very hard, either.

"Not much of a challenge," grunted Nathanson. "Though your arm has healed well, I see." He stepped back. "Switch hands, then." Elizabeth noticed only now that Sommers was fencing right-handed. No wonder Nathanson had not had any difficulty. Sommers tossed the foil into his other hand, and they were about to resume, when there was a resounding tattoo on the door at the foot of the stairs.

"I'll go," said Elizabeth, and dashed down the stairs. It was too early for pupils, and Frau Renner did not knock. Perhaps it was Cox.

But it was not. It was a stranger, a very blond man in an officer's uniform of some sort—Elizabeth could not keep all the different colors and markings sorted out. She thought this one was Austrian, but she was not sure.

"Is there a Captain Nathanson here?" he demanded in French. His tone was more than peremptory, it was hostile.

"I will go and inquire," temporized Elizabeth, wondering who this person was and why he was so angry. Perhaps she should warn Nathanson that the visitor seemed threatening.

"I will see for myself," growled the officer, and he shoved her out of the way with the staff he was carrying and strode up the stairs. Dismayed, Elizabeth followed, and caught him as he reached the door to the *salle.* She grabbed at his damp sleeve, but he shook her off impatiently and opened the door so hard it slammed off the back wall. The two fencers, surprised, looked at the intruder with no trace of recognition.

"I am Rittmeister Karl von Naegel," he announced. "Which of you is the man Nathanson?"

Nathanson lowered his foil and stepped forward. He looked puzzled, but wary. "I go by that name," he answered. "But I do not believe I have your acquaintance, sir."

"Nor will you," said that gentleman coldly. "Apparently, however, you thought yourself able to claim the acquaintance of my sister last night. I am told you danced with her."

"Did you?" Sommers was clearly surprised. "You never dance, Nathanson. I left too early, I see."

Nathanson was still looking at Naegel. "I danced with her, yes," he said slowly. "She was presented to me by

Baroness Reuss at a most awkward moment. A young man had asked her neighbor to dance. Your sister believed the invitation was for her, and stepped out on the floor to take a place in the set. It would have been very cruel to have insisted on my usual rule under the circumstances."

Von Naegel's expression wavered for a moment. Then his face hardened again. "If a footman had been nearby, would you have expected him to dance with my sister, too?"

"Do you call me a lackey?" demanded Nathanson, his face darkening.

"I trust I am not obscure," retorted the Austrian. He flourished the stick he was carrying. With a sick feeling in the pit of her stomach Elizabeth saw that it was not a stick. It was a riding crop. "I will take good care that you do not appear at any dances in the near future, I promise you."

Sommers stepped forward, restraining Nathanson urgently with one hand. "You are under a misapprehension, Naegel," he said coldly, deliberately omitting the officer's title. "If you wish to pursue this matter, you will need to send your friends to call on *Captain* Nathanson."

"Your English army may allow Jews to pretend to be officers," said Naegel savagely. "That does not make him a gentleman in Austria."

"I believe you are in error on that point," said Sommers calmly. "And it is certainly my business to know such nuances of etiquette, as you will concede." He was gripping Nathanson's shoulder very hard, Elizabeth saw, and with good reason; the latter was stiff with fury. "It is no matter, in any case. You cannot possibly refuse to fight him. His real name is Meyer. He is Baron Roth's nephew."

A strangled cry of rage broke from Naegel, and he dashed his crop to the floor. "That dog, Reuss! He and his mother contrived this!" he cried in German. Then he reverted to French, speaking only to Sommers. "Very well, monsieur. Since our emperor has seen fit to ennoble moneychangers, I suppose I must fight him. Please inform *Captain* Nathanson that my own seconds will be more comfortable if those who act for him have a more legitimate claim to be gentlemen."

At this Nathanson gave Sommers a furious shove, broke free and headed for Naegel, his purpose very clear in his eyes. Elizabeth threw herself in front of the Austrian. Once a blow had been struck, she knew, there was no retreat.

"This is disgraceful!" she said fiercely, glaring at them in complete disregard of her position as a young assistant. At the contempt and indignation in her tone, both men faltered momentarily. "Have you no thought for Monsieur Sommers?" she asked Nathanson, her eyes blazing. "Do you realize that if it becomes known that you called someone out here in the *salle*, the emperor will probably order it closed? And that in any case, such a scandal would have the same effect?"

She rounded on Naegel. "Would you ruin a man's livelihood because your sister and the captain were pushed onto the dance floor by someone who knew it would annoy you? For that matter," she continued, totally forgetting herself, "to my mind you would be more justified in calling him out had he refused to partner her. I have been at such a pass myself; a maid can have her pride crushed as easily as a man, I do assure you. And what do you think her feelings will be when she discovers she has escaped a minor embarrassment only to have her brother's duel make her the talk of Vienna?"

She was trembling with suppressed anger, her scorn and her vehemence so unexpected that all three men simply stood for a moment, staring. Then Nathanson stepped back two paces. He looked very uncomfortable, as did Naegel. The silence grew, and Elizabeth suddenly knew, to her horror, that she was about to burst into

tears. Slipping under the Austrian's arm, she fled up
the stairs and ran frantically to the basin to splash water
on her face. It was empty, and when she grabbed the
pitcher to fill it, her hand shook so hard that the pitcher
tilted over and slopped water all over the floor.

"I don't care," she said to herself hysterically, dousing
her flaming cheeks with handful after handful of the
cold water. "I hope it drips on them, those horrid creatures! Posturing and insulting each other because a girl
had one dance, by accident, with someone not quite
socially acceptable." Her shirt was now soaked, she realized. What a mercy she had finally altered her spare
one. She started to yank it off, and then froze just in
time as Sommers's light tread came up the stairs. She
went out into the sitting room. He was looking at her
very oddly.

"What happened, then?" she managed to say.

"They have agreed not to fight, of course," said Sommers. "At least for the moment." He was still considering her, and he did not miss the red eyelids or the
trembling, which she was unable to suppress completely.
She took refuge back in her room, under the pretext
of mopping up the water. But Sommers was still standing
there when she came back out.

"Purcell, how old are you, in truth?" he asked
abruptly.

"How old do you think me?" she parried.

"I would not have believed the sixteen-year-old
existed who could face down Nathanson in one of his
rages," he told her candidly.

He knows, she thought numbly. *He heard what I said
about being in the same situation as Naegel's sister, and he
has seen through my disguise.* She felt sick with shame, and
she closed her eyes. Then she felt a hand ruffle her hair
affectionately. Dubiously, she opened her eyes again.
Sommers was in the sword room, lifting foils off the
hooks.

"Lesson time," he reminded her. "Or are you

minded to take up a new post as a diplomat?'' He headed
towards the stairs, but just before he started down he
stopped and looked at her with no trace of his usual
detachment. "I am in your debt, Ned," he said. "That
could have been a very ugly affair. Naegel's father was
one of the leading figures in the movement to grant
Roth his baronetcy, and the whole incident was obviously engineered by those who opposed that decision.
When he and Nathanson have cooled off a bit, they will
be very grateful. But not as grateful as I am, that you
kept your head when all three of us had lost ours.''

The equipment bag was heavy, and she was—as
usual—having a hard time keeping up with Sommers.
Somehow the last lesson of the day was always the worst;
by then she was always so tired that even walking took
effort. Perhaps that was why, when she first became
aware of the dog, she did nothing about it. She even
had a brief moment of sympathy for the creature.

He was not a handsome animal. His coat was a tangled
mass of wiry gray and brown curls, which nearly covered
his dark eyes. A stubby tail looked as though it had been
through a field of prickleburrs. Elizabeth was not a good
judge of breeds but she was sure it was a mongrel—
part poodle, perhaps. *He's as tired and dowdy-looking as
I am,* she thought, and gave his head a surreptitious pat.

When, three streets later, the dog was still trotting
alongside, Elizabeth began to think it was time to assert
herself. She had not had a dog since she was very little,
but she remembered it was unwise to let one follow you
too far. It might think it had a claim on you. "Go home,
sir!" she said sternly to the dog. He gave her a reproach-
ful look and kept trotting, his tongue hanging out
impertinently.

She stamped her foot and swung the bag in a threatening manner towards his head. He whined briefly, and
then sat back on his haunches. Feeling obscurely guilty,

Elizabeth hurried on. Sommers slowed for her by the Schottenkirche, and they fell into some talk about the pupils who were coming on the following day.

It was only when they were nearly home that Elizabeth noticed the small gray and brown shadow once again at her heels. She stopped and banged down the bag. "Drat and confound it!" she said in martyred tones to the dog. "Can you not take no for an answer?"

The dark eyes gleamed at her hopefully, and the dusty tail thumped on the cobblestones.

"I'm only a temporary resident here, you know," she informed the dog. "You have selected the wrong victim." Sommers was ahead again now, and she picked up the equipment and strode quickly down the lane and into the courtyard.

For the next quarter hour, she was busy cleaning and storing the foils and masks and did not think about the dog. But when she went down at last to get some tea from Frau Renner, a familiar form was huddled patiently at the foot of the stairs. "This is ridiculous!" said Elizabeth. Sommers had come down behind her and was regarding the dog with some amusement. "He followed me home," she muttered shamefacedly.

"And you, of course, did nothing to encourage him."

"I most certainly did not!" said Elizabeth with indignation. "Well, hardly anything," she corrected, remembering that stealthy caress of the curly head. "Anna always said animals had a natural attraction to me."

"Who is Anna? Your sister?" he asked, hoping for some clue to the boy's real identity.

"No, our maidservant here in Vienna." Elizabeth smiled reminiscently. She and Anna had tried to persuade her aunt to get a small dog. Perhaps they would have succeeded if her aunt's illness had not taken a sudden turn for the worse. Observing, Sommers misread that smile. *The boy was sweet on this Anna, I'll wager,* he thought. For some reason the notion made him uncomfortable.

But Elizabeth had forgotten about Anna already. The dog was whining softly and claiming her attention. She inspected him more closely. Now that he was lying down, she could see a dark, matted clump below his right flank. Sommers was there first, bending over, stroking the dog gently, peering at the wound. The dog was licking his face as he tried to pull the wiry hairs away to get a better view. "Just a scrape," he announced. "Probably dragged himself up against something deliberately to inspire your pity." He glanced at Elizabeth and then back at the dog. It would have been hard to say which was wearing a more pleading expression.

"It appears I have another waif on my hands," he said in resigned tones. "Perhaps when he is clean he will be more presentable."

In fact, the dog did have a rather engaging air once his coat had been brushed and trimmed back from his eyes. Elizabeth named him Trumpet. When Sommers asked her why she had chosen that name for a dog who almost never barked, she reminded him of Little John in the Tales of Robin Hood. "It is fortunate he is so quiet," she pointed out. "Otherwise Frau Renner would not have let us keep him."

"Frau Renner is even more besotted about that animal than you are," he said crossly. "Did you know she is going to the butcher at this very moment to get scraps for him? You will be leaving soon, and I will be saddled with this dreadful hound without even an assistant to help me care for him."

But Elizabeth spied him furtively stroking the dog sometimes when he thought she was not looking, and within two days Trumpet had deserted her cot and was sleeping every night at the foot of Sommers's bed.

Six

As always, she had crossed to the far side of the Fleischmarkt to avoid her uncle's building, and was walking with her head tucked well down into her shirt. She therefore almost missed seeing her aunt's pianoforte sitting there, balanced precariously on top of some old crates at the corner of the gateway. The legs had been taken off and were stacked next to the crates. A small boy who looked vaguely familiar was sitting on the ground, laying out stones in some sort of pattern inside the hollow bottom of one of the crates. He looked up as she approached.

"Are you here about the harpsichord?" he asked inaccurately.

"Has it been sold?" Elizabeth was torn between a desire to stay as far away from her uncle's lodgings as possible and a longing to know what was to become of the instrument.

"You're not from Vienna," said the boy accusingly, hearing her pronunciation.

"No," said Elizabeth. "I am English." Instantly she cursed herself for an idiot. If her uncle had made any inquiries after her departure, this boy might well put two and two together. But he seemed remarkably uninterested, and went back to his stones.

"Has it?" persisted Elizabeth. "Been sold?"

"No." said the boy without looking up. "Notice is inside by the far stair."

Elizabeth did not want to go into the courtyard. It was dangerous enough out here at the entrance. If she went in, she was very likely to encounter either her uncle or one of the tenants from the other apartments.

"Do you know how much they are asking?"

"Yes." There was a silence which lengthened out until Elizabeth realized the boy had gone back to his game. This was silly; she should go. Sommers would wonder why it was taking her so long to deliver a simple message to Nathanson's servant. But she seemed unable to make herself leave.

"How much, then?"

"Twenty florins." Elizabeth was stunned. It was a fraction of the true value. Her uncle could not possibly be so foolish as to put it out on the street for that sum, she thought. Something must have happened.

"Who is selling it?" she inquired cautiously. "Herr Stourhead?"

The boy snorted. "Him? He went off so fast he didn't even take all his clothes. My Mutti says the place looked like five of me had been up there making messes. It is my Papa is selling it, to get some of the rent money back for Herr Schneidler. And there's lots of ladies' clothes, too, but they're inside. My Mutti is going through them to see if any of them will fit my sister." Now Elizabeth knew who the boy was; he was the youngest of a large family who lived in one of the attics.

"Is your father here?" she said impulsively. "I will buy it."

The boy shook his head. "My Mutti is, though. Would you like to talk to her?"

Elizabeth bit her lip momentarily. Would the boy's

mother recognize her? Perhaps it did not matter. It seemed her uncle had left. Taking a decision, she nodded and gave the boy a small coin. This produced an instant response; he lit out for the far steps yelling at the top of his lungs, "Mutti, Mutti! Someone wants to buy the funny music box!"

"It is not funny," grumbled Elizabeth indignantly to herself. She loved the little Ermel piano, which her aunt had bought in Brussels. It was painted black, with gold leaf trim which had mostly worn off, and faded gilt scrolls on each side of the rectangular case. The original legs had been painted to match, with gold knobs at the base, but somewhere—she thought it was Zurich—they had forgotten to pack the legs, and had been forced to have new ones made in the next city.

A tired, pale woman emerged from the courtyard behind the boy and came timidly up to Elizabeth. "May I help you, young sir?" she asked politely.

With great relief Elizabeth saw that she had not recognized her. Pitching her voice even lower than usual, Elizabeth informed the woman she was interested in purchasing the pianoforte.

"It is a very nice one, young sir," the woman told her. "It belonged to an English lady. But she died of a broken heart because her husband fell in love with a girl at the Greek tavern, and then her nurse stole the jewels right off the dead body and the husband tried to catch her, but he couldn't."

With a shock, Elizabeth realized that the 'nurse' was herself. Suppressing an outraged denial, she slid a bit more completely into the shadow of the archway.

"And what do you think happened next?" asked the woman triumphantly.

Evidently such scandals conferred a certain status on the neighbors, thought Elizabeth, fascinated.

"Then the *husband* ran away, too, because the secret police were after him!"

Still struggling to adjust to this new view of her uncle's

household, Elizabeth seized on the one detail which might explain his departure. "The secret police?" she inquired in a hesitant voice. The woman mistook her hesitation for a natural awe at hearing the emperor's surveillance force mentioned. Her voice sank to a whisper.

"They say he was selling rifles to the French! They came to our lodgings last week and asked questions of everyone, even the children. And both families across the yard, and all the tenants in Herr Schneidler's, of course. But he was already gone."

This sounded extremely plausible to Elizabeth. Her uncle's business was something illegitimate, she was sure, because there was a tacit understanding that it was never discussed in front of her or her aunt. Emboldened by the hope that Stourhead was gone from Vienna for good, she made a quick series of bargains with the woman. The father and the oldest boy would bring the pianoforte to Frau Renner's later in a handcart; she could give her two florins now and the remainder when it was delivered. As soon as the negotiations were concluded, she reflected how readily the woman had agreed and began to think she could have paid much less, but even so she was exuberant as she started off back towards the *salle*. To have a piano again! Her fingers fairly itched at the thought, and she found herself humming one of her favorite pieces as she danced in the gate and ran up the stairs.

Sommers was reading in the armchair, his feet extended over Trumpet's sleeping form. "Your papers are here," he said cheerfully, pointing to a packet on the table. "They look quite adequate, and were not as expensive as I had feared."

Her eyes flew to the neatly folded documents, stiff with seals. It was as though he had thrown a bucket of cold water in her face. What had she done? She had just spent every florin she had—no, more than what she had; she owed Sommers now for the cost of the forged papers—on a pianoforte which she would be leaving behind. And where would they put it? How could she do this to him, when she was so close to having enough money for her fare? With a groan, she dropped onto the sofa and hid her face in her hands.

"What is wrong?" he said, worried. "Did you find Silvio?"

"Yes, he was over at the coffee warehouse. I found him, and I left your message. But I am a complete and utter idiot," Elizabeth said dully, refusing to meet his eyes. "I did not stop to think at all, I was so happy to see it. And now you will be saddled with me for who knows how long, and with *it*, too."

Sommers was totally bewildered. "It? What do you mean?" A likely explanation occurred to him. "Did you find another dog? Ned, we cannot have two dogs. I am sorry, it is simply impossible."

"Not a dog," she muttered. "Worse. My aunt's pianoforte. It was lying out on the street. They were selling it for twenty florins; it is worth a hundred, at least. And it looked very forlorn, and I have so missed being able to play—oh, I am the most thoughtless creature!" She clenched her fists in misery. "I will tell them I have made a mistake when they deliver it. If I pay them another florin or two they will not mind carting it back."

"Nothing is worse than a dog," said Sommers with mock gravity, giving Trumpet a nudge with his foot. "And what is so dreadful about buying your old pianoforte? I admit it will not be possible for you to take it back to England with you, but if it is in truth worth much more than you paid for it, you can simply sell it for something closer to its real value and be that much nearer to having enough money for your journey."

It had not occurred to Elizabeth that she could resell the piano. "Herr Schneidler did nothing beyond putting up a placard in the courtyard," she said slowly. "And I would wager he had no notion of what it is worth, because it looks a bit shabby. But I could go down to the music school and post a notice there. Then I could get a reasonable price for it. Probably enough for the papers and my travel expenses.''

Sommers's observation ought to have relieved her mind immensely. Not only was the piano not a mistake and a burden, it would provide the means for her to discharge her obligations and leave almost immediately. Instead she found herself feeling more miserable than ever. "I will do so right now," she announced fiercely. "Unless you need me for something before the afternoon lesson."

"Yes, you must be anxious to be gone," agreed Sommers in a flat voice. "It was a fortunate chance you came upon it like that." He gave a sigh. "I will probably have to hire another assistant. You are a luxury to which I have grown accustomed, I am afraid."

There was that wistful smile again, lighting up the hazel eyes, and Elizabeth knew with a sudden and dreadful certainty that she did not want to leave. The reason why was pushing towards the surface of her thoughts, and to hold it at bay she began to babble nervously.

There was no rush. It was quite hot, and traveling in the heat had always made her ill. The children's class had just begun to mind her a bit, and it would hardly be fair to leave them to start again with someone new just like that. And it might take a bit of time to find someone willing to pay full price for her instrument. Indeed, it was a bit late, now, to go down to the school— she might not get back in time for lessons. Perhaps tomorrow would be better. No, tomorrow they were going to the palace. Friday, then.

At the odd urgency in her voice, Trumpet had awakened. He pushed his head up under Sommers's legs and looked at her curiously. When she at last paused for breath, Sommers held up his hand, his face grave.

"Ned, stop. Listen to me." He searched for the right words. "It would not be right for me to keep you here. You are young. You have your future to think of. You should be home in England with your family, going to school. And in any case I may not be here very long myself. But you do not have to leave immediately if you do not choose to. Surely you know I have come to value your help and your companionship." Suddenly he smiled again. "And I would not mind having a piano here for a bit. I used to play sometimes, although I don't know if I still can." He looked down at his right hand. The knuckle on his index finger was at an odd angle, and the middle finger had bumps in the wrong places.

"Did you have an accident?" asked Elizabeth, curious. She had never really noticed the misshapen fingers before.

"Something like that," was the curt reply.

Coming through the gate, Nathanson was abstracted. The sudden, noisy attack of a woolly creature which erupted out of the shadows under the arch caught him totally off guard. It was a dog, and for some reason it was frantically jumping up and trying to reach his throat. After a moment of panic, he realized first that the dog was barking delightedly, and second that it was attacking with tongue, not teeth.

"Trumpet!" Here came that boy, Purcell. Naturally the creature would belong to him. He felt his temper rising, not least because he suspected the boy might have seen his dismay when the dog first launched itself at his neck.

"I am very sorry, sir. Down, down, Trumpet!" Apologies mingled with barks and scuffles; an inadvertent thrust against his leg brought him down hard onto the stone paving, where the dog triumphantly proceeded to plant its feet on his thighs and lick his neckcloth in frenzied happiness. His humiliation was complete when he saw Sommers standing in the doorway, observing dog, assistant, and visitor with a huge grin.

"May I ask why I have been favored with this animal's

attentions?" He stood, brushing off his clothing, and glared impartially at all three of his hosts. "I take it he is yours?"

"I'm afraid so." Sommers was trying to suppress a smile. "Up until now he has been very well behaved. Have you been embracing any female dogs lately?" At this point Trumpet broke free of Elizabeth's hold, leaped up, and tried again to reach the neckcloth.

"Most certainly not," responded Nathanson acerbically. "And if I had, surely the scent would be on my hands. Apparently your hound wishes to become a valet. He seems to believe my cravat requires attention."

"Well, it does," Sommers pointed out. One end of the cloth had come loose and was dangling over the collar of Nathanson's coat. With a muttered oath in French, Nathanson pulled the band off completely, but before he could even unfold it, the dog had seized it and a tug-of-war ensued.

"Oh, take it!" said Nathanson, disgusted, relinquishing his hold. But the embarrassed owners jointly managed to wrestle their pet to the ground and remove the shredded remains. Elizabeth went running off to deposit it in the dustbin, pursued by Trumpet, who stood whining plaintively at Frau Renner's door as his prize disappeared inside.

"I'll replace it," said Sommers curtly as Elizabeth rejoined them. "Purcell, run up and get one of mine for the moment." When she returned, breathless, with the clean linen and a clothes brush, he frowned at the cloth for a moment. "Yours are French, are they not? I think the haberdasher by the cathedral carries something similar."

"No great matter," muttered Nathanson, tying it hastily. "It was a bit stained; something splattered on it at breakfast and I did not have time to change. Perhaps that was what attracted your dog."

Elizabeth, who had been walking away, stopped and

turned back. "Was it smoked fish, by any chance?" she asked.

Nathanson frowned. "As a matter of fact, it was," he said slowly.

"You see?" she demanded of Sommers.

He held his hand out palm up, conceding defeat. "I stand corrected. But who ever heard of a dog obsessed with fish?" Seeing Nathanson's puzzlement, he elaborated. "According to Purcell, the dog dashes down the stairs the moment Frau Renner comes in the gate if she has purchased any smoked herring. I myself had always thought fish attracted cats."

"Fascinating," drawled Nathanson. Elizabeth flushed.

"Pay him no mind, Ned," advised Sommers. "He is not fond of dogs." With the unerring attraction of all domestic animals to the one human who dislikes them, Trumpet had returned now to his critic and was attacking his shins with affectionate snuffles, much to that elegant young officer's dismay.

"I swear I have not put fish on my boots," he growled. "So could you please get this thing away from me?"

"Come here, Trumpet," said Elizabeth, grabbing at the nape of his neck. He eluded her, and bolted through Nathanson's legs out the gate into the street. With a groan of frustration, Elizabeth went running after him.

"First an assistant, now a dog," observed Nathanson coldly. "You become domestic, my friend. Unwise for a man in your situation."

"Purcell seems to attract strays," said Sommers, swiping at Nathanson's uniform with the brush. "Three days ago the dog followed him back here, and yesterday we acquired an orphaned pianoforte."

"A piano!" Nathanson gave a disgusted snort. "Are you mad? You live in an attic, grind yourself to the bone teaching all day, and now you are purchasing pianos?"

"At least I am not—by some strange happenstance— strolling by the Hofburg every morning when a certain

countess is likely to be walking out," Sommers retorted
in sharp tones. "I had thought you a bit more discreet."

"Discretion? You talk of discretion?" blazed Nathanson. "Why is Purcell still here? You cannot possibly imagine you can continue like this?" His face was grim. "Meillet
is here—at least I assume he is. I glimpsed his unlovely
henchman Jean-Luc earlier today in the Renngasse, outside my hotel. I came over to warn you, but perhaps now
that you have an errand boy who is an expert fencer and
a ferocious guard dog you are not concerned."

Sommers had gone white under his tan. "Hell!" he
muttered. "I thought I would have a bit more time. Did
Jean-Luc see you?"

The other man shook his head. "I am not in much
danger. None of them saw me last month in France,
and even if they do notice the resemblance to my father,
I am accredited to the Prussian court and therefore
protected by the armistice. Your case is very different."

"I would not be so sure you are safe," said Sommers,
frowning. "Meillet does not play by the rules."

"Never mind about me," interjected Nathanson,
watching him narrowly. "What of you? What will you
do? Leave?"

"Yes. No. I don't know," said Sommers, pacing back
and forth in a distracted manner. "I know White
thought I could be useful here, but perhaps I should
move on. After all, you believe you can safely stay, and
you are far better connected than I am."

"That is not what Jervyn thinks," said Nathanson.

Sommers stopped pacing. "Who is Jervyn?"

"One of Stewart's aides. He will be in Vienna Monday,
and has requested a meeting with you to communicate
some matters pertinent to Stewart's mission. A private
meeting."

"I know what that means," said Sommers bitterly.
"Some poky little antechamber off of a ballroom. It
means I will have to go to another reception. And why
on earth is our ambassador to Prussia sending his aide

to find me? Have we no one in Prague? Or Schweidnitz? What about you, for that matter?"

"He asked for you," said Nathanson. "By name. By your real name." He held out a large square envelope. "Your card of invitation from the Baroness Reuss."

"Are you going?" asked Sommers, taking the envelope reluctantly.

Nathanson smiled without warmth. "The one thing Rittmeister von Naegel and I agree on, at the moment, is that we will not set foot in the house of anyone named Reuss. Cox will be there. He can tell you where to go to meet with Jervyn." He cocked his head for a moment, listening. Faintly, amidst the noises of the street, they could hear Elizabeth approaching, scolding Trumpet. "I will take myself off," he told Sommers. "But I am beginning to be very curious about several matters. For example, what am I doing here? So far, the answer appears to be: nothing. Or: who is Purcell, in truth? You do not know anything about him. He could be a plant." Sommers's furious protest was waved aside. "I do not believe that, in fact, but you must admit there is something rather odd about him. And then there is the most puzzling thing of all."

"What is that?"

"Why does Doña Maria travel with two priests, one of whom is never seen in public? Why is my cousin Elena with her, pretending to be a *hidalga*? Ask Purcell to find out something about those priests the next time he collects kitchen gossip for your amusement."

Elizabeth came back in the gate dragging Trumpet just as Nathanson left, and did not miss his scowl. "Is he very annoyed?" she asked timidly. "I should have made sure there was no one in the courtyard before I let Trumpet loose. He is not very well trained, and some people do not like dogs." She released Trumpet with a sigh of relief and straightened up.

Sommers shook his head. "Nathanson has a permanent quarrel with the world," he said absently. "I would not pay much attention to his moods, if I were you." He tucked the envelope away and handed her the clothes brush. "On the other hand, he is no fool, and he has just posed a very interesting question to me. Very interesting, indeed. Purcell, if you were a wealthy Catholic traveling abroad into regions where it might not be easy to locate a priest, would you consider paying the expenses of a confessor to accompany you?"

"Certainly," said Elizabeth promptly.

"Two confessors, though?"

"Oh," said Elizabeth, suddenly understanding.

"Did you hear anything about either of the priests when we were at her house?" Elizabeth shook her head. "What reasons can you think of, Purcell, for someone to travel with two priests?"

She thought for a moment. "If one of the priests will not be completing the trip," she said slowly, "and is only traveling part of the way. Or if one of the priests is not a real priest."

"Or both."

"Or both," she agreed. She looked at Sommers. "You do not have to tell me what you and Nathanson and Cox are doing here in Vienna," she said abruptly. "But it is becoming rather difficult for me to pretend to believe you are simply a fencing instructor." Blue-gray eyes held hazel ones firmly for a long minute.

No point denying it, thought Sommers. Nathanson was right, damn him. He should have sent the boy home a week ago. At length he said only, "Ned, I am sorry. I cannot tell you anything. Do you trust me enough to accept that as an answer?"

That horrible bleak emptiness was back, she saw. The planes of his face had settled into a finely carved mask, glittering in the sunlight. Hastily she turned and started towards the stairs, with Trumpet at her heels. Only at the door did she remember to answer his question. "Yes," she stammered. "Yes, I trust you, of course."

"The more fool you," he muttered.

Seven

It was very late, and most of the offices in the Chancellery were dark. Baron Franz von Hager pushed away a pile of papers with a weary grimace and stretched briefly in the large leather chair he had pulled up beside the desk. "Well, Roswicz," he said irritably. "What is it?"

The younger man coughed diffidently. "Your Excellency, you asked me to report to you if anyone made inquiries about the Englishman who calls himself Sommers. A French official named Meillet was here late this afternoon, with a request for assistance in locating someone who matches Sommers's description. Evidently a *mandat* against him has been issued by the *Sûreté* in Lille, and the French are demanding that we honor it."

"And what did you say?" asked Hager, leaning back in his chair and smiling at his subordinate. Roswicz was a deceptively mild-looking young man with pale, thinning hair and sleepy blue eyes. Most people underestimated him, but Hager relied on him heavily; he was one of the shrewdest officers in the Hofpolizei.

"I told him no one like that was known to be in

Vienna," responded Roswicz promptly. "Which was not
a complete lie, since he described the fugitive as having
red hair, and Sommers has brown hair."

"You are certain it is the same man, though?"

"Yes, Excellency. He is left-handed, with two broken
fingers, and the date of his arrival corresponds to the
information we had from England. As you requested,
we have been watching him, and my informant is certain
the brown hair is not natural."

"What does he seem to be doing, besides teaching
fencing? Has he contacted anyone?"

Roswicz frowned. "A 'cousin' called upon him, but
has not visited him more than three times or so. More
significant—and of more concern—is the return of the
English agent Nathanson. They have been seeing each
other almost daily. Also, Sommers has attended a few
functions in Nathanson's company—large, public
events, for the most part. But as I told you last week,
although Sommers had been reported killed, a Bill of
Attainder charging him with treason was drawn up very
quietly just after he fled England. Evidently the intelligence office hopes to keep their error concealed for as
long as may be. It is a great embarrassment, after all.
He was White's chief aide. In any case, I am inclined
not to attach great importance to his contacts with
Nathanson, who is well known to be something of a
maverick."

"I hope you are right," growled Hager, drumming
his fingers on the arm of his chair. "I gave my personal
guarantee that there was no risk involved in allowing
him to instruct Prince Francis. Thank you, Roswicz; let
me know if you hear anything further."

This was clearly a dismissal, but Roswicz did not leave.
"The French are offering a reward for his death, and
even more for his capture," he said pointedly. He
named the sum. It was very large, and Hager's eyebrows
shot up.

"Where is he lodging?" he asked Roswicz after a

moment. Roswicz told him. "Do we have him under surveillance?"

"Only sporadically, Excellency. We are very short of reliable men at the moment, as you know."

Hager sighed. With the French and the allies jockeying for position and pouring agents into Vienna, it was nearly impossible to keep track of everyone who needed watching at the moment, let alone read all the reports. He looked with disgust at the stack he had just finished. "Put two men on, around the clock," he said at last. "It will not take this Frenchman long to find him, and I still believe you were right when you suggested he could be useful to us. And send a précis of what you have just told me to Metternich in Prague."

Elena Roth Mendez, currently known only as Elena Mendez, was edging her head around the corner of the wall again when she became aware that someone walking on the other side of the street had stopped and was staring at her. Distracted momentarily from her task, she looked across, feeling a bit embarrassed. It was not surprising she would attract attention trying to peer around the wall; it must look quite odd. She expected, therefore, to see a curious or even disapproving stranger.

Instead she saw a familiar face: slim, with a high-bridged nose, reddish-blond hair, and intense blue eyes made quite large by a pair of thick-lensed spectacles. The face was attached to a rather thin young man in a dark jacket, who was rapidly crossing the street to accost her, looking both shocked and indignant. Instantly her black-garbed duenna moved in behind her, and Elena just had time to flash a warning with her eyes as her cousin Anselm came up to them.

He gave a small smile to show he understood, and bowed courteously. "Dare I hope that you remember me?'' he said with, Elena thought, a very credible air of diffidence.

"But of course I remember you, Monsieur von Roth," Elena replied promptly. At the sound of the honorific 'von,' the duenna relaxed slightly and allowed the cousins to draw slightly apart from her. Elena switched to German. "You looked at first as though you had seen a ghost," she said tartly. "Pray mind your manners. My guardian will become suspicious."

"You are lucky I managed to keep countenance at all," Anselm Roth retorted in the same language, assuming correctly that Elena had switched to avoid comprehension by the duenna, "given the surprise of seeing you here in Vienna when I thought you were on your way to Naples. Not to mention the surprise of seeing you up and about at this hour of the morning."

"Don't lecture me," said Elena crossly. "My dear English cousin has already done that, and I assure you he did a most thorough job. Your father knows I am here, and he is escorting me down to Naples in a fortnight or so. Doña Maria sent you cards for at least two parties. If you had bothered to come, you would not have had such an unpleasant public shock."

"It was not an unpleasant shock at all," objected Roth with a smile. He had not seen Elena for four years, and although her pugnacious disposition had not changed, her appearance certainly had. The stubby little schoolgirl had turned into a lovely young woman—still short, but with an elegant, rounded figure and those beautiful green eyes in a face which could have been a model for a sculptor. "So you are the mademoiselle traveling with the notorious Doña Maria? I suppose it was not such a bad scheme; otherwise Luis would have had to escort you from Gibraltar. James has already seen you, then?"

Reminded of her original purpose, Elena gasped and stuck her head around the corner again. "Never mind," she said with relief. "She has not come out of the gate yet."

Roth was mystified. "Who has not come out? What gate? What are you doing, sticking your head around the corner? That was what caught my attention, you know, from the other side of the street. It looked very strange."

"I am spying," said Elena loftily. "Everyone else in the family does it. Why should I not have my turn?"

Roth was startled. "Don't exaggerate, Elena," he said impatiently. "I am not a spy, for example. It is only the Meyers. But in any case I do not think you are doing a very good job, if I—a nearsighted, absentminded book-worm—noticed you from across the street. Who is your victim?"

Elena smiled slowly, watching him for his reaction. "James. I am spying on James."

Roth was totally bewildered. "You are spying on your own cousin? Why on earth are you doing that? This is not a game; he is often involved in very dangerous affairs, you know."

"Affairs, yes. Dangerous, no," snapped Elena. "Unless you consider the Countess of Brieg dangerous."

At that name, Roth's eyes widened.

"I find it a bit hypocritical of *Captain Nathanson* to give me a blistering sermon on propriety when he has been coming to the Josefsplatz every morning for the last week and watching the Countess go out for her morning ride with a look on his face like a child who sees a candied plum."

"Has he?" asked Roth, disconcerted.

"Come and see," invited Elena, moving aside so he could peer around the wall.

He shook his head. Perhaps there was still some schoolgirl in Elena, he thought. After all, she was only eighteen. "Now that I am with you," he pointed out, "we do not need to crane our necks and hide. We can walk along onto the Augustinerstrasse and observe matters. If you are walking with me and we are conversing, it will not be obvious that we are watching anyone. It is still quite early and there are not many people about. We should have a good view of everything. In any case, a young lady cannot simply stand on a street corner. If you insist on remaining here, we will stroll back and forth in front of the emperor's statue.''

Bowing, he offered Elena his arm. He had to admit he himself was curious, and a bit worried, at her report. Nathanson was a ladies' man, yes, but only in the passive sense: they swarmed around him like flies. Until now, he had never shown any sign of a *tendre* for anyone. Indeed, Roth's older sister Adelheid had nicknamed him 'the Iceman.' That was a complimentary term, however, compared to the names he had heard for the Countess of Brieg.

Roth swung rather briskly around the corner, forgetting that Elena, who was hanging on his elbow, was more than a foot shorter than he was. She stumbled, and cursing himself for a clumsy fool, he turned remorsefully to support her. But she was not looking at him. Wide-eyed, she was staring down the street.

"Anselm," she gasped, forgetting to call him Monsieur Roth. "She's stopped! She's talking to him!"

Looking down the wide avenue, Roth easily spotted the tall, uniformed figure of his cousin, his face turned up to converse with the countess. She had pulled up her horse and now was bending down, laughing at something Nathanson had said. Other passersby were glancing over as well; the tiny, golden countess in the blue riding habit and the dark-haired officer in his green regimentals made an admirable picture. There was a hiss of indrawn breath beside him, and Elena's arm stiffened in his grasp. Roth did not know what disturbed him more—that Nathanson was indeed embroiled with the infamous countess, or that Elena was so dismayed to see it.

"Have you nothing better to do than trail around collecting gossip about James?" he growled in irritation.

The chaperone was hurrying over now that he had taken Elena's arm. Scarlet, he dropped it and stepped away.

Elena looked at the chaperone and then back at her cousin. The flush was fading; he regarded her soberly, making no attempt to disguise his discomfiture at her interest in the dashing James. Her expression was thoughtful. "*Tía*," she announced in Spanish to her guardian, "Señor von Roth has kindly offered to escort us to the park and then to Monsieur Dehn's confectionery for some refreshments."

"Why, Captain Nathanson," the countess was saying with a mocking smile. "What a surprise."

She held her horse in very well, he noted abstractly, although the animal was clearly fresh and expecting by now to be well on the way to Währing. He had been utterly dumbfounded when she had suddenly turned the mare's head and ridden over to accost him, and even more dumbfounded when he saw she was twice as lovely as he had remembered. But he was used to living by his wits, and he fell into her game glibly enough.

"It should hardly be a surprise," he replied, bowing, "since I am fairly certain you have noticed me here for the past several days at this exact time."

"The hour I go out riding with Johann and Mademoiselle Veidler?"

Nathanson glanced over to where her companion and groom waited for her to return. "As it happens, I have business here at this hour," he said, with a challenging stare.

"You are engaged? What a pity," she said, taking him on with a saucy smile. "I had thought of asking whether you might care to accompany us. But of course, if you have some appointment . . ."

"Oh, I am free now," he assured her calmly.

He had fallen right into the first trap, she thought with a slight pang of disappointment. She had thought he would prove more entertaining. Perhaps his reputation was overblown.

"But you have no horse," she pointed out sweetly. "Perhaps another day, Captain." Anticipating his crestfallen look, she watched his face closely for the moment when he realized he had been outmaneuvered. No such look appeared.

Instead he raised one eyebrow, gave a quiet smile, and lifted one hand briefly over his shoulder. Out of the shadows under the wall of the Hofburg, a manservant leading a beautiful black gelding appeared. With one deft movement he swung into the saddle and now looked down at her, their positions completely reversed, since his horse was a good two hands higher than her own mount.

Nettled, but grudgingly admitting to herself she had been bested, the countess allowed an expression of artless surprise to settle on her face while she considered what to do. She had not had any intention of allowing the man to join her riding party; she had simply given in to the urge to satisfy her curiosity. He was looking at her with something like sympathy, she saw.

"Your friend is waiting," he said gently. "I beg your pardon for teasing you. It would be quite a scandal if I joined you; I am well aware of it. Good day, Madame." He touched his hat briefly and turned his mount back towards the Herrengasse. Torn between exasperation and admiration, the countess bit her lip. Then on impulse, she turned her own horse and came up behind him.

"Captain!" she called. He pulled up his horse and turned in the saddle, clearly surprised. "I am well inured to scandal," she announced, with a wry smile. "If you think your reputation can survive such an expedition, I would be very glad of your company."

He rode in silence as they wound their way out of the city past the walls dismantled by the French and into the fields east of Währing, listening to the countess chattering gaily with Mademoiselle Veidler. The latter's poorly dissembled shock when her companion had introduced him had sobered him quickly. No more than the countess had he had any intention of riding out together. The concealed horse had been a typical courier's gesture: show the enemy you are prepared, show them you can foresee the unexpected.

The problem was, the countess was not an enemy. He had derived no satisfaction at all from trapping her in her own snare. And now here he was, uneasily aware that he was doing something remarkably foolish, all because he was so obsessed with a tiny slip of a woman that the only way he had found to function for the rest of the day was to go and watch her ride out each morning.

Until she spoke to him, he had not realized she had allowed the groom and her companion to ride ahead and had dropped back next to him.

"Regrets already, Captain?" she said lightly.

He came out of his reverie and glanced at her curiously. "Not at all," he said politely. "I did not wish to intrude on your conversation with your friend, however. And it did occur to me you might be the one with regrets."

"Only because I fear my brother may call you out," she said ruefully. "A hole in your side seems a high price to pay for a morning ride. My brother is unfortunately somewhat overprotective, even though my marriage took me—officially, at least—out of the family."

"No wonder you are inured to scandal," he commented dryly, "if your brother creates them so persistently by calling out anyone who speaks with you."

This brought a shaky laugh, but she was not ready to give up her concern, he could see. The blue eyes were very apologetic now, and she twisted one hand nervously in the mane of her horse. They had slowed to a walk. "I am quite serious," she said. "My father was always used to say that I never thought about the consequences of my actions, and now I am feeling very guilty about my thoughtlessness."

"Well, if you are fond of your brother in spite of his boorish behavior last week in the garden, I will promise you not to hurt him much," he said with a reassuring smile.

At this she drew rein and came to a complete stop. "I don't think you quite understand," she said with some hauteur. "My concern was for you."

The eyebrow went up again. "Is your brother an experienced duelist, then?"

"Very much so," she said earnestly. "Please, Captain—perhaps if you turned back now, nothing would happen. Very few people were about when we left, but if we return together, he would be sure to hear of it from someone."

"How many duels has your brother fought, then?" he inquired, his tone carefully neutral.

"Seven or eight, at least," she said, exaggerating slightly to be more sure of intimidating him. To her amazement he put back his head and laughed out loud. Then he turned back to her and studied her for a long moment with a rather odd expression on his face, as though he was making up his mind about something.

"Would you like to know how many duels I fought in my first year as a commissioned officer in Portugal?" he asked after that long pause. "Fifteen. In that one year alone. Of course, that was the worst year."

"Fifteen!" she gasped. "In *one year*? That is more than one a month!"

He bowed mockingly. "Your arithmetic is excellent, Madame. If you wish, you may subtract the one duel in which I sustained a real injury, and take it down to fourteen. Even so, the numbers weigh against your brother quite heavily. In all those other affairs, and in the nine I have been forced into since that year, I have bested my opponent."

She was still struggling with the notion of fighting a

duel every three or four weeks. "Were you such a ladies' man?" she demanded impetuously, and then blushed at her own question.

"I assure you that on campaign there are not so many opportunities for dalliance that fifteen duels would be the result," he said with a cynical twist of his lips. "Especially for a nineteen-year-old. No, my fellow officers objected to my possession of a certain item and took it in turns to provoke me, hoping to persuade me to relinquish it."

Now she was thoroughly puzzled. "Surely such behavior is little better than extortion? What was it you had that they wanted you to give up?"

"My commission," he replied. His tone was still flat, but his lips had tightened. "I am sure your brother would agree with them, too."

"But you did not give up," she said slowly. "It must have been a terrible year."

"It was not as bad as I made it sound, in fact," he said. "Most of the duels were in the first two months, and the rest were more pro forma because the friends of the original challengers did not want to seem cowardly after their comrades had been defeated. Besides, we all knew our colonel would be furious if anyone were killed, which meant it was mostly sword fighting rather than pistols. Indeed, it became somewhat farcical towards the end, because by then we had all been in several battles together and had learned we needed to be able to trust each other for the sake of our men."

"Nevertheless, you left the regiment."

He gave her a considering look. "I still hold my commission," he pointed out. "Unless you think I am wearing this uniform as a souvenir of my happy days in Portugal."

"I am sometimes involved with the emperor's secret police," she told him candidly. "You have not been in the field with your regiment for some time. You are an

English spy." If she had thought to unnerve him, she failed.

"Liaison officer," he corrected smoothly. "You are right in some sense. I have been seconded to administrative tasks recently. But that was Whitehall's decision, not mine. I would have preferred to stay with my unit." He looked ahead at the distant figures of Miss Veidler and the groom, who had also halted, and were clearly awaiting them. "We should ride on," he said abruptly. "Or Mademoiselle Veidler will complain of me to your brother with some justification."

Obediently she spurred her horse, and they trotted on towards the rest of the party. But just before they came within earshot, she slowed to a walk again, and when he turned to her inquiringly, asked in a rush, "It did not seem to surprise you, when I said that I—that I had some contacts with the secret police."

He laughed. "Obviously you have not heard the latest *bon mot* of your minister Prince Metternich. He is reputed to have said that if one goes to a dinner party in Vienna, the likelihood is that the person on your right is an agent for a foreign power, the person on your left is a member of the secret police, and the person across from you is taking money from both." He added with a sardonic smile after a moment, "That tally does not even include liaison officers whose questionable background precludes them from receiving invitations to the dinner parties."

"I am giving a dinner party next week," she said with a flash in her eyes as they came up with the other two riders. "And I will most certainly send you a card."

She was serious, he saw. "I shall look forward to receiving it," he said courteously. "But—"

"But you will not come," she finished for him in bitter tones. "I see in your own way you are as conventional and snobbish as my brother."

Nathanson flushed; that comment had stung. "If I receive a card, I promise I shall come," he said impetuously. "But for the moment I believe I will follow your advice and take my leave."

"Shall I think you are indeed afraid of my brother, then, in spite of all your fine claims?" she flashed, unwilling to let him go so easily.

"As you wish," he said, calm again. He gestured lightly with one hand towards another group approaching them from a distance. "I myself do not care to explain to Monsieur Roswicz why I am in your company. He is a senior officer in the Hofpolizei, is he not?" Wheeling his horse, he cantered away.

The countess bit her lip. Things were not going according to plan. And she had not even noticed Roswicz's group. Was she growing careless?

Eight

Philip Jervyn stared down into the pointed arcs of light over the candelabra. When he closed his eyes he could still see three haloes behind his eyelids. He rubbed his eyes and opened them again. This was going to be just as difficult as he had thought it would be. Worse, in fact. He had not really expected Sommers to take his extended hand when he introduced himself, but he had at least thought he would be willing to look him in the face. The younger man, standing on the other side of the mahogany table, held himself stiffly, eyes lowered, his expression drawn and wary. Jervyn's gaze went back again, involuntarily, to the crooked fingers on the right hand.

"Please sit down, Mr. Sommers," he said at last. He himself pulled a side chair up to the table and sank into it. "This will not take long, I hope. It is very good of you to come."

"Why did you send for me?" Sommers asked bluntly. He had remained standing; the candles were sending little flares of light up over his chin. "Nathanson is here, and King is with you at Prussian headquarters. I cannot imagine what you could ask me to do that they could not do more reliably and more successfully."

"You have access to the palace," said Jervyn, blunt in his turn. "They do not. Is it not true that you are an instructor to Prince Francis?"

"The lessons are in the riding school," Sommers said. There was an edge to his voice. "I have been into his quarters in the palace precisely once."

"Once is more than never," observed Jervyn mildly. "I am sure you could find a pretext to be invited in again. And since you are regularly instructing the prince, it is likely you could simply walk in with some sort of bundle under your arm and announce that he had requested you to bring something."

"What if I said that I felt some loyalty to my employer, the emperor? And to the country which took me in?"

"What if I said that your mission in the palace is for the benefit of Austria?" countered Jervyn. Sommers shot him a suspicious look, but finally sat down across from him in an armchair. *He looks ill,* thought Jervyn. *Not physically ill, perhaps, but emotional strain can ultimately have the same effect.*

"I beg your pardon, Mr. Jervyn," Sommers said wearily. "If I can indeed be of some assistance, I will of course be glad to help. Please go on."

"How much do you know about Prince Metternich and about recent events in Austria?" asked Jervyn.

"Not much," was the reply. "I know after Austria was defeated by Napoleon, the aristocracy divided into two camps, one favoring pacification and one favoring renewed war. I know Metternich consolidated his power partly by manipulating both camps. And that the Bonapartists have been courting Metternich during the armistice, without much success."

"Had you heard that two months ago there was an abortive attempt at an uprising in the Tyrol?" asked Jervyn.

Sommers shook his head.

"It was suppressed before it could begin, through the combined efforts of Baron Hager and Metternich. The emperor's brother was involved. It was an ugly incident, very local, but, as it happens, one which now could affect all of Europe."

"How so?"

"Metternich wrote a letter. It seems his mistress, Wilhelmine von Sagan, has a cousin who was deeply involved in the conspiracy, and Metternich protected him. Which was certainly not so very dreadful; the conspiracy was never really a serious threat. But he was damnably foolish to put it all down in a letter and send it to the Duchess of Sagan, because someone else has now managed to get their hands on the letter. And they threaten to publish it unless Metternich exerts his influence to negotiate peace between Napoleon and the allies."

Sommers's eyes were wide as he absorbed all this. "Good God," he said, stunned. England was counting on Austrian support. It had been a foregone conclusion for months now that when the armistice expired, Austria would declare war against France. Although there were some even in England who argued in favor of a European peace, no one who had fought under Wellington believed for a moment Napoleon could be stopped by anything except military defeat. He leaned forward, looking fully engaged for the first time since he had entered the room. "The letter is in the possession of someone in the palace?"

"It is," confirmed Jervyn. "Someone who is well-connected to Hager's secret police, so that Metternich would have little chance of using one of their agents to recover the letter without exposing himself."

"And you want me to steal it?"

Jervyn nodded. "Or destroy it, as a last resort, but of course it would be better to be able to prove to the prince that the threat no longer exists."

"I haven't done much of this sort of thing," said

Sommers, frowning. "You want Nathanson, I should think. He could probably break into the place ten times for every once I could walk in without looking suspicious."

"Nathanson would not be suitable in this case," said Jervyn, "no matter what his talents—and I think you exaggerate both his skill and your deficiencies. The letter is in the hands of the Countess of Brieg."

Sommers sank back in the chair with a groan and put his head in his hands. "Damn," he said indistinctly. "Damn, damn, damn." There was a long silence, and one of the candles guttered and went out. "Very well," he said finally. "I'll do my best. I know roughly where her apartments are, in fact. There is a lot of gossip at the palace about who visits those apartments, and at what hours. My young assistant may even have been to her rooms. While I am giving lessons, infatuated maids cart him off all over the place to feed him bonbons and ices."

Jervyn handed him an envelope. "This is a letter of Metternich's written at approximately the same time, also to the duchess. The notepaper and envelope will be the same."

"How did you get this?" Sommers demanded, suspicious again.

"The duchess gave it to me," said Jervyn with a cold smile. "She, too, would like to see that letter recovered quietly, since she was supposed to have burnt it the day she received it. When I mentioned we might be able to help, she was delighted to provide a sample to guide our efforts."

"I'll go bail she would have been more delighted if all of us vanished into a chasm in the earth," muttered Sommers, looking at the envelope. He rose.

"Do you know where to reach me?" Jervyn asked.

"Yes, Cox gave me your direction," responded the other man, still frowning at the sample letter. He sighed,

tucked it into an inner pocket in his jacket, and turned
to go.

"Sommers, wait," called Jervyn urgently. The other
paused, his hand on the door. "If something—if you
get into difficulties, I want you to know—oh, hell!" He
stepped closer. "What I mean is, if you need help at
any point, please come to me." He had spoken with
more feeling than he had intended to, and saw a slow
flush creep up Sommers's face in the candlelight.

"Difficulties?" Sommers's tone was mocking. "Once
I add burglary to the other crimes, you mean? My dear
fellow, burglary is nothing in the grand scheme of
things. Your conscience can rest easy on that score, at
least."

The door opened and closed, and Jervyn knew he
should reappear in the crowded salon quickly, before his
absence was noticed, but he stayed motionless instead,
staring down at the armchair where Sommers had been
sitting. On the left side, at the front of the seat, were
four deep dents, where the occupant of the chair had
been digging his fingers into the upholstery. *Well, he is
an expert fencer,* thought Jervyn. *Of course he has strong
fingers.*

"Damn, damn, damn," he whispered, unconsciously
echoing Sommers. His conscience was not, as it happened, resting easy at this moment. Then he adjusted
his cuffs, checked his cravat, and prepared to saunter
back into the brightly lit salons of the Baroness Reuss.

"You never went to sleep last night," Elizabeth said
to Sommers in accusing tones. She had heard him come
in, very late, and now, an hour or so after sunrise, had
found him still in evening dress, writing something at
the table.

He glanced down at his feet, where Trumpet was
sprawled snoring on his back. "The dog has been sleeping for both of us," he said. "But, in fact, if you can

take this note over to Rittmeister von Naegel, I might be able to rest a bit before morning lessons." He handed her the letter. "You had best read it," he said after a moment. "And then I will explain what I would like you to do when you get there."

Elizabeth looked at what he had written. It was a very courteous apology for the incident with Nathanson the previous week. Now she was thoroughly confused. Surely he had given her the impression her intervention had been welcome and justified? He must have decided he could not antagonize Naegel. "If you feel an apology is necessary," she said with dignity, "I am the one who was at fault. I can make my own excuses. You do not need to send a note around as though you were a father acting for a schoolboy."

"Do you think you ought to apologize?" he asked, giving her a searching look.

"If you tell me I should, I will do so." Her chin was jutting out stubbornly.

"That is not what I asked," he pointed out. He looked very tired, but his eyes were starting to twinkle. When she had first emerged, his face had been stamped with that terrible flatness which made her want to throw a bucket of water over him every time she saw it.

"Very well," she said with some asperity. "If you want my opinion, I think Naegel owes *you* an apology."

"Quite so," he said cheerfully. "And from what I hear, he is, underneath it all, rather a decent sort. I think he will agree with you. Since Naegel is evidently a very early riser, I think you should arrive at half-past seven. Give his man the letter and say no reply is expected, but see if you can contrive some excuse to delay your departure—a coughing fit or a flirtation with a maidservant. I am hoping Naegel will in fact send a reply, and if you linger he will be more likely to do so. If not, I will have to think of something else, but this seemed the simplest. I need a sample of his hand-writing."

"What for?" asked Elizabeth, before she could stop herself.

"I am going into a new line of work," he said lightly. "Forgery."

She stared at him. "You are joking, surely?"

At the expression on her face he grimaced. "I wish I were," he said. "Ned, I am going to have to ask for your help with this. My handwriting is dreadful, especially now that my fingers have been rearranged, and this is too delicate a matter to entrust to a professional document maker. Your script is neat, and I am fairly certain you could do a good enough job for the purpose. Nathanson is quite gifted at this sort of thing, but I cannot involve him."

Shaken, Elizabeth sank down on the nearest seat, which happened to be the crate which served as a piano bench. Absentmindedly she reached over with one hand and fingered a chord. Her heart was pounding, and there was a bitter taste in the back of her throat. She should never, never have told him she knew he was not a fencing master. Somehow that had opened the door, and now she was going to be drawn into—what was he doing? Something illegal, she was sure of it. And she did not want to know what it was, she was sure of that, too. How had she ever come to such a pass? She was so overwhelmed she was tempted to simply tell him the truth about herself and leave.

He was saying something, he had her by the shoulder. She twisted away, unwilling to let him see her dismay. Exasperated, he shook her, hard.

"Ned, for God's sake! Will you listen to me? I apologized, dammit! I am a prize fool; I've been spending too much time with cynics like Nathanson. This is no work for a boy your age. If I am very careful, I am sure I can manage." She still had not looked up, but he let her go and walked over to the other side of the room. "You should go back to England," he said in strained tones a minute later. "Presumably you have enough money now. I can purchase the piano from you. I find I rather like having one luxury item in my attic.'' He had tuned it himself and had been playing occasionally, using only his left hand, although he usually stopped when Elizabeth came into the room.

"I cannot leave," she heard herself say in a calm voice. She had finally managed to raise her head and look at him. Luckily, he was now staring down at the hearth, scuffing a log chip back and forth over the floor with his foot.

"Why not?" he asked, surprised, turning to face her.

"Because you are in some sort of trouble," she said fiercely.

To her surprise, he burst out laughing. "Ned, if you remain in Vienna until I am no longer in trouble, you will be here a very long time. Forever, in fact."

"Give me the letter," she said abruptly, getting to her feet. "If I am going to be there at half past the hour, I should be on my way."

He shook his head. "I'll walk over towards the Spieler-gasse and then pay some urchin to deliver it. I cannot imagine why I even considered dragging you into this stupid tangle."

"I said I trusted you, and I meant it," said Elizabeth vehemently. "Now seal up the damned letter and give it to me." She was enraged to feel herself blushing at the use of the oath, but she held her ground and stared at Sommers in what she hoped was a boyishly truculent manner.

Sommers blinked. Thoughtfully, he sealed up the note and handed it over. Then he sank down onto the ancient sofa, put his feet up, and ostentatiously closed his eyes. On her way out the door, Elizabeth saw Trumpet had climbed up between the elegantly breeched legs and burrowed down for a continuation of his nap.

When she returned more than an hour later, neither one of them appeared to have moved at all. Trumpet woke at once as she came in and bounced over to greet her, but even under the mauling Trumpet gave him as he extricated himself from the sofa, Sommers barely stirred.

He's exhausted, thought Elizabeth, looking down at him. His face was softer in sleep, though. He looked even younger, far too young to have gray hair. But of course, as she now knew, that was a disguise. She wondered what color his real hair was under his wig. His brows were dark, but she suspected he was blackening them, because his lashes were far lighter. Mentally, she substituted light brown hair for the salt-and-pepper strands of the wig. It did not seem right. Fair hair? She closed her eyes, picturing a towheaded Sommers. Perhaps. When she opened her eyes again, she gasped to find Sommers staring at her with a sleepy grin.

"What cheer?" he inquired lazily. "Did our noble fish bite?"

"He did indeed," said Elizabeth, smiling in spite of her qualms about her part in the fraud. "I had barely started on a piece of cake in the kitchen when a footman came down with the reply." She handed him the note, which he scanned intently.

"Not a man of many words, Herr Naegel," he said dryly. "We are missing some important letters—capital B, for example. Still, it does not have to pass inspection at a solicitor's. As Nathanson is fond of saying, people see what they expect to see. If the little countess receives an indiscreet missive from our friend and the handwriting is not implausible, she will not check individual letters against an exemplar."

"The little countess?" Elizabeth felt a bit uneasy and suddenly began to have a suspicion of why Nathanson was not available to help. Rumor had it he was quite taken with the tiny lady-in-waiting. "The Countess of Brieg?"

"I am afraid so." Sommers took Naegel's letter over to the bookshelf and tucked it inside an Italian treatise on footwork. "She is in possession of a letter which does not belong to her, and I have been asked to get it back. Needless to say, this is all extremely confidential and I am breaking both my own rules and government rules by involving you, but you seem to have a cool head on those young shoulders, and I have a much better chance of pulling this off if you are helping me."

An ugly knot which had been sitting in the pit of Elizabeth's stomach since he first mentioned the word 'forgery' began to loosen. "Are you saying the countess is threatening someone?" she asked cautiously. From what she had heard from the servants at Doña Maria's, it would not be surprising.

"Let us say she appears to believe her possession of this letter entitles her to special favors," said Sommers.

"But I don't understand," said Elizabeth. "Why should we send her a forged letter from Captain von Naegel? How will that help you to recover the other letter? What happens if she tries to use the new letter against Naegel?"

"That is a good point," said Sommers. "Just in case things go badly wrong, you will have to make two copies of our forgery. We will deposit one with my papers at Roth's bank, together with a statement. The new letter is the bait, you see. I rather suspect the countess has quite a few documents hidden away. And I will not have much time to search her rooms. I will need to be able to abstract the item we need within a minute or two. Ergo, I must have a way of knowing where she keeps her treasures. And the best means of acquiring that knowledge is to send her a new treasure and hope she puts it in the same place."

Elizabeth was still confused. "Surely she will not let you watch her while she puts the letter from Naegel away? And why would you be there, in any case? It would make no sense for you to deliver his letter."

"Oh, I will not be there," said Sommers. "But I should still be able to find the letter later." He held up a glass jar with a cork stopper. At first Elizabeth could not discern what was in it. Then her eyes widened, and she gasped.

"You are completely mad! It will never work!"

"O ye of little faith," snorted Sommers. "Can you think of anything better?"

"No," admitted Elizabeth. She started to laugh. "Nathanson will kill you," she said. "That will be the last straw."

Sommers laughed, too. "It only takes one straw with Nathanson, so I may as well be hung for a sheep as for a lamb." The laugh deteriorated into a huge yawn and he looked over at the clock. "Oh, God!" he gasped. He bolted for his room, ripping off his jacket as he went. "I had no idea I had slept so long. I should have known you could not have gone and returned in under an hour. The students will be here any minute!" He was pulling stockings off very well-muscled calves, and suddenly Elizabeth realized he was about to take down his breeches. Scarlet-faced, she fled to her room and started loudly taking swords off the hooks, making sure to stay behind her door until she heard him run down the stairs to the *salle*.

She was late coming back from her walk with Trumpet, owing to an encounter with a female terrier which had jumped out of a carriage window in a sudden access of passion for her charge. Tired and stiff from dragging an unhappy dog through seven crowded streets, she started up the stairs, hoping there were no afternoon pupils today. She still could not keep track of the schedule, and Sommers apparently did not use an engagement book of any sort.

Her heart sank when she heard voices from the *salle* as she came to the first landing. With a vigorous slap on his woolly rump, she sent Trumpet scrambling up the stairs to the loft, and opened the door. It was only Nathanson, she saw, and they were just getting started.

He had taken off his boots and was shrugging out of his jacket.

"Sorry," she called to Sommers, who was at the other end of the long room, stretching. "Trumpet enticed some pampered female dog out of a carriage window. Are there any pupils coming?"

Sommers grinned. "Just Nathanson here. He anticipates being called out, I gather, and is trying to regain his form." Elizabeth dismissed this as banter; she had seen Nathanson fence.

"Escaping from Cox, rather," growled Nathanson. "All the man ever wants to do is eat, talk, and drink. Mostly drink. I would swear his object in life is to take as few steps as possible between chairs—provided, of course, the chair is adjacent to a table with a decanter on it." He was loosening up, taking some small lunges, and checking the button on his foil, when a cold, wet object pushed into the back of his leg. Instantly he whirled, sword ready, and confronted the adoring gaze of Trumpet.

"Oh, dear," said Elizabeth, trying very hard to control her face. "I sent him upstairs, Captain, truly I did. I am afraid he has taken a liking to you."

"It is not mutual," said Nathanson between his teeth. Sommers was sputtering with laughter. Reluctantly, Nathanson smiled. "Wretched beast," he said weakly. "Nearly gave me apoplexy."

"I'll take him back up and shut him in my room," said Elizabeth. She grabbed Nathanson's jacket and boots and whistled to Trumpet. For once he actually followed her, although she suspected Nathanson's boots were more responsible for his obedience than her whistle. Once in the loft, she took the boots into her room and then moved to the door as Trumpet obligingly trailed in after them.

"Now behave," she said sternly. "And for goodness sake, don't eat them!" She thought Trumpet was old enough to be beyond the chewing stage, but she was not sure. Carefully, she backed out of the room and closed the door before Trumpet could follow. She was still carrying Nathanson's jacket. Eager to get back to the *salle* and watch, she slung it over the back of the sofa instead of hanging it up. Unfortunately, the epaulettes weighted the shoulders considerably, and with a silken hiss, the whole garment slid gently down behind the sofa onto the floor.

"Drat," muttered Elizabeth, hoping Marta had swept recently. Dirt was easy to see on dark green wool.

She darted behind the sofa and picked up the jacket. It looked clean, she saw with relief. More carefully this time, she restored it to the sofa. Then she spied something white on the floor. A card had fallen out of one of the pockets. Stooping, she picked it up and was about to replace it when she noticed the name at the bottom. Her hand froze midway back to the pocket. Sternly, she told herself she should put it back.

It was no use. Temptation was too strong. She sighed, opened the door to her room, and let Trumpet out. She might as well have company, and this way she could keep an eye on the fate of the boots.

"I must be destined for a life of crime," she told him. Fetching the ink and pens from Sommers's bureau, she set the card out on the table and began to copy it letter by letter onto a clean sheet of foolscap.

Nine

Elizabeth and Trumpet reappeared in the courtyard behind the Reitschule just as Sommers was beginning to pack up the bag of equipment. He gave her a quick, interrogative glance and apparently was pleased with what he saw; he was smiling grimly as he tied up the bag. The young prince and his tutor came over to her at once when they saw Trumpet at her side. Elizabeth wondered how he had ever come to be abandoned. In her experience, he drew admirers as honey drew flies. She was bursting with her news, but had sense enough to say nothing until they were well away from the palace precinct.

"I owe you a pound of herring," she confessed, once they were safely out of earshot.

He grinned, triumphant. "It worked, then?"

"Well, you will not know for certain until you go back, of course. But I slipped the lead as soon as we got to the first floor in the old wing of the palace, and he went straight to her suite. The outer doors were open, luckily. I went in after him, just as we had planned, and pretended to stumble so I could not catch him until he ran into one of the inner rooms. It is the one furthest to the right after you come into the entry hall. There is a small black lacquer cabinet in there, and he was sniffing ecstatically at the bottom of it." She added after a moment, "I can make you a drawing of her suite and of the cabinet when we get home."

"Admit you thought the idea totally ridiculous," he prodded.

"Well, I did," she acknowledged. "And I thought that letter you concocted from Naegel was even more ridiculous. How could she believe someone whose betrothal was announced only a month ago would write her such a letter?"

"The letter would not have had any value were he not recently betrothed," Sommers reminded her. "To a very wealthy girl, from a very old-fashioned family."

"Still, I did not think it was a very good love letter," Elizabeth muttered. "If he had really been trying to seduce her, that letter would not have done him much good. Men think all they have to do is tell a woman they love her and she will fall into their arms."

Sommers slanted an amused glance at her. "I take it you are an expert on such matters, halfling?"

Reddening, Elizabeth retreated hastily. "How much fish oil did you put on the letter, then? Do you think the countess will notice the smell?"

"A trace, no more," he reassured her. "And I hope the tobacco will have concealed it, in any case. That was a good thought of yours." He gave her his rare, warm smile. As always, her legs seemed to dissolve underneath her, but she had learned to school her expression, and after a momentary wobble, she strode along beside him in her most boy-like fashion.

"How are you going to get back into her suite?" she asked, trying to sound casual, as they turned down the Tiefer Graben towards home.

He frowned. "Probably climb in," he said. "There is a state dinner tonight; she will be there, I am sure. Once you make me a sketch of the layout inside the suite, I can calculate which window is the right one. It has been quite warm. The window is likely to be open."

"Isn't that a bit dangerous?" she said, warming to her game. "Are there no guards?"

"Well, I have done it before," he said. "Admittedly the two other times involved buildings whose back court-yards were not quite so well illuminated, but I think it less risky than trying to walk in the doors past the guards. At that hour they will certainly stop me. I considered going in during the day, but her rooms are full of visitors and servants then, and I am also reluctant to leave our false love letter in her possession for one hour longer than necessary."

They had turned in the gate to their little yard, and Frau Renner came out to meet them. "Someone was asking for you, Herr Sommers," she said cheerfully. "He left a note." She searched her apron pocket, in vain. "I must have left it in the kitchen. I will go look." A few moments later she was back, empty-handed. "I am sure I have it somewhere," she said apologetically. "I have been losing many things lately; Marta says I am getting old."

"Nonsense," scolded Sommers, smiling at her. "You are simply busy. Bring it up when you find it. I'll warrant it is nothing urgent."

Elizabeth was pacing back and forth impatiently at the foot of the stairs, annoyed at the interruption, but she managed to hold her peace until they had unpacked the weapons and masks and hung them up. Sommers had gone into his room and was sluicing his face in the basin. She followed him as far as the doorway, waiting for an opportunity to tell him what she had done. He turned around, his face dripping. With a smug expression, she handed him a towel.

"You look mighty pleased with yourself, Purcell," he said, eyeing her suspiciously. "What are you plotting?"

"I have a present for you," she informed him. Like

a small child, she wanted his full attention. She made
him come out and sit down in the armchair. Then she
went over to the bookcase and pulled out the sheet of
cream-colored paper. It had taken four tries on very
expensive stationary, but she frankly thought it was quite
good, much better than the false letter from Naegel. It
was easier for her to imitate a woman's hand.

"Here," she said, suddenly nervous, handing it to
him. "I thought this might be better than climbing in
the window. It is her writing; I copied it from an invitation which fell out of Captain Nathanson's pocket."

The note authorized the bearer to visit the countess's
apartments between eight and ten that evening to take
measurements for a custom-built credenza. "If anyone
asks whether one of the countess's servants is meeting
you," she added, "tell them you believe Frau Mueller
is expecting you. She is the only one whose name I
know; she gave Trumpet a sweetmeat this afternoon.
Stout, with dark hair."

He was totally stunned. Twice he read the three-line
note and the signature; twice he looked up and started
to speak. Finally, he folded the note again, very carefully.
"You never cease to amaze me, Ned," he said slowly.
"I predict great things for you." He looked troubled,
though, and she guessed he was remembering again
that he should send her home. Her mute look of appeal
was answered with a faint smile of understanding. "Why
a credenza?" he asked lightly.

"It was the only word I could think of with a 'z' in
it," she confessed. "Her z's are very distinctive. I wanted
to use one."

"What if the footman asks me what a credenza is?"

"Did you think I would use a word I did not know?"
she said, laughing. "It is an Italian word for a sideboard
or buffet without legs. They often go under windows,
and are sometimes designed to match the decoration
of the room."

"How demeaning," he grumbled in mock indignation. "I thought I had sunk fairly low as a fencing master, but now I am an Italian cabinetmaker? What next, an organ-grinder?"

It was a brilliant scheme, Purcell's forgery, he reflected as he opened the middle drawers of the lacquer cabinet. One of the countess's servants had admitted him, glanced at the note, and then ushered him courteously into the small inner sitting room. He did not have to worry about making noise; he had been able to bring in, openly, a measuring tape and level; he had been able to come while it was still light.

The later he arrived, as he knew, the greater the chance the countess might return from the dinner before he was done. He felt carefully at the back of the drawer. Nothing. He had already tried the two lowest drawers, not really expecting to find anything. Only the crudest false bottoms had their latch in the same section of the cabinet as the hidden compartment. He hoped he could find the mechanism. With his stiff right hand he was not sure he could pry open the panel in the bottom without splintering the wood, and that would certainly bring the servant back into the room.

He tried the next drawer and had almost closed it again when his finger brushed against a suspiciously straight crack along one side. He pushed, then tugged. No result, but he could feel that something was ready to give. He tried pushing up. A thin layer of wood slid away from the back corner, revealing a square hole. He glanced around to make sure that the servant was not watching, then inserted two fingers of his left hand into the square and felt, with satisfaction, the familiar shape of the latch rod. A tug, and with a small click the bottom molding of the cabinet sprang forward half an inch.

Soundlessly he eased it open and looked inside. Six neat stacks of paper were sitting behind the false front.

He spotted what he wanted immediately; it was in the middle of the second pile.

Gratefully he invoked the blessings of St. George upon Jervyn for getting a sample of the notepaper to him. Just to make sure, he unfolded it and read the first few lines. Then he tucked it safely away and put the one Jervyn had given him in its place. Next he looked for the false letter from Naegel. This was harder to find; the paper they had used was not as distinctive. In the end he resorted to sniffing for traces of tobacco and located it on top of the right-hand pile.

Time was running out, he realized. And yet it galled him to leave the other letters undisturbed. Who knows how many poor devils had their secrets sitting in this black lacquer prison? He heard footsteps. Just in time, he replaced the panel and moved his tape over under the window.

The servant peered in. Was the gentleman nearly finished?

Sommers decided to take a chance. Unlikely that this young chambermaid knew anything about carpentry.

"Could you by chance get for me a large bucket of water?" he asked in deliberately broken German. "My level is not working, and I must use the floating." He tried a shy smile, and she blushed and hurried off. He heard the outer door close; his guess that she would have to leave momentarily to get such a container had been correct.

In haste, he opened the panel again and took out the first stack of letters. Adding Naegel's to the top, he put the whole lot in a large bronze bowl half filled with potpourri and struck a light. It blazed up at once, with an odd odor of burnt flowers mixed with paper ash. He put in a second stack, stirred the ashes a bit to settle them, and struck another spark. Absorbed in watching the flames, he only heard the voices at the last minute.

"What is this? A cabinetmaker? Where is he?"

He swore under his breath. It was impossible. It was

far too early, but he was virtually certain it was the countess. Quickly he grabbed the top letter of the third stack and stuffed it in his pocket. In another minute, she had pushed the door open and was inside the room. She thought fast, he conceded, and kept her head. There was no scream, no denunciation. Instead, she quickly shut the door and leaned back against it. She had no desire to broadcast the contents of this cabinet to her servants or to the guards, he realized. A faint hope stirred inside him.

"Who are you?" she said coldly. "And what are you doing here in my apartments?"

He looked at her curiously. She was angry, he saw, but not afraid. And yet for all she knew he was armed. "I suppose you would not believe me if I said that I was a physician and was purging the room of pestilence?" he said mildly.

Her mouth twitched. "A pretty conceit," she acknowledged. *God, no wonder Nathanson is attracted to her,* he thought. *Ethereally lovely, and with the poise of a field marshal.*

"I came for a letter I had misplaced, if you must know," he said. "A practical joke which some of us had played on von Naegel." His voice held a warning which he hoped she would understand. "But I was not certain which it was, and I was in haste. So it seemed prudent to burn them all. I thought you were safely occupied at the banquet." He was watching her eyes, and saw them darting to the pile where Metternich's letter had been. An infinitesimal relaxation of her shoulders told him she had seen the replacement and believed that stack undisturbed.

"Did no one ever tell you it was discourteous to pry into a lady's love letters?" she said conversationally. "You are justly served that I am not, in fact, attending the princess tonight. I have a private engagement later." She had moved over to a small bookshelf on the opposite side of the room. Suddenly he found himself looking at a pistol. "Take off your jacket and boots, if you please," she said, her tone belying the courtesy of the phrasing.

He raised his eyebrows, but complied.

Still holding the pistol, she felt with her other hand inside both boots, then inside the jacket. She found the letter he had placed in his pocket, but was not satisfied. "Come closer," she ordered. She pulled his shirt out of his breeches and shook it, then ran one hand over his legs in a thoroughly professional manner.

The pistol was now in his gut. He tried not to think about what would happen if it fired. Her inspection finished, she stepped back. "You may leave your bag," she said scornfully, gesturing with the pistol towards his satchel and its innocent-looking assortment of tools. "I am quite certain you will not say anything about this to anyone."

"What will you tell your maidservant?" he asked curiously as he put his boots and jacket back on.

She gave him a very demure smile as she slipped the pistol back into the bookshelf. "Why, that you are one of my lovers, of course." Then he heard a man's voice raised in irritation out in the hall. She had heard it too, he saw.

"Who is it?" he said quietly, preparing to head for the window if necessary.

"It is my brother," she said, frowning. "I asked him to meet me here briefly, but he is usually not so punctual. This is unfortunate." With one expert tap of her foot, she flipped the panel back into place at the bottom of the cabinet, and just as Frederich Werzel jerked open the door, she fainted gracefully into Sommers's arms.

"What the devil!" exclaimed Werzel, purpling with anger.

"Thank heavens someone has come at last here, *mein Herr!*" exclaimed Sommers, depositing the countess in his arms. "I have been calling with my voice! We were simply talking of the furniture, and the lady has fainted.

So I burn some flowers to wave under her nose, and she wakes, but now she faints again.''

Picking up his satchel, he withdrew, bowing and apologizing profusely, while the slow-witted Werzel stared down in bewilderment at the limp form of his sister.

Elizabeth was trying hard to concentrate on her book, and not succeeding very well. She wished Sommers had some novels. Books about fencing were all very well, but as a steady diet they grew stale quickly. No, she was deluding herself. Not even a novel could distract her tonight.

In spite of the jesting and Sommers's laughing farewell, she knew there was a very significant chance he would be caught attempting to steal the letter. She wondered what would happen to him then. Would they put him in prison? Expel him from Vienna? What if, as she suspected, he was a spy? Didn't they hang spies? She shuddered, and Trumpet, who was sitting near her with his head conveniently available for petting, whined in sympathy.

With a sigh, she went over to the table and climbed on top of it so she could look out the window. The light was fading; it must be around nine. She had tried three times to estimate how long Sommers should take to get to the palace, get to the countess's rooms, and return, and had come up with a different answer each time.

The two men were gone, at least. For the last several days, pairs of them had been loitering in the Zeughausgasse, making her very uneasy. She had finally asked Sommers who they were, and he had told her quite casually he believed they were working for the secret police. He seemed so unconcerned that she had accepted their presence more calmly, but once she knew Sommers was planning to break into the apartments of an imperial lady-in-waiting, her anxieties about the surveillance had returned.

There was a noise from the stairwell, and for a moment she thought it was Sommers, but then she recognized the slower steps of their landlady. Disconsolately she climbed down from the table in time to meet Frau Renner at the top of the stairs.

"Is Herr Sommers gone out, then?" asked the old woman, disappointed. "I found the note the Frenchman left for him earlier. It was sitting right by the sink the whole time, can you imagine? Lucky I did not get it wet when I was washing the vegetables."

"I'll take it," said Elizabeth mechanically, her eyes fixed on the folded paper. It did not look like a personal letter, more like a printed handbill. Her fears when she heard the word 'Frenchman' were unfounded, then. It was probably an announcement for a fencing exhibition. There were many French émigrés in Vienna; perhaps some of them now taught fencing, as Sommers did. "It is a notice," she said to Frau Renner, who appeared reluctant to relinquish it to her. "See, it is printing, not writing."

She unfolded it and her heart stopped beating. All along, she had hoped that Sommers's remark about being wanted in France was a jest. It was not.

The bill announced that good Austrian citizens should be aware that a reward of five hundred florins was offered for proof of the demise of a man calling himself Michael Sommers, a traitor to the Imperial State of France believed to be resident in Vienna. Two thousand florins were offered for his person, if alive and unharmed. At the bottom of the notice was a handwritten addendum in French: *I look forward to our reunion at the earliest possible moment.* It was signed *Meillet.*

"Who left this here? What did he look like?" she whispered.

Frau Renner was frightened, now, too. "A very polite man, very well dressed, Herr Purcell. Tall. Fair hair. Is something wrong? Should it have been delivered earlier?'' She wrung her hands. "Oh, it was so foolish of me to leave it by the sink!"

"It is no great matter," Elizabeth managed to say, quickly refolding the bill. "It is just a notice, as I said. But I think Herr Sommers has been hoping for news of the man who delivered this. I will tell him about it as soon as he comes home, I promise.'' Frau Renner needed some soothing, but Elizabeth heard not one word of the conversation, which some other part of her conducted automatically. Only after Frau Renner had climbed slowly back down the stairs did she go into her room and sit down on the cot, still holding the paper. Trumpet got up and padded in after her. She was thinking hard.

Meillet. It took her a minute to recall the name. Meillet was the man Nathanson had said was loose. He was pursuing Sommers, and now he had found him. Perhaps those two men were his hirelings. Suddenly she was not at all glad that the two men were not on the street any longer. They had probably followed Sommers to the palace. Now it was growing dark, and he would be coming back alone and unarmed. Cabinetmakers did not wear swords, after all.

Panic seized her. She fished frantically under her cot for her boots and pulled them on; scrambling to her feet, she yanked two sabers off of their hooks, dislodging the smaller weapons next to them, which slid off the wall with a crash. She was already tumbling down the stairs, tripping over the sabers, and running out the gate into the street.

Which way would he be coming? She stood frozen in indecision, then forced herself to reconstruct what he had said about his plans. He was not walking straight to the palace; she remembered that. His papers identified him as an Italian craftsman residing in Leopoldstadt, and he must appear to have come from there. He would have gone by boat, then. Very likely he would come back the same way, and would land by the Fishermen's Stair. Reciting the route like a rosary, she took one saber in each hand and set off at a brisk walk. It was foolish to run in the dark carrying unsheathed weapons.

As she hurried along she told herself she was worrying about nothing. Even if the two men had followed him, they would have had difficulty pursuing him once he was on the water. Still, it would do no harm to go to the Ruprechtsplatz. From the top of the stair, she would at least have a good view of the river.

She had come around the north side of the church when she spotted him, climbing out of a small boat. This took several minutes, since his first attempt to leave was forestalled by an indignant boatman; evidently he had forgotten to pay.

Once ashore, he headed along the wharf, evidently intending to go straight past the barracks and around the depot to their little lane behind the armory. Her first reaction was relief that he was out of the palace and unharmed. But her relief was short-lived. Almost at once she saw the two men emerge from the shadows and move steadily along behind him. There was no doubt about it; they were following him, and if he decided to continue towards the barracks, he would be leaving the wharf, where there were crowds and lights, and walking into a dark, quiet area ideally suited for an attack.

She thought of calling out to warn him, but his pursuers were so close and she was so high up that she judged it would be more dangerous than remaining silent. Nor was he likely to hear. A noisy, jostling family which had just returned from some pleasure trip down the river was approaching the bottom of the stair.

Her heart sank as she watched them begin to struggle up towards her, laden with babies and enormous picnic baskets. She would never catch him if she went down that way; by the time she pushed through all those people it would be far too late. There was the smaller stair to the west of the church. Praying that the gate behind the salt warehouse at the bottom was still open, she rushed across the plaza and scurried down the stone steps as quickly as she dared. The first gate was open, and she nearly ran around the corner of the warehouse to the side gate which let out into the lane. It was shut.

Furiously, she shook it. Not only shut, but locked. Too high to climb over, she saw at a glance.

She could go partway back up the steps to the landing and try climbing down the old city wall, which was of rough stone, but she did not think she could make such a climb very quickly. If she went all the way back to the front of the church, she could go down the public stair, but it was twice as long, and if Sommers was headed for the barracks she would never reach him in time.

Think! she told herself furiously. How can you get through this gate? If she had a pistol, she could break the lock, but she knew the sabers would be useless as crowbars. She stepped back and scanned the steep wall next to the gate. It was dishearteningly smooth.

There was a gap—a narrow gap—however, between the wall and the iron grillwork of the gate. No adult man could fit through it, but a child perhaps could. Or a very thin young woman. She stepped into the corner and measured her shoulder against the wall. It was her only chance; she would have to try it. She remembered reading about someone getting their head stuck in a fence and pushed the thought hastily away.

Gritting her teeth, she took the sabers and pushed them through on the ground. Now she was committed. In fact, it was not too difficult, she discovered. There was one bad moment when her foot became jammed sideways, but by pointing her toes she was finally able to free it. Sommers would never make it through, though. She picked up the sabers and hastened down the little lane beside the warehouse, hoping to catch him before he left the safety of the wharf.

Too late. There was a tavern at the far end of the

lane, spilling bright light out onto the cobblestones. A group of five young men were standing at the door, talking—almost shouting. They seemed very drunk. And she saw Sommers stride by them into the darkness, acknowledging some joke or greeting with a lift of his hand, and then the two pursuers behind him.

She was still hurrying towards him, although she knew she would never reach him before the hunters did, when a miracle happened. Three of the drinkers detached themselves from their group and greeted the two men with uproarious hilarity. She could hear laughing shouts, and a snatch of song. Sommers had turned briefly, but now had resumed walking. The two men were now completely swallowed up in the rowdy gang in front of the tavern, and she felt her shoulders slump in relief. They had been heading for the tavern all along, not following Sommers.

She began to feel rather self-conscious. What would Sommers think when he found her, scraped raw from the fence, holding her sabers and running after him? He would think she was an idiot, would he not?

He had told her all along there was a price on his head in France. She had made a mountain out of a molehill. Men hated being protected; she knew that much from Robin. He would be embarrassed and angry. With a sigh she started back towards the gap, but halted almost at once at the sound of running feet. She whirled around.

The singing and laughing in front of the tavern had stopped abruptly. Two figures were lying on the ground, and four men—the erstwhile revelers— were moving with grim purpose to encircle Sommers. He had darted back towards the wharf and was much closer to her now. She could see the defiant set of his shoulders as he turned to face the attackers. He had a dagger, she saw— but all four of the men had thick cudgels. Elizabeth was racing down the lane as fast as she could, heedless of the danger from the sabers, and yelling Sommers's name.

Taken by surprise, the four men stopped momentarily, and that gave him time to sprint past them into the lane and join her.

"Here," she gasped, thrusting a saber into his right hand. He shifted it automatically into his left, switching it with the dagger. The four men moved more cautiously now; it was four against two, not such good odds, and the two were now armed.

"Is the gate beside the warehouse open?" Sommers asked quietly, his eyes on the four attackers.

"No," she said, still breathless. "I squeezed through a gap, but you will not fit."

"Trapped, then," he observed in calm tones. "Move slowly back towards the end of the alley; we need a wall behind us or they will circle around us. Don't turn, though; walk backwards, facing them."

It was like some deadly dance, she thought, as they paced slowly backwards, followed by their sinister partners. The enemy did not know Vienna well, she realized, because when they suddenly saw the wall looming up out of the darkness one of them cursed in French, railing at the other three for fools and cowards. The rough stone felt wonderful against her back, and she gladly forgave the wall for every scrape on her hips.

"Stay exactly where you are," instructed Sommers, stepping in front of her and slightly to the left. "Don't move away from the wall, no matter what. Try to cover my right side, if you can, but be careful with that thing. I have to stay close to you, and I don't want to be sliced open by my own assistant."

Elizabeth gave a shaky laugh.

"Good lad," said Sommers in a low voice. "It's not as bad as it looks. Thank God you brought sabers and not rapiers. A saber can slice a cudgel into bits if it hits at the right angle, and these men are hired help; they have no reason to risk their necks."

The four men were muttering to each other and must have reached some agreement, because suddenly they attacked all together, swinging the cudgels and heading straight for Elizabeth. Sommers immediately shifted across in front of her and caught the leading man a backhanded blow on the wrist. With a scream he dropped his weapon and grabbed his arm, doubling over. The man behind him tripped. The two others were already on top of Sommers, however. One of them managed to land a blow on his ribs; the other had jumped back as the saber swung in his direction.

Sommers staggered slightly and swept the saber out in a glittering arc. The third man had gotten back on his feet, but was staring uncertainly at his disabled companion. "Come on," said the tallest of the three impatiently. "The other one is just a boy, couldn't you see?" He hefted his weapon and the three of them marched forward again.

This time they did not make the mistake of allowing Sommers to engage them one at a time. They stayed together until the last second, then suddenly split up, one on each side, and one bearing down in front, trying to get around him to Elizabeth.

She realized there was a cudgel coming at her head and instinctively parried with the saber. The force of the blow almost knocked the weapon out of her hand, and a spasm of pain shot up to her shoulder. Wrong angle, she thought. The cudgel had not broken. The man came at her again, and suddenly Sommers was in front of her, pushing her behind him. He ducked under the cudgel and smashed the man in the shoulder with the dagger, then stabbed backwards with the saber as a second attacker tried to close in from behind. There was a grunt of pain, and the man retreated. The one who had been hit in the shoulder was down, but he was pulling himself back up to his feet again.

"They'll break in a minute," Sommers said to her in a low voice. "I got that second bastard in the thigh; he won't be good for much longer. Then it will be even odds, and they do not fancy working under those conditions.''

Something was nagging at the back of Elizabeth's mind, something important, something she had noticed. The attackers had regrouped and were approaching again, slowly. He was right, they were hesitating, she realized. Her spirits began to lift. One of them darted forward suddenly and aimed a blow at her knee. With a lightning downward slash, Sommers split the cudgel in two. The Frenchman danced away, shaking his hand with a howl of pain. The man with the gash on his thigh had fallen back and was attempting to bind up his wound. They were going to beat them off, thought Elizabeth, exultant.

Then she heard a slight noise from the wall behind her and suddenly remembered what it was that she had noticed earlier. There had been five of them, not four. One of them must have gone up the public stair and come across to the landing above the gate. With a shout of warning, she pushed Sommers aside. But she was not quite in time. The fifth reveler had launched himself from the top of the wall, and Sommers was lying, limp, underneath him.

A violent rage seized her and boiled up through every muscle in her body. She hit this latest assailant in the head as hard as she could with the flat of her sword. Then she was kicking the stunned man in the stomach and using her saber like a poker to roll him away from Sommers. And she was screaming—a true scream, not a shout or a yell. As a child her screams had been infamous. This one hit a high E.

She saw a horse harnessed to a cart in front of the tavern rear and bolt. Windows began to pop open farther down the alley. One of the two figures lying by the tavern door had gotten up and was pointing to her; she heard a shrill whistle and shouts of *'polizei.'*

The whistle seemed to be some sort of signal. One minute the remaining Frenchmen were moving back in on her; the next moment they were running—or limping—back down the lane, dragging their two disabled comrades and shoving their way past a few curious residents who had begun to come out into the street.

The instant the assailants turned and ran, she dropped to her knees and bent over Sommers. It was so dark down on the ground that she could hardly see a thing; she could not even tell if his eyes were open. She fumbled for a pulse but could feel only her own heartbeat, thudding wildly through her fingers.

Frantically she put her hand over his mouth and forced herself to still her trembling palm until she sensed the faint, damp puffs of air. Other people were arriving; one of them had a lantern. There were exclamations, orders, a buzz of comment. She heard none of it, her eyes locked on the dim shape of Sommers's face. *Don't die,* she prayed silently. *Please don't die. I don't even know your real name.*

A neatly dressed older man with an air of authority pushed through the crowd and knelt down by Sommers. It must be a doctor, she thought numbly; he was taking a pulse and checking under the eyelids. There was a groan from the patient, and his eyes opened slowly. They looked wrong, too dark, the pupils enormous. "Don't move," cautioned the doctor in German, beckoning to someone else on the fringe of the crowd. Elizabeth saw two men approaching with a makeshift litter.

"Have no fear," said Sommers weakly. "I have no plans to move in the immediate future." The doctor had pulled open the wounded man's shirt and was running his hands along his ribs, and Sommers suddenly gave a stifled gasp and closed his eyes again.

"Is he injured badly?" asked Elizabeth fearfully, her heart in her mouth. There was a cut on his forehead, and a huge bruise was already forming next to his collarbone under the placket of his shirt.

The doctor peered again under one eyelid. "He has a concussion," he told Elizabeth. "At least one cracked rib. Perhaps a broken collarbone. He should be taken home and put to bed at once. Do you live far from here? I asked the tavern-keeper to send for a carriage. He should not walk.''

Offers of help were pouring in; many hands lifted the litter and carried it down to the tavern. Sommers lay unmoving on the hurdle, blood trickling slowly down the side of one cheek. Impatiently, Elizabeth knelt down and blotted his face with her handkerchief. Out of the corner of her eye, she noticed a portly man speaking rapidly to the doctor. Elizabeth recognized him. He was one of the two she had thought were pursuing Sommers.

The doctor came over to her. "You must file a report with the police." He nodded to the portly man. "Would you wish to do it now, or wait until your friend is able to talk to them also?"

"I would prefer to wait," said Elizabeth, trying to assimilate this new puzzle. The pursuers were policemen? That explained why the fake revelers had swarmed over them and knocked them down. She took a closer look at the policeman. He had been outside Frau Renner's house yesterday afternoon, she realized. Nothing made any sense whatsoever.

A carriage arrived at last, a rather shabby affair, but she was beyond noticing. The crowd had already begun to drift off, and once Sommers was carefully deposited in the coach, they dispersed completely. Elizabeth gave the doctor their address, requesting him to follow as soon as he could, and then climbed wearily into the vehicle.

They had stretched Sommers across one of the cushioned seats. Someone had lit the small passenger lantern, and she studied the fine-boned face opposite her intently. His cut was bleeding again, she noticed. Gently, she reached across and dabbed at it.

My God, he's even younger than I thought, she realized, her heart contracting. When she had first seen him on the street outside the jeweler's shop three weeks ago, she had thought him in his mid forties. Now she was wondering if he was even thirty.

Sommers's eyes opened again as they began to rumble down the street.

"Are you all right?" Elizabeth asked anxiously. He looked much better already, she noted with relief; his pupils were their normal size again.

"My head hurts like hell, but yes, I think I'll live," he said, with a faint smile. "Mostly thanks to you. Where did you learn to scream like that?"

"I sang in church when I was younger," said Elizabeth, flushing, hoping he was too preoccupied with other matters to put two and two together. No sixteen-year-old boy should be able to make that sound, and she knew it.

"Well, it was an outstanding specimen, that scream," he said. "And this time it did the trick. But your saber technique needs work. It is customary to stab opponents with the saber, or occasionally strike them with the flat. Using the saber as a shovel to push bodies around on the street, however, is not at all *comme il faut.*"

"Can you never be serious?" flared Elizabeth, suddenly and irrationally angry with him for nearly getting himself killed. "Who are these people? Why are they after you? And what are you going to do next time? I am useless in a fight. We were simply lucky tonight."

"You were not useless," he retorted, angry in his turn. He pushed himself up on one elbow and glared at her. "I would be worse than dead now if you had not turned up with those sabers, do you not see that? And you did your share of holding them off. But there will not be a next time, for you at least. You are going home. At once."

"I will do no such thing!" shouted Elizabeth.

"Yes, you will," he said in a steely tone she had never heard him use before.

"So you can brood alone in the loft with your brandy until they chase you down again?"

"Yes, dammit!" They glared at each other until a jolt of the carriage forced an involuntary gasp of pain from Sommers. He sank back onto the cushions and turned his face away. "Don't you understand?" he said, his voice muffled. "They want me alive, unhurt. But there is no reward for you. They will simply kill you to get you out of the way. Did you not realize they all were attacking you?"

"Is that why you kept pushing me behind you?" whispered Elizabeth, her throat tight.

He nodded, then winced again at the motion and eased himself carefully back into a supine position, eyes once more closed. "It is not going to be much fun traveling to Baden tomorrow with my head like this," he commented.

If this was intended as a device to change the subject, it succeeded. Elizabeth erupted again. "Are you mad?" she demanded. "You are not even supposed to walk down the stairs for two days! Do you think I am going to let you ride to Baden? It must be four leagues, at least!"

"More like five," he corrected. "Nevertheless, I have to go. I'll hire a carriage. I'm not a complete fool. I know I should not ride a horse in this condition."

"You have the letter," said Elizabeth slowly, finally understanding. "You found it, and now you have to take it to someone." Caught up in the desperate events by the canal, she had forgotten all about the expedition to the countess's apartments.

"Bright lad," was the sleepy response.

"Why can't Cox or Nathanson take it?"

There was a long silence, and she thought perhaps he had dozed off or passed out again, but when she looked more closely she saw his lips were tightly compressed.

"Because," he said reluctantly in low tones, still not opening his eyes, "I don't trust them with it."

Ten

A groom was waiting to take his horse, and Nathanson paused for a moment before ascending the stairs to the front door of the house. The upper story was in darkness, but lanterns at the end of the drive illuminated the entryway and the lower windows.

It looks like a jewel box, he thought. Probably it was a summer house or hunting lodge. It was too small to be anything else, and was just outside of Hietzing, where many wealthy Viennese spent the months of July and August, but it was the most ornate summer house he had ever seen.

Every window, every gutter, every angle of the roof sprouted into fantastic curlicues and ornaments. Putti with gilded wings topped the pillars framing the door, which was set beneath a roundel depicting Neptune and the Nereids. It was difficult to see colors in the fading light, but he had a strong suspicion the house was painted pink.

The interior, when he was admitted by a soberly clad manservant, was equally fantastic. A huge mirror in a silver frame shaped like antlers dominated the tiny entrance hall. It clashed with an ugly brass chandelier. Mahogany wainscoting gleamed everywhere, and he caught a glimpse of what appeared to be a tiger skin on the floor of a room off to the left. He was shown, however, into a more conventionally furnished space, a small salon done in white and gold, with the unmistakable stamp of the countess's personality upon it. A Sévres clock framed by figures of shepherds showed the time as twenty past nine.

He frowned. Surely at least some of the other guests should be here by now? Supper was often taken very late in Vienna, and it was not fashionable to arrive on time, but the invitation had said nine, and the diners would assuredly prefer to make the trip back to the city before midnight. He was beginning to grow uneasy when he heard the sound of a carriage pulling up in front of the house. Of course, the other guests had come out together as a group. He heard a familiar voice and felt a quiver of anticipation. There was a light step in the hall, and the manservant reappeared to hold the door open for the countess.

She was alone, and it took him a moment to realize that he heard no other voices, no other footsteps, because, as always, he was completely occupied in the struggle to prevent himself from staring at her. A high-waisted white gown *à la Grecque* fell over a gold underslip of taffeta, and her hair was caught up in a simple knot, tied with a white silk band. Gold and white, he realized. She had dressed to match the room.

"Please forgive me, Captain, for arriving too late to welcome you," she said, with a charming smile. "I was delayed at the palace. Has Josef offered you some refreshment? Have you been here long?"

"I have only just arrived," he responded, bowing briefly over the hand she extended. "I was not certain of the route, and feared to be the last arrival, but now I find perhaps I am unfashionably early after all, since none of the other guests are here."

She paused a moment before replying, and he saw the blue eyes consider him, waiting for his reaction. "There are no other guests," she said in level tones.

Nathanson had been trained since childhood not to show surprise, although someone who knew him well might have seen his shoulders stiffen slightly. "You cannot be serious," he said in a carefully neutral voice.

"I certainly hope we will not be too serious, my dear Captain, at a private and informal dinner. But yes, I meant what I said. You are the only guest."

"I am afraid I have just recollected a previous engagement," he said, his face tightening. "Please excuse me, I will call for my horse."

The countess lost her temper first. Eyes flashing, she marched to the door and whirled to face him, blocking the exit. "I had not heard you were so prudish, sir, in Spain," she said angrily.

"I do not know what you heard, Madame," he retorted, "but if you wish me to spend the rest of my stay in Vienna meeting Austrian gentlemen at dawn in the Belvedere Gardens, you have certainly concocted the perfect scenario. I begin to have some sympathy for your brother."

"My brother has no right to censure me," she said stormily. "I am a woman grown, married and now widowed. My conduct is my own affair."

"Then you will allow me to make the same claim for my conduct," he said sternly. "And I do not choose to be a party to this, no matter what rumors may have come to you from Spain." His face softened as he saw her fighting back tears of chagrin. "How old were you when you married?" he asked abruptly.

"Sixteen," she said in a low voice. Anticipating his next question, she added: "My husband was nearly seventy."

"And how old are you now?"

"Twenty."

He had thought her older. It was appalling. "Do you

really wish," he said, looking at her intently, "to claim the privileges of a widowed matron at the age of twenty? To have affairs and lovers, a court of silly gallants who troop into your boudoir to watch you put up your hair and choose your gowns? To never be escorted to an event by the same man twice in one week? To set aside all thoughts of a true marriage, of an honorable life with someone you can respect?"

"I did not find marriage such a desirable state that I should wish to constrain my behavior in order to experience it again," she answered defiantly.

"You will forgive me if I point out that a marriage where the groom is half a century older than the bride is not likely to offer a flattering picture of the institution."

"May I ask, then, why you are not married, Captain?"

"I am still rather young," he said defensively. She was really just a spoiled child, he thought. And it was understandable that the ridiculous arranged marriage had warped her sense of proper conduct.

She looked disconcerted. "Young? Do they marry so late in England, then?"

"I am twenty-two!" he said in exasperated tones, wondering for the hundredth time why everyone persisted in thinking he was nearer thirty.

The door opened and the dour-looking Josef came in with a tray and glasses.

"Thank you, no," said Nathanson curtly. "Please have my horse brought around at once. I am leaving." The servant, confused, looked at the countess, but a glance back at Nathanson's face decided him. "Certainly, *mein Herr*," he said hastily, setting down the tray and disappearing. He started to close the door behind him, but Nathanson's arm shot out and held it open. Josef's mouth made an O and he scuttled away nervously.

She was pouting, he saw. He would have been amused, except that she was so damnably beautiful. For a long moment he studied her face, seeing her delicate features, thinking of the Sévres clock and the incongruous femininity of this room in contrast to the rest of the house. A terrible suspicion began to take hold of him. Was her interest in him based on the same impulse that had led to the tiger skin in the room next door: curiosity, an attraction to the exotic and forbidden, a desire to savor her own aristocratic civility in the face of something uncouth and barbaric?

"My thanks for the invitation," he said bitterly, moving towards the door. To his surprise, she stepped aside. Only after he had gone out into the hall did she release her parting shot. "Your friend the fencing master was not so fastidious in my rooms at the palace earlier this evening."

Elizabeth was inclined to agree with Frau Renner: Sommers was a terrible patient. He had cleverly removed his most formidable antagonist from the scene by sending Elizabeth off at once to the local livery stable to arrange for a carriage and pair for early the following morning. When the doctor arrived, he had refused to let him examine the head injury and only grudgingly permitted his ribs to be taped. And the moment Frau Renner had gone back down to the kitchen to brew an infusion, he was out of bed, staggering to the sofa, where he defiantly remained even after Elizabeth returned and told him frankly that he looked green around the edges.

"You should be in bed," she said, exasperated.

"I'm better off out here," he said, although he did not look very comfortable. He was keeping a wary eye on the basin Frau Renner had posted by the sofa after an earlier bout of retching. "I need to ask you something. The countess, as it developed, was not at the state dinner. She came in while I was making a bonfire out of the contents of that cabinet, at a little before nine."

Elizabeth blanched. "She did? How did you get away? Why did she let you take the letter?"

"Well, she did not know that I had taken it. I put a

similar one in its place. And she did search me at gunpoint before she let me leave." He grimaced as he recalled the feel of the gun barrel in his stomach. "But she could hardly call the guard and let me show them her instruments of extortion, could she?"

"Oh," said Elizabeth, feeling foolish. "What did you want to ask me, then?"

"She told me that she had a private engagement later." He shifted awkwardly, trying to move his head to a more comfortable position. "When you presented me with that lovely authorization to play furniture maker, I should have asked you what the original invitation said. At the time, I had some foolish scruples about reading Nathanson's personal correspondence by proxy. Did you save the copies you made, the ones you used as samples of her writing?"

Elizabeth shook her head. "I burned them."

"Do you remember what they said, by any chance?"

"Pretty nearly," acknowledged Elizabeth. "I copied it twice, letter by letter—" She gasped. "Good heavens, it was for tonight! She invited him for a light supper tonight at nine at her villa in Hietzing! And I sat there and let you tell me she was going to be at the state dinner!"

"My fault," said Sommers apologetically. "I should have asked. Never mind, it makes no difference now. I expect at this very moment Nathanson is hearing all about my iniquities over a glass of excellent Rhenish wine. Go to sleep, Ned. I rather suspect he will be calling here, but not until much later."

Without answering, Elizabeth picked up a book and settled herself firmly in the armchair. It was the same volume she had been attempting to read earlier in the evening: a French work, an octavo bound in calf and entitled, *Of Affairs of Honor. Being a Treatise upon the Conduct of the Duello, the Weapons thereof, and the Duties of the Combatants. Together with a Description of Notable Duels. Translated from the Italian of Fabrizio Sabatini.* Keeping a weather eye on her patient, she doggedly returned to her study of Signor Sabatini's guidelines for the use of the rapier in the duel.

A scant quarter of an hour later, there was a furious pounding on the door at the foot of the stairs. Elizabeth looked up from her book and glanced anxiously at Sommers.

"It's Nathanson," he said in resigned tones. "Supper must have broken up early. Go let him in."

"Are you certain it isn't—those men?"

"There are two members of His Imperial Majesty's police outside our gate," Sommers said dryly. "And I do not think they will be fooled twice in one evening. I have not yet determined why they are guarding me, but I most certainly do not object. If it is not Nathanson, it is someone else they recognize—Fratelli or Cox or one of my students. But from the sound of that knock, I think my hot-tempered former colleague is the best guess."

With some trepidation, Elizabeth went slowly down the stairs, wishing she had a pistol. "Who is it?" she called in German as the knocking resumed.

"Let me in, Purcell," was the instant response, in English. "I need to have a brief word with Mr. Sommers." This last was said so viciously Elizabeth almost told him to leave. But Sommers had said to let Nathanson in, and the voice was unmistakably his.

Reluctantly she slid back the bolt. It was dark at the bottom of the staircase, so she could not see the visitor's face, but something about the way he shoved past her and leaped up the stairs made her run up after him. She arrived at the top landing just in time to see Sommers pulling himself to his feet.

"You canting hypocrite!" said Nathanson, eyes flashing. "You prate to me of my indiscretions, you bait me with my infatuation, and then you sneak off behind my back and take advantage of that child? She is a child, you know, in spite of all her efforts to appear jaded and worldly-wise."

"I take it we are speaking of the little countess?" asked Sommers, trying to draw himself up straight. He was forced to keep one hand on the back of the sofa.

"What were you doing in her apartments?" blazed Nathanson. He took a step forward. "Stand up, you traitor, so I can knock you down!"

Sommers flinched. Obligingly he removed the hand which was supporting his weight and promptly collapsed onto the floor.

"What on earth?" gasped Nathanson. And then, defensively, as Elizabeth rushed over with a horrified cry and threw herself down next to Sommers, "I did not touch him!"

She gave Nathanson a contemptuous look. "No," she said bitterly. "Meillet's men got there first. He has a concussion and two cracked ribs. Would you like to add anything to the inventory? A slap in the face, perhaps? I can tell him about it when he comes to, so that you need not wait here. I am sure your time is very valuable."

Nathanson turned pale. "He was attacked? Where? How many of them?" Briefly, Elizabeth described the confrontation by the warehouse. The anger had vanished from Nathanson's face. "Help me get him into bed," he said abruptly. "What was he doing out here, with injuries like that?"

"Waiting for you to arrive and rake him over the coals," muttered Elizabeth under her breath as she lifted Sommers's feet. But Nathanson heard her. He said nothing until they had slung Sommers onto the trundle bed.

"I will stay until he wakes, if you do not mind," he said slowly. "I suspect I owe him an apology. And I should find out more about the men who attacked you."

There was a movement from the bed, and Sommers tried to sit up. Lazily, Nathanson reached over and pushed him back down.

"Did I hear you utter the word 'apology'?" said Sommers weakly. He gave a shaky grin. "Or perhaps I was dreaming? Delirious?"

"Not so fast," said Nathanson. "Explanations first, then apology."

Sommers looked uncomfortable. "Well," he said, choosing his words carefully. "It seems that the countess is a collector. Of letters. Other people's letters."

"That is ridiculous!" said Nathanson scornfully.

"I saw them, James," said Sommers gently. "A whole cabinet full. Neatly stacked by category."

"She is probably keeping them there for her brother," growled Nathanson, pacing back and forth next to the bed. "He bullies her dreadfully. It would be just like him to decide her apartments in the palace were the perfect place to store compromising documents."

Sommers opened his mouth to object and then closed it again.

Nathanson stopped pacing. "She had something you wrote?"

"No," was the response. "A letter of Naegel's. I owed him a favor, and I was going over to the palace in any case, so I decided to do a quick round of epistolary abduction while I was there. She walked in on me and was not very pleased to find me burning her property. But then her brother arrived, and she needed some explanation of what I was doing in her room. She fell into my arms, but it was simply a masquerade for her brother. That is all, I swear it."

Elizabeth had seen Nathanson clench his fists at the words 'fell into my arms,' and she held her breath. He scowled fiercely for a moment and then sat down on the edge of the bed with a sigh.

"You can have your apology," he said, grimacing. "Now tell me what our friend Meillet has been doing."

* * *

It was very late when Nathanson came out of the back room, but Elizabeth had waited, curled up on the armchair, so she could light him downstairs and lock up behind him.

"You should not have stayed so long," she said accusingly when he finally emerged.

"Took me quite a while to persuade him to let me look at his head injury," he said wearily. "Nothing broken, though, and his eyes are clear. I think he'll be fine in a day or two if he rests."

Elizabeth was about to tell him Sommers was going to Baden in five hours, but remembered in time that Nathanson was not to know of the letter. In fact, she realized, Sommers had not exactly lied to Nathanson about his reason for visiting the palace, but he had certainly phrased his explanation in a way which suggested that it was an actual letter of Naegel's which was in question rather than the false letter they had used as bait.

"He was concerned about you, as well," Nathanson went on as they started down the stairs.

Startled, Elizabeth looked up at him.

"He thinks you are in considerable danger now, living and working with him, and I agree. Cox is going back to England at the end of the week, and I told Sommers I would arrange for you to travel with him. It is far safer than traveling on your own."

Her vision wavered and dimmed, and Elizabeth was aware that she had made some sort of odd noise. She tried to remind herself that this was exactly the opportunity she had been waiting for. Cox would be shocked, of course, when he discovered her identity, but he would not abandon her, he seemed to be a rather kindly man. She could make the long journey back under the protection of a compatriot. He might even be acquainted with her mother's family.

It was no use. She was numb with despair. Unthinking, she put one hand over her eyes, as though that would shut out the pictures inside her head: Sommers, alone in the loft, slumped over the table—or worse, lying on another street, senseless, with no one to help him this time.

"What is it?" said Nathanson sharply. "I never thought to ask if you took any hurt during that melee tonight. Sommers said you saved his life twice."

"I am not hurt, no," said Elizabeth faintly, and then, in a stronger voice, "How could I be? He kept stepping in front of me. Or did he omit that part when he described what happened?"

Nathanson did not answer her for a minute. He had moved to the side and was studying her profile intently. The candlelight flickered up over her neck, and the bottom of her ear. His hand shot out; he gripped her face and turned it towards him.

Seizing the candle from her unresisting grip, he raised it deliberately to the side of her neck—first the right, then the left. Elizabeth froze in horror as she saw his dark eyes narrow, then widen in disbelief. His hand moved down from her face, over her shoulders. With a cry, she backed away before he could pull her shirt open.

"My God," he whispered, dropping his arm. "I've been looking at you nearly every day for two weeks and I never noticed. I kept thinking you reminded me of someone, that there was something odd. Your earlobes are pierced. Your face is too thin, too old not to have any beard. Your shoulders slope too much. My father would have spotted you in five minutes." He gave a crack of bitter laughter. "To think I've been lacerating myself for the past hour for accusing Sommers of flirting with the countess! A fine fool he must think me."

"Do you mean—you believe that—" Elizabeth was

so outraged she could not speak. To her mortification, tears had started up behind her eyes, and she was shaking.

"Are you trying to tell me he does not know?" Nathanson demanded, incredulous.

"Please don't tell him," she pleaded, slumping back against the wall. She closed her eyes in despair. "Please, I beg you. I'll leave at the end of the week with Mr. Cox. Just don't tell him, I could not bear for him to know."

"Of all the blind idiots," said Nathanson in disgust. "Best code breaker in the courier service. Cracked every cipher the French came up with last year. And the only man I know who could live with a girl for three weeks and never see what was right in front of his face." He added stiffly, "I cannot allow you to remain here now that I know, of course. I will go see if I can find a respectable hostelry still open somewhere nearby. Or perhaps Frau Renner is still awake and you can stay with her for the rest of tonight."

"No," said Elizabeth firmly. "I am not a child. I am fully of age, and I can make my own decisions. I understand I will have to leave. I knew that all along. Indeed, I put on boy's clothing in the first place in order to be able to travel home unescorted. But I am not leaving tonight. Mr. Sommers is ill; he should not be left alone. And I need a few days to get ready. It is a long trip."

"What if I said I would tell Sommers who you are unless you agree to leave with me now?" asked Nathanson, drawing back so she could not see his face in the candlelight.

"I do not believe you would do that," she said quietly.

"No," he said, sighing. "I'm afraid you are right. I would not. Although I probably should."

Elizabeth put her hand on his arm. "Captain Nathanson," she said earnestly, "I know you are uncomfortable. You feel that now that you know, everything has changed. But in fact, nothing has changed. I am not so concerned with my reputation that I would leave the man who rescued me from a cutpurse to lie there, dizzy and retching, with no one to look after him. And in any case my reputation is no great matter. I have known for several years that I would probably never marry; I have neither face nor fortune. When I return to England, I will seek a post as a companion. So long as I am well-spoken and gentle, the elderly ladies who need my assistance will not be concerned with where I was for a few weeks in Vienna."

"Very well." He still looked unhappy, she saw. "What shall I tell Cox?"

"I suppose you must ask him if I can travel with him," she said slowly. "Is he discreet?"

"Yes," replied Nathanson with a brief smile. "Even when he has been drinking, you will be relieved to hear." They continued in silence down to the bottom of the stairs and he opened the door to go. Then, impulsively, he turned back to her. "Did you really brain that lout who jumped off the wall with the flat of your sword?" he asked.

Elizabeth nodded. "I should have hacked his head off," she said ruefully. "Better saber technique. Mr. Sommers told me so."

Nathanson laughed, but he said slowly, "That stubborn fool upstairs may not believe it, and when I lose my temper I may not always remember it"—he colored slightly—"but I do count him as a friend. I am in your debt. Not many women, or boys, for that matter, could have done what you did tonight."

"Well, Captain," Elizabeth replied, trying to keep her tone light, "I would not like to leave you under an obligation. You can repay me by trying to keep him alive after I leave."

"So far that is all that I seem to be needed for here in Vienna," said Nathanson enigmatically. "And I am not doing a very good job, either." He bowed briefly in farewell and disappeared into the darkness.

Still numb from the confrontation on the stairwell, Elizabeth followed him, making sure the gate to the alley was closed before she went back in through the blue door, bolting it behind her. The candle cast rippling shadows on the wall as she climbed back up past the empty *salle* and reemerged in the loft. Nathanson would not betray her, she decided. Not until she had gone. For some reason that thought was not as comforting as it should have been.

Mechanically, she went over to the lamp on the table, intending to snuff it out. She should go to bed, she knew, but she did not think she would sleep much. Suddenly she noticed the iron box. It was Sommers's strongbox. She had taken it out of his room to pay the doctor, and here it was, sitting open on the table.

Some larger items which she had scooped out of the top of the box were lying next to it—a watch which he never wore, a gold stickpin with an odd dragon design, a silver folding frame with three miniatures and a blurred shield embossed on the cover.

Idly, she opened the frame. In the center was a girl— about five or six, she judged, very pretty, with red-gold hair and greenish eyes. Elizabeth suspected she had freckles, but the painter had obligingly suppressed them. Something about the eyes and mouth reminded her of Sommers.

On the left was a fair-haired woman of about thirty, even lovelier than the girl, in some sort of classical drapery—it was difficult to tell exactly what it was, since the portrait extended only to her shoulders. Her hair was gathered up in an odd Roman style which must have been meant to go with the costume.

The right-hand frame was empty. There had been something there, but it had been laboriously removed with a penknife. Traces of paint still clung to the edges of the little wooden rectangle.

He's married, she thought numbly, as the significance of the resemblance between the girl and her host sank in. *It is a family group: mother, child, father. He scraped out the portrait of himself so that no one will know what he really looks like under that wig. This is why he is sending all that money home to England. He has a wife. He has a daughter.*

Carefully, she packed everything back into the box, closed it, and locked it. Sommers's jacket was hanging over the back of the couch. She put the key back in his pocket and went into her little room.

Tears were sliding down her face—for herself, for him? She was not sure.

Eleven

Sommers sat in the sparsely furnished hall and tried to adjust his position so that the wooden chair back was not cutting into his injured ribs. How long had he been waiting? An hour, an hour and a half? Occasionally a maid would pass through and give him a curious glance; it was far too early for callers. One cheerful young woman was carrying a tray of coffee and chocolate as she hurried by. He looked at it so longingly that she blushed and promised to try to get him something from the kitchen. But she did not return.

It was no surprise, of course, that he was having difficulty persuading the staff to let him see Metternich. He had been interrogated by three different servants, each more superior than the last, and each stubbornly unwilling to let him disturb their master unless he would state his business. If he had been an accredited representative of some foreign power, it would have been different. The last questioner, some sort of undersecretary, had come in and said encouragingly, "It is Monsieur Sommers of . . ."

Of nothing, he wanted to say. *Of nowhere.* But he merely

shook his head—a painful mistake, which he regretted immediately—and replied: "Sommers, *tout court.*"

A dreadful thought occurred to him: what if Metternich refused to see him before returning to Prague tomorrow? Then he would be forced to make a journey of over a hundred miles to seek him there. The thought was appalling; if necessary, he vowed, he would sit in the hall all day and all night until someone relented.

Thank God he had anticipated some delay and sent the coachman back up the road to an inn. Presumably the man was having a good breakfast at his expense. He himself had not dared to eat anything, fearing that the ride out to Baden would be too much for his still shaky equilibrium. And now it was becoming difficult to decide if he was faint from his injuries or faint from hunger.

There was a sudden stir in the main hallway outside his antechamber. He had not heard the knocker, but he did hear the unmistakable sound of the front door opening, followed by the manservant's voice. It must be someone intimate with the family to arrive at this hour, he thought. Or a courier.

A moment later he heard his own name, a series of murmured queries, and the door to his side passage opened. He recognized the leonine head of the man who came in immediately; it was Gentz, Metternich's secretary. To his great relief, he saw that Gentz also recognized him.

"Monsieur Sommers," ventured Gentz warily, clearly rather puzzled. "I am told you have an urgent message for His Excellency?"

Sommers tried to get to his feet, but he had been sitting too long, and the attempt brought a wave of dizziness that nearly choked him. He gasped, and when his vision cleared he saw Gentz looking at him narrowly, and then back at a younger man who had come in behind him—a slender, fair-haired sort with a somewhat bemused air. "It's true, then, Roswicz?" Gentz said. He turned back to Sommers. "Mr. Sommers, I very much regret you have been kept waiting, and in such a Spartan fashion. I gather you were injured last night when some ruffians attacked you; allow me to express my dismay that such a thing should happen here. I have a small office upstairs. If you would be so good as to come with me, we shall see what we can do to help you."

Ten minutes later, Sommers was a good deal more comfortable. He was in a padded armchair, he had a cup of coffee and a roll on a tray next to him, and the maid had even brought a wet cloth to wipe his face. Nevertheless, he was no closer to seeing the prince. Gentz was curious, and he was a powerful man not accustomed to leaving his curiosity unsatisfied.

"Monsieur Sommers," said Gentz for the third time, "surely you must understand that I cannot disturb the minister for every messenger, every petitioner who arrives here with an urgent affair? He is only back for three days. There are many people who wish to see him."

You had to admire him, thought Sommers. Gentz showed not one trace of frustration or irritation. His tone was as courteous, as warm as it had been the first time he made the statement. The secretary leaned forward, a move designed to suggest intimacy and trust. "Could you not give me at least some notion of why this must go straight to him?"

Perhaps it was the pose, almost seductive in its manner, which gave Sommers the idea. He looked significantly at an undersecretary, who had just arrived with a mass of papers for Gentz. The latter jerked his head, and the young man withdrew, closing the door behind him.

"Monsieur Gentz," said Sommers softly. "It involves a woman. And it is a very important matter, but one which is most certainly not for the public ear. Your discretion is well known, of course"— this was blatant flattery; Gentz was a notorious gossip and was in fact being paid by the British government to relay the gossip to London in writing at regular intervals— "but I have given my word that I will speak, at least at first, only to His Excellency." The 'at first' had not gone unnoticed, Sommers saw. He followed up at once; now it was his turn to lean forward. "Monsieur Gentz, I will not violate my bond if I tell you just this much, knowing it will never leave this room: the lady is the Countess of Brieg."

This was so contrary to what Gentz had expected to hear that he fell back in his chair with a distinct thump. "The Countess of Brieg?" he echoed, at a loss. He had been certain that the woman was the Duchess of Sagan. Now he recollected that he had heard rumors the countess was pursuing an English spy, a Jew—what was his name? And here was this earnest young British aristocrat, currently disaffected from his compatriots, according to Roswicz. Gentz shoved his chair back and stood up.

"Monsieur," he said crisply, "I will endeavor to persuade the minister to see you as soon as he has breakfasted."

Prince Clemens Lothat Wenzel von Metternich pulled his chair up to the desk with a slight frown. He was a little disgruntled that Gentz had insisted he make time for this visitor. He had hardly seen his children at all and was leaving early the next morning to return to Prague. Nor was he intrigued, as his secretary had been, by the mention of the countess. He judged her a temperamental and dangerous woman who was more of a burden than a help to the secret police. A vague recollection that Hager had thought this man Sommers might prove useful, coupled with Gentz's vehemence, had won him over. He hoped the interview would be brief.

"How may I help you, monsieur?" he said brusquely. The young Englishman hesitated. "Are you certain we will not be disturbed?'' he asked, in surprisingly good French.

Something about his manner caught the prince's attention. Instead of a vague reassurance, he crossed to the door and spoke sharply to the two clerks outside. Then he closed the door completely and turned back to the center of the room.

To his astonishment, his visitor was taking off the top of his head.

Metternich blinked, and his vision readjusted itself.

Improbably, the graying hair was a wig. Underneath it was close-cropped reddish-brown hair and a large and ugly bruise, centered around a cut high on the right temple. And from the inside of the wig, his guest was extracting a very creased and flattened envelope.

"I believe this belongs to you," said Sommers, placing it carefully on the walnut desk in front of him.

The prince frowned, stared, and returned slowly to the other side of the desk. Sitting back down, he picked up the crushed wrapper and took out the equally crushed contents. A glance sufficed to assure him that his initial surmise had been correct. His lips compressed.

"Is it not a trifle premature, monsieur, to give me the merchandise before receiving your fee?" he inquired with a cold smile. "Or do you have a witnessed copy hidden away?" He was wondering how much he should offer for the recovery of the letter, and whether Sommers would demand further payments to conceal his knowledge of its contents. Still, without the letter itself, slanders from a discredited man like this would not be a very serious threat. He shot a glance at his visitor and was astonished to see him flushed with anger.

"If I had not thought you would wish to see it destroyed with your own eyes, I would have burned it myself," said Sommers, his voice shaking. He rose and bowed stiffly. "I will take my leave. I am sure you are not accustomed to receiving extortioners at this hour."

The wig was back in place, Metternich saw, and the brief glimpse of a younger and more battered countenance was gone. Incredulous, Metternich realized Sommers was, in fact, moving to the door. Clearly Roswicz's information was wrong, and he had just grossly insulted the young man.

"My dear sir!" he expostulated. "Please let me apologize for my suspicions. I have received so many threats lately from so many quarters that it seemed unlikely I would recover this document in such a fashion. I beg you not to leave so abruptly! How did you come upon that foolish letter? How may I thank you? Is there nothing I can do for you in return?"

Sommers looked embarrassed. "A diplomat of my acquaintance suspected that a certain person in Vienna had possession of this," he said slowly. "And I happened to be a visitor at this person's home." He did not answer the other questions the prince had asked.

"An English diplomat?" asked Metternich, looking at him keenly.

No point in denying it, thought Sommers. He was certain Hager's men knew he had met Jervyn at that reception. "Yes," he answered curtly.

"May I ask why you brought the letter to me instead of to your friend the diplomat, who could easily request a private audience with me?"

Sommers looked very uncomfortable. "It seemed only logical, Your Excellency, to return it to you."

"I assure you diplomatic logic would not have suggested to an English legate that the letter be returned to me. Not immediately, at least," Metternich informed him with a dry smile. "I take it that before you left England you were not in the diplomatic corps."

"No," Sommers said in a tight voice. "You are correct. I was not in the Foreign Office."

Change the subject, thought Metternich. This topic was not a felicitous choice. *Keep the man talking.* He had not been certain who held the letter; the veiled threats had come from Reuss and Werzel, but they were too clever to keep the document itself while acting as the extortionists. "And your injuries?" he inquired casually. "Were they the result of this visit you mention, to the home of the person who had possession of my indiscreet note?" Perhaps Sommers's answer would give him a clue as to who else was involved. To his surprise, the reply was negative.

"A brawl on the street," he said with a slight smile.

"No respect for your gray hairs?" asked Metternich, smiling in turn. "It is a most ingenious notion; permit me to compliment your perruquier. Who would ever suspect that partly gray hair was artificial?"

The younger man relaxed slightly; Metternich saw a twinkle in his eyes. "It is real hair, in fact—extremely expensive," he confessed. "But I was traveling through French-held territory, and my own hair color is difficult to disguise with dye."

Something stirred in the prince's memory. This was indeed the Englishman Hager had mentioned, the one who was wanted by both the French and the English. Hager had thought such a man might have his uses, but Metternich suspected the tasks Hager had envisioned would horrify the quiet figure who stood before him, leaning slightly on the doorknob. This was not at all the sort of person he and Hager had pictured, given the accusations from the French and English governments.

"My young friend," Metternich said in warm tones, using the intimate form of address, "please allow me to express my gratitude, and my dismay that such a rescue was necessary. If there is ever anything I can do for you . . ." he trailed off, hoping he had not insulted his guest again.

Sommers did stiffen slightly, but he recovered and replied, with only a slight flush, "Your Excellency, I am happy to have been of some service."

After his visitor had left, Metternich went to the fireplace and dispassionately burned both the letter and the wrapper. He stood for a few minutes looking down at the small pile of charred fragments. Fortunately, his servants were accustomed to finding such ash heaps on his office hearth. He walked back to the desk and traced the grain of the wood absently with one finger. At last he went out to the small sitting room which had been converted into a temporary office. "Is Roswicz still here?" he demanded.

"Yes, Excellency," responded the more senior clerk.

"Tell him I wish to see him at once." He wanted more information about Sommers. The man did not fit the dossier, and Metternich had learned from long experience that it was usually the dossier which was false.

Long interviews with both Gentz and the prince had raised Sommers's standing with the staff considerably, and when he descended and collected his hat, the same manservant who had grudgingly allotted him a wooden chair in the back hall two hours earlier now offered to send a groom to summon his carriage. But Sommers declined; he felt like a walk. He reckoned it was not more than half a mile to the inn where he had sent the hired coach.

His reckoning was wrong. Evidently Metternich's wife had taken lodgings towards the edge of the little spa town; Sommers passed row after row of elegant stone houses before he finally came onto the main street. He was tired and slightly dizzy again, and his head was throbbing. In other words, he was not as alert as he should have been, which perhaps explains why, when he suddenly found himself in front of a tall young man leaning on a cane, he stopped and gaped instead of ducking his head and moving on.

"Evrett! What are you doing here?"

A quizzical stare was the initial response, and then an incredulous start.

"Good God! It *is* you! What have you done to your hair? Why are you in Austria?"

"I asked first," Sommers pointed out, reasonably.

Evrett laughed, and his dark eyes crinkled at the corners. "My mother has been here for some weeks," he said, "taking the waters." A grimace accompanied this statement. Lady Evrett was a notorious hypochondriac, and her late husband had spent the last years of his life escorting her to every healing shrine on the continent. Evidently she had converted from saints' relics to spas now.

"You got leave to escort her? I thought you would be driving frog-eaters across the Pyrenees, not squiring your mother around to mineral springs."

Evrett gave another grimace. "Had to sell out. My knee never quite recovered. My cousin Rollo brought m'mother here, but once I gave up my command I thought I might as well come and fetch her back. England was pretty bleak; everyone else I knew was either in hospital or on their way back to Spain."

"Sorry to hear that," said Sommers uncomfortably. He was cursing himself for stopping. Evrett would never have recognized him in the wig if he had not called attention to himself.

"You know," said Evrett, frowning as he recollected, "the oddest rumors were going around when you disappeared. We were told you had been killed."

"Not yet," Sommers said lightly, hoping Evrett would take a hint and drop the subject. He did not.

"Well, our friend Drayton nearly was, because of that false report that you were dead." Evrett scowled. "Courthorpe accused him of having you murdered, and called him out; he's quite a good shot, is Corey, plugged him right in the chest—" He saw Sommers's face and stopped. "You didn't know?"

"I knew he had been injured in a duel," Sommers managed, feeling even more sick and dizzy than before. "Nathanson is here, and he told me. But he did not

tell me the cause, or that the injury was so serious." He
groped his way over to a low stone wall in front of a
church and sat down. "How could Corey think Drayton
was responsible for my death? I was reported killed in
action, was I not?"

"Drayton was arrested for treason right before your
demise was announced; the two of you had been working together behind enemy lines . . . *voilà!* Courthope
put two and two together and deduced that Drayton
had betrayed you to the French."

"God!" groaned Sommers. "No wonder Nathanson
was so closemouthed."

"It was very ugly for a time," acknowledged Evrett.
"I was one of Drayton's seconds, and there were some
who cut me for months merely for acting for him. But
I think everyone knows now it was all a huge mistake.
There were even some rumors afloat that you had been
arrested for treason as well, which was patently ridiculous."

"Oh, it was ridiculous, was it?" said Sommers bitterly.
"I'll go bail I know why Drayton was arrested for treason.
Because he tried to put me on a boat for Stockholm.
Did you know treason is contagious? He who shelters a
traitor instantly becomes one himself."

Evrett's smile faded, and he stared, bewildered at the
seated man. "What are you saying?" he asked after a
moment. "You don't mean to tell me the charge against
you is true?" Sommers had gone very pale under his
tan, and his shoulders were rigid. He looked at Evrett
without answering, a twisted smile on his face. When
Evrett clenched his fist and advanced, he did not move.

"I don't believe it," Evrett said thickly.

"Neither did Drayton, at first." Sommers leaned back,
his hands against the top of the wall. He was goading
Evrett to hit him, he knew, and he was not sure why he
was doing it. He could hardly fight a duel with an injured
man.

Evidently Evrett had realized the same thing. He lowered his hand and stepped back. Gradually his face hardened as he accepted the revolting conclusion Sommers had forced on him. "If I still held my commission, I would arrest you, and Austrian sovereignty could go to perdition," he said in a voice of ice.

"I was arrested," Sommers shot back. "And released. Evidently a trial was deemed imprudent. They requested that I disappear." He picked up a loose fragment of stone from the cornice of the wall and examined it carefully. "I am doing my best."

"Are you?" said Evrett scornfully. "It was certainly damned insolent behavior for an invisible man to hail me on the street as you did."

"Sorry," muttered Sommers. "Won't happen again."

"No, it will not, at least if I can avoid it." Evrett's tone was scathing. He walked away without a backward glance.

Sommers had told Elizabeth flatly that she was not going to Baden with him. Indeed, she was not going anywhere with him from now until she and Cox left the city on Sunday. So she was sitting on her cot, ostensibly mending her clothing in preparation for the journey, when she heard what sounded like a knock on the door at the foot of the stairs. It was so timid she was not certain she had really heard it, but Trumpet was on his feet wagging his tail.

Puzzled, she got up and went down. There was a sign on the door announcing that Monsieur Sommers was unavailable today; it would not be a student, then. Nathanson? No, his knock was not so quiet. Cox, perhaps. But when she opened the door, she saw a slight young man who was totally unfamiliar.

"I am sorry," she said politely in French. "Monsieur Sommers is ill; there are no lessons today."

"Yes, I saw the note," he replied, flushing. "I was hoping to consult him, for a few moments only."

"He is away, as it happens," said Elizabeth, and then, realizing she had just claimed that he was ill, "at—at the apothecary's. My regrets, monsieur."

The caller looked rather dismayed. He bit his lip, turned to go, and then turned back. "Are you his assistant?" he asked hesitantly.

"I am," said Elizabeth, hastening to add, "but I should tell you I know very little about fencing. He has been instructing me for the past month, but I am scarcely able to do more than teach the children's class."

"Of a certainty you know more than I do," he said with a bitter smile. "And I find myself engaged to fight a duel tomorrow. I have a few rather elementary questions. Do you think you might be able to at least give me some instruction as to the conduct of the affair? I am embarrassed to ask Captain Naegel, though he is my second; it is so generous of him to act for me that I hesitate to reveal my ignorance."

Not for nothing had Elizabeth been poring over the shelves of Sommers's collection. "We have a small library," she said, "with some volumes you might find helpful." At the word 'library' his face lit up.

"I would be most grateful," he said. "I am afraid I am more comfortable with books than with swords. And perhaps, if it is not too great an imposition—" He stopped, but Elizabeth's friendly expression encouraged him to go on. "If you could just show me how to hold a rapier," he said in a rush. "And a few passes, so that I do not make von Naegel look like a complete fool for standing by me."

A wave of indignation at the male sex swept over Elizabeth. Of all the ridiculous notions, that this nice, shy young man should be forced to offer himself up to be wounded or killed like a sacrificial sheep.

"Forgive me if I intrude," she said, "but could you tell me how this affair came about? One of the duties of your second is to effect a reconciliation. Is there any

chance Captain Naegel and the gentleman acting for
your opponent might be able to prevent the meeting?''

"I am afraid not," he responded. "The affair was
forced on me, and in the presence of a lady I was escorting. Indeed, if Captain Naegel had not alerted me, I
would be in even worse case; we would be fighting with
pistols, and I would not dare even to fire, lest I injure
a bystander.''

"Your opponent is the challenger, then?" Elizabeth
interjected.

He smiled. "Yes. I did not understand it at the time,
but von Naegel explained it to me later. He and three
other gentlemen encountered me strolling with—with
a young lady in the Prater. One of them sought a quarrel
with me, using the very grossest insults, and when I
replied that I found it offensive of him to employ such
terms in front of my companion, he began to saunter
over to me in a very threatening way. Evidently Captain
Naegel must have decided to take pity on me, because
he stepped over to my side at once and advised me, *sotto
voce*, to strike my opponent first.''

"Yes, that is right, if you wish to have the choice of
weapons," said Elizabeth automatically. "Please come
in. I will show you whatever I can. Who is your opponent?
Is he a competent swordsman?''

"Very much so. It is von Werzel.''

The name meant nothing to Elizabeth. She held the
door open and followed her visitor up the stairs to the
salle. "Please go on in," she said. "Take off your jacket
and boots while I fetch some books from upstairs. Oh,
and remove your spectacles, also. The mask will not fit
over them.''

"I do not see very well without them," said the young
man ruefully. "Must I remove them during the actual
duel?''

Elizabeth shook her head.

He gave a sigh of relief. "One piece of good news. I
must hope that when I examine the rules of engagement

I will find more good news. This is my own fault; my cousin warned me I should learn how to fence once my father was ennobled. He has been forced into many such encounters, and I should have known from my experience at the Royal Lycée what happens when someone named Roth is thrust into the company of Austrian aristocrats.''

"Roth?" Elizabeth looked at him. "Are you Captain Nathanson's cousin, then?" It was difficult to imagine that this quiet, fair-haired boy was related to the dark, fierce, impetuous officer.

His eyes widened. "Do you know him?" From her face, he could see she did. He should have anticipated this; the English community in Vienna was quite small. "Please," he said earnestly, "you must not let him hear of this. He will step in and try to take my place. Or he will go to my father, who will summon the guard and have us all arrested."

Privately, Elizabeth thought that would be a very good thing. But she had not spent weeks in a fencing salon without learning to understand the strange, bloodthirsty ideas of honor which dictated that such intervention would disgrace Roth permanently. She started back to the stairwell, then realized that she should find out precisely what his query was so that she could bring down the correct books.

"What was your question about the rules, Monsieur Roth?" she asked. "Is it something specific, or would you merely like a description of the normal procedures?"

"Oh, it is quite specific," he said grimly. "And not at all normal." He told her. Elizabeth went slowly up the stairs, revising her opinion about sheep. How fortunate that she had been reading Sabatini. She was fairly certain Roth's proposal was in fact quite legal. Very dangerous, of course, and practically unheard of, from what she had read. But if it was permitted, it was clearly his best hope of avoiding serious injury.

Twelve

The murmur of the pigeons had faded away, and the plink of rain dripping through the leaky roof into the tin basin by the armchair was growing rarer. Sommers was asleep, had been asleep most of the preceding day, in fact, and after a brief revival in the evening had gone back to bed quite early. Elizabeth was not sure how late it was—very late, nearly dawn, she suspected.

She had been lying awake for a very long time, she was certain of that. All manner of things were chasing around inside her head: that poor Roth boy and his duel, the French reward for Sommers, his haggard exhaustion when he had returned from Baden, her trip back to England, her chances of finding some position once she arrived. And, lying like a festering lump at the bottom of the pile, the miniatures in the strongbox. His wife, his daughter—did he miss them? Would he ever be able to see them again? No wonder he had looked so dreadful that night he had left the reception and raved to her about the mirrors. She recalled his smile as he had extended his hand and said, "Friends, then?"

When her thoughts reached that particular item, she

decided hastily to get up. It was quite warm; she had lain down in her breeches and shirt with no coverlet. Now she got up and went, yawning, over to the wash-stand. The pitcher was nearly empty.

Delighted to seize on a concrete task, she picked it up and went out in her bare feet. For good measure, she went into Sommers's room and took his pitcher as well. Feeling her way downstairs in the dark, she opened the door as quietly as she could and then gave a small shriek. A figure was sitting on the steps. For a moment she was frozen with terror, but then, since the night lantern at the gate was still burning, she caught a glimpse of spectacles reflecting the light.

"Monsieur Roth!" she gasped, remembering to breathe again. He was as startled as she was, she realized. "How long have you been here? Is your engagement not today?"

"I beg your pardon," he stammered, getting awkwardly to his feet. "I have frightened you. I meant to knock when I first arrived, but all the windows were dark, and I did not wish to wake you. I thought I could afford to wait a bit. The meeting is an hour after sunrise."

"Did you leave something here, then, yesterday morning?" asked Elizabeth. With some dismay, she considered the possibility that he had changed his mind about his unorthodox scheme and was hoping for a quick demonstration of proper fencing before the duel. Surely he must know how futile that would be?

"This is most embarrassing," he said, "but yes, I forgot something quite important, and I did not remember it until I was dressing this morning. I am evidently expected to provide the weapons, and I do not own any swords, nor could I think of anyone to approach at this hour on such an errand who would not go instantly to my father."

"The fault is mine," Elizabeth said at once. "I should have offered. I knew you needed to bring a pair to the meeting. Wait here; I will go fetch some." She went in and filled the pitchers at the kitchen pump and climbed quickly back up to her room. After a moment's thought, she pulled on stockings and boots, scrambled over to the pitcher and gave her face a hasty scrub. Then she picked out two matched rapiers, took one of the equipment bags from under her cot, and scribbled a note to Sommers, which she propped on the mantel.

"I will accompany you," she announced as she rejoined him in the courtyard. "You would attract quite a bit of attention walking back to your residence with naked weapons, and we have no sheaths for these. Nor could you take the sack without looking even more suspicious; you are too well-dressed."

"You need not trouble yourself," he protested. "It is not far at all; no one will be about at this hour. And Naegel is coming by shortly with a closed carriage to take me out to the field."

"There are two policemen right outside this gate," said Elizabeth dryly. "Or did you not notice them? Give me directions to your house. You should leave first and I will follow in a few minutes."

Naegel looked quite surprised to find Elizabeth waiting with Roth when he pulled up shortly after dawn around the corner from the hotel where the Roth family lodged, and even more surprised when Roth informed him Purcell would accompany them. Elizabeth had persuaded Roth that she was responsible for the rapiers, whose value she recklessly trebled. The truth was that, given her previous experience with Naegel, she had begun to worry the duel was a fraud and that Naegel had offered himself as a second to prevent someone more disinterested from filling that role. She balanced the possible harm to Sommers's business should she be seen at a duel with the possible harm to Roth if her suspicions proved correct, and concluded she must go and act as a witness. If she stayed in the carriage, no one except Naegel and Roth would know she was there.

Naegel was also clearly surprised by the demeanor of his principal. Roth looked well-rested and composed. His *toilette* was impeccable, and he chatted lightly on insignificant topics as they drove out to the grounds. It was perhaps a bit embarrassing that he had been to a fencing master the very morning of the meeting, but Roth had freely admitted he knew nothing about sword-play, and in any case, he had the justification of the need to borrow weapons.

Indeed, Naegel begged Roth to excuse him for this oversight. He should have anticipated this problem and offered to procure a suitable pair. Sommers's rapiers were of good quality, though, he announced. Werzel and Spier could not possibly object to them.

Spier was there before them, in fact, when they reached the appointed spot, just across the river at Aug-arten. The rain had completely stopped and in the warm breeze the grass was already nearly dry. Pausing only briefly to give Roth the encouraging words, "You'll do, I think," Naegel strode over to Spier to arrange for the inspection of the weapons. Roth gave Elizabeth a quiet smile and followed.

Elizabeth looked around with morbid interest. She had never witnessed a duel and was not certain she wanted to witness this one. It was part of a bizarre male world of arrogance and aggression which had not made much sense to her until the last few weeks. Now, how-ever, if she did not take hold of herself, she could almost believe Roth was doing the right thing to risk his life for the sake of a few insulting remarks on a woodland path.

Another carriage was drawn up on the opposite side of the field—Spier's, presumably. Nearby was a third carriage, and here came a fourth. Elizabeth had thought duels were lonely affairs; evidently there were more par-ticipants than she had realized. Perhaps she need not have insisted on coming. A thick-set young man jumped out of the fourth vehicle and went over to Naegel and Roth. This was the opponent, presumably. Who was the third carriage, then? The surgeon? She remembered that seconds often arranged for a medical man to be present.

But now here came a fifth vehicle. This one was an open barouche, and at the sight of the passenger, Elizabeth gasped. Roth would think she had broken her word. Forgetting the need to remain concealed, she tumbled out of the carriage and hastened over towards the combatants.

Nathanson jumped down before the driver had even reined in the horses and was up with the small group almost at once. Elizabeth halted under a convenient tree, belatedly recollecting the need for discretion. "Just what do you suppose you are doing?" Nathanson demanded furiously of his cousin.

"I believe I could more properly ask you that question," Roth fired back. "I am engaged in a private affair with these gentlemen; what is your business here?"

"To stop you from killing yourself," was the succinct answer.

"I have no such intention," Roth said stubbornly. "May I ask how you learned of this?" He glanced over at Naegel's carriage as he spoke, and Elizabeth shrank back behind the foliage.

"Elena told me."

Consternation showed on Roth's face. "But I said nothing to her, naturally! Someone else must have informed her—and perhaps my father, as well." He glanced anxiously around, as did the other three, concerned that the guardsmen might even now be about to descend on the entire party.

"You idiot!" snorted Nathanson. "Do you think a girl who has been in Gibraltar flirting with scores of young officers would not understand for herself where you were likely to be this morning after that confrontation in the Prater? My only difficulty was staying far enough behind Naegel's carriage to remain out of sight without losing your route."

Reassured no arrests were imminent, Roth recovered his composure. "Be that as it may, I must ask you to leave the ground. Only principals and seconds may be here now."

Nathanson put his hands on his hips. "My, how very learned we are in the *règles du combat,*" he mocked. "Book learning, I take it, since I know you have never held a sword."

"Books have their uses," Roth observed coolly. "Stand aside, James, or I will ask the seconds to escort you to your carriage."

He would have been well within his rights to do so, as Elizabeth knew. Fuming, Nathanson stepped back and stood at the edge of the little field, watching the seconds measuring the weapons and checking the turf for rabbit holes and tree roots. As the two principals were removing their boots, Naegel came over to him.

"Werzel does not intend to hurt him seriously," he said in a low voice which Elizabeth could barely hear. "I told him if he did he would have to answer to me."

Nathanson looked slightly relieved. "It is still a vile scheme," he said shortly.

"I agree," Naegel said, equally curt. "Hence my offer to act for your cousin."

"My thanks, then," said Nathanson. But Elizabeth thought he looked as though the words would choke him.

The seconds stepped back; the opponents gave a brief salute, and the blades engaged. It was all over in less than ten seconds. After the first, preliminary parry, as Werzel satisfied himself that his opponent did not, indeed, know how to handle a rapier, he stepped slightly to the side and beat down his opponent's blade, preparing to feint left and then thrust across into the right shoulder.

Before Werzel could complete the feint, however, Roth had lowered his sword, extended his left hand, and seized the middle of Werzel's rapier. In that brief instant, while he held the blade motionless, he reversed his grip on his own weapon and hit Werzel a stunning blow on the jaw with his right hand, now cased in the hilt. Werzel crumpled to the ground, releasing his weapon, and Roth, who looked slightly dazed at the success of his maneuver, found himself holding both swords. Blood was streaming from his left hand.

He turned to Spier. "First blood to your principal," he said courteously, and stepped back from his opponent's supine form. Werzel was out cold; Roth took out a handkerchief and pressed it against his palm.

The three more experienced duelists looked at each other in astonishment. Spier was the first to regain his voice.

"This is highly irregular," he sputtered. "Naegel, I must protest your man's misuse of his weapons. I demand an apology, from you and from Roth. This is an affair of honor, not a boxing match."

Elizabeth stepped forward. If she did not intervene, Roth would have to fight Spier as well as Werzel.

"It is completely legal," she announced loudly.

Nathanson looked horrified to find her there. Naegel was clearly irritated, but her attention was fixed on Spier.

"Who may you be?" he demanded haughtily, taking in her shabby breeches and lack of jacket.

"I am an assistant fencing instructor," replied Elizabeth, flushing. It did not sound very impressive, she acknowledged to herself.

Spier curled his lip. "And we are to take the word of an assistant fencing master on such a point?"

"Would you take the word of Fabrizio Sabatini?" countered Elizabeth. Everyone recognized the name; he was the greatest living authority on the *duello* in Italy.

"I do not think Signor Sabatini is likely to appear

and favor us with his opinion of this travesty," Spier retorted.

For answer, Elizabeth went back to the coach and pulled out the equipment bag. Turning it upside down, she gave it a slight shake and caught the little volume just before it fell on the ground. She came back and held it out to Spier. "Chapter Four," she said coldly. "Uses of the rapier in the duel. The hilt may be used as a weapon, provided the blades have engaged at least once beforehand."

Spier looked at Werzel, who was now sitting up, though looking a bit groggy. Werzel gave a grudging nod.

"Of all the reckless schemes—" Nathanson was looking at Roth with a strange mixture of anger, relief, and respect. He gestured peremptorily, and Roth turned his injured hand palm up and allowed him to peer at it. "You could have lost a finger, or cut a tendon." He looked over at the third coach. "Where is that fool of a surgeon? Has he fallen asleep? Purcell, run over and roust him out. Cuts on the hand need immediate treatment."

Emerging from his shock, Naegel started over towards the vehicle at Elizabeth's side, but they were both forestalled by the sudden arrival of yet another barouche carrying an elderly gentleman with a mass of curly white hair peeping out from under his hat. "There he is!" said Naegel with relief. The surgeon was alighting, with profuse apologies for his tardy appearance. After a cursory inspection of Werzel, he turned to Roth's hand and began pulling salves and bandaging out of this bag, scolding all the while in a continuous flow of lisping German.

"But—" said Elizabeth, puzzled, looking at the third carriage.

Nathanson had the same thought. "I'll wager a hundred guineas I know who is in there," he said between his teeth. He stalked across the grass at a furious pace and wrenched open the door. Roth and Naegel, with Elizabeth and the surgeon trailing behind, followed more slowly. Doña Maria and her enormous skirts took up one side of the carriage. Opposite her, Elena was sitting, very upright, next to her duenna. Streaks of tears were still visible on her cheeks, and the two older women were pleading with her in Spanish. Probably telling her to order the carriage to leave, thought Elizabeth.

"I take it," said Nathanson grimly, "you will not be traveling to Italy next week, Elena?"

It was Roth who answered. "I am afraid not." But he did not look at Nathanson. Elena had caught sight of his hand, and he was smiling reassuringly at her.

Unexpectedly, Nathanson started to laugh. "Poor Anthony!" he said, between gasps of merriment. "At least I hope you do not plan to honeymoon in Italy. That would be rather cruel."

"Since my bride has been rather publicly visible in Vienna masquerading as a Catholic, I think we will require more than a honeymoon," said Roth, still looking at Elena. "I had thought perhaps Paris. For a year or two. I can study with Berthollet at the Academy."

"You are going to be a scholar's wife?" said Nathanson to Elena, disbelief written large on his face.

"I am going to be Anselm's wife," she replied, green eyes flashing. "If he happens to be a scholar, that is his affair."

"What subject do you study, Monsieur Roth?" asked Naegel courteously.

"Chemistry," replied Roth absently. Then he glanced down at his hand. "I believe, however, that in the more immediate future I will be studying fencing. And perhaps shooting."

"He did *what?*" roared Sir Charles Stewart.

Jervyn flinched and glanced down at the note in his hand.

Sir,

I beg leave to inform you that I have located the silver card case your comrade misplaced in Vienna and have returned it to him. Please advise me if I may assist you in any other way.

Your very obedient servant,

M. S.

"Sommers returned the document to the prince, sir," he repeated, swallowing, and trying to keep his voice low. They were in Stewart's sitting room, but Jervyn knew that out in the antechamber a number of officials, including the mayor of Prague, were waiting. No need to broadcast the affair to everyone in the suite.

A string of curses was the response. Stewart flung himself into a chair and glowered at his subordinate. "I should have had Jackson handle this," he growled. "Did you not instruct the fellow to deliver the letter to you?"

"With respect, sir, I believe that if Mr. Jackson had met the man, he would have decided, as I did, that such a request would be pointless."

Stewart pulled himself up straight and frowned. "What the devil do you mean, Jervyn? If we are paying the man's fee, what right does he have to make stipulations about what he will do with the information he collects?"

Jervyn coughed. "Sir, there was no payment."

"No payment?" Stewart's florid face grew even redder. "Do you mean you simply turned this fellow loose, entrusted him with highly sensitive items, and all the while we had no hold on him whatsoever?"

Jervyn looked bewildered. "Did Lord Castlereagh not explain the situation, sir? This man is a former officer. White sent him here months ago. He is not a paid informant."

"He's a damned traitor, that's what he is," snapped Stewart. "Sells information to anyone who greases his palm, as far as I can tell. Don't know what White and my brother were thinking of. Surely we could have found someone else to help us in Vienna."

Castlereagh had not told him, Jervyn realized. Perhaps he had forgotten, or perhaps he had thought his volatile brother might not keep the news quiet. But it would be as much as his place was worth if Stewart discovered later that Jervyn had known and had not informed him.

"Sir," he said hesitantly. "I believe you may not be acquainted with all the facts of the case." He gave a brief sketch of the dispositions Castlereagh's office had asked White to make.

There was an appalled silence when he had finished. Stewart took out a handkerchief and mopped his brow. "And you sat down at table with him, shook his hand, spoke with him?" he demanded.

"My duties required it, sir," said Jervyn stiffly. "In fact, he refused to accept my hand."

"Not to be wondered at," muttered Stewart. "Not to be wondered at, by Jove. From what you tell me, it is, after all, quite a good thing that he did go straight to the prince?"

"Exactly, sir," confirmed Jervyn. Stewart was choleric and capricious, but he was not stupid.

"And you say French agents have tracked him to Vienna? It would be a shame to lose such a well-placed source; have we anyone there helping him in case of attempts by the French to arrest him?"

"Nathanson is there, sir."

Stewart shook his head blankly. The name was not familiar to him.

"Apparently the emperor's surveillance force is also watching over him," Jervyn added.

"Poor devil!" said Stewart, half to himself. "I take it he does not know?"

"No, sir."

In a rare moment of fellow feeling, professional and amateur diplomat regarded each other in troubled silence. Then Stewart gave an eloquent shrug. "*C'est la guerre,*" he said.

Thirteen

The sun was high in the sky when Elizabeth finally pushed open the gate to the little courtyard. Frau Renner was keeping watch for her while pretending to sweep the pavement. She dropped the broom and hurried over, scolding.

Elizabeth was too tired to respond properly to the thickly accented complaints: Herr Sommers had been very worried; they had not found the note until just an hour ago; what manner of pupil came calling before dawn?

Stammering some sort of apology, she opened the door to the stairway, hopped over the sleeping form of Trumpet, and started up the steps, half-hoping Sommers would be gone so she could postpone the reckoning until later. But at once she heard the notes of the piano. He was playing the melody of a sonata by Scarlatti, rather hesitantly, one-handed. It must be from memory; she did not have the music for that piece.

Slowly she climbed to the door of the loft and looked in. She saw his shoulders stiffen slightly, but he did not turn around or stop playing.

I am in disgrace, thought Elizabeth wearily. Suddenly she was almost glad to be leaving in a few days. It was growing tiresome to pretend to be a schoolboy, to be called to account constantly, ordered about, teased, patronized. Setting her jaw stubbornly, she marched into her room and hung up the swords without saying a word. Sommers was still playing.

Very well, she told herself, her temper rising. *If this is a music hour, let us do the thing properly.* She yanked open her valise and dumped the contents unceremoniously on her bed. Her sheet music was on the bottom. She found the piece she was looking for almost at once and marched back out to the main room to get a chair, which she pulled up by the crate Sommers was sitting on. Now he did look up, startled, but she pretended not to notice him. Indicating the music with a jerk of her chin, she began to play the right-hand part.

It was another Scarlatti sonata, in G major, with a moderately difficult part for the left hand. Sommers was already behind. She took pity and stopped.

"Let me read through it once or twice," he said quietly. "I've played it before, but not for a long time." He fingered through the notes. Slowly, they began again.

At first Elizabeth could not quite keep in time with him, but all at once they seemed to come to some sort of understanding. The music flowed out; the inevitable fumbles and missed notes were ignored and grew fewer and fewer. When they reached the end, without saying a word or even looking at each other, they began again from the beginning, a bit faster.

A fierce joy swept over Elizabeth; she was flushed and breathless, her heart was hammering. She could feel Sommers's shoulder leaning into her, his leg braced against hers as they struggled for space in front of the tiny pianoforte. Her hand seemed to be attached to another being—to Sommers, perhaps; it was moving completely in time with his. Some outside force was making the music.

She did not even need to look at the notes. Her fingers were directed by an unknown agency. Instead she looked at his profile, his clear gaze intent on the music, frowning slightly, his lips parted. The last trill resolved into the final chord, and Elizabeth felt her whole body humming along with it. Sommers was turning to look at her now, smiling, about to say something. But when he saw her face he faltered and stopped.

One touch, thought Elizabeth. *If he touches me, I'll fall to pieces.* She could not breathe. She tilted her head back slightly, looking up at him. He was staring at her, his hand motionless on the piano keys. They were both waiting, suspended in the chord.

Waiting for what? a distant fragment of Elizabeth's brain asked. Suddenly she knew. She was waiting for him to kiss her. And in one more second, he was going to realize it.

She bolted into her room, slammed the door, and leaned back against it, shaking, praying he had read boyish hero worship in place of what she knew had actually been in her eyes.

"Ned?" he called, sounding puzzled.

She did not answer, could not.

"Ned, I'm not going to beat you, you know."

She slumped in relief. He had not understood. How was she going to manage two more days of this? Perhaps Nathanson had been right; she should go to a hotel.

"Purcell!" He was starting to sound irritated.

Good, that was safe. She opened the door. Wrong, not safe. He was looking wary, bewildered, staring at her.

"Why don't you try playing with your right hand?" she demanded, saying the first thing which came into her head.

Taken aback, he blinked and looked down at it. A crooked smile came and went. "Cowardice, I suppose. So long as I don't try to play, I can imagine I will be able to do so."

"You have no trouble holding the swords, or pens," Elizabeth pointed out. "Or sewing." They had mended the burlap sacks a few days earlier. She lifted away the Scarlatti and replaced it with a very simple Mozart minuet.

"Are you by any chance trying to distract me?" Sommers inquired, with a lazy smile. "I already said I would not beat you, you know. But I would like to know where you were. And with whom."

"Full information in return for the minuet," offered Elizabeth, praying her guess was right. If he could not play, his mood was unlikely to be improved by the report of her actions earlier that morning.

Sommers gave her another puzzled glance and sat back down. "Impudent pup," he muttered, loud enough so that Elizabeth knew she was meant to hear. He tried some scales and chords first, and then played the minuet all the way through, slowly, with no apparent difficulty. "I'll be damned," he said softly to himself after a minute, flexing his hand and looking back and forth from his hand to the piano.

"And now . . ." He swung his legs neatly over the crate and faced her. "Information, if you please."

Elizabeth gave him an abbreviated version of the morning's events.

He listened intently, not apparently too perturbed, until she reached the story of her intervention. "Do you mean to say you simply walked up to Spier and waved the book in front of him?" he interrupted.

Shamefaced, she nodded.

"Was Nathanson still there?"

She nodded again.

To her surprise, he burst out laughing. "I would have loved to have seen his face," gasped Sommers. "Especially when it was you who told him less than a fortnight ago that fencing instructors should never appear to be connected with duels."

"He discussed that inconsistency with me at great

length while driving me back across the river," said Elizabeth bitterly. "I told him that since I am leaving, you can always tell anyone who inquires that you sacked me for my improper behavior."

"I would not worry too much about it," said Sommers, who was still laughing and shaking his head. "I doubt very much whether anyone involved in this morning's affair will be eager to discuss it publicly. Roth made Werzel look like a fool and a bully; there will be no gossip from that quarter." He grew serious again. "You cannot imagine that my concern is with your role as arbiter in that trumped-up fight?"

Disconcerted, Elizabeth stepped back a pace. "What—what is wrong, then? Should I not have loaned the rapiers to Monsieur Roth?"

"For God's sake, you young idiot!" he snapped. "You can throw every sword in the place out into the courtyard to rust into the ground, for all I care. But what on earth did you think you were doing, running off before dawn by yourself with those hellhounds of Meillet's out there?" He moved forward until he was looking directly down at her. His face was grim. "You are not to leave this house until Cox comes to fetch you Sunday at noon. Is that clear? I would send you off to stay with him, but I think you are in fact safer here, with the police watching the street."

"I cannot go out at all?" stammered Elizabeth. "Not even with you?"

"Especially not with me!" he shouted, exasperated.

"But—are you going out to give lessons this afternoon?"

"Yes."

"You are not well yet," she objected, glaring at him. "You should not be traipsing across the river carrying heavy bags."

"My thanks for your concern, Dr. Purcell," he said sarcastically. "I have given two lessons already while you were educating Spier and Werzel about the finer points

of sword fighting. And between lessons I went all over
the damned city trying to find you. Maybe I *should* beat
you. And if you disobey me and set one foot into the
street, I will."

Obedience was not coming naturally to her any
longer, Elizabeth decided. Five years of acting as a
demure companion and dutiful niece seemed to have
gone out the window the moment she ran away from
her uncle. She had managed to fetch out the foils and
pack the equipment bag without saying anything when
Sommers went out to give a lesson early in the afternoon,
although she had spent most of the time he was gone
standing on the table, attempting to look up and down
the street. The sight of today's pair of policemen following him had been somewhat reassuring, but by the time
he reappeared two hours later, she had a stiff neck and
was soaked with sweat. Deliberately, she did not climb
down from the table until he had come into the room.

Tight-lipped, he watched her as she stalked off to the
other end of the loft. "Still playing nursemaid?" he
asked in cold tones.

Elizabeth refused to turn around and look at him.
She heard him stomping towards her room to put away
the weapons. "They are not likely to attack me in broad
daylight in the middle of the Kohlmarkt, you know,"
he called.

Suddenly Elizabeth realized in horror that she had
never put her things back into her satchel after she had
taken out the music. In the jumble on her cot he would
see her dress, her shawl, her slippers, and her chemise.
She had never moved so fast in her life; an astounded
Sommers pulled up short as she slammed into the door-
jamb in front of him, unable to stop herself any other
way. Taking advantage of his surprise, she snatched the
equipment bag from him and pushed him away from
her room.

"I beg your pardon, sir. Please excuse me. I am being very childish," she gasped. "I should have come down to meet you and help you with this. I'll go get clean towels and water in just one minute."

In one quick movement she had slipped into the room, closed the door, and flung the equipment bag on top of her garments in case he followed her in. She held her breath until she heard him give a small chuckle and go into his own room. A moment later footsteps approached, and she frantically stuffed all of her clothing under the coverlet. But they stopped before reaching the door.

"I'll get the water and towels," she heard Sommers say. "I'm going down for a wash in any case."

"Fine," she managed to say. After she heard him start down the stairs, she made herself count to sixty. Then, one ear cocked, she carefully repacked her dress and shawl, wrapping them in the cloak this time, so that a quick glimpse into the bottom of her bag would not reveal them.

Afterwards she sat in a kind of trance at the foot of her cot, picturing her dress spread out over the covers, as she had seen it when she darted into the room. "You want him to find out," she whispered to herself at last, accepting the truth. "First that foolish scene at the piano, now this. Make up your mind, Elizabeth De-Quincy. Are you going to tell him, or not?"

He would learn the truth once she had left, of course; Cox and Nathanson would tell him. But when she tried to imagine herself confessing to his face, she shuddered in horror. What would she say?

"Pray excuse me, Mr. Sommers, but before I leave, I would like to point out that I have grossly deceived you, and possibly destroyed your credit with the entire British community in Vienna. Many thanks for your assistance and hospitality, and by the by, you somehow failed to notice that you have been living with a young woman for more than three weeks"?

Her stomach was roiling; she felt slightly dizzy. Any moment now, he was going to come back up, probably half-dressed from the bath, and if she was not careful, she would throw herself at him. What a stupid, ridiculous mess.

"Well, as long as I am a boy, I may as well take advantage of it," she muttered, jumping up and going out to the table. She poured four fingers of brandy into a mug and took an experimental swig. It stung, and she gasped slightly, but it distracted her, which was the important thing. Holding her breath, she drained the cup. For a moment or two, she felt nothing, save for a residual burn all the way down her throat into her chest. That faded quickly, however.

Not enough, she decided, and poured a second dose into the bottom of the mug. Her hand did seem to waver a bit as she poured. Then she heard nails clicking up the stairs. Trumpet emerged happily into the room, followed by Sommers. She turned to meet them and the room kept on going. Instinctively, she put out a hand to steady herself, but she missed the table and hit herself in the thigh. Trumpet was looking up at her with a familiar plea in his liquid eyes.

"Sorry, old boy," she said, her voice sounding thick and awkward in her ears. "Can't take you out right now. I'm under house arrest."

Sommers was looking amused, she saw. Damn him! She should slap his face for him. No, wait, she was a boy. He would have to kill her if she hit him. She tried to focus, but a wave of fire went through her eyeballs and she grimaced.

"Are you not a tad young to be drowning your sorrows?" he queried, after a glance at the decanter.

"I'm older than you think," Elizabeth tried to say. It was not clear whether the words had emerged properly. She could feel herself swaying slightly. There must be some trick to this that she did not know. Surely men did not feel like this after one glass of brandy?

Dimly a fuzzy recollection of her father's fireside drinks came to her. The glasses were much smaller than the coffee mug, she now remembered. And he had sipped it slowly. Perhaps that was the problem: too much, too fast. Something was certainly the problem; she could barely see straight.

"How much of that stuff did you drink?" asked Sommers, beginning to be concerned.

"Half a—half of a mug," she mumbled. "Not that much."

"Half a mug! Are you serious?" His eyes narrowed. "And you gulped it down, I'll wager. And you had no lunch. Did you have anything to eat before you left this morning?" He could read the answer in her face.

"Bacon-brained, witless, ignorant boy," he growled, supporting her as he guided her over to the couch. "Didn't you learn your lesson from that beer?" He brought over the basin from the washstand and shoved it onto her lap. "Don't close your eyes," he warned. "I'll go see if I can get some biscuits or toast for you."

She did not need the basin, as it turned out. Apparently she had a better tolerance for brandy than for beer. It took a while to get some toast and tea into her, and by the time the dizziness passed, she had a splitting headache.

"Serves you right," he announced callously when she informed him of her latest symptoms. But he dipped a cloth into cold water and handed it to her to lay on her forehead. After a little while, to her surprise, she felt very drowsy. She dropped off to sleep with a hazy impression of Sommers standing over her, an enigmatic expression on his face.

She awoke with a start to find the shadows slanting across the room; the sun was setting. Sommers was adjusting his neckcloth in the mirror behind the door of her room. He was elegantly dressed in knee breeches and a dark jacket Elizabeth had not seen before, very well-cut. As she struggled to sit up, he went back into his own room and came out with a pair of black leather pumps.

"You're going out," she said, and then felt foolish for saying something so obvious.

"Reception at the home of Naegel's father," he replied curtly.

"But it will be dark soon!" she protested.

He sighed. "Ned, I am not going to let Meillet make me a prisoner. They caught me off guard that first time. It will not be so easy for them to find such a good opportunity now that I know they are here. I will not walk down dark alleys, I promise."

"We *live* in an alley," she grumbled under her breath. Her head still pounded, but she felt much more like herself. And she vowed that if he would not let the French make him a prisoner, she would not let him make her one, either.

A minute after he had left, she slipped silently down the stairs, carrying her boots and a sword, and stole carefully out to the gate. Glancing up and down the narrow lane, she saw two men lounging in a doorway further down towards the street. Sommers was coming up to them rapidly and had raised a hand in ironic greeting.

She recognized them, they had been on duty the previous day as well. A little further along a carriage had paused in front of a gate. Plenty of people here, then. Everything looked normal. Feeling a bit foolish, but determined to go on with her plan, she sat down on the step by the gate and pulled on her boots.

It was then she heard the scream. It was a woman's voice, shrill and frightened, and it came from further down the alley, towards the blank wall of the armory which closed off the bottom of the lane.

Sommers had stopped and turned around. The woman cried out again, in a language Elizabeth did not recognize. What was someone doing down there? she wondered. Theirs was the last gate; the rest of the alley was blank wall down to the armory.

No, wait. There was a large block of apartments which fronted on the Hohe Brucke, and its rear courtyard had a small door onto their lane. But Elizabeth had never seen it opened; it was latched with a rusty lock which appeared to have sat untouched for years. Weeds grew out of the dirt in front of the wall, and although Trumpet liked to escape down there and eat the plants, she had never spied another living creature anywhere near that door.

Sommers evidently had not paused to ask these questions; he was sprinting towards the end of the street, already almost back to their gate. The carriage, too, was under way, following Sommers at a fast pace. A very fast pace.

Elizabeth froze in horror. The driver of the carriage was one of the men who had attacked them behind the church two days earlier. Sommers was past her now, still intent on the scream he had heard. It was some kind of ruse, she knew that at once.

The carriage was coming up towards her. The driver was leaning forward, urging on the team, his eyes on Sommers. She could see the horses, huge, dark creatures. She could see their hooves flashing up and down in the fading light, could hear the solid 'thunk' each hoof made as it hit the stone paving.

Dear God, they were going to run him down. He had no place to go. She imagined him falling, the hooves flashing and coming down on top of him, striking his head instead of the stones. Where were those idiotic policemen? Now she saw them, puffing along behind the carriage, losing ground with every step.

It would be described as an accident, she realized. A regrettable accident. Some woman had screamed, and the horses had bolted. And if he were only hurt, not killed, the driver of the carriage would kindly offer to convey him to a doctor.

Out of the corner of her eye she saw Sommers turn, saw him stiffen as he realized how he had been trapped. No time to look at him now, no time to think. If horses bolted at a scream, perhaps they would stop bolting at one, too. She stepped out of the shadow of the gate just as the horses came up to her and let out the highest, loudest, scream she had ever produced.

She had a glimpse of the team rearing and backing and of the driver's terrified face as he pitched off his seat. One of the horses was neighing madly, and she heard wood splintering. The window of the carriage was directly opposite her now, and she could see the startled face of the blond man inside; he was clinging desperately to the strap. The body of the carriage tilted away from her momentarily, settled itself back onto four wheels, and then toppled slowly in her direction.

For one instant she looked straight into the gray eyes of the man inside the carriage, into a face contorted with fury. Then a black door panel replaced the window rushing toward her.

She had forgotten how to move. It was too late in any case. There was a stunning shock, an instant of searing pain as though every minute of her earlier headache had been recombined into one horrible jolt, and then nothing.

Fourteen

He was running, his silver-buckled pumps sliding on the cobblestones, and occasionally giving way altogether and pitching his foot to one side. They were meant for ballrooms and carriages, not for mad dashes down half-paved streets. Twice one shoe came off, but he knew enough not to give in to the temptation to discard them. Doggedly he had stopped, uncurled the flattened side of the shoe, and pulled it back on. Until he reached the marketplace, his route was easy: he concentrated on keeping his footing, on pacing himself, on ignoring the pulsing burn in his injured ribs. But in his mind's eye he was seeing, over and over, the carriage and Jean-Luc urging on the horses.

The carriage was a good trick. He had not thought to guard against it, although it should have occurred to him that the cul-de-sac was tailor-made for something of the sort. Meillet must be getting desperate, though, because he had realized at once when he saw the carriage bearing down on him that his chances of being killed or fatally injured were very high. It was while he was calculating how best to position himself that Purcell had stepped out of the gate, just under the right leader's head, and given another one of those tin-whistle screams.

Surely that scream had not lasted very long? And yet, when he pictured it—the horses rearing, the carriage slewing first one way, then the other, the horrible, slow fall onto the boy's slender form—it seemed as though the whole scene was accompanied by the sound of that cry.

No, that could not be right, because the next part had screams in it, too, and of course Purcell could not make any more noise with the carriage collapsed on top of him. Perhaps the screams had been his own, or Jean-Luc's, or Meillet's.

There had been one instant, as he raced towards the boy, when Meillet had looked him full in the face as he climbed out of the other side of the carriage. And in that brief moment of contact, before Meillet had cut loose the uninjured horse and made his escape, he had seen the hatred and frustration in the Frenchman's face.

He skidded around the corner and across the road, sprinted up the stairs by the church, down the Salvator-gasse. Which street was it? He had lost the doctor's card, of course. Taking a chance, he tried the first turn out of the market.

An elderly woman was slowly emerging from a narrow gateway just off to his left. He slowed and jogged over to her, calling out as he approached. She looked up, startled, and directed him to a prosperous-looking residence four doors down. One last dash, and he was pounding on the knocker, praying. A maidservant opened the door, shrinking back instinctively at the sight of a disheveled, panting young man in evening dress.

Yes, the *Herr Doktor* was in. Yes, she could summon him at once. If *mein Herr* would be so good as to wait in the parlor? Certainly he could remain here in the hall if he wished. She understood, it was very urgent.

He must calm himself; the doctor would need to question him so as to pack his bag with the proper medicines.

"Herr Sommers!"

Dr. Walch had a good memory for names, he thought, as he watched the older man hurry into the hall. He, too, was in evening dress, but with no jacket or cravat. Probably getting ready to go out, Sommers decided.

"Herr Dr. Walch, I apologize for disturbing you at home in this fashion, but it is a matter of great urgency. There has been an accident. My assistant, young Purcell"—he closed his eyes for a moment—"a carriage fell onto him." The maid, who had accompanied her master, gave a horrified exclamation.

"Did you see the accident?" asked Walch, taking him by the elbow and steering him into a room. The breakfast room, it looked like. He took a seat mechanically.

"Yes." He shuddered.

"Could you see where Herr Purcell was hit?"

"The carriage pinned him to the wall—by the shoulder, I think. And it must have hit his head; there is a great gash on one side."

"Is he conscious?"

"No, not when I left ten minutes ago."

Walch went out to the hall and gave some instructions to the maid, then returned. "It is fortunate I am still at home," he said. "My wife and I were to leave shortly for a concert."

The maid reappeared with a satchel and a leather-covered box, which Walch opened, selecting several items and packing them into the satchel.

He glanced over at the haggard face of his visitor. "You made good time here for someone with your injuries, Herr Sommers. I take it you came on foot?"

The state of his shoes and stockings left no doubt about the answer to that question.

"Perhaps it is not so wise of me to attend you and

Take **4 FREE** Books!

We created our convenient Home Subscription Service so you'll be sure to have the hottest new romances delivered each month right to your doorstep — usually before they are available in book stores. Just to show you how convenient Zebra Home Subscription Service is, we would like to send you 4 Kensington Choice Historical Romances as a FREE gift. You receive a gift worth up to $23.96 — absolutely FREE. There's no extra charge for shipping and handling. There's no obligation to buy anything - ever!

Save Up To 30% On Home Delivery!

Accept your FREE gift and each month we'll deliver 4 brand new titles as soon as they are published. They'll be yours to examine FREE for 10 days. Then if you decide to keep the books, you'll pay the preferred subscriber's price. That's all 4 books for a savings of up to 30% off the cover price! Just add the cost of shipping and handling. Remember, you are under no obligation to buy any of these books at any time! If you are not delighted with them, simply return them and owe nothing. But if you enjoy Kensington Choice Historical Romances as much as we think you will, pay the special preferred subscriber rate and save over $7.00 off the bookstore price!

We have 4 FREE BOOKS for you as your introduction to
KENSINGTON CHOICE!

**To get your FREE BOOKS,
worth up to $23.96, mail the card below
or call TOLL-FREE 1-800-770-1963
Visit our website at www.kensingtonbooks.com.**

Take 4 Kensington Choice Historical Romances FREE!

YES! Please send me my 4 FREE KENSINGTON CHOICE HISTORICAL ROMANCES (without obligation to purchase other books). Unless you hear from me after I receive my 4 FREE BOOKS, you may send me 4 new novels - as soon as they are published - to preview each month FREE for 10 days. If I am not satisfied, I may return them and owe nothing. Otherwise, I will pay the money-saving preferred subscriber's price plus shipping and handling. That's a savings of over $7.00 each month. I may return any shipment within 10 days and owe nothing, and I may cancel any time I wish. In any case the 4 FREE books will be mine to keep.

Name _____

Address _____ Apt No _____

City _____ State _____ Zip _____

Telephone ( ) _____ Signature _____

(If under 18, parent or guardian must sign)

KN062A

Terms, offer, and prices subject to change. Orders subject to acceptance by Kensington Choice Book Club. Offer valid in the U.S. only.

4 FREE
Kensington
Choice
Historical
Romances
are waiting
for you to
claim them!

(worth up
to $23.96)

See details
inside....

lllnlllnnlllllnlhlllnlllnlllnllllnlllnl

KENSINGTON CHOICE
Zebra Home Subscription Service, Inc.
P.O. Box 5214
Clifton NJ 07015-5214

your young friend," he added dryly. "You seem very prone to accidents at the moment."

"I had just made arrangements to send Purcell home to England," he said bleakly. Walch was no fool; the doctor looked up, startled at this admission that his jest was close to the truth. Then, without comment, he returned to his packing.

The maid reappeared. "*Herr Doktor,* Hansi is taking the carriage around to the corner."

Walch turned to Sommers. "It is difficult to bring the carriage to the front door; the street is very narrow. I usually walk out to the marketplace. Are you ready to go?"

When he and the doctor pulled up outside the gate, the wrecked carriage had been removed, but neighbors were still milling about in the street. Sommers realized he was not even sure where Frau Renner and Marta would have taken Purcell. Into the kitchen? Frau Renner's tiny parlor? Up to the loft? He looked up and saw lights in the windows along the roofline.

"I think he's up in my quarters," he told the doctor, and ran up the stairs. The sole of his right shoe was working loose; it hit each step with a disconcerting slap as he rushed up.

His guess had been right, he saw as he reached the top of the stairs. He could see into his room. Marta and one of the neighbors were fussing about with cloths and a kettle of warm water. Frau Renner had come out into the sitting room and was standing, her arms folded, looking outraged. She blocked his way as he moved forward.

"Herr Sommers." Her voice was shrill with righteous anger, the anger of the benevolent woman who finds that the objects of her kindness have betrayed her. "You must leave my house immediately. And the fräulein, too, as soon as she can be moved. This is a decent, God-fearing place. I'll have none of your sort here."

He had started to push past her and follow the doctor into the bedroom, but now he stopped, totally bewildered.

She was shaking; her face crumpled a bit. "When I think of how you deceived me, a poor, nearsighted old woman! And how I cooked special soups for that hussy, thinking she was a nice young boy!"

He was frozen. He stood staring at her blankly. Walch reappeared, looking very uncomfortable.

"She is conscious," he said stiffly. "She is asking for you."

"She?" He looked in horror at the doctor, at Frau Renner, at Marta, who was standing in the doorway of his room glaring at him. Like someone in a trance, he moved towards his bedchamber, with both women trailing after him.

They had propped the patient up on the trundle bed, with towels underneath the head to try to protect the bed linens from bloodstains. Purcell, or the person he had thought was Purcell, lay there in a torn shirt, the fair curls matted on one side into a sticky dark mass, the blue-gray eyes fastened on him in anguish and apprehension.

It was a girl. How could he not have seen it? She was a girl; no, a young woman. Fine features, wide eyes, slender neck, rounded shoulders. Slim, certainly, and not ample of bosom, but unmistakably a female. And he had sensed it, too, had known the boy was not what he seemed, but had resolutely shut his eyes, closed his mind, because he was so despicable in his loneliness that he was willing to take advantage of whatever threat had forced her to such a desperate masquerade. He groaned and leaned for a moment against the wall of the tiny room, shaking his head in disbelief.

"I'm sorry," she said brokenly, looking up at him. "Mr. Sommers, I am so very sorry." She gave Frau Renner a pleading look. "Frau Renner, I apologize to you, as well. He did not know; I swear it."

The doctor had returned to her side. "Most certainly he did not," he commented testily. "Or he would not have summoned a physician. At least, not a reputable one." He was looking at her shoulder; moving her arm gently first in one direction, then the other.

She gasped suddenly.

"Dislocated," he said curtly. "Herr Sommers, could you hold her other shoulder, please?"

Numbly, Sommers moved to the other side of the little trundle bed and braced his arms behind her. "This will hurt," he warned her in a low voice.

"It already does," she said crossly. But she had taken her eyes off Walch, and now he swept her injured arm up in a great arc. There was a sickening noise, like a bladder popping, and she gave a small cry.

"Fainted again," observed Walch. "Let me get to work on this gash; stay right there, Sommers, so you can hold her still if she comes to while I am stitching it."

Frau Renner was still in the doorway. "Gerda, perhaps you should go to your house and get one of your night-gowns," she said grudgingly to the neighbor woman. "Mine will be far too small."

She believed Sommers. No one was that good at acting; he looked as though he had been hit by a mortar.

After Walch left, Sommers sat on the cot in the sword room, staring at the wall, trying to keep out of the way. Frau Renner had apparently forgiven not only him, but the girl as well. She and Marta traipsed up and down the stairs with an endless procession of hot and cold towels, tisanes, fresh bed linens, rolls of lint, pitchers of water, even a rosary.

The injuries did not appear to be life-threatening— some bruises, a bad blow to the head, the dislocated shoulder, and two rather nasty puncture wounds on the arm, which had not been discovered until she was undressed. But Walch had taken Sommers aside and warned him there might be further internal injuries. There was already a massive brown and black swelling on the patient's back, which Sommers had of course not seen, but had heard described in vivid detail by Marta.

"She must not be moved for several days," Walch had cautioned.

Frau Renner had nodded in emphatic agreement. "Marta and I will stay with her," she announced belligerently. "Tomorrow we can ask Gerda to come and help as well." Sommers heard the message clearly: there would be a chaperone at all times.

"I will move the cot down to the *salle* and sleep there," Sommers had offered, smiling slightly as he saw Frau Renner's approval. In fact, however, he planned once everyone was asleep to keep watch on the stairs. The last thing he wanted was for Meillet's hired men to come creeping in and attack the sleeper in what they believed to be his bed. And the recklessness of the attempt this evening had sapped his confidence that the police surveillance would at least protect them at home.

Marta appeared, carrying a pile of mysterious-looking paper packets which smelled like licorice. "Could you watch her for a moment? I must go down to the kitchen and ask Frau Renner about something. I think *she* is asleep."

She—did she have a name? Her gender, it seemed, was such a shock that the simple feminine pronoun was sufficient to indicate exactly who was meant. Hesitantly, he got up from the cot, aching muscles protesting, and moved stiffly into the next room.

It was as though the entire universe had been taken apart, rearranged, and put back together with everything just the slightest bit different. It was still Ned lying there, bandaged, and propped at an impossible angle with piles of cushions to protect the injured shoulder. The same person he had known for nearly a month: funny, resourceful, indignant, courageous, curious, affectionate. The same open face, the same golden-brown hair, ruffled up now in a peculiar crest by the bandage around her head.

But not the same, of course. A tide of corrections was flooding through him, visiting all his memories of the past four weeks and tinting them with new shades of meaning: the sympathy for Naegel's embarrassed sister, the intolerance for strong drink, the shyness, the complete lack of familiarity with gentlemanly skills. The screams.

He had known since that first scream two days ago, probably. At least some part of him had. The odd feeling which had come over him during their duet, as though he were going to explode with tension—in retrospect there was no escaping it. He had hidden his head in the sand, and now this incredible girl was paying the price, in humiliation and pain and illness.

Marta had returned with the paper packets and was steeping three of them in hot water. A sickly sweet smell stole out from the kettle and he offered up a prayer of gratitude that Frau Renner had not brewed that stuff for him the other day. Now that Marta was here, he should go back to the other room and get to work; the cot would have to be disassembled to be carried down the narrow staircase.

At the last moment, however, something made him look again over at the sleeping invalid. She was lying very still, her face turned slightly towards the wall. As he watched, he could see the tears slipping down onto the pillow.

Squatting down by the bed, he reached over and touched her gently. "What is it—" He almost said "Ned." "What is wrong? Are you in much pain?" He looked over at Marta. "Did the doctor leave some powders for her?" he asked in German.

"No, please," she said, before Marta could answer, her voice muffled by the pillows, still not opening her eyes. "I do not need anything."

"What is your name?" he said, trying to keep his voice light. "I cannot keep calling you Ned, you know." That produced a watery smile, and she opened her eyes and twisted slightly so she could see him.

"Elizabeth."

He waited for a surname, and when none was forthcoming, sighed. "You don't trust me enough to tell me your family name?"

"I am too ashamed," she whispered, turning her face away again. "I don't know how you can bear to be in the same room with me. I meant to tell you, truly I did, but I was too much of a coward. And every day, of course, it grew more and more difficult, and I hated myself more and more, that I could practice such a deception on you when you had been so kind and patient."

He gave a shaky laugh. "The coward in this bed saved my life three times. Please take care how you insult her. And as for deception—" He smiled bitterly. "I will claim the prize there, if you do not mind." He thought of all the lies, months and months of them, piling up until they crushed him, and shuddered.

"Why were you in boy's clothing?" he asked abruptly. "When I first met you, I mean. Did you have an aunt?"

She nodded. "And a wicked uncle, too. It seems ridiculous now, but at the time, I thought it the simplest solution. My aunt died, and my uncle—I was frightened of him, and all I wanted to do was get away from him and go back to England. It seemed so daunting to travel as an unaccompanied female, and I could not afford to hire an abigail."

"Well, we cannot send you home with Cox, I am afraid," he said, frowning. "You will not be well enough to travel for at least ten days, and he must leave long before that."

She stiffened, and he misinterpreted her reaction.

"Please do not worry, Miss—Elizabeth," he added hastily. "I will arrange something suitable. Rest assured that I will do my best to try to make amends for everything you have suffered on my account. I am moving downstairs for tonight, and tomorrow I will find some other lodgings. Frau Renner and Marta will keep you company here. And we will think of some story to explain where you were for these past weeks so that when you return to England there will be no unseemly gossip."

At this she turned her head all the way around, to face him, and he saw her grimace momentarily as the movement jarred her shoulder, but she ignored the discomfort. "I care nothing for gossip," she said fiercely. "It is absurd that you should move out of your own rooms for the sake of a silly chit who could not walk down the street without losing her purse. Nor do I wish to go home. I have not wished to since the first week."

He was going to ask her what she did wish to do, but the question died on his lips as she looked at him. There was no entreaty, no embarrassment, no maidenly reserve, only a simple declaration.

Hastily he scrambled to his feet, avoiding her eyes, stammering something about dismantling the cot, and glancing helplessly at Marta, who gave him a very hard stare as he left.

"Now who is the coward?" he asked himself savagely as he began wrenching the dowels out of the canvas seams of the camp bed, making as much noise as possible. "Why did you not simply tell her at once who you are? That would put a period to any notions of romance in her head."

Trumpet had followed him to the *salle,* and was sleeping on top of a pile of garments he had carried down from the sword room. He had brought down a few books as well, his comb and shaving gear, and a washstand. With each personal item he had removed from the bedroom, Frau Renner and Marta had thawed a bit more. Propriety was clearly weighing very heavily in their minds, he saw, and he was in full agreement with them.

How the devil was he to keep her month-long stay with him quiet, though? He had hoped she would tell him her surname; there might be family friends in Vienna or Prague who would be willing to cover for her. But she had vehemently refused both times he had asked her.

For hours now, he had been pacing back and forth in the dark, ostensibly keeping watch for any further attempts by Meillet, but in reality trying to think of some plan to get her back to England with her reputation intact. He could not accompany her himself. He was a magnet for trouble with that *mandat* out against him, and England was closed to him. Nathanson, supposing him willing, was so controversial a figure that his escort would be worse than none. And even if they could find a suitable party traveling back to England and persuade them to include her, there was still the problem of accounting for the weeks she had been living with him.

A mock growl caught his attention. Trumpet had awakened and was nosing at one of the wooden dowels. Apparently it resisted his advances; he pounced on it and grabbed it with his teeth, shaking it, dropping it, and pouncing again. Sommers was so tired and bemused that at first he could not imagine where the dog had found a stick in the middle of the fencing studio. But then he remembered: the cot.

It suddenly struck him that it was no longer very dark in the room. Dawn was breaking. Marta would be returning soon, and if that cot was not assembled when she arrived, propriety would be offended. After all, if he had not slept down here, where had he slept? Perhaps on the couch, within yards of the young lady!

In some haste he sat down on the floor and began

assembling the pieces. Trumpet thought this a fine game and abstracted the dowels one by one as he retrieved them, racing around the room and depositing them in dusty corners. Finally Sommers had to pacify him by getting out some of the chalk-tipped staffs and trading them for the dowels. Still, his troubles were not over. It emerged that it was much easier to disassemble the cot than to reassemble it.

On his third try, when all the dowels were nearly in place and he was stretching the last corner of the canvas over the frame, the whole thing slipped out of his hands and crashed to the floor, scattering dowels everywhere. Trumpet promptly skidded over and seized the edge of the canvas in his teeth. "Devil take you, you blasted hound!" he hissed in frustration. With a sigh, he pushed the dog away, retrieved the dowels, lined them up, and started over.

His rib was aching, his head was aching, and he felt sapped by that thick-tongued lethargy which comes, early in the morning, to those who have not slept the night before. Still, he was well-trained, and perhaps subconsciously still on guard, because when he heard the noise on the stairs, he whirled at once, grabbing his sword from the floor in one clean movement and leaping towards the door to the landing.

On the steps, leaning shakily against the wall, was Elizabeth. Gerda's enormous nightgown billowed out around her thin frame and puddled slightly on the floor. The sling was still around her neck, but she had taken her arm out of it, and her good hand was holding a saber. Around the bandage on her head the curls rose like a halo, gleaming in the faint light from the stairwell window. She looked like an angel, he thought, like the angel with the flaming sword who expelled Adam and Eve from paradise. Only this time the angel wanted Adam to stay, and Adam was going to leave of his own volition.

"I heard a noise," she explained in halting tones,

flushing in embarrassment as she saw the pieces of the cot and Trumpet racing around exuberantly. "And I looked on the couch and in the sword room, and you were not there . . ." She was growing paler by the second, her flush fading, her good shoulder now desperately banked against the wall. The arm holding the sword was trembling.

"So you came down to save my life again," he finished for her, tossing down his weapon and grabbing her uninjured arm just as she slumped towards the floor. "You little pea-goose!" he burst out savagely. "You are not supposed to leave your bed for three days! Can you never think of yourself?" He pulled her over so that she was leaning on him instead of on the wall, and felt a sudden warmth as she huddled against his chest. "I cannot even conceive of a way to carry you back to your room that will not be extremely uncomfortable, unless I toss you over my shoulder like a sack of flour!"

"Let me just sit down for a moment," she said faintly. "And then I think I can walk back upstairs." He lowered her very gently to a step, and she sank against the wall with a shudder, closing her eyes. This seemed a good opportunity to put her arm back in the sling, and he did so, as carefully as possible. She winced, but kept her eyes closed.

Sommers remained on one knee on the stone floor of the landing, looking up at her. The light was growing stronger; Marta would be arriving very soon. He had to get her back upstairs.

Her color was gradually coming back and her breathing was less ragged. For perhaps a minute he remained motionless, intent on her face, scanning it raptly while he could do so unobserved. The early morning light silvered her skin with a faint luminescence. Every line, every curve of her face, so well known to him, was like an accusation.

"I think I can manage now," she announced suddenly, startling him. She opened her eyes and looked at him expectantly. He should get off the floor and help her up, he realized.

Instead, as though under some enchantment, some spell which robbed him of all his normal cautious devices of concealment, he picked up the bottom edge of the nightgown, bent his head, and slowly pressed it to his lips. He did not dare look at her, but he sensed that she had stiffened.

It was his turn to close his eyes, damning himself for that ridiculous, revealing gesture. Then he heard her draw in her breath, and he felt something heavy tap him on the shoulder: first the right, then the left.

"Rise, Sir Knight," she said gravely, leaving the sword on his left shoulder. At that he risked a glance at her expression, and saw a wry smile. "Do you swear fealty to me, upon your honor as a knight?"

"Forever," he answered lightly.

"Then I require a service of you."

"You have only to ask," he said, relaxing slightly now that that one careless moment seemed to be behind him, and anticipating that she would ask him to help her stand up. He rose and took the saber from her, waiting for her to reach up with her right hand.

"Kiss me."

She was perfectly composed; he was the one who had stopped breathing.

"I understand that you are going to send me away, but I've never been kissed, unless you count my cousin George when I was eleven, and before I leave I want you to kiss me."

"Ask me for something else." His voice was strained. "Please." He was looking at the floor; he could feel himself trembling.

"I know you are married—" She swallowed. "I saw the pictures in your strongbox. But surely you could kiss me, just once, even so."

He was on the point of denying that he was married

when he realized her misunderstanding was potentially his best safeguard.

"Very well," he said stiffly. He sat down on the stairwell next to her, trying to keep his legs from touching hers, and leaned over to kiss her on the forehead. He was picturing the sort of kiss an older married man would give to a girl who had a *tendre* for him, an avuncular peck on the top of the head, conceding the favor but making it quite clear that nothing but disinterested affection was involved.

Unfortunately, the result was not what he had envisioned. Before he could stop her, Elizabeth had twisted slightly, reached up, and pulled his head down so that he found himself kissing not her forehead, but her lips. He gave a little sigh and surrendered, remembering just in time not to put his arm around her left side.

How could he ever have thought she was a boy? How long had he been wanting to do this? His body had known, even if his mind had not; he felt the frustration and longing of weeks pouring out as he pressed hungrily into her mouth. She was kissing him back, tentatively, and now more passionately, one hand curved fiercely across the back of his neck. With a groan, he wrenched himself away and leaned his head against the wall.

"Your family is in England." Her voice was calm.

He could answer that without telling any more lies. He nodded.

"And you cannot go back."

He nodded again.

"I could stay here with you. I have no family, no real reason to return. My uncle has fled Vienna."

He looked across at her, incredulous. "How could you possibly imagine I would let you do such a thing?" he asked, his voice shaking.

"Why not? What is so dreadful?" she retorted. "You are an exile; I am one as well, in effect. My family is gone. I have not lived in England for five years. Is there some reason we must each go off to be lonely and miserable? What do I care for a piece of paper? Do you think I will be happier reading sermons to some crabbed old woman and dosing her with quack medicines? That is what awaits me back in England.''

"No!" he shouted, furious. "For God's sake, have some sense! Get yourself away from me. You're deluded. That blow on your head has addled your wits." He hauled her to her feet, not even caring now to make sure that he did not hurt her. In his agitation he nearly pushed her up the stairs, but she did not resist and settled obediently back into the trundle bed, giving him one last, sweet smile before she turned on her side. Frau Renner, miraculously, was still asleep in her chair.

He grabbed the brandy from the table and staggered back down to the *salle,* collapsing onto the floor next to Trumpet. Damn, he had forgotten to bring a glass. No matter. He took a long drink straight from the decanter.

On top of all the other unbelievable, improbable events of the past two days, he had just been offered the poor man's equivalent of a *carte blanche* by a well-brought-up English girl who was, by her own admission, a virgin.

Fifteen

The cot took him nearly a quarter hour to assemble, and he had barely finished and changed into clean clothing when Marta arrived. She had already lit the stove and heated water, so he shaved while she brewed some coffee and went out to the baker's for bread. Then they went up together to relieve Frau Renner, who by now was fidgeting very uncomfortably in the hard wooden chair. Elizabeth was asleep, or pretending to be asleep. Her face was buried in the pillow, but after a minute he decided her breathing was too regular to be feigned. He relaxed somewhat and prayed she would stay asleep, at least until he had made his arrangements.

"Frau Renner, I have decided we must hire nurses," he announced. It was the right thing to say; he saw a look of relief on her face. "You and Marta have too much to do to stay with the fräulein all day and all night, especially since I will not be here to help." He wondered briefly where he was going to find the money to pay nurses, purchase a proper wardrobe for the girl, and buy passage for her and an attendant back to England. Probably he would have to borrow from Nathanson. Frau Renner tottered off downstairs, promising to send Gerda's oldest boy to inquire about nurses from Dr. Walch, and he left Marta taking up her post by the patient's pillow. He grabbed a roll, swallowed some of the coffee, and went into the sword room, dreading his next task.

This was to search her valise. He had argued with himself about this the entire time he was struggling with the pieces of the cot. Clearly, she did not want him to know her name. Perhaps she was afraid her uncle might return, perhaps she had other reasons, perfectly good ones. It seemed especially contemptible to violate her privacy while she was lying half-conscious in the other room, but he resolved nevertheless to do it. British diplomats and officers were arriving every day now; it was quite possible some family member who could help her might be here without her even being aware of it.

Jervyn owed him a favor, and while he would have died rather than ask for anything on his own account from such a source, he had no hesitation in asking Jervyn, on her behalf, to help him locate anyone who might be here with the allies. In fact, if she did not have family here, he was prepared to ask Jervyn to designate a junior attaché to escort her home. But he could not do anything until he knew who she was.

Keeping his ears open for sounds from next door, he opened her bag and quietly scooped the contents out onto the floor. A cloak, very plain, wrapped around a summer dress and slippers. Good, she had at least one dress to wear right away. No nightgown though, he discovered.

Linens, handkerchiefs, a thick sheaf of music—this in addition to the stack already out on the piano; no wonder the bag had been so heavy. A velvet reticule, with only a few hairpins inside. The miniature. A small jewelry case, with the lone diamond earring sitting in one corner. At the very bottom, a small bundle of papers, tied up with a ribbon. He riffled through them impatiently, and his heart sank. No identification papers save for the forged set he had procured under the name Purcell. She must have had some real ones. Where on earth were they?

The letters did not look promising, either. The envelopes were gone, and the salutation on the first five letters was useless: *Dearest sister, Dear Beth, Dear sister, My dear sister, My dear Beth.* All were signed simply *your Robin.*

He began to think he might have to actually read the letters, reconstruct the regiment of the brother from their contents, and then inquire through Whitehall. The thought of reading the letters of a dead man, especially one who had died in that particular way, horrified him. He reached the last letter, expecting to see the same brief salutation, and stopped.

"Miss E. M. DeQuincy," it said. He turned to the signature. There was not one name, but three, and at the sight of the second signature he choked and nearly dropped the sheet. Then, steeling himself, he read the entire letter.

> *28 September 1810*
> *Coimbra*
> *Miss E. M. DeQuincy*
>
> *Madam:*
> *By now you will have received from London the melancholy account of the loss you have sustained. We will not burden you with further details of your brother's passing, save to assure you that he was not in great pain at the end and spoke often and affectionately of you until the very last.*
> *His only concern, indeed, was that you were left unprotected, and in consequence of that, he exacted from us the pledge, most willingly given on all our parts, that should any occasion arise, now or in the future, when you might require the aid or advice of a brother, we would serve you as he would have, had he lived.*

*We do not expect this pledge will alleviate in any way
the pain of what must be, for you, an even more grievous
privation than for us his friends. But we beg that you
will remember that we remain ever,*

Your most obedient servants to command,

*Captain H. T. Archer, 95th Rifle Corps
Captain J. M. Weyland, 95th Rifle Corps
Lieutenant N. S. C. Trant, 52nd Light Infantry*

Five minutes after reading this epistle, he was in long-
unworn riding clothes, striding at a very fast pace
towards the livery stable in the Tiefer Graben. Surely
he could manage a horse by now. His head hardly ached
at all anymore.

"My lord," an apologetic voice repeated.

Evrett stirred and turned over. Someone had opened
the shutters, he realized. Daylight was filtering in
through the branches of the linden tree which grew up
against the south windows of the villa. The face of his
valet loomed over him, looking somewhat apologetic.

"My lord, a young man is here to see you. He says it
is extremely urgent. I told him you were still abed, and
he begged me to rouse you."

Evrett fumbled sleepily in the little cupboard built
into the head of his bed and extracted his watch. It was
half past seven. Who on earth could be here at such an
hour?

The servant held out a folded sheet of paper. "He
requested that I give you this, and inform you he is here
on behalf of a Miss DeQuincy."

Evrett blinked and sat up. He glanced briefly at the
paper, but the moment the name had been mentioned
he had recalled the letter quite vividly. For the first few
months after DeQuincy's death, he had expected to

hear from the sister at any moment, especially since he
was the trustee for the pension. But as the years had
gone by, he had assumed she was married and settled.
Every once in a while he would remember that he should
dissolve the trust and transfer the funds to her husband,
but somehow he had always forgotten to make inquiries
about it during his short sojourns in England. Grabbing
his dressing gown, which was hanging over one of the
elaborately carved bedposts, he ran his fingers through
his hair. "Show him up, Flynn. Did he give his name?"

"No, my lord. A young English gentleman, though."

Well, that would make sense, thought Evrett. Perhaps
it was her husband; perhaps she was married and had
discovered he was here in Vienna. But then why come
calling at this hour, announcing it was urgent?

He rubbed his eyes and accepted the cup of coffee
Flynn handed him before withdrawing. Over his mother's objections, he had taken this odd room at the top
of the house, with its ancient, heavy furniture, no carpet,
and no curtains. The portly Flynn was getting plenty of
exercise climbing up and down the stairs, and he did
not move quickly. Evrett decided he had time to make
himself a bit more presentable; he swung out of bed
and headed for his dressing room. In the event, it was
several minutes before he heard two sets of footsteps
approaching.

"Mr. Southey, my lord," announced the harassed
valet, and immediately headed back downstairs to alert
the kitchen that his lordship was up two hours earlier
than usual. In his wake a red-haired young man entered,
his buckskins and boots dusty, looking very shaky on
his feet. The hazel eyes met his apprehensively.

"You!" gasped Evrett, his face darkening with anger.
He had assumed that he had misheard the name when
Flynn made his announcement. Jumping out of the
armchair where he had been sitting with his coffee, he
limped purposefully over to the bellpull. "I don't know
how you got hold of this letter, but if you think you can

use it to worm your way in here, you're fair and far out."

"For her sake, Evrett." Southey's voice was raw. "Please. Don't have me ejected just yet. I knew you wouldn't want to see me. I tried to find Nathanson, but he had already gone out somewhere. Probably a duel. If I could have found anyone else I trusted to send, I would have, believe me."

Something in his tone, or perhaps the exhaustion and despair in his face, reached Evrett. He removed his hand from the rope, but he stayed near it, eyeing his visitor warily. "When you say, 'for her sake,' I take it you mean Miss DeQuincy? Where is she?"

"At my lodgings. With a dislocated shoulder and a three-inch slice out of her left temple. She was run over by a carriage."

"Good Lord!" Evrett moved to the bellpull again with an entirely different expression on his face, and this time Southey made no objection. Flynn reappeared, huffing, and Evrett issued crisp instructions before resuming his seat. "How did she happen to be taken to your lodgings?" he asked, once Flynn had left again. "Was it simply because the neighbors knew you were English?"

Evrett was going to call him out this time, wounded knee or not, Southey thought. How on earth could he explain what had happened without sounding like an idiot, a libertine, or both? "Evrett, I must ask for your word that what I am about to tell you will go no further." He stopped, leaned on the bedpost, and asked suddenly, "How long has your mother been in Baden? Has she been entertaining much?"

He's gone mad, thought Evrett, stunned, watching the slight figure swaying and clutching the furniture for support. "Take a seat, for God's sake," he said grudgingly. "Although that bedpost you are holding is remarkably apropos." Southey lifted his hand and grimaced as he saw the wolf's head emerge. "Did the carriage run over you, as well?"

"No. Although it made a good attempt at it." Southey sank down onto a trunk at the foot of the bed. "She was injured trying to keep it from reaching me." He made an abrupt gesture, as though murderous carriages were of no significance. Evrett was beginning to wonder if he was really awake, or dreaming this entire bizarre conversation. "Please, I must know. How many weeks has your mother been in residence here? It is very important."

"Six or seven," said Evrett impatiently. "And she has hosted some quiet luncheons, but nothing elaborate. What of it?"

Southey gave a sigh of relief. "Thank God," he said, leaning back against the bedrail and looking slightly less distraught. "Evrett, four weeks ago, I came upon what I thought was a young English boy, perhaps fifteen or sixteen, who had just been robbed and left penniless on a street near my fencing studio. I—I adopted this waif temporarily, took him back to my lodgings, hired him on as an assistant so he could earn enough money to travel back to England. He told me his name was Edward Purcell." He shook his head helplessly. "I swear to you, I had no idea she was not a boy until I was attacked a few days ago, and she screamed. And even then it was only a vague notion, a momentary qualm. But when the doctor came last night, after that carriage fell on her . . ."

He took a deep breath and looked at Evrett, who was staring at him in horror. "Do you have any idea of what I put her through? She knew nothing of fencing, of course, so I set her to practicing for hours, until she could barely stand. She carried my equipment all over Vienna, scrubbed masks, ran errands. I had to do a bit of burglary and forgery; she helped me with that, too. Then—" He stopped and shook his head numbly. "Then some French bounty hunters attacked me in an

alley and would have taken me had she not come running up with some weapons at the last moment. It
sounds incredible, but at one point she heaved an assailant off my half-conscious body with a saber. Finally,
yesterday they tried to run me down. Only they hit her
instead of me. And that's not the worst of it."

"What do you mean?" asked Evrett warily. He was
only now beginning to grasp that this boy who was not
a boy must be DeQuincy's sister. Nothing was making
any sense. Why would the French attack Southey, of all
people? How had Miss DeQuincy ended up alone, in
boy's clothing, in Vienna? Hadn't she been living in
Switzerland with her aunt and uncle?

With an effort he tried to comprehend the disjointed
narrative he had just heard. "What do you mean, that's
not the worst of it? She's injured, she's lost all her
money, and her reputation may be irretrievably ruined.
What else is there?"

"She's in love with me. She thinks I am married to
someone who has remained in England, and she has
kindly offered to be my mistress while I am languishing
in exile." With a cynical smile he observed Evrett's eyes
narrow in suspicion and contempt. "Don't worry," he
said bitterly, "I haven't taken advantage of her, if that
is what you are thinking. I thought she was a boy until
twelve hours ago. But when I found that letter, Evrett,
it seemed like a gift from heaven. If your mother has
been here for that long, you can presumably say she
took refuge here when she ran away from her uncle,
and has been ill since then, too ill to leave the house.
I'll resume my own name and go into hiding for a bit.
I have already discarded the wig. She'll simply never see
me again, and I'll know she is safe with you and your
mother. Her injuries are painful, but they will mend;
she will be able to travel back to England with you in a
fortnight or so."

Evrett was still trying to untangle Southey's story. "Did

you say she ran away from her uncle? Why would she need to do so? Surely she is of age now?"

"I assume so. When I still thought her a boy, she swore to me that no one here in Vienna had a legal claim to her. I realize now she must have meant she was no longer a minor. Evidently her aunt died, and her uncle was persecuting her, so she disguised herself and ran off to try to get back to England."

"She was living on her own with Stourhead?!" Evrett was horrified once again.

"My God, is that who her uncle was?" Southey was equally aghast. He and Nathanson had heard tales of the renegade arms dealer. "I'd sooner see her living with a toad! No wonder she was driven to such a desperate ruse. He's gone now, in any case." In a fit of nervous agitation, he got up and started pacing back and forth by the bed, absentmindedly stroking the wolf's head on the post as he passed. His initial weariness had dissipated; he was intent on discharging his errand.

"I have enough for her travel expenses, I believe, and to purchase a modest wardrobe—she has just one frock at the moment. When she ran off she took only a small bag with her. As soon as I can find Nathanson, I'll send you funds to hire a maidservant to travel with her. I'm a bit short right now. The nurses—"

"Damn you, Southey, I'll see you hanged before I'll let the sister of Robert DeQuincy take one penny from you!" blazed Evrett, cutting him off. "What do you take me for?"

"It's not charity, or a—a *douceur*, if that's what your foul mind suspects," retorted Southey, stung. "It's her money! She worked for me for three weeks; worked damned hard, too."

"I find it difficult to believe an assistant fencing master earns that sort of money in three weeks," observed Evrett coldly. "What was her wage?"

"Ten florins a week," admitted Southey reluctantly,

sitting down again, and gambling Evrett would not know that was absurdly high.

"Thirty florins, then. Forty at the most. Hardly enough to cover all the items you just mentioned. If you give me, or her, any sum larger than that, I will consider Miss DeQuincy has been grossly insulted and will take appropriate measures. Do I make myself clear?"

Southey nodded wearily. He had no desire to fight Evrett. It would have to be pistols, since both Southey's profession and Evrett's wound precluded swords, and guns were chancy things. Even if Southey himself deloped, Evrett could be seriously injured by a misfire from his own weapon. It was too great a risk to take.

Flynn came in with two breakfast trays and consulted briefly with Evrett before disappearing into an adjoining dressing room.

"Well, I hate to admit it, but you did the right thing to come here," said Evrett, scowling as he reached for a biscuit. "I'd do more than this for DeQuincy's sister, and your idea of using my mother to concoct a plausible story for her is quite sensible. My mother will be delighted, in fact. The only thing she likes more than being fussed over is fussing over someone else. Give me your direction; we will go and fetch her as soon as she can be moved."

"That will be the day after tomorrow," Southey said. He handed Evrett a card. "You may want to call later today, however, to reassure her. My lodgings are directly above the *salle*. Ask for Frau Renner. I'll leave word you are coming."

"You will not be there?" Evrett was puzzled.

"I am going to disappear, I told you. And this time I will try to make a better job of it. Don't tell her my real name. That will make it harder for her to find me."

"You seem very certain she will want to do that," said Evrett in cutting tones. "Are you such a success with the ladies here in Vienna, then?" He realized at once that he had made a mistake. For a moment, he thought the other man would actually strike him.

"Someday, you complacent fool," Southey said softly after a minute of tense silence, "someday a woman will look at you the way Elizabeth DeQuincy looked at me last night. And I assure you that when she does you will have no doubts about her willingness to follow you into Hell itself." He got up and moved towards the door.

"You haven't eaten anything," Evrett stammered, not knowing how to respond to what he had just heard.

"No." Southey paused, his hand on the door. "Tell me, Evrett," he demanded, his face bleak, "tell me again that I am doing the right thing. Tell me it's quite admirable of me to walk away from her and leave her feeling alone and betrayed. That virtue is its own reward, that I will eventually enjoy a great inner satisfaction at the thought of my nobility." His glance fell on his untouched breakfast tray. "Give my apologies to your cook. I am afraid I am not hungry at the moment."

Dawn was certainly an appropriate time for this meeting, thought Nathanson, glancing around the deserted corner of the gardens. It was nearly as terrifying as a duel, and possibly just as dangerous. He had resolved, of course, never to see her again after that travesty of a dinner. And when he had received her note last night, he had vowed not to go anywhere near the Belvedere this morning. Yet here he was, glowering at the rose bushes, pacing back and forth like a nervous schoolboy.

This part of the garden was very private. On one side an old arbor, choked with vines, blocked off the view from the main path. A thick hedge marked the border of the public section of the park. Presumably the carriage road leading back to the palace lay beyond the hedge, but there was no traffic at this hour. The hedge went around the corner, and the fourth side of the little square was a series of elaborately trained rosebushes long past their bloom now, but still giving off a faint perfume.

The secluded nature of the spot made him uneasy. He had been shocked and offended by the dinner and had hoped for something more public. The early hour offered ample protection if she did not wish to be seen with him—which he was fairly certain was the case. She did not need to select a meeting place which suggested the most illicit sort of assignation. He scuffed moodily at the dead leaves under the hedge with the toe of his boot.

Anselm had lectured him after the duel yesterday. Anselm, of all people! His shy, studious, cousin had suddenly turned into a different person. He had sat quite calmly while his left hand had been stitched up, his right hand clasping Elena's while he told her not to be a goose as she wept into his collar. Then he had made arrangements to send Elena off to his house. Doña Maria had agreed to a story about Anselm's mother sending for Elena to help nurse his younger sister, so as to conceal her presence at the duel. And before Nathanson had gone off with Purcell, he had pulled him aside and told him quite bluntly that he was only a visitor in Vienna and might not know quite how to go on in certain cases—for example, the case of the Countess of Brieg.

"She is poison, James," he had said earnestly. "Once, in Florence, I saw a ring in a jewelry shop, a beautiful ring, gold filigree set around a cameo. And the jeweler took it out of the cabinet and showed me how it could be opened, secretly, to sprinkle venom in a man's drink. I do not know if that was the real purpose of the little compartment behind the cameo, or if it truly belonged to Caterina Sforza, as he claimed, but I have never been able to look at the countess since without thinking of that ring." Nathanson had not been able to argue with him. In his mind's eye he could see such a ring: white and gold, like her gown the other night. Cold, hard, lovely.

The top of the hedge was glowing; it was nearly sunrise. He frowned. Where was she? It was long past the time she had set. A few early morning riders were beginning to appear on the carriage road, and another party had entered the garden—two elderly women and an equally ancient servant. He looked at his watch. Five more minutes, and he would leave. Impatiently he stepped out of the little rose arbor and glanced around.

Perhaps she had gone to a different part of the garden, forgetting her instructions. But, surveying the rest of the park, he saw no one except the three old women. Probably she had simply decided to make a fool of him. He was about to leave when he spotted the boy hurrying towards him, dressed in palace livery.

There was a note, of course, delivered by the breathless messenger, a very apologetic note. She was devastated, he would never forgive her. She wrote:

> *I cannot leave the palace. They are watching me. I am growing frightened. Please, don't believe the stories you hear about me. If I need a friend, if I find myself in difficulty, am I deluding myself that I could still call on you, after the way I have treated you?*

"Do you wish to send a reply, Captain?" asked the boy timidly.

"No, no reply," answered Nathanson curtly. He pocketed the note and walked slowly away.

From the behind the hedge, the countess watched him carefully through the leaves. He had come, he had waited. And she had seen his face when he read the note. She did not need a reply.

Sixteen

For some time afterwards, Elizabeth was not sure whether that scene on the staircase had really happened, or whether she had dreamed it. It seemed incredible that she could have gotten out of bed, lifted a saber off the wall, and walked down the stairs, because for the next five days, she could not even raise her head. She lay in a stupor, sometimes sleeping, sometimes dimly aware of her surroundings.

Her only indication that time was passing was the changing nature of the pain when she woke: at first, mostly in her shoulder and head; then a sort of throbbing in her head and neck, and then, suddenly, a hot, angry burn in one arm. The skin on that arm seemed about to push through the sleeve of the nightgown; at one point, she thought she saw the doctor again, cutting the sleeve away.

But the next time she woke, both sleeves were there, although there was a new, lumpy bandage on the arm, and the nightgown had changed from plain white to white trimmed in blue satin. The pain was more diffuse now, aching through all her joints, and she seemed to be having odd hallucinations. People were talking in English, someone was being referred to as 'her ladyship,' and a dark-eyed young man looked straight at her and said, "My God, it's DeQuincy to the life!"

Even more confusing, the doctor seemed to be back, but now he was speaking in French instead of in German. "Perhaps it is best to move her, after all," she heard him say. "It will be easier to care for her in Baden, and it is cooler there, as well." Cooler sounded good. She was so hot, but every time she tried to take off the covers, her arms would not work.

And they did move her, wrapped up in blankets. Two people carried her down the stairs, very slowly and with great difficulty. When she was being lifted into the carriage she suddenly realized she had not said good-bye to Sommers, and she started to protest and try to get back out, but they did not seem to understand her. The dark-eyed young man took her hand and tried to reassure her, saying something about Robin. But she struggled and became so agitated that eventually they went back into the courtyard and brought Frau Renner out to speak with her.

"Herr Sommers is not here, Fräulein," the old woman said. "I will give him your message." There were tears in her eyes; she was wiping her face with her sleeve.

And somehow those tears sobered Elizabeth. She was acting very childishly, she realized, and she simply gave up and let them tuck her into the carriage and drive her away. She did not remember much after that, although at one point she woke up and thought she saw Nathanson talking to the dark-eyed man.

Sensible English voices, like the voices of the servants of her childhood, moved around her and told her to lift her head or turn over. She slept, and sipped strong-smelling liquids from mugs, and slept again.

* * *

When she did at last emerge from her five-day sleep, she came awake suddenly and completely. It was dark, although a lamp was burning on a nightstand by her bed. She wondered where she was. Not the loft, not her room in her uncle's apartments off the Fleischmarkt.

She remembered enough of what had happened to know that she had been ill, and that someone connected to Robin had taken her somewhere in a carriage. Raising her head, she looked cautiously around.

She was in a large bed with a damask counterpane and piles of thick pillows in crisp white cases which smelled faintly of vervain. It was a four-poster, but there was no canopy, and she could see that the room had a low ceiling. Next to the bed on one side was the nightstand, and in the shadows behind the lamp she could see two old-fashioned side chairs and a small table, with a door beyond them. Tentatively, she turned and looked over at the other side of the room. It did not hurt at all to move her head, she discovered.

Emboldened, she sat up. On this side, there were two large windows—she could see the curtains, which had some gold in the pattern, glinting in the lamplight. A massive chest of drawers. An armchair with a very tall back and some odd cushions piled on it. As she watched, the cushions stirred and resolved themselves into the form of a young woman. Two large blue eyes fastened on Elizabeth, and there was a shriek.

"Fräulein! Fräulein Elizabeth! Thou art awake!" Scrambling out of the chair, the figure ran to the door, yanked it open, and darted out into the hall, calling out to someone. She heard another door open, then a third, and more voices—a man's voice, and then a woman's.

She knew at least one of the voices: the shriek had been Anna. This made no sense, of course, but she was feeling very clearheaded and calm, for once. She was not at her uncle's house, and she knew that he had left Vienna. There was no reason to panic.

Anna hurried back in. "Fräulein, you should not sit up yet," she protested, remembering to use the respectful form this time. "Are you truly awake? How do you feel?"

"I would like something to drink," said Elizabeth, suddenly realizing she was desperately thirsty.

Anna brought her a glass of barley water, and she drained it.

Her arms worked, her fingers grasped the glass. How extraordinary that seemed.

There was a knock at the door, although it was open, and an elegantly dressed young man came in, escorting an older woman in a dressing gown and followed by a second woman, rather severe-looking, instantly recognizable to Elizabeth as some kind of superior servant— a dresser, or a housekeeper. Anna was clearly quite frightened of her; she ducked her head timidly in a most un-Anna-like manner as she left the room.

"You see, mother," scolded the young man. "She is doing quite well, just as the doctor said." He turned to Elizabeth. "How are you feeling, Miss DeQuincy? We are very pleased to see you awake."

An Englishman. Was she supposed to know who he was? She rather thought he was the one who had said, "DeQuincy to the life." And the older woman was his mother, but that did not help her remember him, of course.

"I beg your pardon," she said at last, unable to think of any polite way to deal with the situation, "but I am afraid I do not recall who you are, or where I am, or why I am here."

"I am Evrett," he said, apparently not at all surprised by her ignorance. "And this is my mother, Lady Evrett. We came to your rooms in the Zeughausgasse, but you were very ill, and of course would not remember that visit." He turned to the other woman. "Rollins, would you mind seeing if you can find Flynn? Ask him to go down to the kitchen and see what he can arrange for Miss DeQuincy."

She nodded grudgingly and hurried off.

A dresser, Elizabeth decided. The housekeeper would not be so offended to be asked to go on such an errand. She felt so alert, her mind so clear, so easily able to draw conclusions, to follow conversations—God, it was wonderful. She almost laughed for the sheer joy of it.

Evrett had pulled up a chair for his mother, and now came over to the bed. To her surprise, she saw he was using a cane. "Miss DeQuincy, do you remember my speaking with you in the carriage two days ago?"

She shook her head.

"I will repeat what I said, in that case. You are in Baden, in a house my mother has rented for the summer. I was a great friend of your brother, and after your injury, a letter was found at your lodgings, a letter I sent you after he died. It is providential that my mother and I happened to be here, and that I discovered that you were ill and needed assistance to return to England. Please do not worry about anything. It will be my great honor to see you safely home, and we will not leave here until you are sure you feel well enough to travel."

He flushed slightly, and added awkwardly, "Also, you need not be concerned about the time you spent with Frau Renner. My mother has been here for quite some time, and no one will know that you did not come directly to us when you left your uncle."

Patiently, Elizabeth thought about everything he had said. Confusion lurked around the corner, but she refused to let it near her. She would simply ask questions until things became clearer.

The older woman gave her a sympathetic look. Her face was tired and pale and reminded Elizabeth of her aunt. Probably she knew what it was like to emerge from the haze of sickness with a hunger for explanations.

Elizabeth decided to begin with the problem of the name. This young man looked honest, but the three names at the bottom of that letter were engraved on her memory, and Evrett was not one of them.

"The letter that you mention—is it the one sent from Portugal?"

"Yes, from Coimbra."

"Were there others, then, besides those who signed the letter, who felt themselves bound by it?"

He looked totally puzzled.

"You did not sign it, for example," she hinted.

"I most certainly did!" He looked quite upset for a moment, and then suddenly began to laugh. "My apologies, Miss DeQuincy, the fault is mine. I did not introduce myself properly. My father was still alive at the time I sent the letter, and I had not come into the title. I am John Weyland."

"You are John Weyland?" The incredulous question slipped out before she could suppress it. She had actually met him once before, then. Weyland had been her brother's closest friend at school. He had come home with Robin one half-holiday when Elizabeth was ten or eleven—a tall, graceful boy with an infectious laugh and a talent for improvising humorous songs. Robin's letters from Portugal were full of him, of his pranks and jests and high spirits. She looked at the face across from her, the face of a man years older than Evrett's true age, lined with the marks of constant pain, and thought suddenly that Napoleon had much to answer for.

Hastily, she tried her next question. "How long have I been ill?"

He looked quite relieved at the change of subject. "Four days or so, that is all. We planned at first to convey you here on Monday, but your arm became infected, and we were afraid to move you. Then Dr. Walch advised us that you might recover more quickly here in Baden, and we brought you here yesterday morning."

"What day is it now, then?"

"Wednesday, Wednesday evening." He saw her glance at Lady Evrett's dressing gown, and reassured her. "It is not very late; my mother decided to retire early this evening." His eyes twinkled and he smiled at her, suddenly looking much younger. "Something tells me you may not go back to sleep for some time now that you are awake. And I suspect you will be hungry. My valet is arranging for a tray to be prepared for you right now."

She was hungry—quite hungry, she realized. But she still had more questions. "How does it happen that Anna is here? I am very happy to see her, of course, but it was a surprise."

He looked uncomfortable. "Someone—" He started again. "There was some concern that you might be frightened, being brought to a strange place while you were ill, with no one you knew. We thought of Frau Renner, but she was reluctant to leave her employer's house untended. It was most fortunate that Anna could be located and brought here to help take care of you." With that odd sharpness of thought which had possessed her ever since she had come to herself, she noted at once the contorted phrasing and the stiff expression on Evrett's face. But she asked her last question, even so.

"Where is Mr. Sommers? I must write to him to thank him for rescuing me and to repay him for some things he purchased for me." At once she knew she was not going to get an answer to her question.

Evrett looked at his mother, his face white, and Lady Evrett leaned forward, her eyes fixed on Elizabeth.

She recognized the expression in those eyes. It was pity. And she knew what she would hear, what she did hear, in a gentle, compassionate, cultured English voice—her aunt's voice, her governess's voice, the voice of decorum and prudence and conformity. It was for the best, he had gone away, everything would be arranged, she should not fret, but rest and recover her health.

Her newly rediscovered powers of logic and calculation told her not to protest at this point. She murmured something, made a pretty speech of thanks to Lady Evrett, and ate the broth and toast Flynn carried in with a good appetite. Her good night to Lady Evrett was cordial; to Evrett himself she was appropriately shy and missish. She could be patient, because she knew Evrett was right, she would not fall asleep again for quite some time. As she had anticipated, once her supper tray had been cleared away and the rest of the household had retired, Anna returned, slipping in quietly in case Elizabeth had dozed off.

Sitting up against her pillows, Elizabeth pounced the moment Anna came in the door. Since Anna spoke no English, she thought it unlikely that Evrett or his mother would have been able to persuade her to conceal anything. And in any case, Anna was a poor liar. Elizabeth had always been able to tell when she had broken a dish in the kitchen.

"Anna, how did you come here to work for Freiherr Evrett?"

The girl's eyes sparkled, and she pulled a chair up next to Elizabeth. Anna loved to tell stories. "It was the Herr Degenmeister, Fräulein Elizabeth. He looked for me for two days, he told me. First he went to the police and asked for the address of Herr Stourhead. And then he went to Herr Schneidler and asked about me. And then he came to the bakery, and my arms were all over flour"—she showed Elizabeth how high the flour had been—"and he took me out of the bakery, just like that! With my apron on! And he walked to my grandmother's house with me and had a cup of tea with my grandmother while I washed off the flour and changed my clothing, and then he sent me to Baden in a carriage."

She sighed, remembering. There had not been many carriages in Anna's life.

"And the Freiherrin was very nice, but I could not understand anything she said to me, so Herr Flynn had to explain that you were not well and might need me to sit with you, and when they brought you in from the carriage I did not recognize you, because your hair was all cut off and your face was a funny color, but now you look like my fräulein again, even without your hair."

Then she remembered something, too late. "Oh!" she gasped. "The Herr Degenmeister asked me not to tell you he found me." Her pink cheeks grew even pinker, and she lowered her head.

"It's all right, Anna," said Elizabeth gently. It had taken her until halfway through Anna's convoluted story to realize that *Degenmeister* was not a name, but a description: sword master. "I knew already." She let Anna turn down the lamp and told her to go off and get some sleep, that she was feeling quite well and did not need to be watched all night.

The dim light projected a hazy shadow of the bedposts onto the curtains. She stared at it without really seeing it. She had been happy to find Anna here at first. Any familiar face would have been welcome, and the affectionate "Thou art awake," with its endearing impropriety, had made her heart soar. But now she felt like a little girl whose well-meaning relatives had given her a beautiful doll the day after her mother's funeral. Anna was a sop, a bribe. He was feeling guilty. He knew he had hurt her.

The kiss on the staircase came back to her, suddenly distinct and sure in her memory. Had that been a bribe, too? Well, she was not for sale. Closing her eyes, she settled back into the bed and planned her campaign.

"Rollins is right, it does not fit properly. I should not have gone to Frau Wecklein." Lady Evrett was disappointed. It was Friday morning, and Elizabeth was to be allowed up today. She had sent Elizabeth's one dress off to a seamstress so that a few frocks could be made up quickly, and now it was apparent the seamstress had not measured properly.

Rollins said nothing, only pursed her lips. She had advised against giving the work to the Austrian woman; everyone knew the Austrians had no talent for fashion. But the French modiste in Vienna who had enjoyed Lady Evrett's patronage had not been able to promise to finish two gowns by Friday.

"It is no matter, Lady Evrett. I can wear my old one," said Elizabeth. "The ones you had made up will need only a few alterations. And it is a plain blue cambric. That is almost acceptable for half-mourning." But when Rollins had helped her into her own dress, which looked quite shabby next to the soft new muslin Lady Evrett had ordered, the dresser shook her head.

"Beg pardon, ma'am," she said grudgingly, "but I may have been wrong to blame Frau Wecklein. This one does not fit, either. It is too tight in the shoulders, and the waist is too large, just like the other."

Elizabeth looked down in dismay. It was true. The sleeves were so tight they were cutting into her upper arms, the bodice was straining across her chest, and the waist sagged. "It fit me a month ago," she said, bewildered, and then blushed as she thought of how long it had been since she had been properly garbed. Her petticoat was loose in the waist, as well, she realized.

Rollins was holding up the discarded muslin and looking back and forth from Elizabeth to the garment. Producing some pins from one pocket, she placed the sleeve against Elizabeth's shoulder and inserted a pin as a marker, and then did the same for the waist. "If we can set luncheon back just a bit, my lady, Liesl and I should be able to make this one right in time for Miss DeQuincy to come down. And we will have all afternoon to alter her dinner gown."

Elizabeth knew enough not to offer to help with the sewing. Rollins would have been even more insulted than Lady Evrett. Meekly, she allowed Rollins and Liesl to take off the round gown. It was a bit out of style. She was glad Rollins was altering the new one first.

She was a bit uneasy about the cost of the items Anna and Liesl had been folding and putting away in the marble-topped chest under the windows: nightgowns, chemises, stockings, gloves, two pairs of slippers, a very expensive-looking shawl. A large box was sitting by the chest; it looked like a milliner's box. How was she going to pay for all this? She did not think her brother would have wanted her to accept charity from anyone, even a close friend like Evrett.

With a sigh, she shrugged into the wrap Liesl was holding out. This was new, too, a beautiful Swiss cotton trimmed with ruche and threaded with silver ribbons. After lunch, perhaps she could have a private word with Lord Evrett. She sat down in the big armchair with her chocolate, which was now cold, and tried to reckon up how much money she had. In a folded piece of paper in her valise she had found thirty florins; her wages from Sommers, presumably. She had five or six florins in her purse. Then there was her diamond earring. It did not sound like much money, when you totaled it up. There was the piano, though. If she paid Sommers the twenty florins and then resold it, she might be able to afford both her fare home and a few gowns. And perhaps she could sell some of her music. She got up and began sifting through the pieces, which had been laid out on the table, and was soon lost in the painful task of sorting out which ones to sell and which to keep.

There was a sharp knock at the door, and Rollins reappeared with the muslin. "If you can stand here in the light, Miss DeQuincy," she said briskly, "I will take a few tucks in your chemise and petticoat before we try this on again."

Obediently, Elizabeth took off her wrap and stood with her arms out while the dresser whipped a needle and thread quickly through the side seams of her undergarments. Her shoulder did not hurt at all, she realized.

Liesl and Anna came in, and they helped her step into the gown. Rollins nodded in satisfaction as Liesl fastened it up in back. "Very nicely done, Liesl," she said. "You are an excellent seamstress." The Austrian girl blushed. Her English was almost nonexistent, but very few servants in the villa heard that tone from the haughty Rollins.

The dresser moved around her, twitching the fabric here and there, and then led her to a chair. "I am afraid this bedchamber has no dressing room," she said apologetically as she began brushing Elizabeth's hair.

At a nod from her, Liesl came over with a packet of very broad silk ribbons, and Robbins held them up to the lavender muslin until she found one which matched the trim on the dress. Then she set the ribbon very carefully onto Elizabeth's curls.

"Lady Evrett bought these specially, Miss," she commented as she adjusted the silk band.

Elizabeth did not understand what she meant until the dresser's hands brushed over her scar, causing her to wince briefly. It was still tender. She reached up herself, pushing aside the ribbon. Underneath it, the hair was very short. The doctor must have cut it. But the wide ribbon would conceal the scar and the shorn patch. She had to smile, it was all so ridiculous. Two attempts to kill her in three days, an attack of putrefying fever, and Rollins and Lady Evrett were concerned about whether her hair could be properly dressed.

Some bumping noises out in the hall proved to be two blond serving men, who carried in an enormous cheval glass and set it down by the windows. They were followed by Lady Evrett. "Let me see," she commanded, and Rollins stepped aside, helping Elizabeth to her feet. "Very, very nice," approved Lady Evrett. "Come and look, my dear."

No wonder her gown had not fit, thought Elizabeth, stunned, as she looked in the mirror. Was this the awkward, scrawny girl who had looked back at her out of that other mirror in her aunt's room a month ago? Now that she thought about it, she realized that the mirrors

in the *salle* had been showing her someone entirely
different for several weeks now, but she had been too
busy concentrating on fencing to notice. Her bony
shoulders had filled out, her waist had slimmed down,
her small breasts filled the bodice of the gown instead
of sinking into a hollow chest.

The short curls softened the lines of her face and
emphasized her eyes. She was still a bit pale and tired,
but even after a four-day fever she looked better than
that miserable girl in the mirror at her uncle's. This
girl stood straight and seemed elegant and self-confi-
dent. Her gaze was direct, her head gracefully set on
the slender neck.

I'm pretty, thought Elizabeth, hardly able to take it all
in. *Thin, still, and my face is a bit boyish, and I have freckles
from being out in the sun for a month, but I am pretty. Or at
least not bad-looking.*

An incredulous smile trembled at the corners of her
mouth, and for one moment she was so overcome she
almost began to cry. She no longer despised Lady Evrett
for worrying about ribbon widths. If she had to go back
to being a young lady, it was nice to be an attractive
young lady. Is this what he had seen when he looked
at her like that on the stairs?

Anna was hurrying over with a handkerchief,
exclaiming at how lovely the Fräulein looked. Mechanically, Elizabeth blotted her eyes and accepted a shawl;
they were going to eat out on the verandah.

Flynn, who apparently was serving as both butler and
valet, came in, looking somewhat harassed. His sketchy
German was especially inadequate when it came to deal-
ing with the cook, who was Schwabian. "Luncheon is
served, my lady," he announced.

Behind him, Evrett stood in the doorway, staring at
Elizabeth. Her blue-gray eyes were luminous with
unshed tears, but she gave him a shy smile.

Good Lord, he thought, as he came forward to offer
her his arm. *Southey is being very noble, indeed.*

Seventeen

The servants were clearing away the dishes and Evrett had risen, with some difficulty, from the low wrought-iron chairs around the table on the verandah. He came over to assist Elizabeth, and she asked him if she could speak with him for a moment.

"Certainly," he said calmly. He shot his mother, who was looking somewhat agitated, a quelling look.

Lady Evrett subsided, although she strongly suspected that she knew what Elizabeth wanted to discuss. She had seen Elizabeth's dismay when the milliner's box was unpacked and not one but three new bonnets had emerged.

"Would you care to take a turn in the garden?" he inquired courteously.

It was a rather small garden, so they would be making several turns, Elizabeth thought. But it was attractive, with its flower borders and low stone wall, and especially inviting after six days confined indoors. She accepted with a smile.

"Do you not need your cane?" she asked, surprised, as he offered her his arm and turned towards the shallow steps which led down to the garden path. He had left it leaning on his chair.

"Not unless you are planning to walk very quickly," he said gravely. But his eyes crinkled a bit at the edges. She was glad to see he still had his sense of humor, and felt more comfortable about the awkward request she was going to make.

"My lord," she said, as soon as they were out of ear-shot of his mother, "I do not want you to think I am ungrateful for your help, and I particularly do not want to offend Lady Evrett, but I am becoming concerned about the purchases she has made on my behalf." To her surprise, he did not protest or assure her he could well afford a few handkerchiefs.

"You feel you may not have adequate funds in England to repay her?" he suggested, looking at her keenly.

She was very relieved to get to the heart of the matter so easily, and nodded. "So far as I know, I have no funds in England at all. Once I return, I will have to find some paying position as a companion or governess. At the moment, I have only a small sum with me, barely enough to cover my travel expenses. It was very foolish of me to run off from my uncle's as I did, and I know I must have a few gowns and some gloves and slippers, but I wonder if you could have a word with your mother. I think what she has already provided for me is quite ample, and yet she and Rollins are talking of taking me in to Vienna in a few days to have more dresses made up."

"What makes you think you have no monies in England?" he asked. "Did you not realize your brother's pension would go to you? I am the trustee, as it happens; he did not wish your uncle to have access to it. There was some back pay, also, and a small legacy from your mother. I have not looked at it for quite some time, I am embarrassed to say, but I would imagine there is more than a thousand pounds in the account. The pension will continue to accrue, and there is interest as well. The income should be around one hundred and fifty pounds a year."

In the world of the Evretts, this was a very modest

amount, but to Elizabeth it sounded like a small fortune. "One hundred fifty pounds a year!" She could live on that easily, she knew. Dismal visions of a future waiting on crusty old ladies vanished. In fact . . . "How long do you suppose it would take to transfer the funds from England to Vienna?" she asked.

"Perhaps a month, or six weeks," he replied. "But you do not need to do anything so complicated, Miss DeQuincy. I will keep track of the expenses here and on the journey back to England. You can repay me once we arrive." He would make sure the accounting was very generous, he promised himself.

"But I will not be going back to England," she objected. "Now that I know I have some means of support, I will stay here in Vienna. My only reason for returning home was to seek a position. I did not think I could find anything suitable here."

At this he stopped short and looked at her in dismay. He cursed himself for telling her about the pension, and then instantly felt ashamed that he had even thought of concealing it from her. Still, was he to let her ruin herself for a scoundrel like Southey? He had no doubts at all about why she wished to stay in Vienna.

They were all the way at the bottom of the path now, some thirty yards from his mother, who was still sipping tea in her chair on the verandah. He gave an agonized glance towards her, as though she could see his expression from this distance, and then looked back at his companion. She was perfectly calm.

One step at a time, he decided. *It has only been a few days since she left him. She needs some time. And a diversion.*

"Miss DeQuincy—" he began. He glanced again at the distant figure of his mother, and inspiration came to him. It was not even a lie, although it was not the sort of thing one normally confided to an acquaintance. "Miss DeQuincy, I must tell you something about my mother. Her health has not been good for some time."

Elizabeth nodded. She had thought as much.

"She is not, however, nearly as ill as she fancies herself. And she drove my father to distraction traveling to various shrines and springs and clinics. She is here in Baden now because she read a report of a miraculous cure for gout obtained from the waters here." He added dryly, "She has never suffered from the gout."

They had turned and were moving slowly back towards the villa. "My mother usually spends her mornings in bed, rises for lunch, sees a physician or visits a bath in the afternoon, and returns to her bed before dinner. Her doctors—and there have been many of them—have told my father and me countless times that there is absolutely no reason why she should do so. She has a weak chest and catches cold easily, but that is all that is really wrong with her."

"My aunt was like that when I first came to live with her," commented Elizabeth sympathetically. "That was one reason my uncle was happy to take me in when my father died. She needed a companion. But then, unfortunately, she really did become ill."

"Don't you see?" said Evrett. "That is what I am afraid may happen with my mother. Her doctor here, whom I admire very much, has told her she needs to be more active—to walk, to drive out, to dress for dinner. But she believes she is too frail. She has refused to do more than be driven to the springs once every few days. Until you came to us."

Elizabeth raised her eyes to his, startled.

"She has gone twice into Vienna to see you at Frau Renner's. She has been to every shop in Baden, buying ribbons and linens and slippers. Rollins could have gone, but my mother *wanted* to go. Last night she came down to dinner and spent the whole evening persuading me to accompany you on this expedition to Madame Hulot's emporium in Vienna."

He looked at her in appeal. "Please, Miss DeQuincy, do not be in such a hurry to leave us. You are not well yet. It would not be wise to make any hasty decisions.

And I beg you not to concern yourself with the exact sums my mother wishes to spend on your wardrobe. I have not seen her so lively in years; she cannot spend more on your shawls than she spends on tonics and nostrums and sulfur packs.'' He grinned and added, as he looked at her new gown, ''Nor are the tonics as pleasant for the rest of us.''

Elizabeth blushed, but said nothing, and they returned in companionable silence to Lady Evrett. Even that short walk had tired her, Elizabeth found, and she excused herself after a minute or two to retire for a rest.

Evrett remained with his mother, leaning on the back of her chair. She looked up at him, concerned. ''What did she wish to ask you, John? Is she annoyed because I bought her so many bonnets?''

He shook his head. ''She wants to stay in Vienna,'' he answered.

''Oh, dear.'' His mother sighed.

''Would you mind postponing our trip back to England?'' he asked. ''I know we were planning to leave in a week or so, but perhaps it would be better to wait.''

''John, I think you are deluding yourself if you believe delaying will make any difference in this case,'' said his mother in a brisk tone, which was most unusual for her. ''I was there when we put her in the carriage, remember?''

He remembered.

''Nevertheless, it will do no harm to stay here a few more weeks. Perhaps he will leave Vienna. If she cannot find him, then she might return with us to England.''

Elizabeth was dressing for dinner when Lady Evrett hurried in, looking a bit flustered. ''My dear, your pianoforte has arrived,'' she announced. ''Would you like to have it in here, or shall we put it in the drawing room?''

''My piano?'' Elizabeth's face lit up and she whirled, leaving Liesl holding a button which had ripped off the back of her gown. "Did he come? Is he here?" She stopped, seeing Lady Evrett's face. "Was there a note, at least?" she asked after a long moment, her voice barely audible.

"I do not know," answered Lady Evrett, shaken. "The servants were unpacking it when I came up to ask you where you would like it."

Elizabeth looked around. There was really no room in here, although she would have liked to have it close by at night. She could go and sit in front of it and pretend. She shook herself. "In the drawing room, I think, if you do not mind."

"Oh, no, it will be lovely there," Lady Evrett assured her. "Rented houses never have pianos, and this one seems most ingenious, the way it folds up into a box. It will not be difficult to ship back to England at all."

Anna came in, holding a piece of paper. So there had been a note. She recognized the cramped writing at once. "This was with the piano, Fräulein," said Anna—to the empty air. Elizabeth had already seized it and retreated to a chair. There was no salutation and no signature.

I am afraid Lady Evrett is not fond of dogs, or I would send Trumpet as well. But since I will have to keep him, and since, as I am sure you will agree, he is a rather valuable animal, I must ask you not to try to repay the twenty florins I gave the Schneidlers for your piano. I am very glad to hear you are nearly recovered, and wish you a safe and pleasant voyage back to England.

Postscriptum: The piano may need to be tuned. The men who packed it slammed it into the wall at one point. My apologies.

Damn him! How dare he send her the piano! How dare he apologize for the tuning, and not apologize for running away or lying to her or kissing her! Did he think he was being witty with that contrived excuse about Trumpet? She would send him twenty florins tomorrow.

Furious, she crumpled the note and threw it on the floor. Then she broke down completely and collapsed, sobbing, onto the arm of the chair.

Liesl and Anna were looking helplessly at Lady Evrett. Elizabeth knew she was behaving dreadfully, but she could not help herself. She saw Lady Evrett motioning for the two maids to leave.

Seized by a sudden terror they would take the note away and put it in the dustbin, she slid onto her knees on the floor and snatched it up, smoothing it out. To her surprise, Lady Evrett got down on the floor next to her as soon as Anna had closed the door.

"Oh, ma'am!" she gulped, horrified. "You must not! I am so terribly sorry. I will be better in a moment." She took out her handkerchief and blew her nose. What had happened to her calm plan of campaign?

The older woman took her hand and patted it. Elizabeth was sure she was going to say something sympathetic—"It will be all right," or "These things take time." But in fact, all she said was, "I will ask Flynn to put dinner back half an hour. After all, we had a late lunch." A rather timid Liesl returned and sewed the button on her gown, and she and Anna fussed over Elizabeth and arranged her hair and brought a cold cloth for her face. Lady Evrett had gone off to be dressed by Rollins.

By the time Rollins appeared, Elizabeth was looking reasonably presentable again. Her gown for dinner was a quiet gray silk with puffed sleeves and a square neck. Rollins selected a darker gray ribbon for her hair, and then turned to Lady Evrett, who had returned garbed in mauve crepe. She was carrying a box, and Elizabeth saw with a sinking heart that it was, unmistakably, a jewelry box.

"Now, do not make a fuss, Miss DeQuincy," she

warned. "This will simply be a loan. Rollins warned me this dress would not look well without a necklace, and she was right. I have something that will match your earrings. Uncolored stones are permissible for you at a quiet family dinner." She took out a thin gold chain, with a teardrop diamond hanging from it.

"But Lady Evrett, I do not have earrings," protested Elizabeth. Liesl had gone over to the chest of drawers and was bringing her little jewel box over to Rollins. *They must not have realized there was only one,* she thought. And now Lady Evrett would insist on lending her earrings, as well.

Rollins opened the box and took the pendant from Lady Evrett. "This will do very nicely, my lady," she told Lady Evrett. "They could have been made as a set." She turned to Elizabeth and showed her the pendant, holding Elizabeth's earring box up next to it.

In the box lay two earrings. One was her aunt's; there was a tiny dark spot at the end of the gold wire which Elizabeth recognized as a bloodstain from the day of the robbery. The other was an exact duplicate.

And then, of course, she broke down again, and in the end dinner was set back over an hour.

"Would you care to go for a drive, Miss DeQuincy?" Evrett asked, his eyes dancing. Elizabeth was standing in the front hall, her bonnet on, looking longingly at the phaeton pulled up in front of the villa.

She colored. "Your mother did mention . . ."

He laughed. "She commanded me, in no uncertain terms, to get you out into the fresh air. And I will excuse her from coming with us, because she has promised me to walk to the baths today instead of being driven."

She almost ran down the steps, and had to wait for him to hobble down and hand her up. But he sprang into the driver's seat very neatly and grinned as he picked up the reins. "Don't need two good knees to drive," he commented. "Haven't used a coachman for this thing once since I've arrived. Where would you like to go?"

"Vienna, please," she said, hating to spoil his mood, but not knowing when she might get a chance like this again. His mouth tightened, but he nodded, and flicked the reins expertly to set the horses in motion.

It was a beautiful day, rather unusual for early August, with a cloudless sky and a cool breeze. Even when they came into the old part of the city, the air was still pleasant.

The steep roofs were etched against the sky; Elizabeth fancied she could have counted the slates one by one, everything was so distinct. Throngs of afternoon shoppers crowded the streets, and clerks were hurrying home, but there was a cheerful energy to the crowds. It had been hot and humid for several days, and everyone was enjoying the change. They made their way slowly along the Tiefer Graben, and Evrett turned without comment down the little alley and drew up in front of the courtyard gate.

"I will go in with you," he said. It was a statement, not a question. He helped her down, and she went over and read the sign which had been tacked up next to the gate. It was in German and French, and it advised the students of Herr Sommers that the *salle d'armes* was temporarily closed.

"Oh, my God," she said faintly, realizing for the first time all that was involved in hiding from her. "He's beggaring himself. He has no money; he has saved nothing. It all goes home to his family in England."

Evrett looked at her uneasily. It had not occurred to him that Southey was in any financial difficulty. The family was not as wealthy as his own, but their estate in Kent was reputed to be well-managed and productive.

Elizabeth had started crying again. "I beg your pardon," she choked. "I am not usually such a watering-pot; I do not know what has happened to me. When I was pretending to be a boy, I hardly cried at all, even when we were attacked." She retrieved her handkerchief and wiped her eyes defiantly. "I would like to go in, please."

He held the gate open for her, and she walked silently in under the roofed arch. Both blue doors were closed. The ropes in the courtyard were gone, and she could see that the shutters in the loft had been fastened. The door up to the *salle* was locked.

Halfheartedly, she knocked on Frau Renner's door and was surprised to hear movement inside, followed by frantic barking. The bolt shot back, and the tiny old woman peered out, then gasped as she saw Elizabeth. Trumpet was yelping in frustration, trying to wriggle out through the narrow opening. Finally he squeezed through and began to lick Elizabeth's ankles triumphantly.

"Fräulein!" She was torn, Elizabeth could tell—happy to see her, but afraid of awkward questions. "You are well, God be praised! Marta and I were very worried about you. Come in, and you also, Freiherr. I will make you some tea."

"Thank you, but we have just stopped in for a moment," said Elizabeth quickly, afraid Evrett would accept. She did not want to sit in Frau Renner's stiffly furnished parlor and watch the landlady's eyes avoiding hers for twenty minutes. "Do you have the key to the other door, Frau Renner? I believe I left a book in the sword room." This was a complete fabrication, but she had to go up and see it, and she needed an excuse. Frau Renner gave her a key, and she and Evrett climbed slowly up the stone stairs to the loft.

It was dark, of course, with the shutters closed, but some light came in through the cracks and through the unshuttered windows in the two side rooms. She wandered despondently from room to room, going twice into his bedroom as if to make sure.

But there was no doubt. He was gone, utterly gone.

The linens had been stripped from the trundle bed. The swords, the books, the papers—all vanished. No shirts hanging on the hooks in his room. No trunks or boxes. Only the dilapidated furniture remained: armchair, couch, battered wooden table. Even the crate which had been the piano bench had disappeared. The room looked unbearably empty and forlorn in the half-darkness.

"I was so happy here," Elizabeth said, almost to herself. Evrett put his arms around her, and she turned her face into his jacket, closing her eyes. "It was like a dream, a rather crazy one, really. How could I be a boy? How could I teach fencing? The first day, I could not even hold up the sabers; I was not strong enough." She remembered the fight in the alley and shuddered. If it had happened ten days sooner, it might have had a very different ending.

She pulled back slightly and looked up at Evrett. "You must understand," she said urgently. "It all sounds so immodest, so bizarre, and I suppose it was, but it wasn't like that while it was happening. He was my friend. He trusted me. I trusted him. I knew his name was not Sommers, and he knew mine was not Purcell, but that did not matter. It was almost as though this was a secret country, where we could have different names and I could be a boy and all the rules about proper behavior and reputation and appearances did not apply."

There was a lump in Evrett's throat. He understood perfectly what she was saying. How else could he be standing here in a dark room embracing a gently bred young woman, and finding nothing shameful or unseemly in their position whatsoever?

"Miss DeQuincy," he began. His nerve almost failed him, but he took a deep breath and continued. "You realize, I am sure, that you can never have again what you found here for those few weeks."

He felt her head against his chest, inclining in reluctant acknowledgment.

"I know things about Mr. Sommers which make it impossible for me to hope that you will succeed in your quest to locate him. Indeed, it is my duty, as your brother's friend, to try to prevent you from finding him, and I would not have brought you here today if I had not known that he had left. To his credit, he agrees with me completely."

She had stiffened, but he kept on.

"Even with what I know of him, however, I can only envy you those weeks here. Not many people have such friendships. It is what I had with your brother." He set her gently away from him; it was not fair to say what he was going to say next while she was still in his arms. "If you find that you need a friend, I hope that you will trust me as you did him, for your brother's sake. And if you would like me to be more than a friend, I would be honored, and would not expect, at first, that you would feel for me anything more than affection."

Her head was lowered; he saw her take out the handkerchief again. Perhaps he should not have spoken. But she did not wipe her eyes, only twisted it tightly in her hands, as though she had forgotten why she had retrieved it.

"Did you know that I told him I was willing to stay and be his mistress?" she whispered.

"Yes."

"I think Robin was very lucky in his friends," was all she said. They walked down the worn steps in silence, and returned the key to Frau Renner.

Elizabeth gave the dog one last pat, but did not ask any questions. She was very quiet on the drive back to Baden, but when he assisted her down from the phaeton, she held his hand for a moment and said simply, "Thank you."

Eighteen

The piano tuner had come and gone, and Elizabeth was entertaining Lady Evrett by playing the same Haydn piece in several different tempos when Anna appeared at the door of the drawing room and announced with relish: "Herr Hauptmann von Nathanson."

"Not quite," corrected that gentleman, following on her heels. "My connection with the newly ennobled Roths is on my mother's side. Besides, I do not believe the 'von' should be used with a *nom de guerre.*"

Anna understood nothing of this. She had assumed that any captain merited a 'von'. With a quick bob, she disappeared.

"Where is Flynn?" demanded Lady Evrett, looking cross. "Do the maidservants not know to ask if we are at home to visitors before they bring them in to see us?"

"I beg your pardon," Elizabeth said hastily, afraid the volatile captain would take offense. "Anna is not well trained. It is my fault. My aunt fell ill just after she came to us, and I never made much of an attempt to correct her errors."

To her relief, Nathanson looked rather amused. "Are you at home?" he inquired with exaggerated courtesy.

Evrett appeared behind him. "Yes, we are. Under certain conditions." His eyes met Nathanson's, and the younger man grimaced.

"Rest easy, Evrett. The same conditions were imposed by the other party."

"In that case, you are very welcome."

Lady Evrett hesitated, glancing in agitation at Elizabeth and then back at her son. She did not wish to leave Elizabeth alone with the two young men, but her own presence in the drawing room conferred upon Nathanson the status of an acknowledged visitor. An informal call on Evrett by a fellow officer could easily be explained; receiving the man herself could not.

Her son rescued her, although she could see he was very angry. "My mother and Miss DeQuincy were just about to go out for a walk, I am afraid."

"No matter." Nathanson's expression remained studiously polite. "I merely stopped in to inquire after Miss DeQuincy. I am delighted to see that she has recovered so quickly."

Lady Evrett had moved with guilty haste towards the door, and Elizabeth rose from the piano and followed. But at the last moment, she stopped and turned impulsively towards Nathanson.

"It is very kind of you to call, Captain," she said. "Might I ask you something about—about a mutual acquaintance?"

He drew back, looking uncomfortable.

"I do not want to know where he is," she said quickly, afraid he would leave. She had comprehended immediately what was meant by the reference to "conditions." "But I saw the notice on the gate at Frau Renner's. Is he giving any lessons?"

Nathanson glanced at Evrett for permission, and got a reluctant nod. "No."

"Not even in private homes?"

"No."

She understood. She had been to those homes; he was afraid she could find him there.

Her eyes closed, and she made a small sound of protest, but there were no tears this time. She felt dead, hollow. If she looked in the mirror, she knew she would see that same bleak emptiness which had terrified her so often in Sommers's face. The two men were frozen in place, watching her, not daring to move.

"Tell him I am going back to England," she said at last. "Tell him it is safe to come out now."

Nathanson let out his breath in a harsh sigh after the two women had left. "*Peste*," he swore.

"Exactly." Evrett scowled down at the carpet.

"She is rather attractive, in an unusual sort of way," Nathanson said, musing. "At one point she told me she was planning to seek a post as a nurse-companion when she returned home, that she would never be able to find a husband with no looks and no dowry."

"I have already asked her to marry me."

"You maggot-wit," said Nathanson in disgust. "Could you not at least wait until you left Vienna? Or did you want her to say no?"

"It seemed right at the time." Evrett's face softened, remembering. "I do not think I have ruined my chances, in fact."

"When are you leaving, then?" Nathanson picked up his hat, which Anna had forgotten to take from him.

"Thursday or Friday, I suppose. My mother has been ready for days now; she is itching to get home and present Miss DeQuincy to the polite world. She has calculated to the hour when the half-mourning will be over so she and Rollins can dress the girl properly."

"I would advise you not to delay beyond Friday," said Nathanson. "The armistice expires on the tenth."

"Good God, I had forgot all about that!" Evrett flushed. "You are right. I will have Flynn begin making arrangements at once. If my mother and Miss DeQuincy can manage it, we should try to get as far west as possible before the tenth. There are six allied divisions within two hundred miles of here."

"Good-bye, then," said Nathanson, holding out his hand. "I will probably see you back in England; I expect I will be recalled soon."

Evrett shook his hand. "I apologize for my mother," he said awkwardly. "You would think that after living in Europe for six months she would be a bit less provincial, but there it is."

"Ça ira. She did not show me the door, after all. She merely recollected that she had promised to take Miss DeQuincy for a walk." He added, with a smile, "You are a very good influence on me, my dear fellow. It is hard for me to lose my temper when you are losing yours on my behalf before I get a chance to be offended."

That brought a chuckle. "At least I made her take a constitutional, for penance," said Evrett, his eyes twinkling. "Her doctor thinks she should be walking more." He saw Nathanson out, and went in search of Flynn. There was quite a bit to be done if they were to leave in three days. But at the top of the stairs, Elizabeth met him, bonnet in hand, a bit breathless.

"My lord, there is something I must tell you, now that I will be traveling with you after all. Are we leaving very soon?"

"Yes, I hope so, if you feel well enough to travel."

"Oh, that is not the problem," Elizabeth assured him. "I am quite recovered. But I have just recollected something, something important. I have no papers. Or rather, I do, but they are made out for Edward Purcell." She was watching his face anxiously, and saw his dismay. "Oh, I knew I should not have destroyed them!" she said, biting her lip in vexation. "How could I have been so thoughtless?"

"Never mind, we can procure new ones," he said, calculating frantically. If he sent a message off this afternoon, they might be able to leave by the tenth. But Friday was out of the question.

Friday, as it turned out, was the day of the grand expedition to Madame Hulot's. As soon as she had yielded on the more essential question of returning to England, Elizabeth had lost her will to fight smaller battles. With an air of triumph, Lady Evrett had carried her into the elegant shop just off the Graben. Her son, with one appalled look at the half-clothed mannequins, armies of aproned assistants, and cabinets full of gauzy fabrics, had fled. He returned only to escort them to Hugelmann's for a light lunch.

"Have you made all your purchases, or will you need to return to Madame Hulot's?" he asked as the waiter presented a bill for one cutlet, one poached trout, and one *confit* of pheasant. This last had been for Elizabeth, and she had barely touched it; a dreary weight was pressing down on her, flattening everything—her vision, her senses, her appetite.

Lady Evrett was concerned about Elizabeth, but roused herself and answered. "We are finished at the modiste's, but I had thought to go to that German chemist by the Augustinian church. He is the only one I have found here who sells my valerian drops, and I will need them once we are traveling."

"I will have the carriage brought around, then," said her son, rising. "Or would you prefer to walk?"

"May we, Lady Evrett?" asked Elizabeth, coming to life. This might be her last chance to see Vienna, she realized. They were leaving Tuesday, if her papers had arrived by then. Her ladyship graciously consented to go on foot, and they set out at a slow pace up the hill towards the cathedral. A shy young servant who had been carrying parcels was sent off to direct the coachman to drive down and meet them at the chemist's.

The air is not so clear as it was when I was here on Monday, thought Elizabeth, looking wistfully around as they left the cathedral behind and came through the Neue Markt. There was a light haze, and the sun was sitting in a sullen pocket behind some clouds. Workmen were repairing the facade of a large stone building on the other side of the plaza, a merchant's guildhall, and Elizabeth glanced idly over as one of them dropped a tool from the scaffolding and let out a guttural German oath.

A slender figure, a very familiar figure, had stopped, motionless, underneath the rude planking and was staring at her in horror. Next to him was Nathanson, who was speaking to him urgently, pulling at his sleeve. The hair color was wrong, the complexion was wrong, but Elizabeth would have recognized the taut, graceful stance anywhere.

Without a single thought for the riders and vehicles in between, she darted across the square, desperate to reach him before he slipped away. Dimly she heard a shout from Evrett, and was aware of vague obstacles between her and her goal: a cart loaded with furniture, a stocky little horse whose rider pulled it up at the last moment. She would have climbed over the cart, if she had needed to, but she found a space where she could squeeze through, and pushed her way towards the scaffolding, her eyes intent on the two men standing beneath it. He had not moved.

Red hair, she noted. *I did not think of red. And freckles. He must have been staining his face with something to cover them.* At the moment he was very pale, and the freckles stood out vividly. The hazel eyes were fastened on her, with a strange expression that she could not define. Apology? Fear? Evrett had made his way across behind her, abandoning his mother.

"Nathanson told me you were leaving," the red-headed man said to Evrett. He looked dazed. "Today. He said you were leaving today."

Evrett made a helpless gesture, and Elizabeth turned

to him. "My lord," she said very distinctly, amazed her voice did not shake, "Would you please present this gentleman to me?"

"I am afraid I am unable to do so." Evrett was gripping his cane so hard that she could see every vein on the back of his hand.

The red-headed stranger spoke, in a flat voice which she almost did not recognize as his. "I'll tell her, Evrett. No need to do my dirty work for me." He looked straight at her, his eyes unreadable now. "His lordship does not claim acquaintance with kidnappers and traitors."

It was as though the terrible weight which had been lurking in her stomach all day was suddenly pressing remorselessly on every organ in her body. Bile rose in her throat; she thought she might be sick, and she covered her mouth with her hand. For a month, preoccupied with her own secret, she had avoided thinking about his: why was he in exile? What had he done? And now he was flaying himself in front of her, laying it out, bare and bloody, whether she wanted to know or not.

"I do not believe you." The words emerged automatically. She had lowered her hand to her chest, where it vibrated with the harsh rhythm of her heartbeat.

"Allow me to be more precise." His eyes glittered. "I was courting an heiress, and my closest friend was suing for her hand as well. I therefore arranged for this friend to be abducted in the company of another young lady and locked away in a remote hut overnight, so that he would be obliged to marry her."

"Did he?" There was a horrible fascination to this conversation; she could not help herself.

"Yes."

Nathanson made a gesture of protest, and was silenced by a warning glance.

"Also, I held a post as chief aide to an officer who supervised military intelligence for Lord Wellington. When I found myself in need of funds, I sold information about our courier routes to the French." He added brutally, "Perhaps my patrons were the same French spies who contrived the ambush which killed your brother."

The sheer cruelty of it stung her, woke her reason, nourished her doubts. "It makes no sense!" she cried wildly. "If you sold secrets to the French, then why have they put a price on your head? Why is that man Meillet pursuing you?"

"Is it not obvious?" He gave an odd little smile. "Eventually, I betrayed them, too. But I forget myself: we have not been introduced. Your servant, ma'am."

And then, with a mocking bow, he was gone, his light stride carrying him quickly through a crowd of workmen and around the corner of the building. After a stupefied moment, Nathanson gave a strangled curse and hurried off after him.

"I asked the wrong question," Elizabeth said numbly. Evrett had taken her arm, but she was not aware of it. "I only had the one chance, and I asked the wrong question. I should have asked why Nathanson is still his friend, and instead I asked about the French."

Evrett, who knew Nathanson well, found he was beginning to wonder the same thing. He was guiding her gently back across the square, where Lady Evrett had been hovering, fretting at the double impropriety: that she herself should be standing unaccompanied on a public street, and that a young lady in her charge had run off to speak with a strange man.

"You would think," he said, more to himself than to Elizabeth, "that if he were everything he says he is, he would have no scruples about marrying you."

That brought her up short. She stopped, right in front of an impatient wagoner. "But he is already married," she said, bewildered. "I saw the portraits in his strongbox. He has a wife and a little girl."

Now he remembered; Southey had mentioned she was under this misapprehension. In his uncertain new mood, he elected to tell her the truth. "He is not mar-

ried. I suspect the portraits are of his mother and sister.
I believe the sister is much younger than he is."

"He let me think—" She broke off. "What does it
matter, after all?"

The wagoner was ostentatiously holding in his horse,
and Evrett urged her forward again.

Lady Evrett, seeing Elizabeth's expression, did not
ask for any explanation of the sudden dash across the
marketplace. Instead she began a long disquisition on
various remedies for the headache as they resumed their
progress towards the chemist's.

Nathanson came up with Southey in front of the
Church of St. Peter. "Congratulations," he said acidly.
"I consider myself an expert in deception and dissimula-
tion, but I have never seen anyone tell the truth as falsely
as you just did."

Southey shook off the arm which had been placed
on his and stared grimly at his friend. "What do you
propose, Nathanson? Am I to whine and grovel and
make my loathsome excuses? And then offer her my
mortgaged estates?"

"As to that—" His quarry started to move away again.
"Damn you, stand still for a moment!" he shouted.
Nathanson never swore, at least not in English.

Southey swung around, shocked.

"I've been looking for you for two hours, and I'm
not about to let you go without telling you what I came
to say."

"What is it, then?" asked Southey impatiently. He
began to walk slowly towards the river, and Nathanson
fell into step beside him.

"I've had a letter from Drayton. He asked my uncle
to look into the mortgages on your estate."

"And why is your sister's husband concerning himself
with my debts?"

Nathanson lost his temper again. "Because, you stubborn cloth-head, he is your friend! Because he knew there was something fishy about those mortgages and that my uncle would be able to find out what it was! And he did. Those mortgages are not worth the paper they are written on. Your mother should be able to recover at least part of the estate within a few months."

"You are roasting me." He had stopped, astounded.

"I am perfectly serious." Nathanson saw that Southey was deeply shaken. "Surely you will admit my uncle is not likely to be wrong on such a matter."

No, Eli Roth, the most powerful banker in England, was not likely to be mistaken in a case involving loan contracts. "I do not understand," said Southey finally.

"Did it never occur to you to wonder how your father was able to break the entail so that he could borrow against your portion of the estate?"

Southey made an impatient gesture. "He hired some scoundrelly solicitors; they concocted something. What of it?"

His friend sighed. No wonder his uncles were so wealthy, if landowners were this ignorant about legal and financial matters. "South, they cannot simply concoct something. There must be a basis in law for removing the restrictions created by the entail. Your father had no title, so the entail did not extend to other surviving males in the paternal line, but the core of the estate was set aside for you, as the heir. The entail could only be broken if there was no direct male issue."

"I still do not understand."

Patiently, Nathanson explained. "The solicitors needed to prove that there had never been a male heir in the direct line, or that said heir had predeceased your father, or that said heir was legally incompetent. In any of these cases, the entail ceased to exist, and your father would have access to the entire estate."

"Very well; he must have done one of those things. You know as well as I do that before he died he had notes on every acre of the damn thing."

"The notes are not legal; that is what I am trying to tell you. He had you declared incompetent. It was a fraudulent declaration. The estate was not his to borrow against. It reverts automatically to you."

"I'm dead," Southey reminded him. "Or attainted, which is legally the same thing."

"In either case, the estates would go to your heir. Which, failing a valid will and testament prepared on your behalf, would be your mother, as trustee for your sister. The crown has not confiscated the property of convicted traitors for twenty years now."

"It does not signify," said Southey stubbornly. "Bassington holds most of the notes. I would feel bound in honor to repay him even if the mortgages are not legally valid."

"My uncle has purchased the notes. And no, do not tell me you will repay my uncle. He has no intention of losing money on this affair. Drayton writes that he expects a man named Sorell to take them off his hands at face value."

Southey frowned. The name was vaguely familiar.

"Sorell," Nathanson amplified, "is the senior partner in the firm of Sorell, Sorell and Fawcett. The firm in Salisbury which assisted your father in perpetrating a fraud against the Crown. The firm whose junior partner, Mr. Fabian Sorell, is hoping to stand for parliament in the next election."

There was silence while Southey digested this information. "You are trying to tell me that I am not bankrupt—or rather, since I do not exist, that my mother and sister are no longer destitute?"

"Correct."

"Well." A mocking smile lit the freckled face. "In that case, I need only worry about the treason and the kidnapping. A mere bagatelle, don't you agree?"

* * *

It was a silent and preoccupied party which sat in the barouche on the return trip to Baden. Elizabeth was recalling, over and over again, the nightmarish meeting with the man she had thought so well-known to her: the dreadful accusations, the bitter twist of the fine mouth, the oddly expressionless voice. Evrett, too, was pondering what he had heard and trying desperately to recall what he knew of the circumstances preceding Southey's departure from England. And Lady Evrett, glancing back and forth from one young face to the other, was wondering if they would indeed be leaving Baden on Tuesday. The double fees she had paid to the dressmaker to have the gowns ready Monday were beginning to seem very extravagant indeed.

No one in the barouche was paying much attention to the other vehicles and pedestrians they passed as they made their way through the southern sections of the city. And in any case, even had they been looking, it is unlikely they could have distinguished the two men who stood in the shadowed archway of an inn yard and watched them as they went by. One was an older man, clean-shaven, with prominent eyes, slouched against the wooden gate without much thought for the dirt he was acquiring on the shoulder of his frock coat. The other was tall and immaculately dressed, with the perfect carriage of a military man of many years standing.

"By God, it's my niece!" exclaimed the shorter man, his bushy eyebrows shooting up in surprise as his glance fell on the occupants of the open-roofed carriage. His companion was staring intently at Elizabeth as well, and he drew in his breath as the late afternoon light gilded her face beneath her new bonnet.

"You interest me extremely, Stourhead," he said. "Your niece, you say? Who are her companions?"

"Don't know," admitted Elizabeth's uncle. "Toffs. Some relations of her mother, most likely. My late wife's family consider themselves above my touch. Never met any of them."

The tall man turned to a groom who was leading a saddled horse into the stable. "Is that one of your horses?" he asked in German.

"*Ja, mein Herr.*"

"Reasonably fresh?"

"Ridden only half a stage, *mein Herr.*"

A very large coin appeared before the groom's eyes. "Follow that carriage," said the tall man. "Discreetly. Another of these when you return and tell me where they go and who they are."

"*Sofort, Excellenz!*" gasped the boy, and was up on the horse in an instant.

"Not sure I should tangle with the Chapmans," said Stourhead uneasily. "They haven't much family feeling where I am concerned. No need to track the girl down on my account, is what I am trying to say." It had taken some persuasion to convince him to return to Vienna, and he did not feel very secure, even denuded of his mustaches.

"Oh, it is not on your account, not at all," said the tall man. "Just a bit of insurance, as it were. In case my arrangement with the countess is not satisfactory."

Nineteen

Yet another meeting at dawn. Nathanson scowled. He was not an early riser. At least she had appeared on Tuesday—very late and flitting into the arbor only long enough to tell him she could not stay. On Thursday, they had met at the Prater, on horseback. She was late again, but they had gone for a brief ride.

Now it was Saturday, and he had an appointment with the Prussians at eight. If she was not on time, he would simply leave. He looked at his watch. It was past six; she was already late. He amended his resolution and decided to leave at half past the hour. The half-hour came and went.

The morning was misty. It was not easy to scan the whole garden, as it had been the first two times. He had heard faint movements on the carriage path, but had seen no riders or vehicles. Keeping an eye on the rose garden, he walked out into the center of the park and stood, turning slowly so he could survey all the paths which radiated out from the fountain. It burbled gently behind him.

He walked at last around to the back of the fountain

and surveyed the northern edges of the green rectangle. Nothing, no one. It was getting on towards seven. He would go. Wearily he headed back to the little bench under the arbor, where he had left his hat and gloves.

"Captain!" He heard her voice, calling softly, and at first could not determine where the sound had come from. Then he spotted her. She was standing by the hedge, wearing some kind of green loose cloak, very difficult to see against the leaves behind her. The hood had fallen back from her hair, and little drops of mist were glittering in the curls. As he walked over to meet her, he realized for the first time that there was a small wooden gate in the hedge just before it entered the little corner where she had set the rendezvous. Vines and branches hung down over the gate on both sides; she had pulled them aside to open it and was still holding some in one gloved hand. Behind her on the carriage path was a low-slung, dilapidated coach. One door stood open.

She drew back to let him through the gate, and as he ducked under the hedge he saw, to his astonishment, that she had been crying.

"What is it?" he asked in alarm, instantly forgiving her all the missed appointments and tardy, contemptuous appearances.

She looked terrified.

He recalled her note: *I am frightened. They are watching me.* Her brother must have dragged her into one of his vicious schemes. When she did not answer at first, he asked more urgently, "Can you not tell me? What is wrong?"

He saw the men reflected in her eyes before he heard the movement behind him. At once he spun, ducking as he turned and leading with his shoulder, as he had been taught. But it was too late.

A stifling and foul-smelling darkness descended over his head; something heavy landed solidly at the base of his neck. When he struggled under the cloth and kicked out with one leg, a second, vicious blow caught him on the side of the head. He was unconscious when they put him in the carriage.

Cold water, full in the face, woke him. He was in a chair, his arms tied behind him, his feet lashed to the legs.

A brutish young man, stout and well-muscled, was standing over him, holding an empty pitcher. Recognition was immediate and chilling: Jean-Luc. Behind the young Frenchman, a blond man with cold gray eyes sat on a tapestry-covered sofa, facing him, his polished boots stretched lazily out on the parquet floor. He had never seen him up close, but he knew it was Meillet. Where Jean-Luc was, his master was also.

He raised his head further, twisting to look around, although movement was painful. It was a beautiful room, fitted up as a library. The walls were lined with mahogany bookcases, and mahogany pilasters continued up to the high ceiling from the top of the shelves. The ceiling itself was carved into a representation of the four winds, one in each corner, with a central boss supporting a brass chandelier, which looked vaguely familiar. All the curtains were drawn, and the chandelier had been lit. The floor in the center of the room was bare, but elsewhere Indian rugs lay scattered over the polished wood. In a far corner he glimpsed something rolled up and leaning against the wall—presumably the rug which had been under his chair, removed to protect it from the water.

"Nicer than the boathouse in Sangatte, don't you agree, Captain?" The blond man had risen and sauntered over to stand behind Jean-Luc.

"Monsieur Meillet," Nathanson acknowledged wearily. "I gather you are bored with your attempts on my friend Southey. You do understand that in my case you are violating the terms of the treaty?"

Meillet shrugged. "A regrettable error, alas. I will have had no idea that you were attached to the Prussian command. My subordinate here"—he gestured at Jean-Luc—"recognized you as the English spy who ran afoul of our coastal patrols earlier this year. And being both thick-witted and overzealous, he attacked you before we discovered your credentials. By the time you make your complaint, we will be long gone, in any case."

Cautious hope stirred in Nathanson. "You are planning to release me?" he said warily.

"Eventually. On terms."

"What terms?"

"I want to know where your father is." Meillet's eyes gleamed with a sudden fierce hunger.

Nathanson shifted in the chair. Hope was receding again. "I do not know where he is," he said bitterly. "Although I don't expect you will believe me."

"Don't play games with me," said Meillet, coming so close to the chair that Nathanson could feel the heat from his body. He looked down at his captive, the gray eyes menacing. "His servant, the man called Rodrigo, has been seen here twice in the last month. First Southey arrives, then Rodrigo, then you, and you expect me to believe your father is not nearby?"

"If you have seen Rodrigo twice, that is twice more than I have."

Meillet turned to Jean-Luc. "Go down to the cellar and see what you can find to assist the captain's memory. The brother told me he keeps part of his collection here." Jean-Luc gave an unpleasant little smile and disappeared. Meillet returned to his sofa, his eyes fixed on the man sitting opposite him, a brooding impatience on his face.

Feeling gently with his thumbs, Nathanson tried to discern what sort of knot had been used to tie his hands behind the chair. Whoever it was, they had done a good job. The knots were off to the side, far out of reach. He slumped back and considered the situation. It did not look promising. Silvio would know something was wrong when he did not appear for his appointment at eight, but it seemed unlikely anyone could find him here. He had not told his valet about his dawn appointments.

This is your own fault, he thought. *You broke all the rules. Never go to a meeting without leaving word of your destination with Silvio. Never go through a door without guarding against attack from someone behind it. Never disregard unusual noises.* The carriage had pulled up behind the hedge. He had heard it, but because it was too low to be visible, he had dismissed it. Still, self-recrimination would not help. He forced himself to let it go. Could he make up something, tell Meillet his father was in Prague, for example? But he would want specifics, and there was a frightening possibility that any plausible location Nathanson could produce might, in fact, be the real thing. Even if he did decide to fabricate something, he would have to let Jean-Luc hurt him for a while before Meillet would accept the false answer.

There was a noise behind him, of a door opening. There must be two doors, then; the one Jean-Luc had used was off to his left. To his surprise, Meillet rose and bowed to the new arrival. Nathanson could hear a light step behind his chair.

"Madame," Meillet said courteously. The countess walked around to where the Frenchman was standing. She did not greet him, or acknowledge his bow, but simply looked at Nathanson, her lips parted slightly in apprehension, her eyes anxious as she took in the ropes binding his arms and legs. She was dressed for riding; he recognized the blue habit and the silver-handled riding crop.

Anguish flooded him, and he jerked forward so hard in the chair that it nearly toppled over. "For God's sake, Meillet!" he pleaded, his composure gone. "Your quarrel is with me, not her. She has nothing to do with this. There is no reason to involve her. Let her go; she'll say nothing, I swear it."

Meillet raised one eyebrow.

"You dog, I knew you were low," said Nathanson, breathing hard, "but I thought even you would draw the line at abducting innocent women. Her brother is a French sympathizer, for heaven's sake. Are you mad?"

"I fear you are under a misapprehension, Captain." Meillet looked amused. "The lady is very much involved. This is her brother's house. She has been most helpful in arranging your visit here."

It was true. Before Meillet had even finished speaking, he had realized where he was. This was the little house in Hietzing—hers, and apparently her brother's as well. The chandelier was the twin of the one in the entrance hall. The rolled-up cloth in the corner was not cloth, it was the tiger-skin. She and Meillet had planned this perfectly, had even held rehearsals to see how long he would wait, to accustom Silvio to finding him gone in the mornings. His eyes sought hers, and she turned away, unable to meet his gaze. She looked guilty, frightened, and very, very young.

"You sold me to this—this thing?" he asked scornfully, jerking his chin at Meillet.

Her chin lifted. "I did not sell you. You are a Jew, a spy, an enemy of my country. It was my duty to assist Monsieur Meillet."

"Could you not have assisted him without making fools of both of us in the process? Why did you need to invite me riding? To have me here for supper? Surely this plan of Meillet's did not require seven meetings between us." He added savagely, "You are playing very deep, Madame la Comtesse. Can you cover your stake?"

Meillet, he noted with satisfaction, was clearly unaware of the rides and the dinner, and was looking uneasy.

Jean-Luc returned through the main door, carrying a large tin washtub with something black in the middle of it. He set it down on the floor in front of Nathanson with a grunt. "You were right, monsieur," he said to

Meillet. "There were quite a few instruments in the cellar, but most of them are too big to bring up here, and I thought you would prefer to remain in this room."

The countess was staring in horror at the lump in the washtub. Jean-Luc misinterpreted her dismay. "Do not worry, Madame," he said earnestly. "His foot will be in the tub. I will not let any blood get on the floor. Monsieur Meillet is most particular about this sort of thing."

Now Nathanson realized what the object in the tub was. It was a medieval device called *la botte d'enfer*, an iron boot, very large, and hinged to open at the front. Inside, he knew, were rows of metal spikes, which would be slowly driven into the ankle and foot of the victim as the boot was winched closed. His ankle and foot, he reminded himself.

He raised his eyes to the countess's face. It had gone completely white. "I would advise you to leave," he said gently. Some part of him wondered why he felt sorry for her. Surely he ought to be feeling sorry for himself.

She looked desperately at Meillet, at him, back at Meillet. Then, with a choking sound, she turned and ran from the room.

They heard a door slam and her voice shouting something, nearly screaming, at the back of the house. Then a man's voice answering, and, after an interval, the rapid thud of hoofbeats.

It was an ugly room, with a stained ceiling which reminded him of the leaky spot in the loft. The bed had a trough in the middle which gave him nightmares of being buried alive when he did manage to fall asleep, which was seldom. Earlier this morning, he had forced himself to get up, shave, and put on some clothes, but then he had lain back down on the bed. Sometime later today he should go back over to Frau Renner's; there was no point in hiding any longer. He might as well make it easy for Meillet to find him.

There was a noise on the stairs. Someone was ascending rapidly, almost running. He did not move. All the visitors were for the other attic room, a much larger one, which housed two ladies who entertained a number of different gentlemen at some rather surprising hours. Apparently the morning was as good a time as any.

Now the steps had stopped at his door, and there was a sharp knock. He did not answer. The man would find the right room quickly enough.

There was an exclamation from the hall. A small knife blade appeared under the latch of the door and lifted it, and a very agitated black-haired man burst into the room.

"Silvio!" Southey sat up, heaved himself out of bed, and went over to the doorway, where the Italian servant was trying to recover his breath. "What is it? Has something happened to the captain?"

"He has vanished, sir." Nathanson's valet took another gulp of air. "He left before dawn again, and he has not come back. He had a meeting at eight with some Prussian officers, and he was nowhere to be found."

"Do you think he was engaged in a duel and has been wounded?" Southey was concerned. It was most unlike Nathanson to be late for an appointment, especially an official appointment.

Silvio shook his head. "He did not take his rapiers, or the dueling pistols. Only his short sword. And he always tells me when it is a duel. He has been going out quite early several mornings a week, but until today he has returned well before eight."

"Do you have any notion where he has been going in the mornings?"

Reluctantly, the servant held out a crumpled sheet of paper. "I found this in the pocket of his jacket the other day, sir. Do you recognize the writing?" Southey did. The note was in French, and one phrase caught his eye:

Pardonnez-moi. It was just as Elizabeth had said: the z's were very distinctive.

"Go on down; I'll join you in a minute," he said as he started pulling things out from the valise at the foot of the lumpy bed. He tugged on his boots, and, after a moment's thought, put on a clean shirt and his best jacket. From under the mattress he extracted a sword belt, a sword, and a pistol. The pistol went into his pocket, and he belted on the steel as he clattered down the stairs. The sword would look ridiculous with his jacket, but he felt defenseless without it; he had always hated guns.

Silvio was waiting on the first landing. Without stopping to see if the Italian was coming with him, he kept on going and headed out the door and onto the street.

Silvio followed hastily. "Where are we going?" he asked, nearly jogging in an effort to stay up with Southey's determined strides.

"The Hofburg," said Southey curtly. "I believe I will have a word with the Countess of Brieg."

They reached the palace a scant quarter hour later, but the gates were still shut, and the guard was not inclined to bestir himself to carry messages for a fencing master and his servant. Was the countess in residence? Or out at Schonbrunn?

The guard could not take it upon himself to answer such an inquiry, nor to speculate about where the noble lady might be.

Southey swore under his breath. He knew the countess had a house somewhere outside the city; he remembered that much about the dinner invitation that Elizabeth had copied, but he had forgotten the name of the village.

"Let's go back to your hotel," he said despondently to Silvio. "Perhaps he has returned by now." Ten minutes later, they were standing in an empty suite, and Southey was beginning to be very perturbed. He searched for a note, for anything Nathanson might have left to indicate where he was going, and found nothing. "What was he wearing this morning?" he demanded.

The valet thought for a moment. "His uniform. He must have decided he might not have time to change before meeting with the Prussians."

Southey shook his head. "That does not help, then. Has he been using a particular horse? Did you check in the stables? Had he taken one out this morning?"

Silvio had already thought of this. No horse had been requested.

"I know he is with that dreadful woman," muttered Southey. "If only I knew where her house was." He closed his eyes, picturing her suite in the palace, hoping something he could remember would give him a clue—perhaps one of the letters had been directed to her there. His eyes popped open, and he started for the door, dragging a bewildered Silvio with him.

"Now what?" panted the valet, breaking into a run this time as Southey set off towards the Spielergasse.

"I thought of someone who can help us. He might even be willing to do it. But he is a very early riser; we must find him before he leaves for the day."

"That is the house," said Naegel softly, pointing to a stucco building at the foot of the hill. It did not look very imposing: a small, ornate villa, with a circular drive in front and stables and outbuildings on the side facing the hill. The garden in back had a wall, but there was no wall at the bottom of the hill, nor on the side with the drive.

"Go and see if you can find out anything without being seen," Southey told Silvio. The smaller man slid down the hillside and then disappeared into the shrubs next to the stables. After what seemed to Southey and Naegel like a very long time, he reappeared.

"He is there, I am sure of it." The Italian's face was streaked with dirt. "Some time ago, a carriage arrived, and an unconscious man was carried into the house. Then, about an hour ago, the countess came out and rode off in a great hurry, with just one groom. There is one room on the east side with all the curtains drawn; all the other rooms are open and empty. In the stable there are two grooms, one French, one Austrian—well, there were." He raised an eyebrow and shrugged. "They are sleeping now. In the house, two men guarding the front door: one inside, one outside. One man at the back. Two maids and a cook in the kitchen. A gardener and a gardener's boy."

"I thought I told you not to be seen," said Southey, exasperated.

"It was only the grooms," Silvio protested. "And they will not be talking for a bit. I gagged them and tied them up."

"Well, we will have to go in right away, now, before anyone stumbles onto them." Southey turned to Naegel. "I am in your debt. It was very generous of you to guide us. We could have found it ourselves, but it would have taken longer."

The Austrian's face hardened. "You do not suppose I will let you go in there without me?"

Southey was nonplussed. Had Naegel brought them all this way only to interfere at this point?

"Monsieur Southey," Naegel said, very slowly, emphasizing each word. "I am a captain in the Imperial Cavalry. An officer attached to one of our allies has been kidnapped, possibly killed, by a foreign *provocateur* whose government is likely to be at war with us in a matter of days. And this criminal is occupying the home of a lady-in-waiting to the Princess Maria Louisa."

"My apologies." Southey flushed. "I was grateful you were willing even to give us the location of the house. I thought Werzel was a friend of yours."

"No, merely an acquaintance," said Naegel. "And possibly not even that, after the events of the last few weeks. Shall I take the man at the back? The room with the curtains drawn is the library, it has two doors, one from the front hall, the other from the drawing room on the south. The maids and cook will give us no trouble, nor will the gardener. They are old family servants who are likely as appalled as I am at what is happening. I can go through the kitchen.''

Southey nodded. "Silvio and I will climb in the windows on the west side and take the guard in the front hall. There is no way to approach the man outside the front door without being seen from quite a long ways off, and I am inclined to ignore him unless he hears us and comes in to interfere. If either guard makes any noise, we will have to proceed into the library immediately and take our chances. But if we can disable them without creating a disturbance, we will have time to coordinate and rush both doors of the library at once.''

Naegel gave him an odd look. "For a fencing master, you are rather well-informed on the subject of breaking into villas guarded by hired bullies.''

"I am not a fencing master," said Southey. He was tired of lying. "I am a failed spy. Let us hope this is not one of my failures.''

Twenty

Southey, who measured his own skills against those of Nathanson and his father, had always thought himself rather clumsy and slow. In comparison to Naegel, however, he was a master of stealth. The Austrian clearly had no notion whatsoever of how to approach a sentry and take him by surprise. He clattered up the stairs from the kitchen, making so much noise that Southey hastily abandoned the man in the front hall to Silvio and rushed towards the back of the house, hoping at least to prevent Naegel from getting a knife in his throat.

The bungled attack proved a blessing in disguise, as it turned out. The French guard, scheming to catch the intruder unawares at the top of the steps, did not raise the alarm, and Southey was able to tackle him from behind before he could call for help.

From the front hall, he heard a soft thud, and prayed Silvio had been equally successful. There had been no shouting, which was promising. The thud might have been audible in the library, though. Gesturing urgently for silence, he let Naegel lead him through the dining room and into a small white-and-gold drawing room.

There were double doors at the other end; he took them at a run. White and gold gave way to dark wood and brass.

Just two of them, he realized, his eyes scanning the room automatically for opponents. Meillet stood frozen, facing him. There was a seated figure lashed to a chair—he could only see the back, but it was clearly Nathanson. The dark head was slumped forward, not a good sign. Jean-Luc was kneeling on the floor, and came to his feet at once, snarling.

Southey ignored him. Drawing his sword as he went, he headed straight for Meillet. The hilt caught on his pocket, which was weighted down with the pistol, and he jerked the gun out and tossed it aside without pausing.

Meillet was reaching into his own pocket for a pistol, but evidently it was not there; as Southey advanced, he grabbed a candlestick from the table and flung it, backing quickly to the sofa, where he snatched up Nathanson's sword.

"We never were able to finish our duel in Sangatte," Southey said softly, his hazel eyes fastened on Meillet's gray ones. Behind him he heard a series of crashes as Naegel tangled with Jean-Luc. Silvio burst through a second door to his left and skidded to a halt as he saw Southey's face. Making a wide detour around the swordfighters, he scuttled over to assist Naegel.

Neither Meillet nor Southey even noticed him. Taking a step forward, the intruder raised his blade, still holding his opponent's gaze with his own. "My arm has healed, as you see. This time I can fight two-handed." Southey stretched out his right arm and opened and closed the crooked fingers to demonstrate.

Pressed back against the sofa, the Frenchman stood at bay, breathing heavily.

"Oh, this is ridiculous," said the younger man suddenly. With five quick passes he disarmed Meillet and slashed open his right shoulder; then, as his disabled opponent instinctively grabbed at the wound, he dropped the sword and backhanded him with his clenched fist as hard as he could, straight across the side of the neck. The blow sent Meillet reeling to the floor. He did not get up.

Silvio and Naegel had rolled the limp body of Jean-Luc under a table and were already at work untying the bound figure in the chair. Nathanson was conscious, but drenched with sweat, his mouth pressed down to a thin, tense line. He could not suppress a low cry as Silvio released the boot.

"Good God," said Southey, horrified, as he took in the bloody tub and the iron-jawed device. "What did they think they were playing at? The Spanish inquisition?"

Naegel was looking distinctly queasy; he averted his eyes as he finished loosening the ropes. Southey squatted down and examined the ankle and foot. They had not bothered to cut away the uniform trousers, which made it difficult to see the damage. There was blood everywhere.

"It's not as bad as it looks," Nathanson said faintly. "The spikes—this thing is quite old. A lot of them gave way. I could feel it."

"Plenty more went in," said his friend, grimly assessing the bloodstains on the shredded green cloth. "Can you stand?" Silvio and Naegel supported him, but after two attempts, Nathanson gave up.

"Sorry," he gasped.

Southey turned to Silvio. "Is the coach still here, the one the grooms mentioned?" The little man nodded. "Hitch up some horses and bring it round front. Go and fetch the ones we rode, if you have to, although I don't know if they have been trained to harness. Watch out for that last guard, the one outside. Perhaps you should go with him, Naegel." Looking relieved to have an excuse to leave the room, the Austrian hurried out towards the stables.

At the far end of the room, Meillet was stirring.

Southey strode over and dropped to his knees beside the blond head, pulling off his own neckcloth. The gray eyes were open, and widened in resentment and surprise as he realized what Southey was doing. "Leave me be, damn you," he said weakly in French. Without replying, Southey pressed his makeshift pad over the wound. Meillet gave an involuntary hiss of pain. With an unfathomable glance straight up into his enemy's face, he closed his eyes again.

Nathanson, flexing his hands to restore the circulation, peered groggily over across the room. "What are you doing?" he asked after a few minutes, his voice a bit stronger now.

"Bandaging his shoulder," said Southey impatiently. "Or do you think I should let him lie here and bleed to death?"

"As a matter of fact, yes, I do. Or at least you should bandage me first." This last was said with some indignation.

Without looking up from his task, Southey commented: "I am no medical man, James, but it seems risky to me to bandage those holes until they are cleaned properly and painted with basilicum. That boot looks to me like a recipe for gangrene or lockjaw."

"I still do not understand why you are patching up that monster."

The other man sighed. "Claude Meillet has seen the command he deserved go to an enemy impostor; he bought documents from me and then watched me turn on him; when he tried to act on his suspicions of his false commander, he ended up under arrest in his own quarters because of information supplied by me. For my own part, I think I have done him enough harm. If you want him dead, come over here and do it yourself."

He looked up at Nathanson, expecting an angry response. But the reply was never destined to be heard, because as he glanced over, Southey caught sight of the square shape of Jean-Luc out of the corner of his eye.

He was crawling furtively over to Southey's own pistol, which lay discarded on the floor; snatching it and rising up on one knee, he cocked the trigger and aimed straight across the room at the wounded man in the chair. Naegel, coming back in at that moment, rushed forward desperately, knowing he would not be in time.

Southey was closer. With a running leap, he hurled himself on the Frenchman just as the pistol went off, blocking it with his chest. Jean-Luc subsided to the floor, with Southey crumpled on top of him.

Heedless of his foot, Nathanson pitched himself out of the chair and began crawling in a frenzy of anger and despair towards the two bodies.

"You cheat, you coward!" he shouted furiously, pulling himself along on his hands. "I never should have told you about those mortgages! I knew the only thing that was keeping you from throwing yourself into the Danube was your mission to send money home to your mother! I could have ducked, you know, I'm not paralyzed! Did you think you were my bodyguard, that I was the Holy Roman Emperor?!"

Naegel had arrived first and rolled Southey's body gently over, dragging it off to the side, away from the stunned Jean-Luc. There was a huge black powder stain over the front of his shirt. In appalled fascination, Naegel and Nathanson stared at the dark patch, waiting for the red to begin seeping through. Instead, Southey blinked and sat up, causing the other two to shrink back instinctively, as though a corpse had suddenly climbed out of its coffin.

"It was my pistol, you know," he said, trying to sound calm. But his voice was trembling slightly. "I never have been very handy with guns. Quite frequently I do not load it properly." He looked down at his shirt. "No bullet, it appears. Just wadding and powder."

Nathanson had collapsed completely onto the floor, and lay staring up at the ceiling. "I'm going to kill you one of these days," he said to the chandelier. "Between you and my father, I'll end in Bedlam.'' He propped himself up on one elbow and examined the trail of blood along the floor from the chair. "I take it the carriage is ready?"

Numbly, Naegel nodded.

"Haul me off to Doña Maria's, then. It's just north of here, and my cousin Elena is a reasonable nurse."

It transpired that Doña Maria traveled with her own physician as well two priests and a cook. Dr. Allais was a genial, silver-haired man who accepted the bizarre nature of his patient's injuries quite calmly. While examining each of the eighteen holes, a lengthy and painful process, he even calculated that the boot must have had four rows of six spikes, so that exactly one quarter of the spikes had broken before piercing the trousers.

Nathanson accepted equally calmly the doctor's warning that his ankle was seriously injured, and would never recover its full motion. "Not to mention," the doctor added in his placid voice, "the possibility of severe infection. You may still lose your foot. I am, however, optimistic in that regard. It is a good thing you did not try to stop the bleeding; in the case of these deep, narrow wounds, cleansing by outflow is often the best. I will clean them each now, of course. Would you like some laudanum? It will be a rather unpleasant process, I fear."

"I have no tolerance for pain," said Nathanson promptly. "Dose away to your heart's content, *Monsieur le médecin*." Allais withdrew to mix up the sedative, promising to return in five minutes.

Naegel and Southey, who had finally been admitted to the sickroom, were just in time to hear this last exchange.

"If you have no tolerance for pain," said Southey skeptically, "would you care to explain why you had not told your hosts in that charming library everything they wanted to know before we arrived? I assume, at least, that you had not satisfied their curiosity, since they were still skewering your ankle when we arrived."

"They only asked me two questions." Nathanson gave a bitter smile. "Although they repeated each question many, many times. One: where was my father? And two: why had I been sent to Vienna? Since I did not know, and still do not know, the answer to either of those questions, I was delighted to have my conversation with Jean-Luc interrupted." He looked at Naegel and added stiffly, "I have no idea why you were involved in rescuing me, Rittmeister, but I am very grateful."

The Austrian turned brick red. "I will be reporting this incident to the minister immediately," he said, equally stiff. "Unfortunately, I doubt Monsieur Meillet will be arrested. I think I can promise you, however, that he will be required to leave Vienna."

At this point, Elena, who had gone off to organize nursing supplies, bustled in, accompanied by a wrinkled Spanish maidservant, and attempted to chase the visitors away. "We are going to take all of his clothes off," she announced. "And if you are still here, it will be very embarrassing." She ostentatiously unfolded an enormous nightshirt and laid it out on the bed. Naegel took the hint and left, but Southey merely withdrew to the door and propped himself there against the wall.

"It will be embarrassing even if they are not!" protested her cousin. "Why must you strip me naked when my injuries are confined to my foot?"

"First of all, they are not confined to your foot," snapped Elena, pressing down with her forefinger on a large bruise which was visible on his jaw. He winced. "And besides, you are likely to develop a fever. If you are going to be an uncooperative patient, James, I will ask Dr. Allais to cup you."

"Been cupped plenty already, if you ask me," muttered Nathanson, looking at the blood-spattered sheets under his leg.

Elena's glance followed his. "What did the doctor

say? About your injury?" This was the information Southey had waited to discover, and he listened intently to the answer.

"He said I would probably never walk normally again." Nathanson used precisely the same unemotional tone the doctor had used in speaking to him.

"Oh, James!" Elena's eyes filled with tears. Behind her, Southey ground out a muttered oath.

Nathanson looked across the room at the white face of his friend. "It could have been much worse, South. Would have been, had you and Naegel and Silvio not appeared."

Southey did not respond for a moment. In his mind's eye he was seeing a cliff top in Spain, with a dark-haired figure at its edge. Nathanson had jumped across a small chasm to a spire opposite, and was looking down, laughing, at the earthbound figure of his companion far below. That leap, the graceful body suspended in the early morning sky, was imprinted on Southey's memory.

And now, he thought, *I suppose I can promise Naegel his sister is safe from any future dances with Captain Nathanson.*

"Don't thank me, for God's sake," he said hoarsely. "Would Meillet have pursued you so obsessively had I not duped and betrayed him? Why does everyone who comes near me end up with holes in them? You, Drayton, Miss DeQuincy?"

"Have you forgotten that I am my father's son, an ample reason for Meillet's interest in me? Or that I ignored warnings from four different people, including you, about the Countess of Brieg?" Nathanson pushed himself up on his elbows and glared at the man in the doorway. "You cannot seriously be proposing to blame yourself for this affair?"

But Southey had left, brushing past the doctor on his way out.

Frowning, Nathanson turned to Allais. "How long will I sleep if I drink that?" he asked, eyeing the vial in the physician's hand.

"Six to eight hours. It is difficult to say, precisely; some are affected much more strongly than others."

"I shall have to do without, then." He turned to Elena. "Could you ask Silvio to ride over to Baden and find Lord Evrett? I need to speak with him urgently. I must hope they did not leave today."

It had taken nearly an hour to clean and bandage his foot, an extremely long hour during which Nathanson had frequently regretted his decision to forego the laudanum. He had been reduced to asking Elena to count the punctures for him as each one was cleaned, so that he could at least have some illusion that the doctor was making progress.

Once Allais had gone, his leg had started to throb with a pulsing ache so forceful he almost expected the bedclothes over the bandages to tremble. For another two hours he had lain there, keeping his face turned away from the beckoning vial of laudanum, calculating over and over again how long it would take to get to Baden and back.

As a result, Evrett found a very irritable and impatient Nathanson waiting for him in the corner bedroom of the massive stone house. Silvio had told him something of what had happened, but he was still taken aback by the drawn face and glittering eyes which greeted him as he came in hesitantly behind the valet.

"Sit down and stop staring at me," snapped Nathanson. "You'd think you had never seen an injured man before."

Evrett dropped into a chair which Silvio had tugged over to the bedside. "Silvio said—what he told me—they *tortured* you? With some sort of iron clamp?"

"A hollow boot, with spikes in it. Fourteenth century, I would guess. An heirloom."

"You are an English officer," said Evrett incredulously. "In uniform. I can't believe this. You remember how it was in Portugal, Nathanson! We used to tell jokes across the picket lines! When our fellows were captured, the French officers would take their paroles and then they would all go hunting for rabbits. This—this is barbaric! I cannot believe Napoleon or his marshals would countenance it.''

''In their eyes, I am a spy, so my uniform does not protect me,'' said Nathanson moodily. ''And the *Sûreté* is not part of the army. In any case, Meillet is a law unto himself.'' His eye fell on the laudanum and he sighed. ''I did not ask you here to fuss over me, though. I thought you would have had enough of that with your mother. Did Silvio tell you Southey was there?''

Evrett leaned back against the wooden bars of his chair. ''Yes. I confess, I do not understand it. Ever since that meeting in front of the guildhall yesterday, I have been wondering why you still associate with him. You have always been unpredictable, and I am surprised you were not cashiered the way you defied orders sometimes when you were still with the regiment, but I would have sworn you would never cry friends with an avowed traitor. And now Silvio tells me that he not only organized this rescue party, but threw himself in front of a pistol which was aimed at you.''

''He claims that since it was his gun, he knew there was a good chance it would misfire. And I do not believe him.'' The injured man shifted restlessly under the bedclothes. ''Southey is the reason I asked you to come here. I gave him my word I would not say anything to Miss DeQuincy, and I suspect I may be violating the spirit of that promise in telling you, but I will leave it to your judgment whether to tell her the truth or not.'' He raised his eyes to his friend's face. ''This will put you in a rather difficult situation; I am sorry for it. But I cannot simply watch him destroy himself like this. That litany of self-abuse he favored you with yesterday was grossly misleading.''

''Do you mean to say that he is not, in fact, a traitor?

Why would he accuse himself of something like that, if it were not true?" Evrett was bewildered.

"He believes it to be true. He did sell information to the French. Most of it was false, painstakingly cobbled together to be plausible. There were some real items—there had to be—but it was an ingenious and superbly crafted mix. And as it happened, it was a godsend for my father, who needed reports from England to maintain his pose as a French intelligence commander. But Southey did not know that at the time; he played this game without any authorization from Whitehall, because he needed money desperately. His father had mortgaged every acre of land the family owned, and when he died last year, South found himself facing debtor's prison, with a mother and a young sister to support."

He struggled up higher on the pillows so that he could see the other man without turning his head. "I *know* he is not guilty of treason, because when Drayton and I turned ourselves in for trying to help him leave the country, his own commanding officer told me so. And Whitehall itself faked his death and sent him to Vienna to keep an eye on affairs here. Even if you doubt my opinion, you surely cannot think two senior colonels would be accepting reports from a man they believed to be a traitor? Or that they would have let such a person walk out of the Horse Guards alive once he did eventually learn that my father was masquerading as the chief of the *Sûreté* in Lille?"

The other man was struggling to make sense of what he was hearing. "Is that why you and Drayton were arrested?" he asked. "Because you attempted to help him flee?"

"It was more than an attempt, I suppose. We put him on a boat; Drayton drugged him." He glanced wistfully over at the little vial. "But when he woke up he forced the captain to turn back and then surrendered himself in Dover. The whole affair was absurd. At one point three out of the five junior officers in the courier service had reported themselves as traitors."

"And the kidnapping?"

"Equally absurd. Drayton and Southey were both courting Miranda Waite. She and her mother came down to visit the Barretts, and Drayton's sister was hoping to match them up. My sister Rachel, however, was also visiting the Barretts, under an assumed name"— that phrase produced a chuckle from Evrett—"yes, I know, a repulsive family habit. In any case, Drayton's sister claims anyone could see within five minutes that her brother was fascinated with Rachel. Southey was just hastening the inevitable."

"You cannot imagine I would condone plotting something like that against one's oldest friend, even if, as you say, the eventual outcome was a foregone conclusion?" Evrett's face was flushed with indignation.

"I didn't say he was a saint," retorted Nathanson. "He was a desperate man in a dreadful situation, and he took some rather ugly measures. If Drayton has forgiven him, who am I to hold a grudge?" His visitor did not appear to be swayed by this argument. Nathanson played his trump card. "You have not asked about his final claim, that he betrayed the French. Are you not curious as to why they have posted a reward of two thousand florins for his person? It is exceeded only by the reward for my father."

"Very well," said Evrett grudgingly.

"He rescued my sister. The French had captured her and were holding her in a little boathouse near Calais, and South managed to smuggle her out in his clothing. But of course, in order to get my sister out, he had to take her place. So he did. By the time Drayton and I got back there and hauled him out, Meillet's thugs had broken half the bones in his right hand and arm. When we arrived, in fact, Meillet was forcing him to fight a duel one-handed, with the broken arm strapped to his body." He shuddered. "That man is a snake."

His visitor sat in silence for a minute. "Why are you telling me all this?" he said at last.

"Because I did not think you would want to propose to Miss DeQuincy again without knowing the truth. Because if someone does not convince him he is not a traitor, he will step in front of another pistol. Now that he knows he is not needed to support his family, he considers himself *de trop* and is looking for the nearest exit. Drayton and my uncle discovered that the mortgages his father had signed were nearly all invalid, and I was fool enough to tell him his mother and sister would have the income from the estates back within a few months."

"The mortgages covered the entailed portion?" asked Evrett, who had a much better understanding of the law than Southey.

Nathanson nodded. "His father had him declared incompetent to break the entail. Presumably they hired some redheaded actor to pretend to be feeble-minded at the competency hearing. My uncle has the situation well in hand now, though. And the notes are only fifteen months old, most of them; the estate has not lost much in interest payments."

"He was declared incompetent fifteen months ago? That is impossible. He already held his commission at that point."

It was Nathanson's turn to be puzzled. "What does that have to say to the matter?"

"A soldier on active duty cannot be declared legally incompetent without consulting his commanding officer. The hearing would not have been able to proceed without proof that your father's attorneys had notified Southey's colonel. And the determination of the hearing would then have been forwarded to Whitehall also. A declaration of incompetency results in the immediate revocation of an officer's commission. Who was his colonel?"

"Colonel White," said Nathanson numbly. A horrible suspicion was forming in his mind.

"I suppose they forged something," muttered Evrett.

"Yes, probably they did." Nathanson twisted over and picked up the container of brown liquid. "If you will excuse me, Evrett, I have been waiting for my medicine for what seems like an eternity. Having saddled you with this mess, I now propose to dose myself into oblivion." With a grimace, he drained the little glass.

Evrett hoisted himself out of the chair and absently took away the empty vial, setting it on a chest by the door. "Would you tell her?" he blurted out, his hand on the doorknob.

Nathanson had closed his eyes, but he opened them again. "I don't know," he said slowly. "But I know you will do the right thing. I have great faith in you." His eyes closed again.

"Many thanks for that vote of confidence," said Evrett in acid tones as he opened the door. "As soon as I discover what the right thing is, you may be sure I will do it."

Twenty-one

He told her, of course. Not only that, he sent a stiffly worded note to Southey in care of Frau Renner, informing him that should he wish to call on Miss DeQuincy, he would be received.

The departure from Baden was no longer mentioned. The entire household was in a state of suspension, as though time had stopped. Elizabeth moved around the house like a ghost, not daring to go out lest he call, hoping one minute that he would and the next that he would not.

Sunday passed, and Monday, and she had heard nothing. On Tuesday morning, when Anna brought in her chocolate, she saw the envelope on her breakfast tray and her heart stood still, but in another moment she had recognized the writing. It was her uncle's. She had written:

> *My dearest niece,*
>   *Upon my return to Vienna I was relieved to discover you were well situated with friends and would not trouble*

*you, save that I knew you might think hardly of me did
I not inform you of my illness.*

*For your aunt's sake I hoped you might wish to bid
me farewell and receive from me some small items of hers
as a last gift from both of us. If I frightened or misled
you in any way in those difficult weeks after her death,
I beg you to forgive me; I scarcely know now what I did
or said. It grieves me to imagine you fleeing, alone and
friendless, in a foreign city.*

*Should this letter not find you in time, or should you
choose not to come, I will at least have some peace in the
knowledge that you are safe and happy.*

Shaken, Elizabeth looked at the address at the top of
the letter. It was completely unfamiliar. *He must truly be
ill,* she thought, *to have written so courteously.* In any case,
surely he was no threat to her now. Would it not be
disloyal to her aunt to stay away?

But her suspicions and reservations were unimport-
ant, in any case. She would have seized any excuse, even
one far flimsier than this, to drive into Vienna.

The maid was still in the room, collecting the spent
candles and replacing them with fresh ones. "Anna,"
she called, "do you know where this is?" She indicated
the address.

Blushing, Anna confessed that she did not know her
letters very well. Elizabeth read out the address. Anna
knew it. It was in the Spittelberg, not a genteel neighbor-
hood.

"I must go there at once," said Elizabeth decisively.
"My uncle is there, very ill. Please help me get dressed,
Anna. Could you come with me and show the coachman
how to find the place? If not, I will see if Liesl can go."

"If you wish it, then of course I will go, Fräulein,"
said Anna. Her blue eyes were troubled. "Perhaps we
should ask if one of the footmen could come with us?
Nice young ladies do not visit that street very often."

But Elizabeth was in a hurry. Once she was dressed,

she stopped only to scrawl a note to Lady Evrett. She
did not even take the time to eat anything.

In the back of her mind was the thought that if she
left now, before Lady Evrett or her son had emerged
from their rooms for breakfast, she would not have to
answer any questions—for example, the question of
where she might go with the coach after she had called
on her uncle. As soon as the driver pulled up, she ran
out the door and down the stairs, leaving Anna to follow
with her gloves and bonnet.

"I will put them on as we ride," she said impatiently,
as Anna looked at her reprovingly. But then she had to
smile. At least, she thought, the other servants in Lady
Evrett's establishment were beginning to teach Anna
the rudiments of etiquette.

It was a long ride. The shabby little street was out on
the southern edge of the city, and traffic was very slow
as they made their way across the Vienna river. When
they arrived at last at the address, even Elizabeth was
somewhat dismayed by the dirty windows and peeling
paint on the narrow town house. She glanced again at
the letter to make sure, and then resolutely stepped out
of the coach.

"This does not look like a very nice place, Fräulein
Elizabeth," said Anna in unusually subdued tones. Both
were relieved when a sour-faced woman answered the
door; she did not look friendly, but at least she looked
somewhat respectable. Anna glanced nervously around
as they went in. The only house on this street that she
knew of was a house she had been warned never, ever
to enter, where ladies took off all their clothes and wore
paint even in the daytime.

"I am looking for my uncle, Herr Stourhead,"
announced Elizabeth.

Relief showed on the woman's face. "Ach, Fräulein,
I am very pleased that you have come. He has been

asking for you, very often, and fretting. And it is fortunate you brought your maid; I am all alone here, and
there is no more medicine. Do you suppose she could
go down to the apothecary and fetch more? It is only
down at the corner," she added hastily, seeing Anna
shrink back. "And I must take him up his infusion."

"The coachman can walk the horses down the street
with you, Anna," Elizabeth reassured her. "It will take
only a few minutes."

Reluctantly, Anna left, clutching the empty medicine
bottle and a few coins, and Elizabeth went slowly up the
cramped staircase. The woman had vanished into the
back of the house, presumably going to the kitchen to
finish preparing her brew.

At the top of the stairs she paused. All the doors were
closed. The hall was dirty, and smelled slightly foul.
"Uncle?" she called doubtfully.

"Here, Elizabeth," came a faint reply from behind
the left-hand door. It was his voice, and she pushed the
door open, scolding herself for imagining things. Her
uncle was sitting in a chair by the window, fully dressed.
This struck her as somewhat odd; she had expected to
find him in bed. Even more implausibly, he rose at
once as she entered, and came over to her, appearing
perfectly healthy, although slightly unfamiliar without
the huge mustaches.

"My dear, I am very sorry," he said. She smelled
schnapps on his breath, and his eyes were bleary. "He
has promised me he will not hurt you." His gaze darted
involuntarily to a point above her head and behind her.
Only then did she become aware of the other man.

She turned very slowly, dreading what she would see:
the blond hair, the gray eyes. It was the man from the
carriage window. One arm was in a sling, but the other
rested suggestively on a bulge in his pocket.

"I regret, Miss DeQuincy, that I must inconvenience
you for a short while," he said politely. His English was
excellent. "Let me assure you that your confinement

will be only temporary, and in far more salubrious quarters than this. If you will be so good as to precede me?" He indicated the door, and the staircase beyond.

When Elizabeth hesitated, he added softly, "If we have not left before your maid and coachman return, I might grow worried that they would carry a misleading tale back to Lord Evrett. And that would not do, not at all."

The implied threat to Anna and Georg sent Elizabeth down the stairs in a hurry. Her captor steered her out through the kitchen, where the sour-faced woman was waiting with a shawl and a small valise.

"You see, I have even provided an abigail," he said mockingly. "This way." They went out the back gate and emerged into a different street. A closed carriage was waiting.

Faintly, Elizabeth could hear Anna's voice calling, and the knocker pounding on the door of the house they had left. Tears welled up behind her eyes, but she forced them back. She would pretend to be Purcell again. It was too terrifying to think of herself in this man's power if she was only Elizabeth DeQuincy.

Afterwards, Southey could never decide whether he would have gone out to Baden if he had received Evrett's note immediately, nor whether anything would have been different if he had done so. But he was not in Vienna Sunday afternoon when the note arrived. He was on his way to allied headquarters south of Schweidnitz.

Early Sunday, he had been awakened by a frenzied knocking at the blue door and had gone sleepily down the steps to find a messenger from Gentz requesting his immediate presence at the Chancellery. The messenger had brought a spare horse. Southey understood: it was urgent. He dressed hastily—in riding clothes, at the messenger's suggestion—and followed the messenger through the empty streets, wondering what this was all about. Certainly he owed Gentz a favor, but with the armistice on the verge of expiring, he had thought the man would be too busy to remember him. Rumor had it Austria would declare war as soon as the treaty ended at midnight on Tuesday.

To his surprise, he was received by Metternich. Gentz was there also, and a blond young man who looked vaguely familiar. Various undersecretaries were hurrying in and out of the office, in spite of the reminder from the church bells that this was the Lord's day.

"Monsieur Southey," the minister greeted him affably. "Please come in." Apparently the emperor's police were more successful at discovering names than at protecting the owners of the names.

A serving man came over and offered him coffee in a low voice. He accepted gratefully and the man hurried away.

Metternich waited until he had been served and had taken a seat before presenting the blond man, whose name he could not quite hear, and inquiring politely if he had recovered from his injuries.

"I find myself in an awkward position," the prince said, once the servant had left. "As you will recall, I owe you a favor, a rather significant one. And yet I must now ask you for another favor."

Southey began to utter some courteous phrase in reply, but Metternich held up his hand and stopped him.

"Please, I beg you, wait until you hear more." He added dryly, "I would not want you to make an empty promise to serve me and only then discover what I require of you." Gentz and the blond man were conferring in low voices, their eyes on his face; now they stopped and waited for their employer to continue.

"You know, of course, that the emperor is likely to declare war against France in a few days."

Southey nodded.

"Quite some time ago, in June, when the present

armistice was first negotiated, the emperor sent a letter to the English government, asking under what conditions, if any, they would agree to a European peace with Napoleon. We have never received a reply."

Metternich sat back in his chair and tapped his fingers against the carved armrest. "Now I have today a new and disturbing report that there is considerable sentiment in Britain in support of such a peace, that there is less commitment to the war against France than we had been led to believe. Naturally, the presence or absence of British forces as allies in the projected war would weigh heavily in any decision the emperor might make at midnight on Tuesday."

Southey swallowed. His mouth was dry. He had a feeling he knew what the request would be. Nevertheless, he managed to appear unruffled as he inquired how he might be of assistance.

"Could you arrange to call on Stewart's secretary, Monsieur Jervyn? He is presently at allied headquarters with Stewart. I understand you are acquainted with him."

He looked for confirmation and got a wary acknowledgment.

"Do you think he would tell you why we have received no reply, tell you truthfully, if you asked him without revealing that you came from me? Could you ascertain from him whether these tales that the British may withdraw from the war are correct?"

He was so relieved that he sank back into his chair with an audible gasp. He had been certain that Metternich was going to ask him to purloin documents from the British commanders.

"I believe I could gain admittance to Jervyn's office, yes," he said cautiously. "And I could ask him what he knows of both these matters. But if he were to ask me in turn who had sent me, I am afraid that I would have to tell him the truth."

"What if I were to offer you a commission in the Austrian army?" countered Metternich.

Silently, the younger man shook his head, although a brief spasm of longing flickered across his face. To be in the field again, in uniform, in a world where the choices were simple and temptations were few—he had not realized, until that moment, how deeply he felt the loss of his captaincy.

"I see," said the minister with a sigh. "England has washed her hands of you, but you are not yet ready to do the same."

"I would be willing to go to Jervyn, but only under the conditions I have just stated." The freckled face was totally impassive now.

Gentz was whispering to his neighbor again. Metternich frowned at him and sat for a moment tapping his fingers on the armrest once more. Unconsciously they mimicked the rhythm of the church bells. "Why not?" he said suddenly. "What do we have to lose? Provided you can go and return with all speed, monsieur, we shall at least be no worse off than we are now. And perhaps Jervyn will be willing to give you some information, or perhaps you yourself will be able to discern, from the actions of the British officers, what is intended. Does that sound fair enough?"

"Fair enough," agreed the other.

Metternich turned to the blond man. "Roswicz, issue him a *laissez-passer* and a voucher for the Imperial Post-Houses. Make sure it specifies that he is my courier. Otherwise they will give him those slugs that the tax collectors use and he will take twice as long to get there." He swung back to Southey. "It is fifty leagues or more, on some very rough roads. Can you get back by Tuesday?"

Southey grimaced, but nodded. He would have to ride straight through without stopping in both directions. It had been a long time since he had ridden so far, and his ribs had been intact on the earlier journey.

But the discomfort and exhaustion which he knew awaited him had a certain appeal. They deadened thought. They postponed decisions. They gave him the illusion of penance. If he was lucky, she would be gone by the time he returned.

Jervyn, too, must be busy, he thought, and might have forgotten him. It had been a long and weary trip. At a few of the post-houses where the roads were better, he had requisitioned a chaise instead of a horse, and had snatched a few hours sleep that way. Now here he was, filthy, staggering with fatigue, with no papers or credentials beyond his own name and the pass issued by Roswicz. What if he could not, after all, get access to Stewart's office?

It was very early Monday morning, but the hallway of the village mayoralty, where the British delegation had temporarily set up offices, was already crowded with visitors hoping to be received: young attachés, a few officers, both British and allied, an English family who had been driven from their vineyard on the Elbe by one of the armies. The two women in the family drew back quite pointedly as he walked by them, wrinkling their noses at his dirty boots and breeches.

His hair was damp with sweat; it had not cooled off much during the night, and there had been almost no breeze. *I must be quite a sight,* he thought, amused, as he withdrew to a corner of the hall.

After a moment he decided no one in his condition would be expected to observe the amenities. He slid down onto the floor and sat back against the wall and closed his eyes, anticipating it would be quite a while before he would be summoned, if at all.

He had reckoned without the cachet conferred by his pass. "Where is he?" It was Jervyn's voice. A moment later, he was being ushered up the stairs; Jervyn was pushing aside all the neatly dressed, clean folk who had been waiting there far longer. He was so tired it took him a moment to realize he was in an office with Jervyn, and that the door had closed.

"You look completely done in," said Jervyn roughly. "Here." He handed him a small glass of brandy; Southey gulped it and took a deep breath. The bite of the liquor woke him somewhat. He took the chair Jervyn offered and perched warily on the edge of the seat.

"Who sent you?" asked Jervyn abruptly. "You have an imperial pass; I assume this is not a social call?"

Good; he could lay his cards out on the table at once. "Prince Metternich," he replied. "He is disturbed that he never received a reply to his inquiry about British participation in a peace treaty. Now he is hearing rumors that Parliament is thinking of withdrawing from the war, and he is concerned the lack of reply might indicate not, as he originally thought, an unwavering commitment to fight, but quite the opposite. And obviously, he would like to know where you stand before he advises the emperor how to act when the armistice expires tomorrow."

To his astonishment, Jervyn came around the desk, strode over to him, and clapped him on the shoulder, beaming. "Congratulations, my dear fellow!" he exclaimed. "I'll own I thought this scheme had very long odds, but Castlereagh is a genius, an absolute genius. Just a moment; let me bring the ambassador in." He vanished through a side door, leaving Southey completely mystified, and wondering whether in his weariness he had not misspoken somehow and told Jervyn that Metternich was to marry the Princess Charlotte, or that Austria had decided to cede the allied command to Wellington.

Jervyn burst back in, accompanied by a handsome man in his thirties who was smiling even more broadly than his secretary.

Stewart, thought Southey. Castlereagh's young half-brother had not been a popular choice as ambassador to Prussia; he was rumored to be a temperamental womanizer.

"This is famous, my boy, simply famous!" Stewart was ebullient. "By Jove, if my brother hasn't done it!" He noticed for the first time the haggard appearance and stained clothing of the prodigal. "Jervyn! Order refreshments at once, and some hot water and towels. And fetch Mr. Sommers's file." He leaned over and said sympathetically, "You'll have been asked to return straight away, I assume? We'll send you in a chaise as far as Josefstadt, at least."

"No need; I have a courier's pass," he responded mechanically.

"That's right, so you do." Stewart laughed and rubbed his hands together.

Jervyn, who had disappeared briefly into the hall, returned, followed by a maid with a hastily assembled tray of coffee and some local pastries, triangles of dough baked around jam. Southey normally found these rather sweet, but he was ravenous, and ate two or three quite hungrily before his stomach revolted.

Stewart had perched on the edge of Jervyn's worktable and was watching him eat with a paternal air. Jervyn had vanished again.

"Now, first of all, you'll want to know what to tell the prince, of course," said Stewart briskly. "In this case, I think you might want to pass on something close to the truth."

The side door opened, and Jervyn came back in with a small portfolio. "Ah, there it is," said Stewart with relief. "I thought I had lost it. Where was it?"

"In the bin with the Russian correspondence, sir." Jervyn kept his eyes lowered. Every night he went through all the dossiers in Stewart's office and tried to put them back in their proper places. It was a futile endeavor.

The coffee was fighting with the brandy and the pastries in Southey's gut, but he knew he needed to wake up. He drank off half a cup, choking slightly as the hot liquid burned the roof of his mouth. What had Stewart said? Something about telling Metternich the truth? He was not sure whether he was really *compos mentis*. Stewart and Jervyn were behaving so oddly that he did not trust his own senses.

"You were saying, sir?" he prompted, looking at Stewart.

The latter looked blank for a moment, and then recollected his train of thought. "Yes, the question of what answer to give Prince Metternich. I think you will tell him that whilst there are some in England who are pressing for an end to the war, they are in the minority and are unlikely to prevail, but their demands and protests made it inexpedient for my brother to send a quick reply to Austria. The reply is therefore on its way, but it has been routed through Silesia, to avoid interception by the French, and is consequently very delayed." He looked at Jervyn for approval.

"But is that in fact the case?"

"It is," Jervyn assured him. "Which is all the more fortuitous, since Metternich will probably receive the reply within the next few weeks. That will confirm your story and establish your *bona fides*. In the future, of course, you will not always be passing on information which can so easily be proved or disproved; thus, it is essential to give the Austrians confidence in you."

"What future?" Southey had stiffened. "I undertook this journey as a personal favor to Prince Metternich; he did not propose any permanent arrangement." But then he remembered the offer of a commission, and fell silent.

Stewart sprawled across the desk top, swinging his booted legs idly back and forth. "This was all my brother's idea," he explained. He asked the senior intelligence officers to find someone competent who could be thoroughly discredited, exiled, accepted by the Austrians as an expatriate. Gentz has been sending us

reports for years, but we have never been able to introduce our own information, to influence Metternich in
any way. My brother realized that we needed to let the
Austrians think *they* had discovered our man. We knew
if you could get that letter back, Metternich would be
grateful, and would have you investigated. And *voilà!*''
He laughed.

"Look," he commanded, handing Southey a neatly
written memorandum with a sheaf of papers attached.
"He had the whole thing mapped out, just like a chess
game. Sees ten moves ahead, he does. This will mean
a promotion for you, of course, but you will have to wait
until the war is over to be reinstated."

Stunned, Southey read a chilling and very professional description of how discretionary funds were to
be paid out to an intermediary, who would bribe an
English officer to sell copies of various minor documents to the French. The items thus obtained would
be forwarded to Nathanson's father for his use in his
pretended role as Arnaut. The memorandum then pro-
pounded a number of hypothetical scenarios, one of
which was indeed that the corrupted officer should be
induced, by a promise of amnesty for his crimes, to go
into exile and insinuate himself into the confidence of
the Austrians.

Clipped to the memorandum, carefully arranged by
date, was a series of letters and documents. White's
request for funds to assist a junior officer who was in
financial difficulties. Castlereagh's inquiry: would this
young man be a suitable candidate for his scheme? A
reply: unlikely, and in fact, it now looked as though the
creditors could not enforce collection; there were some
suspicious irregularities, including an apparent forgery
of White's own signature. Castlereagh's response, marked
for delivery by special messenger, requesting that White
do nothing until he had spoken with him personally.
An authorization to disperse monies from the secret
service account, payable to a Mr. Jean Vachelet, of Brus-

sels. Assignment and purchase of a majority in the name of Michael Southey, currently holding the rank of captain and serving on the Adjutant-General's staff. A report of the death of one Major Michael Southey, killed while on a reconnaissance mission behind enemy lines, 17 May, 1813. A bill of attainder against the same Michael Southey, dated 22 May, 1813. A copy of identification papers in the name of Michael Sommers. Summaries of the reports he had sent to White from Vienna.

"It all worked out, did it not?" His voice was amazingly calm. "In fact, I was an ideal subject. I sold the French false information; we did not have to give up any secrets. And I cooperated beautifully in sending myself off into exile." He pocketed the memo, detaching it from the accompanying papers.

"Here, we'll need that back," Jervyn said sharply. More astute than his employer, he had read Southey's expression and was suddenly afraid.

"I think not." A long, slender, and very deadly looking knife appeared from the cuff of one muddy boot. Although Southey held it casually in his left hand, the glittering blade was aimed straight at Stewart's throat. "I imagine Prince Metternich will be very interested in this document. It is my intention to convey it to him immediately. Along with, of course, your reply to his query."

Stewart was astounded, and outraged. "You will do no such thing! I order you, as a British subject, to return that paper to me at once!"

"I am no longer a British subject," Southey reminded him. "You may take your pick. I am either dead, or I am a traitor. As a matter of fact, I am an officer in the Austrian army."

"You are?" Jervyn was horrified. He had been quite certain after the interview at the Reuss's reception that Southey had remained completely loyal. "When did this happen?"

"Just now." Holding the knife like a short sword,

Southey backed out the door, closed it behind him, and with an expert twist of the point of the blade, jammed the lock.

Stewart sprang to the door and turned the handle, cursing. He looked back at Jervyn, who had a thoughtful expression on his face. "Don't just stand there, you fool!" he barked. "Go after him! Stop him!" And with a series of vicious kicks he shattered the bottom panel of the door and wrenched the handle off from underneath.

"Hell," muttered Jervyn. He walked over to his desk, pulled a pair of pistols out of the bottom drawer, and strode out through the mangled door.

Twenty-Two

The journey north had been a brutal slog. The journey south was a nightmare. He had been lucky, he knew. Lucky the trick with the door handle worked, because Jervyn and Stewart would have caught him halfway down the stairs otherwise; he was so stiff he could barely walk. Lucky there had been an Austrian platoon just down the street whose officer had surrendered his horse after one glimpse at the pass. Lucky that it was not raining. Lucky that the posting stations maintained excellent mounts.

He had not dared to risk the delay involved in harnessing up a coach; Stewart would have sent someone—perhaps several someones—after him. So he rode, clinging grimly to the back of an endless series of horses, his legs aching, his rib burning through the side of his chest, his temples pounding. The sun beat down on his head; he had lost his hat somewhere.

At each posting station he asked only for coffee, and gulped it as they saddled a fresh horse. After the third stop, the grooms had to help him on and off the horse, because his knees had stopped working. At the fifth posting house, in Brünn, a young Hussar came over to him and inquired courteously if he could be of assistance.

The Hungarian, who was taking new recruits up to Königgrätz, was motivated more by curiosity than anything else. Why had the entire station ignored him and his men to fuss over this bedraggled civilian?

At first Southey could hardly understand the man; his German was heavily accented. But then the words, and the meaning behind them, penetrated through his fog of weariness. He held out his pass. "I have an urgent message for His Excellency, Prince Metternich," he tried to say, but it came out as a croak. He cleared his throat and was more successful the second time. "I am an imperial courier. I am being pursued. Would it be possible for me to have an escort to Vienna?"

The Hussar and his men were delighted. They had been journeying in easy stages up from Presburg, wondering what would happen at midnight on Tuesday, whether they would be deployed at all or sent back as part of the home guard once the regiment was organized. Now they would be right in the capital as decisions were made. Perhaps this foreigner was carrying some vital document.

A nightlong ride was a small price to pay for such interesting doings. With a smug air of importance, the novice cavalrymen formed up in front of the vehicle which the grooms were now wheeling out.

"Pursuit," Southey reminded them. "Comes from behind." He and the young officer exchanged rueful glances.

Abashed, the soldiers regrouped. He did not care. Any escort would be sufficient, even these amateurs. If he had an escort, he could ride in a chaise, which would mean he could sleep. The roads were rather bad between Brünn and Nikolsburg, but he felt sure no jouncing would keep him awake. And he had made very good time up until now; he could afford to use a carriage for the last twenty leagues.

He was awakened by the Hussar officer about an hour south of Brünn. A messenger from the English ambassador had come up with them, accompanied by some Prussian Dragoons. The man urgently requested speech with Major Southey.

So, he thought, *suddenly I am a major. And eventually a lieutenant-colonel, if I play their game.* He smiled grimly to himself. The Hungarian, observing his expression, understood at once.

"This is the pursuit?" he asked, his eyes flashing below his black brows.

"Yes, but I am perfectly safe, with your men here," Southey assured him. He climbed awkwardly out of the tiny carriage. Jervyn sat motionless on a lathered horse some five yards behind them, at the edge of a pool of light created by the coach lanterns. A half-dozen Prussian soldiers were drawn up next to him, drooping slightly in their saddles. They had developed a healthy respect for the riding ability of the foppish-looking secretary over the course of the day.

"My apologies, Jervyn," said Southey. "It did not occur to me that I could commandeer an escort and travel at a reasonable pace until the last station. Otherwise I could have let you catch me eight hours ago and saved you a rather grueling afternoon and evening."

The secretary stared at the gaunt figure standing by the chaise: unshaven, clothes plastered to his sides with dirt and sweat, flushed with sunburn, boots caked with mud. He was clutching the door handle with one hand for support. And he was looking at Jervyn the way a mother might regard the hangman who had executed her son.

It was your duty, that look said. *I accept that. But I loathe*

*you and those who employed you, nevertheless, for what you
have taken from me, in the name of serving your country.*

"I am sorry," Jervyn said in a low voice. "I am truly
sorry. I've been with the diplomats too long, I suppose.
I felt badly for you when I learned of it last month, but
I never thought about it, really, until today. As God is
my witness, I'd undo it if I could. If you choose, I'll hold
myself ready to meet you, on your terms, at any time
you name. I will stand in for Castlereagh and Jackson.
I'll take responsibility." He added bitterly, "It's the only
satisfaction you are likely to be offered from anyone in
my office, I fear."

Then, recollecting his charge, he leaned over the
neck of his horse, pleading, "Think as badly of us, of
me, as you like. But I beg you, by anything you still hold
dear—your comrades among our troops, perhaps, if
not England herself—I beg you, please, consider carefully what you do before you give that memorandum to
the prince. Metternich is another Castlereagh, for good
or for ill. He will use that document as unscrupulously
as we have used you."

There was no change at first in the drawn face, no
movement. Then suddenly, with an awkward gesture,
the battered figure let go of the door and straightened
up. The lantern, jostled, swung crazily behind him, sending jagged arcs of light dancing out over the road.

"Do you know what I was dreaming in there?" he
demanded hoarsely, ignoring both the apology and the
plea. "I suppose I was asleep, but perhaps not. Perhaps
it was a vision, a memory, rather than a dream." Dark
shadows filled the hollows of his face. "I dreamt that a
pack of dogs were pursuing me across the downs. I was
running, terrified, trying to keep ahead of them. And
then I came to a cliff. I stopped, and the hounds came
up, and they stopped, too. And then some men ran up,
and physically dragged me over to the very edge of the
cliff. But they did not push me quite over; in fact, they
let go of me. There I was, with the hounds all around

me, and these men menacing me, and the cliff behind
me. So I jumped."

He closed his eyes and leaned against the coach. "Do
you understand me, Jervyn? I jumped off the god-
damned cliff. Myself." His voice was shaking. "They
brought me to the edge, but I was the one who took
that leap. No one touched me—no one shoved me or
tripped me. *I chose to jump.* And I can never, ever get
back to the top of the cliff again. No matter what I do,
no matter how long I live."

The Hussars and the Prussians were glancing back
and forth between the two men, unable to understand
the words, but grasping that something was very wrong.
In an instinctive gesture of sympathy, the young Hungarian officer laid his hand on Southey's elbow.

Startled, he turned and saw the fierce black eyes,
warm with concern. How old was this Hussar lieutenant?
Twenty-one, twenty-two? Did he have a sweetheart who
was in church right now, praying he would be assigned
to the home guard? How many more lieutenants were
wondering what would happen tomorrow—no, tonight;
it was well past midnight. Austrian, French, Prussian,
English, Spanish, Russian: thin ink lines on the maps
in Metternich's office, representing thousands of men
like this one.

Without a word, Southey reached into his jacket and
extracted the memorandum. Reaching up, he
unhooked the lantern and pulled off the cap. It burned
his fingers slightly, but he ignored the pain, and carefully fed the paper into the low flame, watching it blaze
up. When it was completely consumed, he looked over
at Jervyn.

"I will still tell him."

Jervyn nodded. Without the actual document, Metternich could not work much mischief, and both men knew
it. Southey got back into the coach. The seven mounted
men sat, like guardian statues, until the last gleam of the
bobbing lanterns had disappeared into the darkness.

* * *

It was nearly noon when they arrived in Vienna, and he elected to go straight out to Schonbrunn. Metternich was presumably waiting upon the emperor; if not, his magic pass would ensure an immediate escort to the minister's actual location.

This time the guards received him deferentially, in spite of his appearance, and tumbled over themselves in their eagerness to provide information. A pity he had not possessed the pass three days earlier when he had been frantically hunting for Nathanson. Perhaps his former colleague would still have the use of both his legs.

A uniformed official was conducting him through a series of sparsely furnished reception rooms and then into a narrow hallway behind the imperial suite. They emerged again in a large antechamber, where the official consulted with a harried-looking man in a tie-wig and old-fashioned frock coat, who was sitting by a marble-topped table near some massive double doors. There were guards at the doors.

"His Excellency is with His Imperial Highness at the moment, *mein Herr*," the official said, returning to his side. "We will notify him of your arrival the moment he is free. Would you care for something to eat? Some wine, perhaps?" He recollected that the British had rather peculiar tastes. "Beer? Tea?"

Southey looked around at the gilded room, the damask upholstery on the chairs, the cream-colored wainscoting. He hardly dared move, lest he befoul the place.

"I would like a bath," he said at last. "And some clean clothing, if possible. The prince has offered me a commission in the army; perhaps I could be given a spare uniform?"

"Of course," the official said, leading him back through the maze of tiny corridors. He ushered Southey through a narrow door in the wall and they entered a small sitting room. It was empty, but two maidservants appeared almost immediately when he rang. He spoke sharply to them and they disappeared. "They will prepare a bath at once, and I will go and inquire about a uniform. Do you know which regiment it is to be?"

Southey had spotted a wooden bench under the window and sank down on it with a sigh of relief. "Not Grenadiers," he said. "I do not handle rifles very well. Something in the cavalry. Hussars, perhaps," he added, recalling the friendly Hungarians.

"Very good, sir," said the official, eyeing him doubtfully. How could someone have forgotten which regiment they were to join? But the man did look exhausted, and he was a foreigner, unfamiliar with the tortuous Austrian system of overlapping German and Hungarian military units. He started out the door, then paused. "And your rank? Do you recall what it was to be?"

The reply came back with no hesitation whatsoever. "Lieutenant." The lowest rank possible. And he would do his best not to get promoted, he vowed. Unless it was posthumously.

"I will go and see what I can do," the official promised, wondering why a man who held an unrestricted imperial pass was only being offered a lieutenancy. He disappeared, and Southey sat rigidly upright on the bench until the maids returned, followed by a small army of footmen with a bathtub and hot water, which they set up for him in a closet adjacent to the sitting room.

It was a proper tub, not a hip bath, and he sank into it with a sigh of profound satisfaction, savoring the sting as the hot water hit the blisters on his legs. He immersed himself completely, scrubbing his hair, his neck, his face, his chest. They had brought a razor, and a very competent servant, some kind of assistant valet, held a basin over the tub and shaved him and combed his hair. A maid had come in with towels and a silk dressing gown.

When he had been shaved, she and the manservant withdrew.

He stared down into the soapy water. What would he do now? Should he really accept a commission in the Austrian army? The water was cooling, but even cool, it felt delightful. His limbs were so grateful to have assistance in supporting their weight that the water would have to be very cold indeed to be uncomfortable. His thoughts were sliding away from him; he could not make a decision yet. In a few moments, he would be able to reason more clearly. Certainly he must think it all through before he saw Metternich. Water sloshed gently around his thighs. He fell asleep.

The official woke him, very apologetic. The minister would see him now, but he would have to wear the dressing gown. The prince had sent back the uniform; it was the wrong regiment and the wrong rank. Under the circumstances, of course, the prince was coming here to the sitting room. Some food and drink was waiting for him. If he could dry himself quickly he would have time to eat something before His Excellency arrived.

Since he found that he was not able to move very quickly, or even to move some muscles at all, he had barely started on the luncheon platter which was set out in the sitting room when Metternich swept in, accompanied by Roswicz and a footman. Southey managed to get up, but was immediately waved back to his seat.

"Please, do not interrupt your meal," Metternich said. "I am told you arrived more than an hour ago, in which case I imagine you have not eaten properly for quite some time. By the way, the record from Vienna to Breslau, which is just beyond Schweidnitz, is twenty-two hours." He sat down on a tapestry-covered sofa across from Southey and signaled the footman to pour him some wine.

"I think the record still stands," Southey answered

dryly. "Something I am having a bit of difficulty doing at the present."

"Is that why you requested a cavalry regiment?" Metternich maintained an air of pleasant banter, but the footman knew his job; he withdrew. "I am delighted to hear that you have changed your mind, of course. May I ask what prompted your decision?" Then he saw the younger man's expression. "Perhaps it is best if I do not."

"No, you may as well know." Against his better judgment, Southey took a sip of his own wine. He should not drink much, not in his present state of exhaustion. "First of all, I should tell you the British did send a reply to your query about the peace negotiations. It was sent via Stockholm and Berlin, to keep it out of French hands. You should have it shortly. The delay was useful for Castlereagh in appeasing the group opposed to continuing the war, but I have Stewart's assurance that they will not prevail, that Britain is firmly committed."

"Did you learn the contents of the reply?"

He had not thought to ask, since it would be moot before it arrived. He shook his head.

Metternich raised his eyebrows and turned to Roswicz. "Roswicz, would you care to take a small wager? I will stake fifty florins the reply professes a sincere and earnest desire to negotiate peace, provided the terms are reasonable."

"I never bet against you, Excellency." Roswicz smiled sleepily. "Why would Castlereagh forego the chance to have proof of his support for peace? True, the letter arrived too late, and Britain must back her allies now, but there it is in writing. Should the war go badly, he need only display his copy of the letter."

Southey breathed a silent prayer of thanks that he had listened to Jervyn and burned the memorandum. These men moved in a world of shadow and gesture which bewildered him, a world where nuances reigned, and actions meant their opposite.

Metternich turned back to him. "Did the English learn that you came from me?"

"Yes, it was the first question they asked me."

The minister's brows rose again. "And what was their reaction?"

Southey told him.

There was a long silence after he had finished his story. Roswicz had lost his sleepy look; he had taken out a small notebook and was scribbling furiously. Metternich sat lost in thought for a few minutes, sipping his wine absently.

"And so it was at this point that you decided to accept my offer?" he asked abruptly.

"Exactly." Southey's voice was flat. "You need not feel obliged to go through with the appointment, now that you have heard this sordid tale."

"On the contrary, my dear young man, I am more than ever convinced that I am doing the right thing," said the prince, "although I feel you will be wasted on the Hussars." He shuddered. "One of our more picturesque institutions. Sometimes I think they truly believe they are sweeping across the steppes behind their legendary chieftains. Did you know we have frequent requests from Hussar troopers to ride bareback?"

There was a knock at the door, and the official entered, looking even more flustered than he had earlier, carrying a pile of red and green clothing, a large feathered helmet, and the most beautiful boots Southey had ever seen. "Your uniform, Captain," he said to Southey, adding apologetically, "His Excellency insisted."

"At least it isn't major," muttered Southey to himself.

Metternich rose, and Roswicz sprang up to pull back his chair. Suddenly very self-conscious in his dressing gown, Southey rose also, hastily setting down his glass. "I am very grateful, Monsieur," he stammered. "For the commission, that is."

"Nonsense, I owe you far more than that," said the

prince sharply. He paused, and took stock of the
exhausted figure across the table. The young man would
not last two weeks in the Hussars; they would bore him
to tears. He would find something better for him as
soon as the declaration of war was official. "It is never
very pleasant to find that one has been used," he
observed. "You may console yourself with the knowledge that in this most recent game, you were not a
pawn. A knight, at least. Possibly even a rook."

It was mid afternoon by the time he arrived back at
Frau Renner's. First the uniform had proved to be too
big. The valet-servant had reappeared and altered it.
Then he had been sent to the Hofburg barracks. There
were papers to sign; he was assigned a horse—a massive
bay—and introduced to a lieutenant-colonel of his new
regiment, who informed him he would be expected to
grow a mustache before reporting for duty the following
week. Seeing Southey's horrified reaction, he hastily
amended the mustache to an optional item. To his
astonishment, he was also issued a substantial sum of
money in gold. He had forgotten that only in Britain
did officers purchase their commissions.

His ancient concierge was outside sweeping the paving behind the gate, working deftly around the recum-
bent form of Trumpet. He sometimes supposed they
must be the cleanest stones in Vienna. Apparently it was
not permissible to sit outside and watch the neighbors,
as elderly ladies did at home. Curiosity carried a price
here in Austria.

Sure enough, she dropped the broom as soon as he
came up to the gate and hurried over, delighted to see
a distinguished stranger—as she thought. The dog had
already recognized him, and bounded across to slobber
on his new boots and then cast himself on his back in
an orgy of submissive greeting.

"No wonder Nathanson would have nothing to do

with you," he told Trumpet in disgust, surveying the smears on the new leather.

"Herr Sommers!" gasped Frau Renner.

"Southey," he corrected automatically, but she ignored him.

"This is of all things the most wonderful! That I should see you in my country's uniform!" She had tears in her eyes. Defiantly, she produced her spectacles and popped them on in order to survey him. "Look at you!" She beamed proudly. "All the braid and lace!"

Southey had been a bit stunned by the amount of these two items on his jacket and shirt, and had been told by the valet that he was lucky his rank was not higher, or the coat would be so stiff with braid it would not bend. "I am very, very happy. Now my nieces will be sorry they criticized Herr Lang for renting the rooms to a foreigner."

He laughed, enjoying her pleasure, and then bent over and searched in his new valise for the key to the blue door.

"Oh," she said, remembering. "I unlocked the door already; you have a visitor . . ." The valise was abandoned. He ignored his protesting muscles and leaped up the stairs, pushing himself off the stone walls to get there faster.

At the entry to the loft he paused, scanning the disordered room frantically. He had barely started bringing his equipment and books down from the attic Saturday evening. Sword bags, still dusty, were lying everywhere, and there were crates piled up in front of the sofa. Fiercely he reminded himself that he did not want to see her, could not see her. But when he recognized Evrett, rising like a fury out of the armchair, he felt a pang of grief and disappointment.

"Where is she?" demanded Evrett, his expression savage.

Astounded, he stared at him. No need to ask who "she" was, of course. But why would they seek her here?

"Damn you!" Evrett stepped closer, clenching his fists. "What have you done with her, you villain? I suggested that you call on her, not abduct her!"

"She is missing?" He was so dazed he could barely get the words out.

"She took the coach and came into Vienna this morning. And then she disappeared. You arranged it, did you not? You planned it with her."

Numbly, he shook his head. "I have been gone since Sunday morning. Metternich sent me up to allied headquarters."

For the first time, Evrett took in the uniform, the circles under the other man's eyes, his stiff posture. Doubt crept into his eyes.

"How could you possibly imagine—" Southey broke off. He knew very well how Evrett could imagine. He had arranged abductions before, after all. "You can write to Philip Jervyn, if you wish, Stewart's secretary," he said wearily. "He saw me last night near Brünn. And I was escorted from there by a troop of Hussars under the command of a Lieutenant Ferencz. Since arriving at noon, I have been at the summer palace."

"But then—I assumed—what has happened to her?" Evrett whispered. "Her maid told us she went to a house somewhere in the city, and then vanished."

"Where was this house? What did the maid say?" Southey asked sharply.

"Somewhere in Spittelberg—a very rough place, evidently. The maid was so terrified that she asked the coachman to walk down the street to the apothecary with her. She could tell us only that Miss DeQuincy had a note from her uncle this morning and told the maid he was ill and she must go to him at once. When they arrived at this house, the maid was sent off on the pretext of refilling some medicine, and the place was empty when she and the coachman returned a few minutes later."

"Who rented the house? Did you inquire of the neighbors?"

Evrett shook his head. "We thought we knew . . ."

"I know what you thought," said Southey grimly. "Never mind. Can you send someone over to the house to make inquiries? Do you still have the letter with the address?"

"No," admitted Evrett, looking uncomfortable. "Miss DeQuincy has the letter, unfortunately. I would have to go back to Baden and see if the maid can find the house for us."

"I would recommend that you do so. At once." His face was very stern. "It is possible that she has run away, that she will indeed come seeking me. I will wait here in case that proves to be what has happened." But he did not think it very likely. The uncle was a real piece of work, that was certain. Perhaps he had decided the wealthy Lord Evrett would pay something to recover his house guest.

"And if she does come here?" Evrett persisted doggedly.

"I will escort her back to Baden. Whether she wishes to go or not." Frowning, the other man nodded slowly and raised his eyes to Southey's. *Don't apologize, damn you,* he thought, as he saw Evrett hesitate. *Get out, leave me alone. I've had a bellyful of apologies from my compatriots today.* With every fiber of his being he willed the other man to walk to the door, to go down the stairs.

His prayer was granted. Evrett had picked up his cane, taken his hat, was already in the doorway. But wait— he was turning for one last remark. "Are you certain you can fulfill that threat? I gather from Nathanson that you were not very successful at persuading young Purcell, as you thought him, to do as he was told."

"That," said Southey, "was when I was still unwilling to hurt her."

Twenty-Three

The carriage blinds had been drawn so that Elizabeth could not see where they were going. She tried at first to keep track of turns, but soon gave up when she realized she had no idea which direction the carriage had been facing when they left.

They drove for quite a while, and she did not hear the noise of pedestrians, nor did they encounter many other vehicles, so she supposed they must have left the city fairly quickly. When they did at last stop, a shawl was wound around her head and she was guided up some steps and into a building. She heard a door closing behind her before the shawl was removed.

This is a good sign, she told herself, trying to stay calm. *It means they intend to release you eventually.* As the shawl was tugged away, she looked about her attentively.

They were in the lower hall of an old house. The floors were crooked, with irregular, wide planks. The ceilings were low and beamed. All the doors leading out of this hall were closed, but there was an air of emptiness and disuse about the place.

She realized there was not one piece of furniture in

the hall—no hat rack, no table, no chair, no carpet. A flight of wooden stairs, dark with age, rose straight up ahead of her, and Meillet gestured politely with his head. His good hand remained in a pocket of his jacket. In any case, the crabbed woman stood between her and the door.

Slowly she mounted the staircase, noting the creaking treads. It would not be easy to come down these stairs without making noise. At the top, she emerged into another hall. This time one of the doors was open, and she walked quickly inside. If this was not her destination, she wanted to know what was in here before she was shut away somewhere else. But Meillet followed her calmly, surveying the room with satisfaction as he ducked through the low door.

It was rather pleasant, in fact. A gnarled wooden bed stood in one corner, covered with feather mattresses and a cheerful embroidered counterpane. There was a little footstool to use to climb onto the bed, which was quite high. A very plain chair was next to a washstand, which had a pitcher and basin, already full.

On the other side of the chair was a small sideboard, of the same dark wood as the bed, and on the sideboard was a tray with food and drink: a capon, some kind of fruit compote, bread, a little dish of custard, a flagon of some kind of wine. There was even a dish of comfits.

Opposite the door was a window, but a large armoire had been dragged in front of it, blocking her view. The upper half let in plenty of light, however, and the room had a cheerful air, as though some comic folk hero might appear at any moment.

The first order of business was to get some food. She had had nothing except half a cup of chocolate, and she could not think clearly, or move very fast, on an empty stomach. Without looking at Meillet or at the woman, who had followed him into the room, she went over to the sideboard and served herself.

There was a fork, she realized, but no knife. No matter. She would eat the capon with her fingers. Apparently a knife was deemed too risky for the prisoner. At least there was a napkin. She sat down in the hard little chair and began to eat.

"Very sensible," approved Meillet. He took a last look around and left, giving some low-voiced instructions to the woman in French. When Elizabeth had eaten a leg and a wing and all of the custard, she decided that was all she could manage for the present. Since she did not want to drink wine, she filled the glass on the sideboard with water from the pitcher and drank that. The capon had been salty; she was thirsty. Then she turned to the woman, who was standing by the door, watching her.

"Could you clear the dirty dishes, please?" she said in French. "And bring clean ones, in case I wish to eat more later? Also, is there anything to read?"

The woman gave her a suspicious look and made her sit on the bed in the corner before she opened the door. Elizabeth heard the lock click and then the telltale creaking as the woman descended the stairs. She wished she had thought to count which stairs were the worst.

Although she was itching to try to look out the window, she knew the woman would come back to check on her, and forced herself to stay on the bed. Sure enough, her guardian reappeared shortly, clutching a venerable German Bible and clean dishes. Elizabeth settled down on the bed with the Bible, and ignored the woman. She had not heard anyone else in the house, and she hoped the woman had chores to do and would decide it was safe to leave her. Eventually, she did.

Cautiously, Elizabeth got up, testing the boards before she put her weight on them. Then she lifted the chair and carried it over in front of the armoire, setting it down very gently. With some trepidation, she took off her slippers and stockings and climbed onto the seat.

She was high enough to see over the top of the armoire now, and the scene before her was very disheartening. It was lovely, or would have been lovely, in a painting. A great chestnut tree spread out beneath the window. Through its leaves she could see fields stretching away to low hills and a blue sky dotted with clouds. The closest field was planted with dozens of small saplings. But there were no people in the fields, no other houses. If she screamed, no one would come, except her captors.

What would he do, if he were here? Well, first of all, he would quietly put away the chair, in case anyone came into the room. She did so, resuming her stockings and shoes.

Then he would look all around the room, inventory everything, take stock. She opened the armoire. It was completely empty. The sideboard held only some clean napkins and an ancient decanter, with some brown residue in the bottom. The feather mattresses on the bed were of the old kind, with the covers sewn shut around the down. No sheets to tie together. The counterpane was too thick to tear, and she had nothing to cut it with.

She sat down on the floor, leaning her back against the bed, and tried to think. The room was spotlessly clean, she realized, looking at the floor. There was no dust at all, even under the bed. Poking her head under, she saw something gleaming in the corner. A brief flare of hope was quenched when she wriggled far enough under to seize it: it was a small coin. Disconsolately, she brushed off her skirts, although they were not dirty, picked up the Bible, and climbed into bed. If she could not think of any plan, then she should rest.

The woman came and brought more food, which she got up and ate. Gradually the light faded. Meillet stopped in and bade her good night very courteously, apologizing for his failure to provide nightclothes. "It is only for tonight," he reassured her.

But she was not reassured. Something was nagging at the back of her mind. There was some reason she had to get away, even though she believed that he meant what he said; he did not intend to keep her here long.

Why? Someone would ransom her, she supposed. Evrett; he was wealthy. But that did not make sense.

Impatiently she shook it off. She must simply trust her instincts. It was imperative she escape. And now was the time, while it was dark, so that it was more difficult to find her in the fields. She looked down with satisfaction at her lavender dress. Half-mourning had its advantages.

Very carefully, she stripped off her shoes again, put the chair back under the armoire, and climbed up once more. It was quite dark outside, no moon. Good. She went back to the sideboard and, using the fork, ripped a small section of the flounce off of her petticoat. Then she picked up the footstool and set it on top of the chair, holding her breath. It balanced. Next she went back to the sideboard, removed all the dishes, and brought the heavy brass tray over to the armoire. Climbing carefully, first onto the chair, and then onto the stool, she slid the tray gently onto the top of the armoire and pushed it back as far as it would go towards the window.

Now was the noisy part, the risky part. Her skirts were in the way; she hoisted them up and twisted them over to one side. Then she pulled herself up as hard as she could, flinging one knee over the top of the armoire and praying it was sturdy enough to hold her. It was; there was the window. She was up, crouching beneath the low ceiling. Averting her face, she picked up the tray and smashed it as hard as she could through the window, taking a second swing to clear a bigger opening. A flying shard cut the palm of one hand, but she hardly felt it.

There was an immediate outcry from the room below her, and footsteps pounding up the stairs. Still, it would take them a moment to unlock the door. Hastily she tossed her scrap of petticoat out into the branches of the tree and slid off the armoire, holding her bloody hand well away from the wood. She had just made it under the bed when the woman burst into the room.

"She has gone out the window!" she screamed, seeing the tray and the broken glass atop the armoire. An answering shout came from below, and the noise of a door opening. From under the bed, she could see beams of light sweeping through the branches of the tree.

Then there were angry voices outside her window. More men must have come later; she was fairly sure when she arrived the house had been empty. There had been only herself, the woman, Meillet, and the driver of the coach.

Circles of light moved away from the house; they were going out into the fields. The woman had run back downstairs. It was working.

How long should she wait? A count of twenty, perhaps. They might return soon, if they found no footprints in the fields. Twenty seemed very short, but she forced herself to move. Still barefoot, carrying her slippers, she stole out into the deserted hall and inched down the stairs.

In front of her, the door at the foot of the staircase stood wide open, and the cool night air wafted up to her, scented with apple. It must be an apple orchard, she thought, those little trees. Testing each stair, she crept down, skipping the two she thought had creaked most loudly. There were only a few little squeaks.

At the bottom she held her breath, listening. A door to the right was open, and a lamp shone out from behind it. But she heard nothing, saw no one. Moving very slowly, she paced her way to the open door, slipped through it and glanced around, noting the wavering lanterns of the searchers. Four of them. She could elude them now that she was behind them and could see where they were going.

A surge of triumph ran through her; her feet danced down the steps to the drive where the coach still stood, looking naked in the darkness without the horses. The rough ground hurt her feet, and she paused to slip on her shoes. But as she straightened, an amused voice spoke from the shadows at the bottom of the steps, and a tall form unfolded, blocking the faint light streaming out from the open front door.

"Good evening, Miss DeQuincy," Meillet greeted her urbanely. "Apparently you have been spending too much time with Messieurs Southey and Nathanson. I am afraid I will have to put you in the cellar after all."

Eventually, he could not endure the waiting any longer, and he hired a horse and rode out to Baden. His lordship was not at home, Flynn informed him. He had gone to consult Captain Nathanson.

Cursing, he climbed back in the saddle, and headed back towards the city, wondering why on earth he had asked for a cavalry regiment when he never wanted to see a horse again. It was another three quarters of an hour before he rode up to the elegant stone house and slipped awkwardly off his mount. "Some Hussar I must look," he muttered as he handed the horse over to the snickering groom.

A supercilious Austrian butler informed him, to his surprise, that he was expected, and led him through a series of rooms to a corner suite, brilliant just now in the light of the setting sun. Nathanson was ensconced on a chaise longue upholstered in a livid green, and Evrett had pulled up a chair next to him. At the sight of the new arrival, he sprang to his feet eagerly.

"Have you any news?" The words burst out of him.

"No. I hoped perhaps you did."

Evrett's face fell.

"Pull up a chair," Nathanson commanded. "We are having a council of war. I think perhaps her uncle intends to hold her for ransom."

"Did you find out anything at the house?" Southey asked, dragging over an ottoman and taking a seat next

to Nathanson's bandaged foot. He saw his friend look
curiously at his uniform, but evidently Evrett must have
already mentioned it to him, because he accepted it
without comment.

"The house was rented for a week only, in the uncle's
name," Evrett answered. "None of the neighbors saw
anything, save for one boy, who saw a coach in the street
behind the house this morning. He remembered it
because coaches are rare enough in that district, and a
coach in his own street is a prodigy beyond belief."

"And the maid? Could she recall anything?"

"The woman who answered the door was perhaps
fifty, plainly but neatly dressed, and spoke German, but
with an accent. The house was very dirty and neglected."
He grimaced. "I saw it myself. We went in and combed
the place, found nothing. They had left it empty and
unlocked. At least she is not there. Let us hope she is
someplace more comfortable." He looked at Southey.
"Have you thought of anything since I left? Is there
someplace we should be looking? Something we have
forgotten?"

Southey frowned. The uncle. What did he know of
the uncle? He had been forced to flee Vienna, but had
now apparently returned. He was an arms dealer, had
sold rifles to both the Prussians and the French. Certainly he would be acquainted with some desperate and
unsavory characters. A particular example of such a
person suddenly occurred to him, and he asked, dreading the answer, but trying to speak casually, "Did this
boy see the driver of the coach?"

"Yes, but it was not the uncle. A young man, rather
stout, he said. He thought perhaps he was a boxer; he
was built squarely and had a black eye. Seems the sort
of fellow the uncle might hire for something like this."

A faint chill spread through Southey as he heard Jean-
Luc described. His eyes met Nathanson's at once, and
a silent warning was exchanged. Evrett must be kept in

the dark. If he blundered around trying to rescue her, Meillet would have no scruples about harming her.

Get rid of him, Southey's hazel eyes demanded.

Nathanson's dark head nodded, almost imperceptibly.

"Evrett, I think you should get back to Baden," Nathanson announced. "It looks as though my theory is the best one we have so far, and if I am right, he will send you a demand sometime very soon, perhaps even tonight. He will not want to hold her any longer than necessary; the police are already looking for him for other reasons. I suspect he is desperate for money. Otherwise he would never have returned here."

He shifted uncomfortably, and allowed a spasm of pain to run across his face. This, more than the argument about the ransom, propelled Evrett out of his chair, apologizing profusely for abusing his friend's patience and promising to send word of the latest developments first thing in the morning.

Southey got up as though about to leave also, and then turned back casually as Evrett went out, inquiring loudly about the injured foot as a pretext for lingering. As soon as the uneven footsteps had faded away, he collapsed back onto the ottoman and looked in despair at Nathanson.

"It is Meillet, I am sure of it."

Nathanson nodded. "You should have killed him," he said flatly. "Or at least not helped him back to life. Why do you think he has taken Miss DeQuincy?"

"He wants one of us." Southey smiled bitterly. "I believe it is my turn, no?"

"I am afraid you are right," said Nathanson, looking unusually agitated. "Curse this foot! I am useless. I can get along on crutches for a few yards, but that is all. Would Naegel help again, do you think?"

"I can take care of it." He opened his arms, displaying the lace at his cuffs. "You are looking at an officer of the Imperial Hussars, you know."

There was a knock at the door, and they froze, worried that Evrett had returned, but it was Elena.

"James, you should be in bed," she announced sternly.

"Yes, madam," he grumbled. "Can you find my crutches, South? I put them under this thing, and now they've moved out of reach."

Obligingly, Southey got down on one knee and retrieved the crutches. They were of polished walnut, quite the most elegant examples he had ever seen.

Nathanson caught his glance. "I am in the lap of luxury here, believe me," he said, as he pulled himself to his feet. "Velvet cushions, silver egg cups, gilt mirrors"—he waved his hand at the mirror hanging over the mantelpiece—"nurses garbed in Italian silk . . ."

Elena blushed. She waited for Southey to hold the door open for her and Nathanson, but he was standing motionless, looking in the mirror.

"What is it?" asked Nathanson sharply. "Did you think of something else, some problem with your scheme to rescue Miss DeQuincy?"

With an effort, Southey pulled himself together. "No, nothing so serious," he said lightly. "Just caught sight of my finery in the mirror. Took my breath away, as it were." He held the door open and watched Nathanson swing easily down the hall and begin the complicated process of maneuvering up the staircase. Even on crutches the man was graceful. A footman stood at his elbow, waiting to escort him out and call for his horse.

He walked slowly out towards the entrance hall, pondering what he had seen in the glass. Someone had been peering cautiously into the room. It was pure chance he had caught him at that one moment, and an instant later the face had vanished.

The man had been wearing a priest's habit, but Southey would have recognized him anywhere. It was Rodrigo.

Probably here to protect Elena, he told himself. After all, she was a Roth, and the eccentric Doña Maria might not be the best judge of servants and outriders for this odd journey across Europe.

Still, something nagged at him as he hoisted himself into the saddle and set out in the twilight towards Vienna. Whatever it was would have to wait, he reminded himself. His job at the moment was to sit in the loft and wait for a message from Meillet. He had no doubt it would be coming.

Twenty-Four

The cellar was not so dreadful, after all. They had offered her a choice: a lantern with her hands tied, or darkness with no bonds. Evidently they were afraid she might use the lantern to make mischief were she not restrained.

She had been tempted by the dark; the cellar was small and just as clean as the rest of the house, but she had caught a faint odor of turnips and a stronger one of apples. If food had been stored here, there would be mice. She chose the lantern. Meillet supervised a thin young man who brought down blankets and two of the featherbeds from her chamber upstairs. Then they left her, and she heard a bolt shoot across the door into the kitchen. She had seen the door; it was very stout.

Her hands had been bound in front of her, and she suspected that if she knew anything about knots she might be able to untie the ropes with her teeth. But she did not, in fact, know anything about knots, and she had the lowering suspicion that she would end by losing some teeth to no purpose.

Even if she could get her hands free, she was helpless, unless she wished to burn herself to death by setting the wooden stairs on fire. With a sigh, she positioned herself carefully on the little nest of featherbeds on the floor, tugged a blanket over her shoulders, and rolled over to face away from the lantern.

For a long time, she lay awake, thinking about the story Evrett had told her. She had thought of little else since the moment when he had sought her out on Sunday morning, his dark eyes troubled, and suggested that they take another short walk in the garden.

She felt sorry for them both: for Sommers, as she still thought of him, and for Evrett. The latter's honesty had compelled him to pass on what he had heard from Nathanson, but it was clear he still despised and mistrusted the fencing master and was reluctant to give Elizabeth any excuse to reconsider her decision to leave.

And then there was Sommers. Unbidden, the picture of him slumped despairingly over the table in the loft rose up before her, followed by the even more frightening image of his face under the scaffolding in front of the guildhall. No, that was not how she wanted to think of him.

Closing her eyes, she tried to superimpose the smile of the young-old Sommers onto Southey's head, with its paler face and red-brown hair. It worked perfectly. He was still the man she knew. Satisfied, she fell asleep.

The woman woke her just past daybreak and took her back up to the bedchamber. It was not as bright as it had been yesterday; they had tacked oilpaper over the hole in the window. The oilpaper would be easy to tear off, she thought, but it soon became apparent she was not going to be left alone for even a moment.

Her bad-tempered warden stayed with her even while Elizabeth washed and dressed. Whenever anything was required from below, she knocked on the door, where the thin young man was posted, and he hurried off to fetch it.

At sunrise, Meillet came in and genially assured her that it would not be long now before she would be at liberty. He was dressed for traveling and had a valise. She heard the carriage wheels on the drive after he had gone downstairs.

Where was he going? What did he intend to do with her? Would he truly let her go?

She considered the alternative: would he kill her? She thought not. Certainly he had had no compunction about ordering the death of Purcell, that inconvenient obstacle to the capture of his prey. But she was of no use to him now, except as a counter to exchange for money.

Calmly, she went back to the bed and her perusal of the psalms. They struck her more forcibly than ever before—perhaps because of her situation; perhaps because reading them in German took away the familiar sameness and forced her to pay attention.

"I will lift up my eyes to the hills, whence comes my help," she said softly in German, reading out loud. Startled, the woman looked up from her tatting and glanced at the window, as though Elizabeth had been referring to something real. But then she saw the Bible. A thin smile appeared, and she resumed her work.

Meillet had chosen well, thought Southey, surveying the open countryside around him with a professional eye. Few trees, no buildings, no place to conceal anyone. The junction of the two roads was adjacent to another, smaller intersection some fifty yards north. It would be impossible to watch so many different approaches simultaneously. And in any case, the Frenchman held all the cards: he had her.

The instructions, very precise and with no mention of alternatives, had been delivered by a ragged boy late last night. He was to come to this crossroads, alone and with no concealed weapons. His horse was to be released and driven off; he was to stand facing east, and should not turn until specifically asked to do so.

With a whimsical smile he dismounted and gave the horse a slap on the rump. It snorted and stared at him indignantly.

"Get on," he told it. "Go home. Don't pretend you're too well-trained to leave me. I've been hiring mounts from your master's rotten stable all summer." He had to hit it twice more before it finally sidled off and trotted back towards the city.

Turning, he set his face towards the rosy sky in the east. Meillet had thought of everything; the sun had just come up, and he was facing into the light. He tilted his shako down so the brim shaded his eyes a bit and stood in the rest position, hands clasped behind his back, legs slightly apart.

To his surprise, he did not feel as tired or stiff as he had thought he would. Shortly thereafter, he heard horses' hooves and the sound of a wheeled vehicle. Obedient to his instructions, he remained motionless. Footsteps came up behind him, and he had to exert some restraint not to turn; it went against all his training.

"Monsieur Southey." It was Jean-Luc's voice. "Please remain still while I search you."

He could smell the unwashed body and the greasy hair, could feel the thick hands moving over him. His saber was removed, scabbard and all, and the small dagger from his belt. He had not bothered to bring any guns.

"Now walk backwards, ten steps."

He did so, sensing the shadow of the carriage behind him. The door opened, and he heard Meillet's voice.

"Turn slowly, and get in."

The sling caught his eye first, and he could not repress a quick surge of savage gratification. Beneath it now he could see the gleam of the pistol, but Meillet read his thoughts. "Force of habit, *mon cher ami*. Should you try anything to curtail your stay with me prematurely, Miss DeQuincy would pay the price."

"You will release her, though, if I cooperate?" he demanded, trying to see his enemy's face in the shadowed seat of the carriage.

"I will," affirmed the other. "I have no use for her, save as a lure to capture you. A lucky chance that Stourhead and I spotted her. I have been ordered out of the country, and might have had to leave with my work unfinished."

Now Southey saw the valise and the coat folded neatly over the seat. "Are you going on a journey?" he queried, apprehension rising. He had thought he would at least be able to make certain that she was safe before he surrendered.

"We are going on a journey," corrected Meillet. "Miss DeQuincy will be released as soon as I send word we are safely away. I will not make her wait until we reach the French lines; as soon as we have a decent head start—say four hours or so—she can have her freedom."

"No," said Southey flatly. "You told me you would release her as soon as I gave myself up."

With an exasperated sigh, Meillet climbed out of the carriage and stood in the road facing his prisoner. "I do not see that you are in any position to set conditions here," he said coldly. "But I am a reasonable man. What do you propose?"

"Release her at once and convey her to safety. In my presence. In return, I will give you my word to offer you no resistance whatsoever until we cross into French-held territory."

The Frenchman shook his head. "She would notify the Austrians; we would be pursued. I am already beyond the deadline given me for my departure from the country. I cannot take the risk."

"How were you planning to convey me north if I did not give you my parole?" countered Southey. "Drugged?

Surely you would not chance my giving the alarm every time we were stopped and asked for our papers?''

He saw that he had been right, and relief welled up in him. "Take a look at this," he said tersely, extracting the pass from his inside jacket pocket.

Meillet scanned it narrowly, his eyebrows rising, and started to put it away in his own coat.

"Now, now! Not so fast, greedy man," chided the other, holding out his hand for the paper. "You will notice that it is made out to me and contains a very full description, including the red hair, the freckles, and the broken fingers."

Silently, the Frenchman re-read it, shrugged, and handed it back.

"Use your sleeping potion on Miss DeQuincy; then she cannot give the alarm. Once she has been taken to safety, I pledge to escort you, under the protection of this pass, to St.-Cyr's lines, or any other place you choose. This document is useless to you if I am asleep. The Austrians will never let a proscribed Frenchman hand them a pass for an unconscious officer."

He waited, holding his breath, until Meillet eventually nodded. "She has not exactly been cooperative," the Frenchman observed as Southey climbed into the carriage beside him. "How do you suggest I get the drug into her? Hold her down and pour it into her? I have only the one dose, and we are not near an apothecary."

"I'll do it." Southey smiled bitterly. "She trusts me."

The thin man had brought up breakfast and had cleared the dishes away, so she was surprised to hear a knock on the door only a few minutes later. Her guardian rose grudgingly to open it, and Meillet came in. "You have a caller, Miss DeQuincy," he announced, as though he were a butler, but then left again, taking the woman with him and pulling the door shut behind him.

Puzzled, she climbed off the bed and straightened

her gown. Was it her uncle? Surely Evrett would not have had to come in person to pay her ransom? She heard low voices in the hall speaking in French and froze. She had heard that voice speaking French many times. The door opened, and he was there.

The odd uniform registered distantly, and the empty sword belt, which she would later remember. But she looked only at his face, the face she had constructed so carefully before falling asleep in the cellar.

It was the same, smiling gently, the hazel eyes warm. He was scanning her anxiously, and an exclamation broke from him as he saw the bandage. He had no time to say anything, however. She ran over to him, laughing and crying at once, and flung her arms around his neck.

At once he stiffened and began to pull away. Elizabeth would have none of it. She put her hands on both sides of his face and forced him to look straight down at her. With an exasperated sigh he yielded and kissed her—first briefly, and then, when she resisted his efforts to remove her arms, a long, fierce response which left her giddy.

"You have no modesty whatsoever," he said, taking a deep breath. He looked down at her injured hand again and his voice hardened. "Tell me how you came by that bandage."

"It is nothing, it is a scratch," she insisted, clinging to him, resisting his efforts to examine it. "They bound it up it very nicely. I have been quite well treated."

He held her at arm's length, searching her expression to reassure himself she was telling the truth.

"Thank God," he said faintly. "You are truly unharmed? How were you cut?"

"I climbed up and broke the window with my supper tray," she confessed. "And a piece of glass flew into my hand."

His eyes went to the oilcloth over the window, and he started to laugh.

"Do you ever behave?" he asked her, trying to look

stern. "Could you not simply wait patiently, like a good young lady, to be rescued?"

"I suppose it was foolish," she admitted. "I should have known Lord Evrett would send the ransom and Meillet would not harm me. You should be grateful I did not in truth go out the window. I could have broken my neck." She felt him start at the word 'ransom' and looked up at him, alarmed.

"Is something wrong?" Could Evrett not pay the ransom? Was it that high? "Why did you have to come yourself?" Horror filled her; she suddenly knew the truth. "There is no ransom," she said, anger and incredulity rising inside her. "You are the payment." Her eyes blazed. "I won't have it! How can you imagine I would wish to be freed, at such a price!"

He had gone white; in her rage and despair, she took him by the shoulders and shook him. "Why did you come? He would not have hurt me; we would have contrived something eventually!"

"No, you are mistaken," he stammered. "Circumstances have changed. I have accepted a commission in the Austrian army." She looked at his uniform, realizing its significance for the first time. "There is a ransom. I am paying it, but I do not have the funds on hand; I am here to give my bond to Meillet and make arrangements to deliver the money."

She looked at him suspiciously, and then at Meillet, who was standing in the doorway, left hand lightly holding his pistol. The Frenchman gave a cold nod.

Slowly her stance eased slightly. She began to believe him. "I will pay you back. I have some money in England, it appears," she said, and then asked anxiously, "It is not more than a thousand pounds, is it?"

"No." He did not seem to want to say more. She supposed he was embarrassed to hear her offer to pay him back. Stepping away from her, he took a small bottle out of his pocket and uncorked it. "I am afraid you will have to drink this."

She looked at it doubtfully; it smelled vile and familiar. Some kind of sedative. "Why?" she demanded, instantly on guard.

He smiled. "Believe it or not, my French colleague took my word not to raise the alarm once he was gone, but he will not take yours. He insists you must be safely asleep before he will release you."

"You swear this is true? We will both be released? This is not a trick?"

"I swear it," he said emphatically. "Ask your host. He has been ordered to leave Austria immediately. He cannot afford to play any games now. The emperor will be declaring war against France at any moment. What he needs is money."

Again she looked at Meillet, and saw his confirmation. Obediently, she took the little bottle and drank it, wrinkling her nose against the bitter smell.

Southey looked at Meillet and raised one eyebrow; the Frenchman bowed and withdrew, closing the door behind him. They were alone.

Already the drug was making itself felt. A sluggish tingle ran across the back of her neck and she swayed slightly.

"Here," he said roughly, scooping her up and carrying her over to the bed. He would have backed away once he laid her down, but she caught his hand.

"Stay with me, please," she said, her voice already thick with drowsiness.

Sitting down on the bed beside her, he stroked her hair, pushing the curls away from her brow. "You are the most remarkable woman I have ever met," he said softly.

She looked up, saw his face growing misty, and closed her eyes with a contented sigh. Only at the very edge of sleep did logic suddenly reassert itself. If Meillet needed ready money, why was he accepting a bond for future payment instead of coin?

How could she have believed that the Frenchman

wanted anything save the prize he had been striving
for ever since his arrival in Vienna: the person of the
sometime spy and fencing master, Michael Southey?
Why had his sword belt been empty? Officers always
wore their swords, unless they had surrendered to the
enemy.

Frantically she struggled to sit up, to look at him. She
had started to cry, but her eyes refused to open.

"You lied," she managed to say, "You lied to me."
The words would barely come out, it was like trying to
talk through a blanket. "Damn you! You always lie to
me!" Her eyes were glued shut; she could not raise her
head. It was just like the fever, only infinitely more
dreadful.

"Ah, Christ, Elizabeth," he said helplessly. "I've bungled it all so badly. But I'll make it right, I promise."

She felt his arms go around her, and his head came
down on the pillow beside her.

"I should not have come up here. I told Meillet it
would be easier if I gave you the sleeping potion, but
that was not the real reason. I just wanted to see you."
He pulled her closer and wiped the tears away.

She could feel the lace on his cuffs sliding across her
cheeks, but she was powerless to move. She had never
been affected so strongly by a sedative.

That must have been a very large dose, she thought, just
before the blackness closed in completely. *Perhaps I'll
have my revenge by dying first.*

They left her in the garden behind Doña Maria's
house. Southey had wanted to take her to Lady Evrett
in Baden, but Meillet had refused. Did he think he
could walk up, ring the bell and hand the footman an
unconscious woman without arousing suspicion? Besides, Baden was too far south. She must be left someplace secluded, where they could set her down without
being observed, and then get away. Several suggestions

were rejected by Meillet before Southey recalled the tangled walkways behind the big stone house. Meillet had been to the place and agreed.

He picked the lock on the back gate himself and returned to the carriage for Elizabeth, shadowed by Jean-Luc. The sullen Frenchman dogged his steps again as he returned, carrying her limp body, and put her carefully down under one of the little cherry trees.

The house was still quiet, the windows shuttered; it was not yet eight o'clock. Jean-Luc had wanted to take her, but Meillet had pointed out acidly that he would not be much use weighed down with a comatose female should Southey decide to attack—and after all, his parole did not begin until she was safe. He glanced back one last time as he reached the gate. The fair hair glittered against the shawl he had put behind her head; her hands were lying gently in her lap. Her pose under the tree was so natural and graceful he almost expected to see a painter with an easel behind her on the path.

His captor considered him thoughtfully as he climbed into the carriage. "I wonder why I took your parole," he mused. "If you were prepared to give a false oath to the woman you love, what value does your word have for a declared enemy?"

"One of life's little ironies," observed Southey, stretching out his booted legs onto the opposite seat. "I take it we have a long ride ahead of us?"

"Eight hours or so." Meillet relaxed also. "It will be much shorter now that we have proper documentation. We can use the main road, since I need not avoid the checkpoints."

Twenty-Five

He had not anticipated that the posts would be manned so far from enemy lines, nor that there would be any concern about parties traveling north, but he was wrong on both counts. They were held up at Stockerau, a scant four leagues upriver, and by an unfortunate coincidence, the young officer who was supervising the checkpoint was a distant connection of Naegel's and had heard the story of the vicious French kidnappers in great detail. Southey was obliged to get out of the carriage, which he and Meillet had both hoped to avoid, and exert the authority of his pass. By a second unfortunate coincidence, Evrett drove up behind him just as he was emerging from the vehicle and watched in silent disgust as Southey explained to the guardsman that Herr Meillet was under his protection, and was now hastening to comply with the request that he leave Austria.

The inn yard was crowded, and he was not aware of Evrett until the uncomfortable glances of the soldiers alerted him that there was someone in back of him who was more than just another traveler. He swung round and looked up into two contemptuous dark eyes.

"Switched sides again, Southey?" drawled Evrett, flicking imaginary dust off of the cushion of the phaeton.

"As you see," he replied, feeling the blood drain away from his face.

"Seems only fair," commented Evrett brutally. "Why should the French and the British have all the fun? Surely the Austrians merit your favor as well." His eyes rested on the carriage. "I assume you will not object if I search your vehicle?"

"Not at all." He stepped back and waited while Evrett's groom made a thorough search of the passenger compartment and the luggage boot. "Did you think I had her under the seat?" he inquired caustically.

Tight-lipped, Evrett gathered up his reins. "If I find she has been anywhere near you, you will pay, and pay dearly," he promised. His face was haggard, and Southey felt a sudden surge of pity for him. Probably he had been up since before dawn going around to the various posting-houses to try to get word of her.

"She is not with me," he said wearily. "Go home. Get some rest. You'll do her no good exhausting yourself like this." He added, as Evrett looked speculatively over at the puzzled officer, "Don't bother telling him what a villain I am. I have a *laissez-passer* signed by Metternich."

Meillet had stood next to him, completely unruffled, during this entire exchange, as though he had not understood a word. But, as Southey knew, his English was fluent.

When they at last were able to get back in the carriage and proceed on their way, the Frenchman said slowly, looking at the receding figure of Evrett, rigidly upright on the seat of the phaeton, "Who was that? Another of Miss DeQuincy's admirers, I take it?"

"Her fiancé," answered Southey shortly.

Meillet looked a bit surprised. "It does not bode well for their marriage that she should throw herself into

your arms in that bedchamber. But perhaps I am old-
fashioned in my attitude towards such matters."

Southey thought of Meillet's reputation as a ladies'
man and wondered whether his wife thought him old-
fashioned. "Her future fiancé, then. I anticipated matters slightly. He is a friend of her late brother, very
wealthy. Quite a nice chap, when he isn't righteously
indignant."

"So you have it all settled," commented Meillet dryly.
There was an awkward pause. "I must commend you
on your fidelity to your parole," he said at last. "And
now that I think of it, I never thanked you for bandaging
my shoulder the other day."

"No great matter," muttered Southey, embarrassed.
But then something occurred to him. He leaned forward, and caught Meillet's gaze. "What if I gave you my
word that I do not know where Rover is? Perhaps we
could omit your imitation of Torquemada then, and
proceed immediately to the tribunal."

"Nathanson tried to tell me that he did not know,
either," said Meillet, curling his lip scornfully. "I find
that impossible to believe."

"You have a son," the other man shot back. "If you
knew that anyone who could locate you was in danger,
would you tell him where you were?"

For a moment he saw a rare flicker of uncertainty in
the gray eyes and pressed his advantage. "Think, man!
Would you tell me, with my history, where Rover was?
Why should you waste Jean-Luc's time and make both
of us sick to our stomachs? I swear I know nothing of
any use to you. I have not been in England for three
months, and although I send reports to London, they
send no information back to me. Let it go. Just hang
me and be done with it."

There was no reply, but that moment of doubt he
had seen gave him hope. He did not pursue it, but
leaned back in his seat and gazed absently out the window, watching the farmland give way to hills. They

passed some cattle pastures and went through several small towns.

The land leveled out again: there were more herdsmen, and a series of prosperous-looking farms. The sun was nearly overhead when the village came into view, carved out of a steep glen, with a tiny white church nestled up at the top of the defile. The road climbed up along the glen, right through the middle of the cottages.

As they went by, he could see a small figure dressed in a priest's cassock scurrying eagerly down the hill. *Lunch time,* he thought, amused. Then he stiffened.

"Hell," he said.

Meillet, who had been dozing, came instantly awake, glancing out the window to look for soldiers. Seeing none, he looked over at his companion. "Well?" he demanded, eyebrows raised.

"I find I am more devout than I would have supposed." Southey attempted a light tone. "With my demise imminent, I am reluctant to perjure myself twice in one day. I have suddenly realized that I do, indeed, know where Nathanson's father is."

"That is rather unfortunate," commented the blond man in placid tones. "For you."

"Don't be so damned phlegmatic, Meillet," retorted Southey. "You're a Frenchman, for heaven's sake, not an Englishman. You should be delighted at this news."

"Strangely enough, however, I am not," said Meillet. "In the first place, it is not clear Jean-Luc will be able to persuade you to confide in me. And in the second place, I may no longer be in a position to act upon the information. I am *persona non grata* in Austria now, and I do not possess Rover's talent for disguise. But the location of your principal courier will be valuable to us, even if we cannot touch him for the moment. Under the circumstances, in other words, I am afraid that the tribunal will have to wait." He adjusted his back against the cushions. "Still, we have many hours to go before these unpleasant events. Do you play chess?"

"I have played, yes."

"Without a board? Pawn to king's fourth."

"Pawn to king's fourth," came the automatic reply. "Knight to king's bishop's third."

Southey tilted his head back and examined the ceiling of the carriage. "Knight to queen's bishop's third," he said at last. "Trite, but effective."

"James?" Elena's voice was soft, but insistent. He groaned and burrowed under the sheets. Last night had been very bad, and he had not fallen asleep until three or four in the morning. She stepped away from the bed and ruthlessly opened the curtains. Still early, he concluded, assessing the light with a practiced eye. Too early.

"Leave me be," he grumbled. "I'm an invalid, remember?"

"What does Miss DeQuincy look like?" she demanded, ignoring him.

Outraged, he sat up and glared at her. "You woke me for that? What on earth are you thinking?"

"I am thinking," she responded frostily, "that Jurgen has just discovered a well-dressed young woman asleep in our garden. Deeply asleep. Drugged, in fact, if I am any judge. And since you have been talking of nothing but the missing Englishwoman since yesterday afternoon, it occurred to me that this event might be of interest to you."

He was out of bed in one bound, forgetting his foot, which promptly gave way and pitched him onto the floor. "*Sanglante cheville*," he cursed, and hauled himself up by hanging onto the side of the bed. Then he realized he was only wearing a nightshirt, which had ridden up over his thighs. "Don't tell Anselm," he warned her, grabbing his crutches and hobbling over to the enormous dressing room. He threw on a dressing gown and headed out to the hall.

"Aren't you going to get dressed?" asked Elena, scandalized, as she hurried after him.

"Where is she?"

"Downstairs, in the small drawing room."

"Naturally there would be steps involved," he muttered. "I am rapidly learning to detest steps and all their progeny." But he lowered himself down the great staircase quite nimbly, and clattered quickly through the two dining rooms into the small drawing room. One glance at the figure on the couch was sufficient.

"It's Miss DeQuincy, all right," he said grimly to Elena. "Wake her up. At once. Walk her, pour water on her, give her coffee, call Dr. Allais. Do whatever it takes. I'm going to get dressed. I am an idiot." And he disappeared back down the hall.

Openmouthed, Elena stared after him. But she obeyed. The fluttering maidservants who were hovering over the sleeping woman were dismissed, a footman was sent to fetch the doctor, two more footmen were delegated to haul the limp figure to its feet and drag it back and forth across the carpet.

At the moment it did not seem as though they would be able to get anything into the patient's mouth at all, but she ordered coffee anyway. After a moment's consideration, she asked that a breakfast tray be brought in as well.

In an astoundingly short time, her cousin reappeared, looking even more irritable than usual, trailed by an apologetic Silvio. He was in a shirt and pantaloons, but the latter had been slashed at the bottom to accommodate the bandages and resembled nothing so much as a partially peeled scallion.

"Don't say anything," he snapped to Elena. "Usually we change the bandages before I get dressed, but there is no time. How is she?" A glance at the stolid footmen and the rag doll between them answered his question. "Where is that doctor?"

The gentleman in question arrived at this point,

breathless and in a state of partial dress similar to his own. At his request, the footmen placed their burden back on the sofa, and he examined her carefully.

"Drugged," he said at last, straightening up. "A large dose, too. She will not wake for many hours."

"We have to wake her," insisted Nathanson, frenzied. "There must be something we can do."

The doctor frowned. "It will do no good to precipitate matters. I admit I am uneasy; her pulse is very sluggish. Nevertheless, it is best to wait. The drug will dissipate in time."

"You don't understand," said Nathanson desperately. "I didn't think; I let him go off last night. He is a dead man if we cannot wake her and find out where they have gone."

"Who is a dead man? What are you talking about, James?" asked Elena, bewildered.

"Michael Southey. The other man who was here last night with Lord Evrett. Miss DeQuincy was kidnapped by the same Frenchman who seized me four days ago. And if she is here, safe, it can mean only one thing. He has exchanged himself for her. I ought to have realized that was what he intended. He has done the same thing before."

The doctor grasped the situation more quickly than Elena. He sat down next to the sleeper and took her pulse. Then he looked up at Nathanson. "It would be pointless to try to rouse her now," he said. "I will take her pulse every quarter hour. If there is no change in an hour, we will consider what to do then."

During the first quarter hour, he sat watching the clock and waiting for Dr. Allais to reappear. The Swiss had gone off to finish dressing. During the second quarter hour, he ate breakfast. During the third quarter hour, he allowed Elena to replace his bandages, but he refused to go upstairs and change clothing. For the last quarter hour, he paced, or whatever the equivalent of pacing is, if it is done on crutches.

"It is no good," said Allais, rising from the couch at the end of the hour. "You may try to wake her if you wish, but she will not be able to swallow, so a restorative is out of the question. I would advise you to wait."

"Go get dressed properly, James," said Elena, giving him a small push. "If she does wake and you need to go off somewhere, it would be as well to be ready to go."

Fuming, he followed her advice. This meant removing and then reapplying the bandages, so as to get his clothing on over his foot. It took nearly half an hour. The moment he was dressed, he hopped back down the stairs and returned to his vigil. During his absence, Doña Maria had come in briefly and had advised Elena to try burning feathers under the young lady's nostrils.

"Feathers!" snorted Nathanson. "Does she think this is a swoon?" He did not think much of his hostess, and saw less of her, which suited him admirably.

Punctually at ten, Dr. Allais reappeared and checked on the patient. "No change," he said briefly. A footman came in, and halted when he saw the doctor and the little group clustered around the couch. "Pardon me, Captain," he said hesitantly, "but Lord Evrett has called. Should I ask him to wait?"

For answer, Nathanson swung over to the door, leaned out and shouted at the top of his lungs, "Evrett! She's here!"

The footman stood gaping, but Elena, hearing the cane tapping uncertainly through the warren of reception rooms, sent him off with a sharp command to bring his lordship in at once. A minute later a breathless Evrett came in the door.

"What is wrong with her?" he gasped, seeing the doctor holding a limp wrist. "My God, is she hurt? What did Southey do to her?"

"She is drugged," said Nathanson curtly. "And at the moment, we cannot wake her." He did not bother to defend Southey from Evrett's prejudiced assumption of villainy, since he rather suspected that in this case prejudice was correct.

Evrett looked horrified. "He *drugged* her?" He looked down in anguish at the marble-hued face on the cushions. "That blackguard! My God, and to think he stood there in front of me and told me to go home and get some rest!"

"You saw him?" Nathanson grabbed his arm, shook it. "You saw South? Where?"

"I am grieved to be the bearer of this news," said Evrett heavily. "But you need to know. He was with Meillet, traveling north in a closed carriage. Quite the boon companions, the two of them. I came upon him at the guard post at Stockerau explaining that Monsieur Meillet was under his protection, and waving a ministerial pass."

"I knew it," whispered Nathanson. He whirled on Elena. "Elena, if you asked her, do you think Doña Maria would lend us her carriage? Doesn't she have a large one, a berlin?"

"For heaven's sake," interrupted Evrett. "You can't imagine you will catch them? They'll be behind French lines in less than six hours. He's not worth the trouble, in any case. Good riddance to him."

"Didn't you understand anything I told you the other night?" demanded Nathanson furiously. "He hates Meillet like poison. The only person he hates more is himself. He has exchanged himself for Miss DeQuincy. Meillet's carting him off to interrogate him about my father. When that is over, if he is still alive, they'll hang him. And the worst part is, he is probably happier right now sitting in that coach than he has been for the last six months."

There was an appalled silence.

"I'm sorry," said Evrett numbly. "He fooled me completely. And Meillet, too. Not a care in the world, it appeared, either of them." He swallowed. "They are well on their way by now; it is nearly two hours since I saw them north of the river. You will never catch them."

"Stockerau," muttered Nathanson. "He's headed up to St.-Cyr's division, I'll wager. That is the closest."

Elena was still standing next to him, frozen.

"I'll still want the carriage," he told her.

She nodded and hurried away.

"Fetch me pen and paper," he snapped to the footman who had guided Evrett into the room. He sat down at the foot of the couch, absently pushing the sleeper's feet back to make room, and drew up a small side table. When the footman reappeared, he snatched the paper and scrawled five quick lines. Without bothering to seal it, he handed it back. "Deliver that at once," he said. "Send a good rider on a fast horse. And tell him to bring the reply to the Tabor bridge and await us there."

"What are you doing?" asked Evrett. "You'll never catch them, I tell you. Not even on horseback, let alone in a carriage."

"I don't have to catch them," said Nathanson, stuffing food from the breakfast tray into a napkin. "I just have to get there before they actually hang him. Drayton told me once that South could hold out for quite a while under interrogation. Evidently his father used to spend his leisure time beating him. If he can last for a bit, I can make the French give him back. He's an officer in the Austrian cavalry. They can't hold him."

"You're wrong," said Evrett flatly. "Austria has declared war. The bells were ringing as I came back through town."

"Doesn't matter." Nathanson restored Elizabeth's feet to their proper place on the couch as he struggled up from his seat. "The terms of the armistice were that the cease-fire and all its conditions would continue for a seven-day beyond the expiration of the treaty. And one of the conditions was that no prisoners could be taken."

Elena hurried in with a napkin which looked as though its contents were similar to the one in her cousin's hand. "You can have a carriage," she said breathlessly. "The small one, the landaulet. Apparently it is faster. And in any case, Doña Maria will be using the large one. She will follow you. She claims Meillet is an old acquaintance. It may even be true. She has certainly spent enough time hounding the French commanders this past month."

Seeing Nathanson struggling to carry his bundle and manage the crutches simultaneously, she relieved him of it and went off with both bundles towards the front of the house.

"I could drive," Evrett offered unexpectedly. "I have my phaeton here. It's quite well sprung."

Nathanson shook his head. "Someone should stay with Miss DeQuincy," he said, glancing down at the still figure below him. "Eventually, she will wake up. Tell her I have gone after him. Tell her I will do my best."

The small drawing room was at the side of the house away from the stables, but Evrett could dimly hear the confusion and shouted orders as the carriages were harnessed and servants ran in and out of the house with messages and supplies. Eventually the noise died away, and he was left perched on his chair across from the couch, watching the slight rise and fall of Elizabeth's chest. A prim older woman, some sort of superior maid-servant, had come in as soon as Elena had gone, and was sitting silently on the other side of the room. Her principal duty, Evrett knew, was to serve as guard, in case he should suddenly prove to have a tendency to ravish unconscious females. But she would remain, even if he went away. They would not leave her by herself.

Should he go? His was not the face she would want to see when she woke, he knew. And yet he could not leave her to come to herself in a strange room, in a strange house, surrounded by someone else's servants.

With a sudden stab of remorse he remembered Southey's frantic efforts to locate Anna. "I hope they find him," he told the sleeping Elizabeth. "It is difficult to apologize to a dead man."

Twenty-Six

"Any progress?" Meillet rose impatiently as a sweating Jean-Luc came into the guardroom where he had been waiting.

Jean-Luc shook his head. Meillet could read the scorn in his square face. The scorn was for him; he should be present at the questioning. In his subordinate's opinion, he was too fastidious for the *Sûreté.*

It was true. Perhaps he should have joined the army, where this sort of thing was frowned upon. But then, he did not like blood or broken bodies even under honorable conditions. Jean-Luc, on the other hand, found it quite satisfying to serve his country by brutalizing prisoners. His attitude was straightforward: these are spies, we are a police force, the rules of war do not apply.

Normally, he agreed. It had not bothered him much to watch Nathanson, defiant, gritting his teeth as the spikes went into his leg. For one thing, the tub had blocked his view of the blood. It had not bothered him to watch a trooper break the bones in Southey's right hand and arm, one by one, three months ago; his rage at the Englishman's double-dealing had been too fresh. He had even, on that occasion, landed a few blows himself.

He had intended to stay this time, as well. It was his duty. Southey might let a phrase slip, might mutter something—something meaningless to his thick-witted henchman, but revealing to him. But when the shirt had come off and he had seen the scars, he had grown uneasy and decided Jean-Luc would do better on his own.

He had ordered him to report immediately if the Englishman said even one syllable, but apart from four words early on in the proceedings, there had been nothing but silence. The four words had been the reply to Meillet's offer to hear anything he might wish to say before the formal interrogation began.

Southey had thought for a moment, then said, "Queen to king's fourth." Meillet had left.

"Has he said anything? Anything at all?"

"No, monsieur. I think he is in a trance. I have seen a few like this. He understands nothing now except that he must not speak. At the moment he is unconscious, so I came to see if you had further orders."

"Leave him be," muttered Meillet. "Let him think it is over for the moment. It will be more difficult then, when you resume. Go down to the commissary, get yourself and Julien something to eat and drink."

"I have no pass, monsieur. They will not let me through to the main section of the camp."

He had forgotten that. The relationship between the *Sûreté* and the army was not a cordial one. Properly speaking, the surveillance office was a glorified border guard, whose original mission during the revolutionary period had been to patrol the French coast for English agitators and escaping *aristos*. In the sanguinary atmosphere of those chaotic days, the *Sûreté* had developed a ruthless character which had persisted even after Napoleon's rise.

The army sneered at its recruits, deplored its tactics, refused to recognize its officers as military men—and gladly profited from the information it provided. Even now, with a captive who surely must be regarded as a major prize, he had been treated coldly.

They had grudgingly allotted him a small room in a market hall being used as a temporary barracks for the interrogation, and he had been forced to wait here in the guardroom rather than being allowed to use one of the private chambers reserved for visiting officers. Luckily, it was empty at the moment. The contemptuous glances of the soldiers when Jean-Luc had come in earlier had been disagreeable.

That first time, still shaken from the sight of the marks on Southey's back, he had considered letting the whole thing go. The tribunal would be a simple affair. The man had been in French pay, had entered the country six or seven times in civilian clothing, and then had betrayed his employers and rescued an English captive. He and Jean-Luc were both on hand to testify—if Southey even bothered to contest the charges. Was it worth it to wait through what was likely to be a long and hateful process for information he might not be able to use?

But then he had remembered the months of Arnaut's imperious commands, the ignominy of house arrest, the shambles the false Arnaut had made of his network of British informants. It was possible he was here, in this very camp, posing as another French officer. He would have to go through with it.

Jean-Luc was still standing there, scowling at him truculently. He looked tired, thought Meillet. Flogging was hard work. The scrawny Julien was not much use. He was only there to assist and usually left everything to his larger cousin.

"Here," he said impatiently, pulling out a purse and extracting a few coins. "Go down the road, then, to the inn." He himself had no interest in food at the moment.

Colonel Michel Sénard was a harried man. For the last few days he had been absorbed in the delicate task of preparing his troops to engage Schwarzenberg—who would almost certainly move towards Dresden—without violating the terms of the just-expired armistice. The orders had been very clear: let the allies be the ones to break the agreement if hostilities were indeed to be resumed before the week-long cease-fire was over.

St.-Cyr, a difficult commander at the best of times, was furious at the restrictions these orders imposed and had promptly delegated responsibility for maintaining the truce to his colonels, who were simultaneously told to be ready for an allied attack at any moment.

And now, in the past few hours, all sorts of distractions had risen up to plague him. First, a courier had come galloping in with the news that Austria had declared war. This was expected, but caused some excitement among the men.

Shortly thereafter, an official of the Lille *Sûreté* had arrived, claiming to have a valuable prisoner and demanding facilities to interrogate the man. And five minutes ago, just as he had begun to think he might have time to eat some supper, two very stern Austrian officers had appeared, with a safe-conduct in St.-Cyr's own hand, demanding that he account to them for his possession of this same prisoner. With them, even more improbably, was a wounded man in civilian clothing who had introduced himself as a British captain attached to the Prussian command.

"Meillet informed me the man was a British spy." Sénard tried to keep the irritation out of his voice. Of all the ridiculous situations, that three enemy officers should be here in his camp, days—hours, perhaps—before their forces would attack. He hoped his duty officer had had the sense to bring them to his staff room through the village, rather than taking them through the camp proper. At least it was dark now.

"He has renounced his English citizenship," one of the Austrians said coldly. "His commission was granted to him, for services rendered to Austria, by Prince Metternich himself. I have a copy of the commission with me." He extracted a folded wad of papers from his jacket.

Sénard waved the papers away impatiently and turned to his orderly. "Have the corporal ask Monsieur Meillet to step in here, if you please." He did not ask the visitors to be seated, nor did he offer them refreshment. They stood impassively across from him, the wounded man leaning on his crutches. Three or four minutes later, Meillet appeared, escorted by the corporal. Sénard was watching his face closely and saw the dismay and anger as he took in the identities of the other men in the office.

"You are very bold, Captain," Meillet said to the man on crutches, who made no reply.

"These men are here under safe-conduct, Meillet," Sénard said sharply, reminding him by his tone who was in charge. "And they have come to me with a rather disturbing allegation, that the prisoner you brought in a short while ago is in fact an officer in the Hussars."

"He is an English spy, as I told you," answered Meillet angrily. "He will admit it. Ask him."

Sénard turned to the corporal. "Did you see the prisoner, Leleu, as you were escorting Monsieur Meillet to the barracks?"

"Yes, sir," stammered the corporal, a boy of nineteen.

"Was he wearing a uniform of any sort?"

"Yes, sir. Green jacket, red breeches and helmet. Quite distinctive, sir."

"Fifth Hussars," said Sénard in disgust, looking down at a letter in his hand. "Just as the minister states. What are you playing at, Meillet?"

"I do not care what he claims to be now," said Meillet,

his voice edged with frustration. "He was, is, a spy. I met with him personally more than a half dozen times near Calais. Not only was he not in uniform, he was *in our pay!* And then he sold us back to the English. Just four days ago, he gave me this." And he gestured towards the sling.

"You may not care what he is now, but I do," snapped Sénard. "If this is reported as a violation of the truce, St.-Cyr will have my head." He turned to the corporal. "Fetch the prisoner at once." The corporal disappeared.

"Look at your orders," insisted Meillet. "There is a *mandat* out against him, with a reward for his capture."

Uneasily, Sénard gestured to his aide-de-camp, who went into a back room and reappeared with the order books. "What is the date of the *mandat?*" he asked, untying the laces which fastened the covers of the huge portfolio.

"Late May, perhaps early June."

Sénard was leafing through the stack of papers and stopped, scrutinizing one of them closely. Then he pulled it out, set it on his desk, and continued to search through the folder. At last he looked up, his face stern.

"This *mandat* is invalid," he announced, pointing to the paper in the folder. "It is signed by Arnaut, the English impostor. At your own request, all orders issued by him were declared null and void. I have the minister's endorsement of your request right here." And he held out the second paper, the one he had extracted and placed on his desk.

A strangled sound, which quickly turned into a cough, came from the man on crutches. Meillet whirled. "There is a *mandat* out against this one as well," he said fiercely, pointing to him. "He is one of their couriers, the son of the man who impersonated Arnaut."

"Captain Nathanson is under safe-conduct," Sénard reminded him.

The corporal reappeared, an odd expression on his face.

"Where is the prisoner?" demanded the colonel, suddenly apprehensive. If the man had died in his camp, there would be hell to pay.

"He is—he cannot walk, sir." The corporal swallowed, remembering. "I am not sure if he is conscious or not. Should I have him carried here?"

"No—please." The English officer, looking very agitated, had interrupted. "Could we have a doctor look at him before he is moved? I have had some experience with Monsieur Meillet's interrogations," he added, his face grim.

"See to it, corporal," said Sénard curtly, cursing under his breath. A protégé of Metternich, captured illegally and tortured right in his camp. What could be worse? The answer arrived immediately, in the person of his duty officer.

"Colonel," he announced, saluting smartly. "Doña Maria de Izalza has called again. She begs your pardon for troubling you once more, especially at this time when she understands you will be very preoccupied, but she has been given a safe-conduct by the marshal. Evidently she is a family friend of some young Austrian officer who has mistakenly been detained here."

With an inward groan, Sénard abandoned all hopes of supper. "Show her in," he said wearily. "And bring chairs for her and that woman who comes with her, whatever her name is, Señora Muñoz." The two women had already spent many hours in his office this past month.

"There are four of them, colonel," said the duty officer respectfully. "The two ladies and their maid, as before, and an older gentleman, a Dr. Allais. She heard the young man had been injured and brought her physician."

"Well, there is one bright spot in this absurd *gâchis*." Sénard stood up. "Conduct the doctor to the east barracks immediately. Come to think of it, perhaps the ladies should accompany him, reassure themselves about the young man's condition."

"With respect, sir." The corporal was very pale. "I am afraid I do not think that is a good idea. At this time, that is. Sir."

He had laughed to himself when they had stripped off his shirt and he had seen Jean-Luc's eyes fastened on the scars. The gloating expression which followed immediately made him hold his breath, hoping. Was it possible they would think this a weak spot?

His luck was good; they had rebound his hands in front of him and pushed him down over a bench. Incredibly, they had not even bothered to go in search of a proper scourge. Jean-Luc had simply used his coachman's whip.

They were in a hurry, he decided, hoping to discover Rover's whereabouts while there might still be time to send someone to Vienna. As soon as hostilities resumed, it would be much more difficult for anyone connected with the French forces to travel so far south.

It was all so familiar: the sting, the sound of the leather hitting his skin, the oddly gentle feel of the drops running down his back. That did not last long, of course. He knew all the stages by heart. First you could count every blow. Then you began to notice only the parts of your back that had not yet been cut, mapping the blank spaces and adding them, one by one, to the roster as the lash sang across them.

Jean-Luc was not very good at his trade; he missed quite frequently. Once the whip became tangled around his neck, and he found himself almost irritated, because he lost his rhythm as they unwound it. Quite a few times, Jean-Luc aimed too low and smacked the thong with a loud echo off of the stiff cloth of his breeches. But that was all early on, while he still could hear and see.

From long experience he knew when to withdraw, when the distractions of Julien's face or the changing light on the wall or the sound of the blow would not be able to compete with the pain. That was when he closed everything and went inside. A small part of him was afraid, was warning him that this was not like all those other times. His father had always stopped, eventually. These men would not. What would happen when he retreated into his shell, and then, instead of stomping away, as his father did, they simply kept on going?

He passed out. He had never fainted before when his father had beaten him; the surprise and horror when he came to and the blows were still falling was indescribable. That was when he understood: pain was pain. The initial advantage his father's brutality had given him was gone.

It could have been burning irons, or broken bones, as in Sangatte, or that sickening boot they had put on Nathanson. At first, one might be more horrifying or painful than the other, but in the end, it was all the same.

He cursed himself. What sort of ridiculous bravado had impelled him to tell Meillet that he knew where Rover was? Now they would keep going until he told them. And he would eventually, unless Jean-Luc miscalculated and killed him first. He toyed briefly with the idea of taunting the man, goading him, but rejected it. He did not dare speak. His only hope was to forbid himself to utter a single word.

His sense of time was gone. He knew that they stopped at intervals and then started again, but he could not have said how long those intervals were. Odd impressions danced in and out of his head; he could no longer will himself to close his eyes or not to listen. Jean-Luc swearing. Julien drinking something; he realized he was desperately thirsty and spent some uncountable number of minutes absorbed in that pain instead of the sensations from his back. His breeches, soaked with sweat, clinging to his thighs—was there that much blood? Then he remembered: they were red.

Someone was talking, and he panicked, thought that the voice was his, that some part of him had betrayed his resolve not to speak. He began to scream and struggle. Jean-Luc was so taken aback that his hand stopped in mid-air. He realized with relief that the screams were coming from a different person than the person who had been talking. He passed out again.

But the next time he awoke, he realized he was talking, babbling, the words spurting out so quickly he himself could not understand them.

It was over. He had given in. This time he let the blackness take him without fear.

When he awoke once more, there were too many people in the room. Julien and Jean-Luc were gone. Someone was sponging his back, very carefully. It was worse than the flogging.

He started to go under again, hoping it was a hallucination. But now another someone was forcing his head up, telling him to open his mouth, to drink.

With a giant effort, he willed his face to turn away from the tempting contents of the mug. God, he was thirsty. But if he drank, he might wake up and remember what he had told them. Better not to know.

A voice, a familiar exasperated voice, was speaking in English, telling him not to be an idiot. Startled, he opened his eyes. It was Nathanson and, next to him, a silver-haired man in shirtsleeves with blood all over his hands.

"What do you think, that I'm trying to poison you?" demanded his friend roughly, thrusting the mug at him again. "Open your ears, you blockhead. You're safe. They're releasing you—if your lordship will deign to accompany us."

He did not listen, did not drink. Behind Nathanson, in the doorway of the little room, were three elderly women in gowns which had not been worn in Spain for nearly thirty years. No, it could not be true. He stared in a daze at the walls, checking to make sure: he was still in the French camp. He had not been moved.

The most dreadful, horrible coincidence in the whole dreadful, horrible course of the last year had materialized in front of his eyes to damn him. From somewhere he found the strength to raise his head, to move. "Go!" he croaked urgently, flailing his arms and then stopping in surprise when he realized they were no longer bound. "I told them. They know. You have to go, quickly!"

"Nonsense," said Doña Maria briskly in her lisping French. "I am quite sure you did nothing of the sort." She turned to Allais. "Can he be moved right away?"

"No," answered the doctor baldly. He had taken the mug from Nathanson and now Southey did finally dare to take one sip. He hoped it was brandy, but it was only water. Still, it felt wonderful.

It felt so good that he took another sip. The room swam, and he blinked. It settled. The women were still there, looking quite calm. Had they not heard him?

"I did tell them," he insisted, frenzied. "I heard myself talking in French. You must leave, they will be back at any moment."

"We heard you talking, also," Doña Maria informed him. "When we came in, you were reciting La Fontaine's fable of the fox and the crow. Your accent is quite good, but you made rather free with the meter."

Nathanson had suddenly frozen in place and was looking at her in horror.

"I am afraid we must remove him, in spite of his condition," she said to Allais, ignoring Nathanson. She signaled to someone who was outside the room. Her skirts blocked his view from where he was lying on the floor. Whoever it was replied in Spanish and moved away.

"If we leave him here and the allies attack, they will be able to take him prisoner legitimately. As soon as we

are clear of the French lines, we will stop so you can
tend him properly."

Two French soldiers came in with a litter and lifted
him on, face down. After a brief consultation, they
draped some kind of cloth over him and carried him
down the hall, which was crowded with curious troops.
Gasps as he went by were suppressed by a stern command in French from one of the litter bearers.

Then there was a brief glimpse of the night sky, cloudy
and heavy with moisture. The cloth was already sticking
to his back; he could feel every one of the coarse threads.
A sickening, jolting, heave, and he was face down on
the padded seat of an enormous carriage. He could
hear the creaking of hoops and the rustle of skirts as
Doña Maria took her seat on the opposite side.

"If you do not mind, Señora Nuñez, I would like to
ride with my friend." It was Nathanson's voice.

"Come in then, Captain," he heard Doña Maria say.
"Señora Nuñez can ride in the other carriage with Dr.
Allais and my maid." More skirts rustled, and the floor
shook as two passengers exchanged places.

The door closed, there was a painful jerk as the carriage got under way, and he accepted the fact that they
were leaving. He was still alive. They had not arrested
the party in the coach. Perhaps, in fact, he had not told
them after all? Relief began to bubble up, cautiously,
as the wheels jolted forward. Each jounce was like a
blow, but he would gladly have lain under the wheels,
bloody back and all, if it would speed them out of this
camp.

It was very quiet; the others must be nervous, too.
Long after the last sentry had waved them through, an
anxious stillness prevailed. A sudden hollow noise under
the wheels told him they were crossing the bridge.

It was true. He was safe. They were all safe.

Unconsciously, he had been tensing his body, prone
on the seat. Now he relaxed, only to wince as the movement stretched the lacerated muscles of his back.

Nathanson broke the silence the moment they reached the other side of the river. He was livid with rage. "Can you never, ever treat me like your son?" he asked Doña Maria passionately. His voice rose. He was almost shouting. "Can we never meet face to face and converse, as ordinary people do, without the tricks and the paint and the mockery? Is it some sort of test to prove how good the disguise is, that you must flaunt it in front of me every time?"

"I will be very glad to leave off this particular disguise," Doña Maria admitted, dropping into English. "Crouching inside a hoop skirt for six weeks has played havoc with my knees."

Nathanson was not pacified by the mild tone or the attempt at humor. He turned grimly to Southey. "How long have you known?"

"Only today, during the journey north," he said faintly. "I saw a priest, and I suddenly remembered— I had glimpsed Rodrigo, you know, that evening, when I came to visit you and Evrett. You were the one who asked me why she traveled with two priests. I don't know why I didn't figure it out as soon as I recognized him. But I would not have told you even had I realized it earlier."

A blistering curse in French was the only response.

"Be reasonable, James," said his father. "What was the point of telling you? You would only have been distracted from your real purpose in Vienna. You would have constantly been trying to protect me and making me conspicuous either by avoiding me or calling too frequently."

"Another matter apparently deemed too subtle for my feeble brain to comprehend," said Nathanson savagely. "Perhaps you would care to enlighten me now. Why, precisely, was I in Vienna?"

"To keep the French from killing your colleague here, I assume," said Meyer. It was very odd to hear the urbane British voice emerging from the bewigged form of a Spanish noblewoman. "I was not told all the details, but evidently White had sent him here with something quite specific in mind, something rather important."

He closed his eyes, hoping they would think he had swooned again, but Nathanson was in no mood for any more deceptions. Taut with anger, he leaned over. Southey could feel him, almost see the dark eyes fixed on him intently.

"Well?" he demanded. "Was I an adequate body-guard? May I be trusted, now, with this great secret? Or do the bodyguards not need to know? What special mission did White entrust to a man who had taken French gold and abducted my sister?"

"Ask Philip Jervyn," he said. And then he turned his head away and willed himself to pass out again. It worked.

Twenty-Seven

He was looking at the fireplace. It was all he did: he lay on the couch, staring at the fireplace. The weather had grown cooler, especially at night. He supposed he could actually light a fire in it soon. Occasionally, for variety, he would turn and stare up at the ceiling, but his back was still tender, even a month later. And in any case, the fireplace was more attractive.

It had become a little routine now, since he had returned to the loft from Schwarzenberg's camp: get up at dawn, wash, dress, go out to the bakery with Trumpet. Come back, fetch a mug of coffee from the kitchen, lie on the couch. Have some bread and coffee. Look at the fireplace. Change positions.

He did not allow himself to drink the brandy until quite late in the day. But then, he did not sleep much, which meant that there was still plenty of time to drink. Every so often he went down to the tavern on the Tiefer Graben and bought more brandy.

Once a day there was an interruption when Frau Renner brought him a hot meal at noon. He thanked her politely, stirred it with his fork, and scraped most of it into Trumpet's dish. The dog was getting fat.

Only once, since the return from the Austrian field hospital, had he gone out for more than a few minutes. When he had received her letter, he had been afraid he might weaken and go out to Baden. Just after midday on the twenty-ninth, therefore, he had hired a small boat and set off down the river towards Hainburg. To be safe, he had waited until the village of Wildungsmauer to turn back.

The boatman had been absolutely mystified by this odd passenger who sailed to a tiny village and then turned around without seeing anyone or conducting any business. Forgetting his place, he had ventured to argue rather vehemently that *mein Herr* must surely have forgotten some errand and would reproach him if they left too hastily.

At last, grumbling, he told the crew to turn the boat, but he was barely civil when he left Southey off at the fishermen's wharf several hours later. That had been more than a fortnight ago, and he had seen no one except Frau Renner since.

Bells rang out from St. Mary's, booming across the quiet city, and faintly echoed by other clocks chiming the hour. Two o'clock. Normally at this time he would hear delivery carts, errand boys shouting, children playing. But the city these days was hushed, holding its breath for news from the front.

After the siege of Dresden, Frau Renner had tried to give him a report when she brought up his dinner. In the face of his listless indifference, however, she had fallen silent in mid phrase. He had no idea whether Napoleon was even alive. In fact, he was not certain whether he himself was alive.

What happens, after all, when you are sure you are going to be dead, but then you are not, and you have nothing planned for the rest of the interminable time until God corrects the error? The couch seemed as good a version of limbo as any.

He had received other letters, of course, and visitors, whom he had refused to admit. Nathanson four times. On the table lay two unopened notes in the familiar spiky handwriting. Evrett twice. One unopened letter from same. Jervyn once. Naegel once. An unknown Austrian captain. He had resigned his commission; presumably the man had come to see why.

In his letter to Metternich he had simply said that an old injury was troubling him and he was no longer fit for duty. Frau Renner had tried her best to salvage the breeches of his uniform, but there were too many rips in them. So he had sent back two extra gold pieces when he returned everything.

He did regret the boots, for a brief moment. Trumpet probably regretted them more; he had been forced to put them in the sword room and close the door to protect them until he was well enough to arrange to ship his gear back to the quartermaster's office at the Hofburg.

He looked at the clock. Five past two. Perhaps he should take Trumpet out and purchase more brandy. Instead, he found his hand snaking over towards her letter. It no longer seemed worthwhile to fold it and put it away between readings. He left it open on the armchair, which he had pulled up next to one end of the sofa.

Besides, a few of the creases were beginning to be so worn he was afraid they might tear if he kept folding and unfolding it. Without even glancing over, he found the paper by feel and picked it up.

26 August
Baden
Dear Mr. Southey:
      Lady Evrett tells me it is most improper for young
ladies to write to gentlemen, especially gentlemen who

have not been introduced to them. According to her, the only exception to this rule is that a young lady may write to her betrothed. My aunt was of the same opinion, save that in her view the only exception was a brother.

Since I cannot in good conscience pretend to Lady Evrett that you are my brother, I have temporarily deemed you my fiancé, which presumably also answers the objection that we have not been introduced. I stress that it is purely temporary, since Lord Evrett tells me we are leaving on the thirtieth, and once I am gone, I would not be so cruel as to hold you to an engagement to a girl who is hundreds of miles away.

I am told you are not receiving any visitors, and in any case it would not be right for me to call on you at your lodgings. Should you wish to be introduced, however, and to say farewell, I will be at home on the twenty-ninth between two and four at Lady Evrett's villa in Baden.

There was a space, and then, in different ink and larger, less carefully formed letters:

I am sending this by Anna. She has no notion of propriety, fortunately. The above is all nonsense, although I will be there on the twenty-ninth. I will understand if you do not come. Indeed, I do not expect you. I will never, never forget you.

Your Elizabeth

Sometimes, as now, he read the whole letter. Sometimes he read only the part above the space. Occasionally he would read just the last few lines. Very carefully, he put the letter over the back of the sofa, face down, and put his arms behind his head, wincing slightly as the last of the scabs stretched out across his upper back.

After a few minutes he concluded he had done his duty by that position. He rolled back onto his side and contemplated the fireplace.

He must have dozed off, because the next thing he knew, he was blinking groggily and listening to footsteps coming rapidly up the stairs. Too fast to be Frau Renner, and in any case, she had tried to come up once to persuade him to see one of his visitors, and he had been so upset that she had promised never to do so again.

Half past three. Who was it? Meillet? Had the man decided it was worth the risk to come and finish the job? Well, he would not stop him. Deliberately, he picked up the letter and began reading it once more. Then it hit him: rapid footsteps, but uneven. A hoarse panting as Trumpet followed the interloper into the room. *Damn.*

He raised his eyes. Nathanson was sitting in the armchair, regarding him grimly and, for once, allowing the dog to snuffle all over his boots.

"How did you get in?" he demanded. "I told Frau Renner no one was to be admitted. Did you bully her into giving you the key?"

"So you are speaking to me?" asked his visitor, raising one eyebrow. "Here's a change. Ever since you came to in Schwarzenberg's camp and demanded that we hand you over to his surgeons I have had the distinct impression I was *de trop*. Perhaps being denied four times might have contributed to that impression."

"Answer me. How did you get in here?" he repeated, his voice tight.

"I have my own key." Nathanson sat back in the chair and put his feet up on the couch, right next to Southey's legs. Trumpet instantly shifted his theater of operations and wriggled triumphantly between the two leather-clad feet. "It seemed unlikely you were going to decide to be hospitable, so I took a wax impression and had one made." He held it up. "You are not the only one in the courier service who knows something about burglary."

"Go away," Southey said wearily. "Leave me be. I am no longer in the courier service."

"So I gather." Nathanson leaned forward. "No longer a courier. No longer an Austrian officer. No longer teaching fencing. No longer eating." A glance at the hollows under the too-bright hazel eyes. "No longer sleeping. May I ask what you *are* doing, besides wallowing in self-pity?"

"Drinking." He indicated the decanter. "Not yet, though. I always wait until eight to begin. Wouldn't want to be like my father." There was a brief silence. "I'm not going to offer you any. I'm nearly out. Please leave."

"Not quite yet. I have a few things to say to you first," said Nathanson, settling back in the armchair. He looked over at the table, where his two letters lay conspicuously unopened. "Couldn't even do me the courtesy of reading my apologies?"

"Apology accepted. Get out. What are you apologizing for, by the way?"

"For what I said in the carriage. Or had you forgotten? You told me to go ask Jervyn what you were doing here. So I did." He was watching the freckled face closely and saw the mouth tighten. "Ah! You do remember. Did you know Jervyn has resigned? That Sir Charles Barrett has demanded a closed-chamber inquiry in London? That the bill of attainder has been canceled?" No movement. "Did you know that I am selling out?"

Finally, he got a reaction. Southey sat bolt upright, and said furiously, "The hell you say! Why would you do an idiotic thing like that?"

Coldly, Nathanson looked him full in the face. "You call me an idiot? I have only renounced a minor command in the army because I can no longer trust my colonel. You, on the other hand, seem to have decided to renounce everything and everyone you have ever known. Did it never occur to you that there are other people involved in your life besides you? What of your mother? What of my father, who blames himself for the whole thing, since it was his idea to impersonate Arnaut? What of that lovely girl who stood for two hours in Lady Evrett's drawing room last month, looking out the window and pretending she was not crying?"

"Unfair," whispered the other man, slumping back down onto the sofa. "Fight clean, damn you."

"I can't fight this"—Nathanson swept a savage arm around the shabby room, taking in the decanter, the couch, the unopened letters—"cleanly. It's filthy. It's a fraud. It's as revolting as what they did to you. More revolting, perhaps. At least they had a reason. There is no justification for what you are doing to yourself."

To his horror, Southey felt tears welling up, and he turned his face away hastily. "You don't understand," he said brokenly. "It's almost worse, that I was tricked into it. I'm still a villain, and now it seems I've been a fool, as well."

"You are certainly a fool," commented his friend. "But you are not a villain, except perhaps in your dealings with Miss DeQuincy." He waited for a reply, and when Southey kept his face turned away, he sighed and stood up, pushing the dog aside. "Well, my exercise in locksmithing appears to have been pointless. I confess I thought you would at least ask me about your former assistant. She almost died from that laudanum, you know. It would have been a large dose even for a man."

Alarmed, he sat up. "She did? You never told me! Is she better?" Then his eye fell on the unopened letters on the table, and he flushed. "I suppose she is well now; I had a note from her."

"Did you open it?" asked Nathanson in acid tones. He nodded. "And you could not even come out to Baden to say good-bye?"

At the time he had been sure it was right not to see her, he thought. All the more right for being painful and difficult. How could he explain? He stared helplessly at his tormentor.

"Try again," said Nathanson gently. "There is such a thing as a second chance, little though you seem to believe it." He walked lightly over to the doorway, with only a trace of a limp, and vanished down the stairs.

"What do you mean?" Southey asked the empty air, puzzled. Then he heard another set of footsteps.

Trumpet raised his head suddenly and scrambled wildly towards the staircase, yelping in delight, and he understood.

She came hesitantly into the room and halted two or three feet away, holding her bonnet by the strings. He had a vague impression that she was wearing some sort of shimmering silver dress, and he noticed she had taken off her gloves. Her hands were clenched around the bonnet ribbons very tightly. The dark-ringed blue eyes were fixed on him, and he watched their expression change: first anxiety, then anger, and then—something else. What?

Terrified that it was pity, he dropped his own gaze and concentrated on Trumpet, who was pushing his nose into her hand. She gave the curly head an absent-minded pat.

"Will you not ask me to sit down?" Her voice was very low. He had risen automatically when she entered, and now looked about him in a panic, as though the couch and easy chair might have disappeared while he was not paying attention.

"I thought you had left," he stammered, and then, recollecting himself, he pulled the armchair away from the sofa and gestured for her to sit. Very stiffly, she did so.

"Are you quite recovered?"

For a moment, he could not recollect what he was recovered from. "Oh—yes. And you? I apologize for asking you to drink the whole bottle of laudanum. It was very thoughtless of me." God, he sounded like a sapskull. Thoughtless? To lie to her under oath and then nearly kill her?

"I am well, yes." She knotted her hands in her lap, twisting and untwisting the ribbons of the bonnet.

"Has Lady Evrett left?" he asked, groping for something to say. She nodded. "Where are you staying, then?"

"Mr. Meyer kindly invited me to stay in the house he had rented. He is no longer there, but Miss Mendez is, and several rather fierce Spanish ladies. It is all exceedingly correct."

"Good, good." He nodded inanely. There was another awkward pause.

"Perhaps you should ask me about the weather," she prompted. "That is always an acceptable topic for the morning call. But I had forgot; it is afternoon now. I believe in the afternoon it is more usual to converse about the events of the coming evening. Shall you be going to the opera tonight?"

"What are you doing?" he whispered, abandoning her script, his throat constricted.

"I am being proper, of course. That is what you wish, is it not? That is the deity we must both worship. In the name of that mighty goddess, you ran off and hid from me and handed me over to Lord Evrett like some schoolgirl who has developed a taste for low company and must be removed to a different household for her own good. In her name you concocted this tale that Lady Evrett had been sheltering me since I left my uncle. And with that well-meant falsehood, you force me to forget, to deny, the most wonderful month of my life. I am not to be allowed even to speak of it." Her voice was still calm, but her eyes had begun to glitter angrily.

"Naturally," she continued after a moment, "I resented, at first, the notion that you and Lord Evrett knew better than I did what was right for me. But I soon came to see that you were far wiser than I"—her glance swept scornfully around the room, just as Nathanson's had—"far more mature and reasonable. I am now prepared to follow your advice and return to England. A very suitable party of three elderly Belgian ladies is leaving day after next. You need only reassure me about my decision, and I will mince off in a docile fashion which would warm Lady Evrett's heart.''

"I approve," he said instantly, going white. "Surely you could not have doubted that?"

"That is not the reassurance I want."

He swallowed. "What do you want, then?"

She looked up and fastened her eyes on his. "I want you to tell me that you do not care for me, that you will be happier when I am gone."

His incredulous, outraged expression brought a strange smile to her face.

She sat, clutching her bonnet, and waited.

"You are being absurd," he said stiffly.

"Just so. You are the rational one, remember?"

He walked over to the table and stood facing away from her, absently stacking the unopened envelopes into a neat pile. "What if I were to say that it is precisely because I do care for you that I wish you to go—that your happiness, not mine, is my object?"

"You believe, then, that I will be unhappy if I remain here with you?"

"Is it not obvious?"

"Not to me. Prove it. Else I shall not go." There was a pause. "You can lie, if need be. It would not be the first time. For example, you could say you have taken a mistress," she prompted helpfully. "Or that you plan to assassinate the emperor."

"I have no need to lie," he said harshly. "How could you possibly be happy with a criminal? A convicted traitor?" He swung around, came over to the chair, and planted his arms on the back of it, staring down at her. "Didn't you understand me when I told you I had kidnapped an innocent girl, had sold information to the French?"

"And is that the whole story?" Her eyes flashed, her chin was jutting out. She seemed not in the least intimidated by the way he had pinned her in the armchair. "From what Lord Evrett told me, I gather that this celebrated kidnapping was more like a crude form of matchmaking. And that most of the information you sold to the French was false."

He stood up and flung his arms out in frustration. "And so?" he shouted. "Granted, I am a prince among kidnappers. The gentlest and most apologetic of traitors. *It changes nothing.*"

"Exactly," she said quietly, looking up at him. "It changes nothing. I still love you. You still love me. I am happy with you. I will be unhappy without you. You have proven nothing save that you are willing to punish both of us for crimes whose victims, if that term is even valid, have long since forgiven you."

He did not answer. His wits apparently had deserted him; nothing came to mind—no argument, no persuasive example, no crushing retort. In a despairing fog he turned away and gazed blankly down at the table, willing himself to tell her that he did have a mistress, that he was a professional forger—anything to make her go.

A rustling noise. She had risen. Perhaps she was leaving, was giving up. At that thought a cold hollow opened up inside him.

When she materialized at his elbow, he could not at first believe she was still there. It took him a full minute to see that she was holding out the little triptych of portraits.

"Who are they? Is the little girl your sister?" she asked softly, tilting her head up and turning the unfolded case so both could see it in the afternoon light spilling in from the high windows.

But he was caught by something compelling in the angle of her cheek against the sunbeams and stood frozen, gazing at her. This was a disaster. He was weakening, was beginning to consider absurd actions such as kissing her. And look where that had led, that morning on the staircase.

He collected his wits and looked down at the portraits.

"Yes, that is my sister, Alice," he said mechanically. "She is much older now, of course. The miniature was done some five years ago. And the picture of my mother is older still. There was a masque or a fete of some sort and she and two friends were dressed as the Antique Virtues. I believe she was Fidelitas. In any case, my father had her portrait done. It was before Alice was born."

"Why did you remove the third portrait? It was of you, was it not?"

"It was." His jaw tightened. "I did not remove it. My father did, while I watched. I was too big to whip. He had to content himself with gouging my face out of the frame flake by flake with his penknife. When it came to me after his death, I left it. It seemed a good portrait of him, as well as of me. A nothing, a blank. A drunken, lecherous cheat who gambled away one of the loveliest estates in Kent and then rode his second-best hunter into a ditch."

Her arm touched his. When he shook her off, roughly, she reached up and turned his face until he was looking at her. Instinctively, he tried to step back, but he could not move; he was already between her and the table.

"You are not your father," she said intensely. "You are nothing like him." His fists were clenched at his sides; she picked up the right one, unrolled the fingers, and laid the hand down flat on the table. "Look," she commanded.

Unwillingly, his eyes went to the crooked knuckles.

"Yes, you were in the wrong." Her voice was firm. "I will not try to tell you I approve of what you did. It was foolish, possibly even spiteful, in the case of the abduction. But they were not great crimes, your desperate schemes to stave off bankruptcy. And you have made recompense to everyone who was hurt by your actions, tenfold recompense, a hundredfold even."

She laid her own hand next to his on the table: smooth, white, graceful. "Your hand healed. You can play Mozart." Soft, warm fingers closed over his; she lifted his unresisting hand and clasped it firmly between both of hers. Her face was taut with the effort of convincing him, of making him understand: her brow furrowed, the great eyes fierce.

"Both things cannot be true," she said, very slowly and clearly, as if to a child. "You cannot be the vile wretch you believe yourself to be, and be the man I love."

"Yes, I could." He forced out the words. "You might be mistaken."

"I lived with you for nearly a month," she said simply. "Are you telling me I am a fool who cannot form a reasonable estimate of a man's character after lodging with him for a month? Was I wrong, for example, in my judgment of the Countess of Brieg?" Her expression hardened; she looked almost stern. "Choose," she bade him imperiously. "Tell me which it is to be. The epic renunciation? The noble exile? Or me and England and your family? Renunciation is easy: a brief moment of resolve and it is over. Coming back to life will require many moments of resolve, some of them probably very uncomfortable. When your mother discovers what happened to you, for example. When you are cut by old acquaintances. When you have to face your colonel. When we bring your sister out, and you hear the whispers as she enters the assembly rooms."

His voice was not working; he made some kind of inarticulate sound and pulled his hand away.

"Do you not trust me?" she asked, so softly he was not certain he had heard her.

Desperately, he closed his eyes, but it was no use. He was lost. Shutting out the sight of her did not help, not while he could sense her standing so close to him, catch the faint scent of her hair, hear her breathing just below his ear.

"I give up," he said at last. "I surrender. After all, even when you were my assistant I never did manage to make you do anything you did not want to do. If I

drive you off now, you will just come back and harass
me another time." He opened his eyes, saw the tears
sliding down her cheeks, the slow, disbelieving smile.
"God forgive me if I am doing the wrong thing. If by
some cursed mischance you have decided you need me,
I suppose you must have me."

"The real you," she warned. "Not that frozen ghost
who drinks brandy. If you stomp about glowering and
reviling yourself all the time, I shall feel cheated."

"I could manage a smile occasionally," he conceded.

"How about right now?" she said, with a wobbly
attempt on her own part to set an example.

He hesitated for a moment, and she reached up
and touched her lips gently to his. Something collapsed
inside his chest; some blockage, some restraint, was suddenly gone.

He gripped her so hard her feet came off the floor
and pulled her over on top of him as he dropped into
the chair, kissing every bit of her face he could reach
until he finally found her mouth. By the time he let her
go, he was dazed and breathless, her dress was sliding
off one shoulder, and they were both trembling.

When he attempted to help her off his lap, she pushed
him back into the chair and kissed him again.

"You're smiling," she said triumphantly.

"You," he predicted, panting, "will be a dreadful
influence on my sister."

Nathanson gave a discreet cough. They paid no attention, which was not surprising, given the circumstances.
There was no door, which meant he could not knock.
He tried retreating down the stairs to the landing and
stomping loudly back up. At last he was reduced to
rapping on the wall at the top of the staircase.

"I beg your pardon," he said. They did not move
apart, but at least they looked at him. He found himself
taking an almost proprietary satisfaction in the glow on

their faces, and sternly repressed an unwelcome memory of the countess looking up at him with an expression very like Elizabeth's. "I came up to see if you would care to be introduced to Miss DeQuincy," he said to Southey dryly.

"No, I think not," said his friend, emerging from his trance and glancing at her with a possessive air. "I would prefer to be her fiancé, which I believe is one of the alternatives. I most emphatically do *not* wish to be her brother."

"A pity," mused Nathanson. "The travel arrangements would be so much simpler."

"What do you mean?" demanded Southey, looking wary.

"I mean that it strikes me as unlikely that you would permit Miss DeQuincy to journey back to England unchaperoned in your company, even as your fiancée. Not to put too fine a point on it, unless you wish to spend a week in a badly sprung carriage with three ancient ladies from Antwerp, one of whom has a very frail digestion, I would advise you not to keep the Reverend Mr. Leswell waiting."

"The Reverend Mr. Leswell?" Southey echoed, his face brightening.

"A most obliging gentleman, who has been in Vienna conducting researches into Dioscurides at the Imperial Library. It has, however, finally reached his ears that there is a war going on, and he is leaving town tomorrow afternoon. Hence my rather high-handed behavior in breaking into your lodgings today. You can find him at the University Commons until six."

Southey had remembered something. "It will not answer; we have no license," he said in disappointment. "It was a kind thought, Nathanson, but you could not have known, of course, since you are Hebrew. A pity."

With a wry smile, the younger man dug into an inside pocket of his jacket and retrieved a crisply folded paper. "Courtesy of Philip Jervyn," he commented, handing it over. "Although I suspect the ambassador would have been glad to provide it even without his intercession." He saw the predictable stiffening. The hand which held the document dropped suddenly.

"I would prefer not to accept any favors from Mr. Jervyn," said Southey coldly.

"Very well." Calmly, Nathanson reached over and took the little square of parchment back, watching Elizabeth's face as he did so. She gave a smothered exclamation, but made no other protest. Perhaps this was more effective than overt disagreement would have been. Her lover flushed, looked at the floor, and reluctantly held out his hand.

"Oh, give me the damned license," he growled, then reddened. "I mean—confound it, Elizabeth! How am I to remember not to swear in front of you when I swore *at* you for weeks? And," he added indignantly, "you swore back!"

"Nonsense," said Elizabeth primly. "I was with Lady Evrett, remember?"

Epilogue

Chanterfield, near Haythorn, Kent
November 1813

The last leaves were coming down off the great oaks, and Elizabeth's boots made a satisfying crunch as she hurried up the path from the stable. She had seen the curricle in the yard when she had arrived back from the village, and now, bursting with her news, she did not wait to change out of her riding clothes, but went straight to her husband's bedchamber.

It had been a good guess. She spotted him standing by the dressing room the moment she came in the door. Sievert was unpacking the valise and scolding simultaneously while Southey stood meekly in front of the open clothespress.

He looked tired, but as soon as he saw her he brightened and came over to embrace her, turning her slightly so that she faced back towards the door. The valet moved at once between her and the pile of clothing.

Her suspicions were awakened. She pivoted in his arms and casually glanced over. Sure enough, there at the bottom of the pile was a neatly folded uniform. Probably it meant nothing, she told herself. Since he had been reinstated at half-pay once the charge of treason was dropped, he would have to formally sell out at some point. Perhaps that was what had delayed him.

"You've been gone for ages," she said accusingly. "You said you would be back on Tuesday, and it's Saturday." He had been traveling to London frequently, trying to untangle the legal snarls created by the fraudulent mortgages.

"Something came up. Did you not get my letter?" Collapsing into a faded armchair, he sighed with relief as Sievert removed his boots. Army boots, she realized. "I should have kept those Hungarian boots and told the Hussars the dog ate them," he commented. "Those were the most wonderful boots I have ever owned." He looked down at Trumpet. "See? A dog of discrimination. He shows no interest in these stiff monstrosities whatsoever."

"He is simply growing more mature," said Elizabeth tartly. "Unlike some people. What are you concealing from me? Do you fancy you can come home four days late with an officer's jacket in your luggage and tell me vaguely that something came up?"

Sievert discreetly vanished.

She saw an opportunity to hint, and took it. "What if I were to tell you that something came up here while you were gone?"

The hint sailed right over his head. He was deciding whether or not to tell her. "They held the closed-chamber hearing," he said finally.

That got her attention. It certainly explained the uniform. He would have to appear properly dressed. "But you said it had been delayed until December, that they could not find anyone to act as Colonel White's advocate!"

He looked very uncomfortable. "They found someone," he muttered. "Thank God it is over, at any rate."

"Well, what happened?" she demanded. "Were you exonerated? Was White cashiered? Did the secretary come to the hearing?"

"Yes, no, and no," he said wearily. "White wanted to resign, but I persuaded him not to. Nathanson sends his regards, by the way, as does his father. They have just returned. It took almost as long to copy and distribute the notes in that leather book of Doña Maria's as it did to collect the information in the first place. All the allied generals insisted on having their own version, with personal visits by either 'Rover' or his son to explain the camp layout under each of the marshals."

His attempt to move the conversation to the travels of the Meyers was ignored. "What do you mean, you persuaded him not to resign?" She was outraged. "You convinced Nathanson not to sell out by telling him White was to be investigated. How does he feel about this?"

"Are your riding lessons going well?" he asked, pointedly changing the subject. For a moment she was tempted. This was a good chance to try again: "I may have to give them up for a bit," or "Well enough, considering." But something about his determined efforts to distract her renewed her suspicions.

"Who acted for White?" she asked suddenly.

A home thrust: he froze.

"*You* did?" Stunned, she sank down on her knees next to the chair. "Are you insane? The man ruined you! Or very nearly," she corrected as she looked around the lovely old room, with the late morning sun angling off the crooked glass of the windows.

"Nathanson, in his usual sarcastic way, said it was very Christian of me."

Tentatively he reached over and brushed his hand across the back of her neck, but she drew away and glared at him.

"Well, I certainly knew the facts better than anyone else," he said defensively. "And after I refused to see him when he came down here two weeks ago, I started remembering things. How he had virtually adopted me, took me home with him several times when my father came to London and made scenes. How he had arranged for my mother to see Dr. Gideon when she was ill. How he himself had planted the idea of forging documents to mislead the French in my head, talking about someone who had done something similar during the wars in Canada sixty years ago. Perhaps I am deceiving myself, but it seems too much of a coincidence, that he should suggest such a thing and then let Castlereagh's office try their scheme on me."

He leaned forward and stared off over her head towards the windows, not really seeing anything. "He lent me a book once, by some Russian general, written in execrable French, and told me to read one particular chapter. It is a long chapter, but in the most memorable section the general is quizzing his colonels, and he asks them: who should be sent on a dangerous mission which is likely to fail? The bad soldier, whose loss will not be felt, or the good soldier, who has a slightly—only slightly—greater chance of succeeding, but who will be sorely missed? And the colonels argue amongst themselves. Most decide to send the bad soldier. A few of the wiser ones hedge their bets and make the decision conditional on the importance of the mission. Only one declares that the good soldier is always the right choice. The general asks him why, and he replies: because the good soldier will understand why he was sent. And the general turns to the other colonels, and says, 'This is the man who will be your next general.' " He looked down at her. "I decided I would rather tell my grandchildren that I was a good soldier than that I was a fool and a traitor. And once I made that decision, I had to defend him."

He looked calm, she realized. Tired, but content. It was an expression she had rarely seen—understandably, given his circumstances when they had met. For a moment she was tempted to let her news wait. But only for a moment.

"Speaking of grandchildren—" she began.

Sievert reappeared. "Beg pardon, sir, but McLean is here. Shall I ask him to come back later?" McLean was their bailiff, a tyrannical little Scotsman who believed they should be keeping count of every lump of sugar in the pantry.

Southey grimaced. "No, I've been fobbing him off for two weeks. Tell him I'll be down shortly. Could you have Joseph bring some coffee into the study?" He pulled on the faded old boots Sievert brought him and stood up, stretching stiffly. She tried again.

"Dearest, could you ask Mr. McLean about the carpenter? He was meant to come see me about some renovations I want done, and evidently Mr. McLean told him there would not be enough money."

She had been sure the mention of renovations would catch his attention; in his eyes every inch of Chanterfield was sacred. But instead he simply said absently, "Certainly. There should be ample money now. I have arranged for the rents to come directly to us for this year instead of going into the funds as they did before."

"Good," she said breathlessly, "because some of the renovations are quite urgent."

He headed out to the hall, helping to her feet and giving her a quick kiss.

"Especially the ones to the nursery," she called after him. She heard him start down the staircase and then stop, turn around, climb back up. She met him at the top of the stairs.

"Did you consult my mother?" he said, frowning. "She is very attached to the old nursery."

"Yes," she said, grinding her teeth. "I have consulted your mother."

"Well, that's all right then." He started back down the stairs.

"Also, we will need to look at the market this spring for a pony."

He looked a bit surprised. "Do you not like your horse? She seems very gentle to me. I know you have not ridden for a long time, but you are somewhat tall for a pony."

"It is not for me." Admittedly he had quite a few things on his mind, but was the man completely obtuse?

"I do not think my mother will care for it. Still, now that you are here—Alice is such a hard goer, my mother could never ride with her, so she gave it up. Perhaps it is a good notion, after all. I will ask Hickman, over at Leigh End, if he knows of any good ponies for sale. The market is no place to purchase an animal like that; all the best ones are sold privately."

He started back down the stairs again.

"Wait—" she tried. "Oh, never mind."

"What is it?" He turned around, looked at her carefully. "Is something wrong?" Instantly remorseful, he leaped back up to the landing and took her gently by the shoulders. "Sweetheart, I have been so full of my own affairs. I have not asked about you. Do you mind if I go down to speak with McLean for a bit? And then we can have luncheon, just the two of us."

"I'm afraid my appetite has not been very good," she said in a failing voice. "Especially at breakfast and luncheon."

Now he was concerned. "Are you ill?" he asked. A new thought struck him. "Do you suppose it is some residue of that dreadful laudanum I made you take? Have you seen the doctor?"

"Yes, I have seen the doctor," she snapped. "And there is nothing wrong with me save that I have married a half-wit! I am amazed they did not draw and quarter Colonel White, if you were defending him!"

"Why? What have I done?" he stammered, taken aback.

"Do you see anything different about me?"

"No," he said hesitantly.

"Well, you will. In about two months. And in about eight months I will look like myself again, and we will need a new nursery and a pony and heaven knows what else. From the way your mother talks, these creatures require so many furnishings and gowns and bonnets and swaddling clothes and toys and teething rings and porringers that it will be a wonder if we can fit it all into the biggest nursery ever created. Do I make myself clear?"

"Are you serious?" he whispered in joyous astonishment. She smiled tremulously in reply. "Good thing I was exonerated," he said faintly. He sat down on the top step, and drew her down beside him. "And everything is going well?" he asked anxiously. "The doctor is satisfied?"

"Everything is fine," she reassured him. "The doctor said I was an exceptionally strong young lady." Actually, the doctor had rather rudely observed that she had muscles like a milkmaid.

"When?"

"July. Perhaps late June."

He looked somewhat dismayed. "That seems rather long—I mean, a long time for you to be indisposed—" He was floundering and turned bright red.

She took pity on him, although she was tempted to let him stew for a bit to punish him for ignoring her hints. "You need not worry, or treat me as though I am ill," she said gently. "I can do anything I please until the last few months. I need only eat well and rest."

"Anything you please?"

"Riding, dancing . . ." her voice trailed off as she saw his expression. It was her turn to blush.

He stood up, and lifted her into his arms. "Sievert!" he called, striding towards her room. From nowhere the blond manservant suddenly materialized, unfazed by the sight of his master, still in his traveling clothes, carrying an equally disheveled mistress towards her bedroom at noon. "Tell McLean to come back tomorrow."

"What about the carpenter?" she protested feebly.

"I am a cabinetmaker, remember?" He gave her a slow smile which made her feel faint. "I think we should retire to your bedchamber so that you can rest. And if you suddenly need a credenza, I will be right there."

Historical Note

For the backdrop to a romantic tale of espionage and international intrigue, it is hard to do better than the summer of 1813. There was indeed a European armistice. Metternich did treat with both the allies and Napoleon, and Britain did send (by a circuitous and very slow route) a conciliatory answer to Austria's query about her willingness to participate in peace negotiations. At the last minute, it was decided to conceal the letter from Austria. It never reached Metternich.

The involvement of Wilhelmine von Sagan's cousin in the Tyrolean plot is a fabrication, but the plot itself did exist. In fact, although my hero, Michael Southey, is fictional, the unscrupulous attempts by Castlereagh's foreign office to manipulate Austria are quite plausible. One of the major players in that Tyrolean affair was a British agent, John Harcourt King, a handsome aristocrat who was reputedly a rival of Metternich for the favors of the Duchess of Sagan.

Readers interested in the role played by Anglo-Jewish families in Wellington's campaigns or in the capabilities of British army intelligence during this period may wish to consult the note at the end of the first book in this series, *A Question of Honor* (Zebra, 2002).

Stella Cameron

"A premier author of romantic suspense."

__The Best Revenge
  0-8217-5842-X $6.50US/$8.00CAN

__French Quarter
  0-8217-6251-6 $6.99US/$8.50CAN

__Key West
  0-8217-6595-7 $6.99US/$8.99CAN

__Pure Delights
  0-8217-4798-3 $5.99US/$6.99CAN

__Sheer Pleasures
  0-8217-5093-3 $5.99US/$6.99CAN

__True Bliss
  0-8217-5369-X $5.99US/$6.99CAN
